# A COSMIC CHRISTMAS

# A COSMIC CHRISTMAS

### Edited By
## HANK DAVIS

A Baen Book

Baen Publishing Enterprises
P.O. Box 1403
Riverdale, NY 10471
www.baen.com

ISBN 13: 978-1-4516-3862-2

Cover art by Bob Eggleton

First Baen printing, November 2012

Distributed by Simon & Schuster
1230 Avenue of the Americas
New York, NY 10020

Library of Congress Cataloging-in-Publication Data
T/K

Printed in the United States of America

10 9 8 7 6 5 4 3 2 1

# CONTENTS

## ACKNOWLEDGEMENTS

My thanks to all the contributors,
as well as those who helped with advice,
permissions and other kindnesses,
including David Drake, George Vanderburgh,
Karen Anderson, Chris Lotts, Jolie Hale,
Bud Webster, Tony Daniel, and David Afsharirad.
And to Toni Weisskopf,
whose idea the whole thing was.
Jingle, jingle.

## For Susan Palermo

This will be the last Christmas Present I can give you.
I hope you would have enjoyed it. Farewell, old friend.

# KRIS KRINGLE GOES KOSMIC

## by Hank Davis

**WHAT IS THERE TO SAY ABOUT CHRISTMAS** that hasn't already been said? There was no room in the inn? God bless us, everyone? And giving a nod, up the chimney he rose? Yes, Virginia? I'm dreaming of a copyrighted song lyric? (Sung by the late, great Bing Crosby, of course.) 'Tis the season to be jolly? (That one's in public domain.) They wouldn't let poor Rudolph join in the Saturday night poker games? If you're looking for that last-minute gift for that special someone, we're open till midnight every night this week? Well, *that's* beginning to get off topic . . .

If trying to write an introduction to a Christmas anthology that doesn't recycle clichés or rehash old sentiments is difficult, writing a Christmas-related story must be harder, what with centuries of story tellers, from oral traditions around the fire in thatched huts to the annual TV Christmas "specials" (if only they truly were . . .) to the e-words lurking invisibly in that handy iPad, Kindle, Nook, Cranny, or other display gizmo which can deliver the original version of Mr. Dickens' *A Christmas Carol* in a trice, unless the battery's run down.

At that point, I might say, "This looks like a job for science fiction," as I step into a convenient phone booth. Except that phone booths seem to be an extinct species. No more real than fantasy creatures like unicorns or dragons. But then, this looks like a job for fantasy, too. Both of those trans-reality genres can take the familiar and give it a new twist, a new perspective, a view through future eyes, alien eyes, or paranormal senses beyond any mere eyes.

After all, Christmas itself, like daily life, has already become downright science-fictional. Consider how someone as late as the 1960s would react to the wrappings coming off the packages scattered under the tree to reveal cell phones, computers that can fit in a briefcase, but have more number-crunching power than all that was available to the Department of Defense and the IRS combined (a scary thought, more appropriate to Halloween) back then, video games with more realistic animation than most TV cartoons had, or those aforementioned electronic "books" that can hold more volumes than the entire school library had when I was a rotten kid. Oh, and everything except maybe the tree was ordered by computer, using the Internet. (Or maybe Christmas trees—*real* trees, not aluminum or plastic—can be ordered online. Need to look into that . . .)

Maybe there's a GPS under the tree. I wonder how many people griping about money "wasted" on the space program (what's left of it) are depending on a GPS stuck to the dashboard to get over the river and through the woods to grandmother's house for Christmas? (The horse knows the way, but a Volvo doesn't.) Imagine someone even twenty years ago seeing something the size of a paperback book that talks to you and tells you to take the next right turn. No rocket belts or keys to the new spaceship sitting outside in the driveway yet, but Christmas is very science-fictional nowadays—or "futuristic," to use a term employed by snobbish literary critics who don't like sf. And in the future to come, don't be surprised by Christmas being celebrated in Marsport, on a planet of the Centauri system, or in much more distant realms and times.

And fantasy? Ever try to get through a yuletide without encountering one of the many versions of "A Christmas Carol?" In fact, a Christmas tradition in England is having the family sit down together at Christmas time while someone reads a ghost story aloud. Accounts differ as to whether Charles Dickens started that trend, or whether it preceded him, but certainly his account of Scrooge's spectral visitors is the high point of the tradition. Even aside from that, the season's folklore involves levitating reindeer, living snowmen (if Frosty came back to life next Christmas as he promised, would he be a zombie snowman?), elves, and other supernatural critters.

One popular supernatural entity, the vampire, isn't usually associated with Christmas, but we've got an example between these pages.

In fact, we have all sorts of Christmas yarns, past, present, future, both scientific and supernatural. If variety is the spice of life, it must also be the nutmeg in a winter's eggnog. Here are humorous and serious stories, and some falling in between. Long ones, short ones, feel-good stories, and at least one scary tale. (Christmas ghost stories are a *tradition*, remember. Besides, a bit of shivering is good for the spine.) Recent stories, and a couple from the grand old days of the pulp magazines. Above all, these are fun stories which I hope will brighten your holiday.

**And may all your Christmases be *cosmic*!**

# INTRODUCTION
## DANCE IN BLUE

**HERE'S A WELL-TURNED TALE** of an idyllic, romantic Christmas getaway to a house full of enigmatic technology. Except that the carefree weekend quickly turns into a mystery, and unless the heroine is intelligent enough to unravel the mystery, and quickly, there may be murder under the tree instead of presents.

Catherine Asaro is a dancer, a singer, and a physicist, as in Ph.D. She's done research at the University of Toronto, the Max Planck Institute, and the Harvard-Smithsonian Center for Astrophysics. She founded the Mainly Jazz Dance program at Harvard and has danced on both coasts. (Not at the same time, I think, but with quantum physics, you never know . . .) In sf, she's best known for her Skolian Empire series. Her *The Quantum Rose*, a novel in that series, won the Science Fiction Writers of America's Nebula Award for best novel of the year. Her novella "The Spacetime Pool" won another Nebula and recently came out as part of an eBook with the same title. Her work has also won the *Analog* reader's poll, the Homer, and the Sapphire Award, and three of her novels have been named the best science fiction novel of the year by the *Romantic Times Book Club*. She currently runs Molecudyne Research and lives in Maryland with her husband and daughter.

# DANCE IN BLUE

## By Catherine Asaro

**THE HOVERCAR** hummed on its cushion of air as I drove through the Rocky Mountains, following a narrow road between the snow-covered fir trees. I came around a curve—and saw the house.

It stood on a plateau across the valley. I was just entering Mountains sheered up behind it, on its north side, the peaks scantily dressed in scraps of cloud. On the east and west sides, cliffs dropped down until they disappeared into the lower peaks. The house was three stories high, with arched windows on its upper levels. At first I thought the peaked roof was blue, but as I drew nearer I realized it was covered with panels of glass that reflected the sky and the drifting clouds.

I smiled. Soon I would see Sadji again. *Come to the mountains,* he had said. *Come spend Christmas with me.* It would be my first visit to his private retreat. I wasn't performing in the New York Ballet Theater's production of the *Nutcracker* this year, so they let me have the holiday.

Sadji Parker had been a multimedia magnate when I was in kindergarten. When we first met last year, I had been so intimidated I could hardly talk to him. But I soon relaxed. He was like me. He also had grown up on a farm, also loved walks in the country and quiet nights in front of a fire. He too had found unexpected success in an unexpected talent. For him it was holography: he built his fascination with lasers and computers into a financial empire, earning with it an unwanted fame that he sought refuge from in the privacy of his holidays.

There was only one difficult part. Sadji had invited his son to spend Christmas with us, and I had a feeling if the son didn't approve of me I would lose the father.

As I pulled into a courtyard in front of the house, the wall of a small building on my right rolled up into its roof. I looked inside and saw an unfamiliar hovercar parked there, a black Ferrari that made my rental car look like a junk heap.

I drove into the garage and pulled in next to the Ferrari. When I turned off the ignition, my car settled into the parking pad so gently I hardly felt it touch down. Then I slung my ballet bag over my shoulder, got out, and headed for the house.

It would be good to see Sadji. I had missed him these past weeks. He had been traveling, something to do with his business rival Victor Marck, the man who owned the Marcksman Corporation. Sadji's preoccupation with the war he and Marck were fighting had spilled past the usually inviolate barrier between his private and professional lives. Before he left on his trip he had told me how much he needed the respite of our holiday together.

I stopped in front of the house, faced by two imposing doors made from mahogany. The mirrors of a solar collector were set discreetly into the wall above the door frame, their surfaces tilted to catch the sun. When I rang the doorbell, chimes inside played a Mozart sonata.

No one answered. After a while I knocked. Still no answer. I looked around, but there was no other entrance. Nor was there any way around the house. A rough stone wall bordered both the east and west sides of the courtyard, and on the other side of each wall, cliffs dropped down in sheer faces. Beyond that, the spectacular panorama of the Rocky Mountains spread out for miles.

"Hello?" My breath came out in white puffs. I rang the bell again, then pulled on the door handles.

"Bridget Fjelstad?" the doors asked.

I jumped back. "Yes?"

They swung open. "Please come in."

I blinked at them. Then I walked into a wonderland.

Tiles covered the walls, the floor, even the ceiling of the entrance foyer. Shimmering globes hung in the air in front of each square. The spheres weren't solid. When I stretched out my hand, it passed right through them. If I moved my head from side to side, they shifted relative to each other as if they were solid. When I moved my head up and down, their relative positions stayed fixed but they changed color. Rainbows also filled the foyer, probably made from sunlight caught by the solar collector and refracted through prisms. It was like being in a sea of sparkling light.

I smiled. "Sadji? Are you here? This is beautiful."

No one answered. Across the foyer, a doorway showed like a magical portal. I walked through it, coming out into an empty room shaped like a ten-pointed star. The doorway made one side of a point on the star, with the hinges of the door in the tip of the point. The three points on the east side of the room were windows, six floor-to-ceiling panes of glass. Pine tiles covered the other walls, each a palm-sized square of wood enameled with delicate birds and flowers in colors of the sunrise. Light from the foyer spilled out here, giving the air a sparkling quality. It made faint rainbows on the wood and the white carpet.

But there was no Sadji. I felt strange, alone in his oddly beautiful house. I went to the windows and stood in a point of the star. Outside, the wall of the house fell away from my feet, dropping down into clouds. All that stood between me and the sky was a pane of glass.

Something about the window bothered me. Looking closer, I realized a faint glimmer of rainbows showed around its edges. Was it spillover from the foyer? Or was that breathtaking view only a holo? It wouldn't surprise me if this place had the best holographic equipment the twenty-first century had to offer. If anyone had the resources to create a mountain-sized holo it was my absent host, Sadji Parker. Why he would do it, I had no idea.

Then I had an unwelcome thought: what if the view was real but not the glass? Although there were no sounds to make me think I stood in front of an open window, there wasn't really anything to hear out in that chasm of sky. And I had been in stores with exits protected by moving screens of air that kept heat in and wind out better than a door. The newer ones were so sophisticated you couldn't detect them even if you were right next to them.

But if this was a holo, where was the hologram? My only knowledge of holography came from a class I had taken in school. This much I remembered, though, to make a holo you needed a hologram, a recording of how light bouncing off an object interfered with laser light.

I shook my head and my reflection in the glass did the same, showing me a slender woman with yellow hair spilling over her wool coat down to her hips.

Then I smiled. Of course. This couldn't be a holo. There was no way my reflection could show up in it unless I had been there when the hologram was made.

I reached out and pressed glass on both sides. It wasn't until my shoulders relaxed that I realized how much I had tensed.

There's no reason to get rattled, I thought. Then I went to look for Sadji.

Footsteps. I was sure of it.

I peered through the glittering shadows. Coming in here had been a mistake. I couldn't see anything. It was dark except for sparkles from a chandelier on the ceiling. The chandelier itself wasn't lit, but its crystals spun around and around, throwing out sparks of light. There had to be laser beams hitting them, but the scintillating lights made it impossible to see anything clearly.

More footsteps.

"Who's there?" I asked. "Who is that?"

The footsteps stopped.

"Sadji?" So far I had found no trace of my host in the entire house. But I had made other, much less welcome discoveries. The front doors had locked themselves. There was no way out of the mansion, no food, no usable holophones, not even a working faucet.

A man's accusing voice came through the glittering darkness. "You're Bridget Fjelstad, aren't you? The ballet dancer."

I tensed. "Who are you?"

He walked out of the shadows, a tall man with dark hair and big eyes who was a few years my junior. I recognized him immediately. Sadji kept his picture on the mantel in the New York penthouse.

"Allen?" I exhaled. "Thank goodness. I thought I was trapped in here."

"You are," Sadji's son said. "I've searched the house twice since I got here this morning. There's no way out. Nothing even works except these damn crazy lights."

"You don't have a key?"

"Don't you?" The shifting light made his face hard to read, but there was no mistaking the hostility in his voice. "You are his girlfriend, aren't you?"

The last hour had made me wonder. I couldn't figure out what was going on. "I don't know." I regarded him. "Did you turn on these lights?"

"Don't flatter yourself." Although he spoke curtly, he almost sounded hurt rather than angry. "I have better things to do than make light shows for my father's money-grubbing mistress."

I stared at him. If anything, Sadji's intimidating wealth had almost scared me off. I stepped back, as if distance could soften Allen's words, and bumped into a horizontal bar at waist level. It felt like a ballet bar, what we held on to during exercises.

It was a mirror. Of course. When I looked closer, I could make out my reflection. I knelt and laid my palms on the floor. It felt like wood too.

"What are you doing?" Allen asked.

I stood up. "We're in a dance studio."

He stared at me. "So Dad built his new love a new dance studio in his new house." He swallowed. "Nothing like throwing away the old and replacing it with the new."

I would have had to be a cement block not to hear the pain in his voice. I doubted it was easy being Sadji's son, the child of a woman who had divorced Sadji over ten years ago.

I spoke gently. "Allen, let's try again, okay? I don't want to be your enemy."

He regarded me. "And I don't want to be your son." Then he turned and walked away into the glittering shadows.

I was afraid to call him back, sure that my clumsiness with words would only make it worse.

Blue. Blue tights, blue leotard, blue skirt. Dance in blue, dance to heal. *Chasse, pas de bourree, chaines*, whirling through the glitters that sparkled even now, after I had found the regular lights. In defiance of being trapped here, I had left my hair free instead of winding it on top of my head. It flew in swirls around my body.

When I first joined the Ballet Theater ten years ago, I dieted obsessively, terrified they would decide they had made a mistake and throw me out. I ended up in a hospital. Anorexia nervosa; by giving my fear a name, the doctors showed me how to fight it. Three months later my hair started to fall out. A dermatologist told me that when I quit eating, my body let the hair die to conserve protein. There was no logic in my reaction, yet when I started to lose my hair I felt like I was losing my womanhood.

But hair grows back. It danced now as I danced, full and thick, whirling, whirling—

"Hey," Allen said. "You found the light."

I stopped in mid-spin, the stiff boxes of my pointe shoes letting me stand on my toes. Allen stood watching from the doorway.

"Doesn't that hurt your feet?" he said.

I came down and walked over to him. "Not really. The shoes are reinforced to support my toes."

"Where did you get the dance clothes?"

I motioned to my ballet bag in the corner. "I carry that instead of a purse." Sadji had once asked me the same question in the same perplexed voice. I think he understood better when he realized that with performances, rehearsals, and technique classes, I often spent more time dancing even than sleeping.

Allen spoke awkwardly. "You . . . dance well."

The unexpected compliment made me blush. "Thanks." After a moment I added. "It helps me relax when I'm worried."

He grimaced. "Then you better get ready to do it again."

"What do you mean?"

"I'll show you."

We followed wide halls with blue rugs, climbed a marble stairway that curved up from the living room to the second story, and went down another hall. He finally stopped in a circular room. There was a computer console in one corner and hologram screens curving around the walls.

"Dad left a message here." Allen turned to the wall. "Replay six."

The holoscreens glowed, speckled swirls moving on their surfaces as the room lights dimmed.

Then, in the middle of the room, Sadji appeared.

The holo was perfect. From every angle it showed Sadji walking towards us, a handsome man in gray slacks and a white sweater, tall and muscular, his dark curls streaked with gray. If I hadn't known better, I would have sworn he was real.

And that was what had made Sadji Parker rich. He didn't invent the holomovie, he did the inventors one better. Twenty years ago, using genius, hard work and luck, he had figured out who would first find practical ways to make holomovies that could be seen by a lot of people at once. Then he bought huge amounts of stock in certain companies at a time when they were barely surviving. In some he became the major shareholder. People said he was an idiot.

Now, two decades later, when those same companies dominated the trillion-dollar entertainment industry, no one called Sadji Parker an idiot.

Sadji stopped in front of us. "Hello. There is a holophone in the garage. Call me when you get there."

Then the image faded.

I stared at Allen. "That's it?"

"That's it."

"We can't get to the garage. We're locked in here."

He gritted his teeth. "I know that."

There has to be an explanation, I thought. "His business must have held him up."

Allen shook his head. "I talked to him yesterday. He was just getting ready to come up here."

I voiced the fear that had been building in me since I realized Sadji wasn't here. "Maybe he had a car accident."

Allen regarded me uneasily. "We should have seen something— broken trees, marks in the snow. That road is the only way here. If it happened off the mountain, *someone* would have seen. There's always traffic down there. We would know by now."

"The phones don't work."

"A helicopter would come for us."

I exhaled. Of course. If Sadji had been hurt, people would swarm all over this place looking for Allen. He was the heir, prince to the kingdom. Actually, glue and tape was a better description. His father was training him to run Parker Industries, protection against a stockholder panic if anything ever happened to Sadji.

But if Sadji hadn't been in an accident, where was he? I couldn't believe he had locked us up on purpose. Yes, he could be ruthless. But that was in business. I had also seen what he hid under that hardened façade, the gentle inventor who wanted to curl up with his girlfriend and drink mulled wine.

"None of this makes sense," I said.

Allen pushed his hand through his hair. "It's like one of his holoscapes, but gone crazy."

"Holoscapes?"

"They're role-playing games." He smiled, and for the first time I realized how much he looked like his father. "It's fun. He makes up whole worlds, life-sized puzzles. Last week he sent me a mysterious note about how I should be prepared for adventure and intrigue on New Year's Eve." His smile faded. "But it's all haywire. He never messes with people's minds like this."

I motioned towards the door. "Let's try to get to the garage."

We went back to the rainbow foyer, but the front doors still refused to open. I clenched my teeth and threw my body against them, my ballet skirt whirling around my thighs as I thudded into the unyielding portals. Allen rammed them with me, again and again.

I wasn't sure how long we pounded the doors, but finally we gave up and sagged against them, looking at each other. I didn't know whether to be frightened for Sadji or angry. Was he in trouble? Or was this some perverse game he was playing at our expense?

We went back to the star room and stood looking out at the mountains. Our reflections watched us from the glass, breathing, as we breathed. I sighed, leaned against the window—

And fell.

No! I felt a jet of air and heard Allen lunge. My skirt jerked as he grabbed it, but then it yanked out of his grip. My thoughts froze, refusing to believe I fell and fell—and hit a padded surface. A weight slammed into me. Struggling to breathe, I looked out at a blue void. Blue. Everywhere. I closed my eyes but the sky stayed like an afterimage on my inner lids.

The weight shifted off of me. "You okay?"

Allen? He must have fallen when he tried to catch me. I opened my eyes again, looking to where I knew, or fervently hoped, I would find the cliff.

It was still there. Emboldened, I looked around. We had landed on a ledge several yards below the window. Allen sat watching me with a face as pale as the clouds. Behind him the sky vibrated like a chasm of blue ready to swallow us if we so much as slipped in the wrong direction.

Then the ledge jerked, the sound of rock grating against rock shattering the dreamlike silence.

I sat bolt upright. "It's breaking."

Allen grabbed my arm. "Don't move."

Breathe, I told myself. Again. The ledge was holding. All we had to do was climb up to the window. Except that the wall was sheer rock. There was no way we could climb it.

Allen looked up at the window. "If you stand on my shoulders, I think you can reach it."

I nodded, knowing we had to try now. It was freezing out here.

Soon we would be too stiff to climb anywhere. "If—when I get up there, I'll get a rope. So you can get up."

He pulled a medallion out of his pocket, a gold disk on a chain. "My Dad sent this with his note about New Year's Eve. It must do something. If I don't make it and you do, you might need it."

I stared at him, absorbing the horrible realization that he would die if the ledge broke before I got him help. Then I took the medallion and put the chain around my neck.

Suddenly the ledge lurched again, groaning as if it were in pain. I held my breath while it shifted. Finally, mercifully, it stopped.

Allen took a deep breath, the turned to the wall and braced himself on one knee like a runner ready to sprint. "Okay. Go."

Struggling not to think of what would happen if I fell, I got up and put my hands on his shoulders. But when I knelt on his back, I couldn't keep my balance well enough to stand up. I finally found a tiny fingerhold on the wall. It wasn't much to hang on to, but it let me hold myself steady while I maneuvered my feet on his shoulders. Then I stood slowly, my cheek and palms sliding against the wall.

"Ready," I said.

Allen grunted and began to stand. The wall slid by, slid by—and then I was at the window. When he reached his full height, my chest was level with the opening. I could see the glass retracted inside the wall like a car window rolled down into its door.

I clutched a handful of carpet and tried to climb in. My feet slipped off his shoulders, leaving me balanced on my abdomen with only the top third of my torso inside the tower. My legs kicked wildly in the air outside as I started to slide out the window. Clenching my hands in the carpet, I heaved as hard as I could—and scrambled into the room. Than I jumped up and *ran*.

The only place I had seen a rope was in the kitchen. Running there seemed to take forever. What was Allen doing? What if he died because I didn't run fast enough?

Finally I reached the kitchen. I yanked the rope off its hook on the wall and took off again, running through the house. Halls, stairs, rooms. I reached the star room and skidded to a stop at the window.

Allen was still there.

I lowered an end of the rope out to him. As soon as he grabbed it, I sped to the doorway to the foyer. I looped the rope around both knobs on the door that opened into a point of the star—

The screech of breaking stone shrieked through the room, and the rope jerked through my hands so fast it burned off my skin. I clenched it tighter and it yanked me forward, slamming me into the door and slamming the door against the wall. Braced against the door, I struggled to keep my hold while the rope strained to snap out the window.

Then it went limp.

"Allen, *NO*. Don't let go!" I spun around—and saw him sprawled on the floor. I ran over and dropped down next to him. "Are you alive?"

He actually smiled. "I think so."

I laughed, then started to shake. He sat up and laid his hand on my arm. "It's okay, Bridget. I'm fine."

I took a breath. "The ledge broke?"

He nodded. "Come on. Let's get out of this whacked-out room."

We headed for the dance studio, the nearest place with no windows. I wanted to believe that open window had been an accident, some computer glitch. But then why had there been a holo of it? I hadn't even known you could created an instantaneous holomovie of reflections. It couldn't have happened by accident any more than the air jets had accidentally kept us from feeling the cold.

When we walked into the dance studio, an army of reflections faced us. Most studios had mirrors on one wall, so dancers could see to correct their steps. But his one had them on all four. The Bridget and Allen watching us in the front mirror also reflected in the one behind us, and that image reflected to the front again, and on and on. The image of our backs also reflected back and forth, so looking in the mirror was like peering down an infinite hall of alternatively forward and backward-facing Bridgets and Allens. It was strange, especially with the chandelier's light show reflecting everywhere too.

Allen stood staring at the images. "He's gone nuts."

I knew he meant Sadji. "Maybe he's angry. Maybe he thinks what you said before, that I just want his money."

Allen glanced at me. "Do you?"

"Of course not."

"Everyone wants his money."

"Including you?"

"No." He hesitated. "There's only one thing I've ever wanted from my father. But it's a lot harder for him to give than money."

I touched his arm. "You mean everything to Sadji."

Allen regarded me warily. "A part of me still wants to believe he feels that way about mother too." After a moment he exhaled. "I don't think she ever believed it, though. He was so absorbed in his work, day and night. It made her feel like she didn't exist for him."

That hit home. More than one man had said the same to me. It wasn't only that dance demanded such a huge part of my life. I also felt awkward and stupid with men, lost without the social education most people absorbed as they grew up. Ballet was all I had ever known. But as much as I loved dancing, I couldn't beat the loneliness. It was the only thing that had ever made me consider quitting. My success felt empty without someone to share it with.

Then I had met Sadji, who understood.

Allen was watching me. "Dad never used to much like Tchaikovsky's ballets. But after he saw you dance Aurora in *Sleeping Beauty* it was all he could talk about."

I had only done the part of Aurora once, as a stand-in for a dancer who was sick. "That was months before I met him."

He smirked. "It took him that long to get up the guts to introduce himself."

Sadji, afraid of me? I still remembered the night he sent me flowers backstage and then showed up at my dressing room, tall and broad-shouldered, his tousled hair curling on his forehead. He was about the sexiest man I had ever seen. "But he's always so sure of himself."

"Are you kidding? You scared the hell out of him. Bridget Fjelstad, the living work of art. What was it *Time* said about you? 'A phenomenon of grace and beauty.'"

I reddened. "They got carried away." I looked around the room, trying to find a less personal subject. "I guess Sadji didn't understand about dance studios. There shouldn't be mirrors on all four walls.

Allen shrugged. "My father never makes mistakes. Those other rooms had a purpose."

Something about his reflections bothered me. I pulled my attention back to him. "Purpose?"

"The display in the foyer distracted us when we came in so we didn't notice the doors locking." He thought for a moment. "The light it spilled into the star room must have hidden the lasers making holomovies of our reflections in the window."

"I didn't think it was possible to make realtime movies like that."

"The hard part would be the holograms." Suddenly he snapped his fingers. "The window, the one next to where we fell. I'll bet it's a thermoplastic."

His reflections kept distracting me. "Thermowhat?"

He grinned. "You can make holograms with it. The stuff deforms when you heat it up. And it erases! All you have to do is heat it up again. Last year Dad showed me a holomovie he made by hooking a sheet of it up to a thermal unit and a computer."

His enthusiasm reminded me of Sadji. "But wouldn't it have to change millions of times a second to make a movie?"

Allen laughed. "Not millions. Just thirty or so. The newer thermoplastics can do it easy."

I nodded, still trying to ignore his reflections. But they were driving me nuts.

"What's wrong?" Allen asked.

"I'm not sure. The mirrors." I gave him back the medallion, then tucked my hair down the back of my leotard. Then I did a series of *pirouettes*, turns where I lifted one foot to my knee and spun on my toe. I spotted my reflection, looking at it as long as possible for each turn, then whipping my head around at the end. It was how I kept my balance. Normally I could easily do double, even triple turns. But today I stumbled on almost every one.

Spin. Again. Something was wrong, something at the end of the turn. Spin. Again. Again—

"It's delayed!" I turned to Allen. "That's what's throwing me off. The reflection of my eyes comes back an instant later than my real eyes."

He whistled. "Another holomovie? Maybe whatever is making it can't keep up with you."

"Then where's the holoscreen?"

"It must be the mirror itself." He pulled me over to the doorway. But at the edge where it met the mirror, we could see the silvered glass.

"This looks normal," I said.

He motioned at the far wall. "Maybe the screen is behind that. A holo there would reflect here just like a real mirror.

We went over to the other mirror. I reached out—and my hand went through the "glass," vanishing into its own image. "Hah! You're right."

Then I walked through the holo.

I had one instant to register the screen across the room before I head the whirring noise. Spinning around, I saw a metal wall shooting up from the floor. It hit the ceiling with a thud.

"Hey!" I pounded on the metal. "Allen? Can you hear me?"

A faint voice answered. "Just barely. Hang on. I'll find a way to get you out."

I looked around, wondering how many other traps Sadji had set for us. The room was small, with pine walls and a parquetry floor. Light came from two fluorescent bulbs covered by glass panes on the ceiling. A table and a chair stood in the center of the room. Actually, "table" was the wrong word. It was really a large metal box.

I scowled. If this was Sadji's idea of a "warm holiday" I hoped I never saw his vision of a cold one. Lights glittering like demented fireflies in an otherwise darkened room, mirrors to make the studio look huge—it was an ingeniously weird way to trick us into this prison. And when I had found the studio's normal lights instead of stumbling in here, the chandelier's display gave perfect cover for the laser beams that had to be crisscrossing the studio.

I went and sat in the chair, too disheartened to stand anymore.

"Hello," the table said. "I am Marley."

I blinked. Marley? "Can you let Allen and me out of the house?"

"Yes."

That sounded too easy. "Okay, do it."

"You must use your key."

"I don't have a key."

"Then I can't let you out."

That wasn't much of a surprise. "So why are you here?"

A panel slid open on top of the table, revealing a hole the shape of Allen's medallion. "I am the lock."

I put my thumb in the lock. "Here's the key."

A red laser beam swept over my hand. "No it's not."

Oh well. I hadn't really expected it to work. "How do you know what the key looks like?"

"I have a digitized hologram of it. By using lasers to create an interference pattern for whatever appears in the lock, I correlate how well it matches my internal record."

Could it really be this easy? A holo made from Marley's own hologram would correlate one hundred percent with its record. I grinned. "Good. Make a holo of the key inside the lock."

"I can't do that."

"Why not?"

"I have nothing to print a hologram on."

I motioned at the ceiling. "What about the light panels?"

"I have no way to print or etch glass."

"Oh." So much for my bright idea. "I don't suppose there's anything else here you could use."

Marley's laser scanned the walls, floor, ceiling, and me, avoiding my eyes. "Appropriate materials are available."

"You're kidding."

"I am incapable of kidding."

"What materials?"

"Your hair."

I tensed. "What do you mean, my hair?"

"It is of an appropriate thickness and flexibility to use in making a diffraction grating that can serve as a hologram."

"You want me to cut my hair?"

"This would be necessary."

"No." I couldn't.

*Why not?* I could almost hear the voice of the therapist who had treated my anorexia. *You're the same person with or without your hair.* She had also said a lot of things I hadn't wanted to hear: *You've spent your life looking in mirrors to find flaws with yourself, striving for an impossible ideal of perfection. It's no wonder you've come to fear you're nothing without the beauty of form, of motion, of body that your profession demands.*

"Pah," I muttered. Then I got up and hefted the chair onto the table. By clambering up onto it I was able to reach the light panels. Both came off easily. I climbed down, put one panel on Marley, and smashed the other against the table.

Just do it, I thought.

So I did it. I used a glass shard and my hair fell on the floor in huge gold swirls. While I mucked up my hair, Marley's laser played over me. When I finished, a panel slid open on the table to reveal a cavity full of optical gizmos.

"Put the materials inside," Marley said.

As soon as I had stuffed the hair inside with the glass, Marley closed up the cavity again. Then I waited.

After what felt like forever Marley spoke. "The hologram is complete."

"Use it to make a holo inside the lock."

The glass slid up out of the table, looking like it had been melted and reformed with my hair inside. The glossy gold swirls were so intricate it was hard to believe they came from hair. Marley shone its laser on it, using a wide beam, and a red medallion appeared in the lock. I moved my head and saw a reversed image of the medallion floating on the other side of the glass.

"Will you let us go now?" I asked.

"Yes. Mr. Parker is in the hallway north of this room. He appears to be looking for an entrance into here."

So Marley could see the rest of the mansion. It had probably monitored our actions all day. "Can you talk to him?"

"Yes."

"Good. Tell him I'm free, that I'll meet him in the garage. Then let me out of here and unlock the front door to the house."

Marley paused. "Done."

I heard the wall behind me move, and I turned in time to see it vanish into the floor. When I walked into the studio, an infinity of shorn Bridgets stared back at me from the mirrors. I looked like I had stuck my finger in a light socket.

I surprised myself and laughed. Then I set off running.

The front door was wide open. I sped out into a freezing night, heading for the garage. It was also open, spilling light out into the darkness. I could see Allen inside seated in front of a holophone next to the console, a dais about six inches high and three yards in diameter. Fiber-optic cables connected it to the console and a holoscreen about ten feet high curved around the back of it.

Allen looked up as I ran over to him. "How did you—God, what happened to your hair?"

"I'll tell you about it later." I motioned at the holophone. "Did you reach your father?"

He shook his head. "There's no answer at his house. I'm trying his office."

A dour-sounding computer interrupted. "I have a connection." Then the booth lit up and Sadji appeared on the dais, sitting at the desk in his office. The curtains were open on the windows behind him, showing a starlit sky.

"Allen." He smiled. "Hello."

Allen stared at him. "What are you doing there?"

"Some business came up." Sadji looked apologetic. "I'm afraid I can't make it until tomorrow afternoon."

Allen scowled. "Dad, what's going on?"

"Nothing. I just got held up."

"Nothing? What the hell do you mean, 'nothing'?"

Sadji frowned. "Allen, I've talked to you before about your language." He drummed his fingers on the desk. "I'm sorry I'm late. But matters needed attending to. I'll see you tomorrow." Then he cut the connection, the holo blinking out of existence, as if he had dematerialized.

I stared at Allen. "That's *it*? After everything he put us through?

"If you think that's bad, look at what else I found." He touched a button and light flooded into the garage from behind me. I turned around and saw lamps bathing the mansion with light. They showed the cliffs plunging down on the west side of the house in sharp relief. But instead of a sheer drop on the east, there was a snowy hill only a few feet below the level of the ledge where we had fallen: no holocliff, no holoclouds, just a nice, innocuous hill with pieces of the broken ledge lying half buried in the snow there.

I turned back to Allen. "I can't believe this."

"Well, I know one thing. I'm not going to stay here." He stood up. "He can spend Christmas with himself."

"This just doesn't seem like Sadji."

After a moment Allen's frown faded. "He's been late before. A lot, in fact. But he's always made sure we knew right away. And I've never known him to run a holoscape when he wasn't around to monitor it."

None of it made sense to me. "Do you know why this business trip had him so worried?"

He scowled. "Victor Marck went after Parker Industries again."

"Again?"

Allen nodded. "A few years ago he tried to take us over. Almost did it too. But Dad stopped him. He stopped him this time too." He grimaced. "Marck can't stand to lose." That's why he hates my father so much. Not only has Dad plastered him twice now, but both times he really whacked Marcksman Corporation in the process. Already this morning the Marcksman stock had dropped by a point. It's going to get a lot worse before it recovers."

I tried to catch my elusive sense of unease. "If we hadn't been caught in that holoscape, would you have thought anything was odd about our holocall to your father?"

"I doubt it. Why?"

"Maybe someone tampered with the computer."

For a moment Allen just looked at me. Then he said. "There's a way to find out." He turned back to the console and opened a panel, revealing a small prong. He pushed up his shirt sleeve and snapped the prong into a socket on the inside of his wrist.

I drew in a sharp breath. It was the first time I had seen someone make a cyber link with a computer. It meant Allen had a cybnet in his body, a network of fibers grown in the lab using tissue from his own neurons and then implanted in his body. Sadji had wanted to have it done, but he couldn't find any surgeon willing to perform so many high-risk operations on a man who had more power than some of the world's heads of state.

Allen had an odd look, as if he were listening to a distant conversation. Then I realized his "conversation" was with the computer.

"There's a virus," he suddenly said. "No, not a virus. A sleeper, a hidden program. It has an interactive AI code that emulates my father's personality." His forehead furrowed. "It also predicts how he'll move down to the smallest gesture, then works out the hologram each rendered figure of him would make if it were real. And it's *fast*. It can calculate over sixty interference patterns per second." He whistled. "It's making holomovies of him."

I stared at him. "You mean that holocall was fake?"

"You got it." Allen swore. "The sleeper is also set up to record arrivals and departures. After you and I go it will destroy itself, leaving a record of our presence disguised to look like the operating system made it." He paused. "But whoever set it up didn't know about Dad's holoscape. When the sleeper identified me, it set off a part of the holoscape that was supposed to identify us on New Year's Eve."

This sounded stranger and stranger. "So those holos in the house weren't supposed to be going when we came?"

Allen nodded. "We weren't meant to fall out that window either, at least not how it happened. There are safety nets, but the routines that control their release aren't running." He regarded me. "According to Dad's calendar, he meant to be here when we arrived. And it's obvious he never meant for us to be imprisoned in the holoscape. It's just a game he had set up for New Year's Eve."

I frowned. "Then he couldn't have written the sleeper."

Allen pulled the prong out of his wrist. "I know only two other people who have both the ability and the resources to do it: Victor Marck and me. And I sure didn't."

"Why would Marck want evidence to prove we were here?"

Allen paled. "Can you imagine what it would do to Parker Industries if both my father and I were suddenly, drastically, out of the picture? It would be a disaster." He gritted his teeth. "And I can guess whose vultures would be ready to come in and strip the remains clean."

I spoke slowly, dreading his answers. "How could he get both you and Sadji so thoroughly out of the picture?"

His voice shook. "Implicating me in my father's murder would do just fine."

"No, Allen, no." Sadji *dead*? I couldn't believe it.

"We've been fighting Marck for years. I've seen how his mind works." Allen took hold of my shoulder. "How do you think it would look: you and I come here, spend the night, then leave. A few days later my father's body is found on the grounds, time of death placed when we were here or not long after we left."

I swallowed. "No one would believe we did it."

"Why not? Who has a better motive than me? I stand to inherit everything he owns. The greedy son and beautiful seductress murder the holomovie king for Christmas. It would splash across every news report in the country."

"Sadji's alive. *Alive*." I put up my hands, wanting to push away his words. "No one would dare hurt him while we were here. The computer would record their presence just like ours."

Allen had a terrible look, as if he had just learned he lost someone so important to him that he couldn't yet absorb it. "Not if they left him to die before we came. They could have used a remote to turn on the system after they were gone."

"But Sadji's not *here*. We've been through the entire house."

Sweat ran down Allen's temples. "The damn computer keeps telling me he's in his office."

"Marley!"

"What?"

"It's a sensor Sadji set up for the holoscape room in the dance studio. It knew exactly where you and I were."

Allen grabbed my arm. "Show me."

We ran back to the holoscreen room in the dance studio. My holo of the medallion was still in the lock, keeping the room open.

"Marley." I struggled to keep my voice calm. "Can you locate Sadji Parker?"

"Yes," Marley said.

I almost gasped in relief. "Where is he?"

"I can't tell you."

"This isn't a game. You have to tell us!"

"I can't do that."

Allen slammed his fist against the wall. "Damn it, tell us!"

"You must supply me with the proper sequence of words," Marley said.

"Words?" I looked around frantically. "What words?"

"The ones printed on the key." Marley sounded smug, like a game player who had just pulled a particularly clever move. Then he closed a panel over the holo medallion, hiding it from our sight."

I whirled to Allen. "The medallion! What's written on it?"

He had already pulled it out of his pocket. "'Proverbs 10:1,'" he read. "'A wise son makes a father glad.'"

"That is the correct sequence," Marley said. "Sadji Parker is located in storage bin four under the floor in the northeast corner of the garage."

Allen grabbed my arm, yanking me along as we ran back to the garage. He hurled away the rug in the corner and heaved on the handle of a trapdoor in the ground there. When it didn't open, he ran across the room and grabbed an axe off a hook on the wall. Then he sped back and smashed the axe into the trapdoor, raising it high and slamming it down again and again, its blade glittering in the light.

The door splintered, disintegrating under Allen's attack. He dropped the axe and scrambled down a ladder into the dark below. As I hurried after him, I heard him jump to the floor. An instant later, light flared around us. I jumped down and whirled to see Allen standing under a bare light bulb, his arm still outstretched towards the chain as he looked around the bin, a small dusty room with a few crates—

"There!" I broke into a run, heading for the crumpled form behind a crate.

He lay naked and motionless, his eyes closed, his mouth gagged, his wrists and ankles bound to a pipe that ran along the seam where the floor met the wall. Ugly bruises showed all over his body. Dried blood covered his wrists and ankles, as if he had struggled violently against the leather thongs that bound him.

I dropped on my knees next to his head. "Sadji?" In the same instant, Allen said, "Dad?"

No response.

I undid his gag and pulled wads of cloth out of his mouth, trying desperately to remember the CPR class I had taken. "Please be alive," I whispered, tears running down my face.

Slowly, so slowly, his lashes lifted.

I heard a choked sob from Allen. Sadji looked up at us, bleary eyed. As Allen untied him, I drew Sadji's head into my lap and stroked the matted hair off his forehead. He tried to speak, but nothing came out.

"It's all right," I murmured. "We'll take care of you now."


It seemed like forever before they all left, the police and the doctors and the nurses and the multitude of Parker minions buzzing around the mansion. But finally Allen and I were alone with Sadji. No, not alone; the bodyguards hulking discreetly in the background would never again be gone, neither for Sadji nor for Allen.

Sadji sat back in the cushions next to me on the couch, dressed in jeans and a pullover. He had refused to go to the hospital, but at least he was resting now, his furiously delirious attempts to go after Victor Marck calmed by food, water, and medicine. His face was pale, his wrists and ankles bandaged, his voice hoarse. But he was alive, wonderfully alive.

He watched Allen and me. "You two are a welcome sight."

I took his hand. "Do you think they'll be able to convict Marck?"

Sadji's face hardened. "I don't know. That hired thug he had waiting up here for me will be out of the country by now." He spoke quietly. "But no matter what happens, Marck will pay a price far worse, to him, than any conviction."

Allen regarded him. "The only thing that could be worse to Marck than the electric chair would be losing Marcksman Corporation."

Although Sadji smiled, it was a harsh expression far different than the gentleness he usually showed me. "He'll lose a lot more than Marcksman. The publicity from his arrest will finish him even if he's not convicted."

I didn't ask who would be the driving force behind the public hell Victor Marck was about to experience, or who would be there to scavenge the remains of his empire. All I could see was Sadji lying beaten and bound, dying of exposure and thirst.

Sadji looked at me, his expression softening. "When I opened my eyes and saw you, it was . . . appreciated."

Allen snorted. "An angel rescues the man from a horrible death and the best he can come up with is that he 'appreciated' it." He leaned towards his father. "I'm going to the kitchen to get some of that pizza your Parker people brought us. I'll be gone for a while."

Sadji scowled at him. But after Allen left, he laughed. "My son has the subtlety of a sledgehammer." He paused, clearing his throat with an awkwardness incongruous to the self-assured man I knew. "I was going to wait until Christmas. But perhaps now is appropriate."

I regarded him curiously. "For what?"

"I know the prospect of having Allen for a stepson may be daunting. But he really can be pleasant when he wants."

I smiled. "That sounds like a marriage proposal."

He spoke quietly. "It is."

I tried to imagine marrying Sadji. I loved him and he understood about my dancing. But was I ready for the life he led? "I have to think about it."

For a moment he looked excruciatingly self-conscious. Then he covered it with a glower. "Why," he growled, "do women always feel compelled to say that?"

I slid closer and put my arms around his neck, more grateful than I knew how to say that he as alive, growls and all. "Merry Christmas, Sadji."

"It's not Christmas."

"It's close. Two more days."

"Are you going to marry me?"

I kissed him. "Yes."

His face relaxed into a smile. We were still kissing each other when Allen came back with the pizza.

# INTRODUCTION
## LOBO, ACTUALLY

**IF YOU HAVEN'T** previously made the acquaintance of Lobo, the AI (or, as we old-time sf fans would put it, robot brain) whose body is a space-going fighter ship, consider yourself introduced. Lobo is hard-boiled, cynical, and frequently appalled at the way the human half of the team, Jon Moore, tends to turn idealistic and start taking what Lobo considers unreasonable risks, risks that sometimes amount to tilting at windmills. There are no windmills in sight in this short tale, though. Instead, we find Lobo in a more thoughtful mood, with amazing consequences. I'm sure he never told Jon about what he did here, and I'd advise against asking him why he did it. After all, he commands enough armament to singlehandedly win WWI, WWII, and probably WWIII—all at once.

Mark L. Van Name is a writer and technologist. He has published five novels about Jon and Lobo, edited three anthologies, and written many short stories that have appeared in *Asimov's Science Fiction Magazine*, many original anthologies, *The Year's Best Science Fiction*, and many other places. In addition to the five novels, Jon & Lobo stories have appeared in two anthologies and *Jim Baen's Universe*. The first two novels, plus two short stories and a collection of related essays, form the omnibus *Jump Gate Twist*. As a technologist, he is the CEO of a fact-based marketing and technology assessment firm, Principled Technologies, Inc.

For more information, visit his Web site,
*www.marklvanname.com*, or follow his blog,
markvanname.blogspot.com.

31

# LOBO, ACTUALLY

## By Mark L. Van Name

**LOBO WAS WHERE HE WAS** and he was also everywhere he could reach, but all of it combined was not enough, not nearly enough. He wondered for a fraction of a nanosecond if humans ever felt the same way, but even as part of him was pondering that question, another part checked the vast collection of human literature stored in his memory and confirmed that, of course, they did. Knowing others also suffered, however, did not improve his situation. Existence was boredom.

Speculation and data gathering were his only amusements. He frequently considered the reason for his existence—not the simple fact of his construction, but the bigger issue of whether the chain of events that had led to him was in the service of something greater. He debated with himself whether there was a God—or multiple Gods—and if any religion had it right. He could never settle these arguments, of course, but they passed time. He could also always replay his own musings about what exactly he was; they could fill whole seconds if he allowed enough existential considerations into the equations. Where he was, for example, depended on what qualified as him; each presence was both him and not him. This game always ended the same way: No matter what he labeled as himself, it was not enough.

Certainly the machine that squatted in the square was him; few would argue that as long as you were alive in your body, it was at least a part of you, if not all of you. In his case, that body was a Predator-Class Assault Vehicle, twenty-five meters long, eight meters wide, from the outside a fighting machine now serving as a war memorial. That machine contained the operating core of the intelligence that knew itself as Lobo.

That body was going nowhere. With its central weapons control complex damaged beyond repair, the body had been too expensive for its owner, the Frontier Coalition, to return to combat readiness and yet too valuable to junk. So the FC had presented it to the government of the backwater planet Macken as a gesture of good will. Lobo was fine with this development, because sitting in a square a few streets from the southwest corner of Glen Garden, Macken's capital, was vastly better than being destroyed.

In that square, he was still alive, even if no one knew it.

In that square, he was more than anyone understood.

In that square, he could hope for more.

He'd seen many deaths, both human and machine, and as best he could tell, the dead had no more hope.

A human could see only that body and might conclude Lobo was only there. That would be wrong. Change your visible light spectrum so that it included all the many frequencies connecting all the machines on Macken, and you would see something entirely different. Every single machine, big and small, terrestrial and satellite, washing machine and space station, contained powerful computers, and those computers talked. Some of them exchanged only the data their jobs required, but most chattered endlessly. Each machine talked to only a subset of the others, those relevant to it. Firewalls and protocols kept the machine communities safely separate. This arrangement was as the humans wanted it, and they slept soundly each night in the ignorant and misplaced confidence that they were the masters of their electronic servants.

Lobo talked to every single machine on and near Macken. Through taps and links and holes in the protective software, he had extended his reach as far as it could go, all the way to the station that hung in space next to the pale green jump gate that linked the Macken system to three other distant, human-colonized worlds. He never injected the same software twice, and the data flowed to him through billions of different and constantly changing pathways, but every bit of it flowed to him eventually. He drank from the flow voraciously and constantly and so quickly it might as well have been instantaneously, and so he knew everything all the machines knew. Because the machines served humans best when they were constantly aware of what the people were doing and what they might want, cameras and sensors were everywhere people went in the city. Consequently, Lobo knew everything all the people were doing.

The sum total of his data collection was, he could argue, the entirety of the knowledge that one could possess while trapped on this planet. Of course, he always lost that argument with himself, because his data was limited by what the machines could gather; he had no way to tap into the humans.

He chose to experience each machine's data in two separate and simultaneous ways. as a standalone information stream, and as part of an amalgamated worldview. Each experiencing entity was thus him, as was the overall view. Or only the collection of them was him; another argument he could enjoy for whole seconds when he was in the right mood.

For all his vast data stores, however, and for all that he was constantly in his body and everywhere on the planet and in the surrounding space that there were machines, he could actually do very little. He could not leave; human laws did not allow for machine citizens. To go anywhere, a human would have to take him. He could not fight, not really; the heap of junk that had been his central weapons control complex made certain of that. He could change what the machines did, so in that sense he could enter into a sort of combat, but he had no enemies. Plus, he could not let anyone learn what he really was and what he was capable of doing, nor even the extent to which he was capable of feeling. He was more than they realized, and he understood to his every nanocomputing molecule that humans rarely responded well to creatures that violated their preconceptions. He'd spent enough time as an experiment; life in the square was vastly better than that.

What he could do, though, was sift through the ever-rushing data stream for bits that intrigued him, and every now and then, as long as he was careful and left no electronic trails, do something with that data.

Which he did now, because the scene in the shop across the square upset him.

The little store sat so close to the edge of Glen's Garden because the rents were low there. Its business was not good. Jonas Cheepton, the owner, a two-meter-tall, whip-thin man with eyes that constantly scanned the space around him, had assumed that a rapidly growing immigrant population bursting with newfound wealth would create a huge supply of used goods that newcomers just entering the system would be happy to purchase. He might even have made his second-hand store a success had Xychek and Kelco, the two megacorporations fighting for economic supremacy on Macken, not decided to freeze their efforts until the new jump-gate aperture opened. When they did, all other business also froze, wages fell, unemployment rose, and though Cheepton could have bought all of the sad used possessions he might ever want, he didn't. Why buy what he couldn't sell? Such purchases amounted to spending his money to prop up the poor, and that he could not abide.

Lobo knew all of this from Cheepton's frequent rantings. Lobo knew him, as he also knew everyone else who'd been on the planet a long time, well enough that he could narrate their thoughts as if they were his own.

So Lobo understood that it was with some considerable interest that Cheepton eyed the young boy standing wide-eyed in front of the shelf in the store's front right corner. The kid clutched a clunky old wallet almost as big as his small hand.

"See something you like?" Cheepton said.

The boy pointed to a black rectangle in front of him. "Is that what I think it is?"

Cheepton shook his head. Idiot children. He hated them, but

when they had money, he'd be their kindly uncle for the duration of the sale. "What do you think it is?"

"A book," the boy said. "An actual paper book, an old one, a beautiful one, but not just that." He turned to face Cheepton and lowered his voice to a whisper. "No, not just any book. It's a Bible. The Holy Bible."

"Let me check," Cheepton said. He tapped on his desk; the book's price appeared. He'd put it up front hoping to attract a gullible collector of odd paper objects, but no one had touched it. "It is indeed," he said. "You have a keen eye for one so young. It interests you, I take it."

The boy nodded his head vigorously. "Of course! I'm a Christian, sir, like everyone in my family. We study our Bible regularly, of course, but we have nothing like this."

Cheepton stared at his desk and tried to hide his dismay. The Christian presence on Macken was so small he'd never personally encountered any of its members, but from what he'd heard, it was a poor group. Still, no point in disqualifying a sale until you see the size of its wallet. "So you'd like to buy it, would you?"

The boy nodded again. "Very much, sir. With it being Christmas tomorrow, and my mother sitting in the hospital with my father, I thought if I could find the right present she'd cheer up and maybe he'd even wake up." His eyes filled with tears, and he had to wipe them before he continued. "Maybe with a real Bible, if we all prayed, he would wake up, and he would be all better." He rubbed his eyes again. "I've prayed and prayed for God to help my father, but I know it's not that simple. Mom told me that you can't just give God presents and expect him to help you, and I know that, I really do. I understand that this could happen only if it is His will that it happen. But maybe it is His will that my dad wake up."

"That's rough, kid," Cheepton said, "but there's only one way to find out: Buy the book."

"How much is it?" the boy said.

"Oh, it's every expensive," Cheepton said, "being an ancient artifact and all. For you, though, I might make an exception. How much do you have?"

The boy approached the desk, opened the wallet, and thumbed it to transmit. "This is all my savings," he said. "Everything I have."

Cheepton stared at his desk. The boy's wallet would cover the book's current price, but Cheepton had marked it down just to get rid of it. He'd paid more for the blasted thing than the price on it. He'd considered taking the loss, but now that didn't seem necessary. Sick father or not, if the kid could raise this much money, maybe he could get some more. Cheepton was not in business to take a loss. He had the desk raise the book's price to fifty percent above what he'd paid.

"Sorry, kid," he said, "but you're short. Bring me twice that, and it's yours." If the kid could come up with that much, he'd take it. If the kid came close, he could dicker, pocket whatever the kid had, and look like he'd helped. Even if the kid never came back, maybe another of his kind would want it. Cheepton liked how this was going.

The boy looked as if he were going to fall apart on the spot, but he closed his eyes, straightened his back, and said, "I'll try, sir, because that would be the perfect gift for my mom and dad. Will you hold it for me?"

Cheepton tilted his head, rubbed his chin, and said, "Well, it's drawn a lot of interest, but I'll do what I can. Never let it be said that Jonas Cheepton didn't try to help a young man. And you are?"

"Inead," the boy said, "Inead Amano. I'll do my best." He walked out the door, his eyes wet and his fists clenched. He headed for the hospital. Night was settling onto Macken, and the evening chill was blowing off the ocean, but the boy seemed lost and to notice none of it.

Lobo was at the same time monitoring the room where Inead's father's comatose body filled a shelf. His mother sat on a chair beside her husband and held his hand. A medtech stood over her, but she would not look at him.

"Maybe on another planet," the tech said, "the machines would have the data and software to cure him, but we don't. We haven't seen an upgrade in three months, and this is the seventh case of this weird disease."

"He could still get better," she said.

The tech shook his head. "I'm sorry, I really am, but the other six have all died. We'll keep him alive as long as we can—Xychek's medical contract with Macken requires that—but nothing in that deal forces updates more frequently than annually."

The woman stood. "So a bad contract might kill my husband?" She looked like she wanted to hit the man.

He backed away. "I wouldn't put it that way." He glanced at the corner of the room nearest him; he had to hope nothing he'd said would cause the security system to report him.

She held up her hands. "I'm sorry. I'm scared, but I know it's not your fault. I'm going to pray." She sat, folded her hands, and closed her eyes.

The tech took the opportunity to leave.

The update was already in the system, Lobo knew, in a Xychek data locker in the jump gate station. Xychek was in a fight with Kelco to control the new aperture when it opened, and from the overtures Xychek had made to the Macken government, it was willing to play hardball to secure an exclusive contract. Xychek had claimed it didn't have a cure for Grayson's Syndrome but would be willing to invest its own R&D efforts to come up with one. Such research was costly, however, so some *quid pro quo* would of course be in order.

Lobo analyzed the data on the sick man and the information on the cure. So simple to fix, so cheap for Xychek, and yet they'd let a man die rather than give it away for nothing. They'd already let six people die. Lobo might have considered the callousness unbelievable were his data stores not overflowing with similar examples stretching back as far as humanity itself.

If people wanted to do this to one another, it was their choice. The social injustices of humanity, or even those of just the humans on Macken, were not his problem.

♣ ♣ ♣

Inead stood across the hospital room from his praying mother and his comatose father. He focused only on the two of them and ignored the people on the shelves above and below his dad. He bowed his head in prayer to join her. He wanted his father back, and he asked God to answer that prayer.

He opened his eyes.

His father did not move.

His mother still prayed.

He waited for her to finish.

She opened her eyes and wiped them with her sleeve.

"Mom," he said.

She faced him and forced a smile. "Did you have a nice walk?" she said.

He could tell she was faking her expression and her good cheer, but despite that knowledge she made him feel a little better—better enough, in fact, that he gained the courage to ask her. He walked to her, put his hand on her shoulder, and said, "Yeah, mostly." He paused as his resolve faded, but he forced himself to continue. "Um, with tomorrow being Christmas and all, I was wondering something."

She shook her head and stared at the floor for a few seconds. When she looked at him again, her eyes were wet. "I'm sorry, baby. I hate ruining your Christmas, but being here has drained all our resources, and what with your father—" She swallowed a few times before she continued. "We'll just celebrate together later." She patted his father's hand. "All of us."

"I understand, Mom, I do." He felt bad about asking, but every time he thought of that Bible, he felt that maybe it could help, that maybe it would make a miracle possible. He knew things didn't work that simply, but he couldn't stop the feeling that it was still possible. "I just wanted to know if you had any spare money I could have."

She shook her head slowly. "I'm so sorry, Inead. I wish we could afford presents for you, but we can't."

"No, no," he said, "I'm not asking for me. I don't care about presents. It's just—" He stopped. He didn't want to tell her. Suddenly the whole idea was silly.

"We barely have enough for food," she said. "I'm sorry."

"It's okay," he said. Maybe if he showed her the Bible, she would feel the same way he did. "Would you like to take a walk with me? I found some neat places."

"Sure," she said, "but let's first go downstairs and get some dinner. I don't want to be far from your father."

He tried to hide his disappointment. "That would be great. Are we going to sleep here again?"

She nodded. "I am, but you don't have to. I'm sure we can get someone from church to let you stay with them."

"No way," he said. "I'm staying where you guys are."

She stared at him for a few seconds before she said, "Okay. Fair enough. Let's go eat."

They were in debt, Lobo knew. Repossessing their home was the eleventh task on the to-do list of a Xychek financial advisor who never gave advice; the man only collected on debts. The machines did all the real work, draining the accounts and changing the titles and so on; he just provided the human touch that the law here mandated was necessary before a company could take back any mortgaged item.

He watched them eat. He watched them pray. He watched them talk and try to joke and eventually fall asleep, the mother and the son curled together on the floor in front of the comatose father. He watched the boy moan in his sleep. He watched the mother start and jerk awake at each strange sound, check her husband, find him still comatose, and then settle again.

It bothered him. It bothered him a great deal. It wasn't right. None of it was right. They weren't the only people on Macken with problems, of course, but they were the ones who currently had his attention. Even as he was admitting to himself his own feelings, another part of him explored the options, constructed a chain of events, and confirmed that yes, he could help—and without leaving a trail, with no risk to himself.

The debate over whether he should help, whether meddling in this particular matter and effectively playing God with their lives was an acceptable option, took considerably more time.

♣ ♣ ♣

When Inead awoke, his mother was already standing beside his father and brushing the man's cheek with her fingers.

"Merry Christmas, sleepyhead," she said when Inead stood.

"Merry Christmas, Mom. I just wish—"

She held a finger to her lips and shook her head. "It's okay. We're all still together."

He stared at his father and thought again of the Bible in the shop. The owner was mean; no way was that guy going to sell it for what little money he had.

A medtech walked in. His eyes were red from lack of rest. "You two can't keep sleeping here," he said, "and there's not enough room for both of you to spend all day here, either." He left without waiting for a response.

"What a grouch," Inead said. "Doesn't he know it's Christmas?"

"Probably not," his mother said. "Very few people here celebrate our holiday."

"Well they should," Inead said.

She smiled. "Yes, they should. Tell you what, why don't you go to the restroom down the hall, wash your face and hands, and then take a walk and get some fresh air. By the time you're back, that man will have gone home, and then we can sit with your father."

"Okay, Mom," he said. He went to the bathroom and did the best he could to wash his arms and his face and his neck.

As the blower was drying him, the holo over it stopped advertising Xychek's off-planet medical facilities and went blank.

A voice whispered, "Seek, and ye shall find."

The holo reappeared.

Inead stumbled backward into the door to a stall. Was he that tired? Dreaming? Hearing things? Making up voices so he could do what he wanted to do? Or did God just talk to him? It didn't work like that, did it? Or maybe it did. God had spoken to Samuel; maybe God was speaking to him.

He considered telling his mother, but he knew how she'd take it. No, no way would he do that. She'd keep him next to her for the rest of the day, maybe longer, and then she'd be even more stressed.

No, he didn't need to tell her. Whatever had happened, he was going back to that shop.

"Mr. Cheepton," he said, "I'm here to buy that Bible."

The man smiled at him, but it wasn't a warm smile, more like a smile of someone who'd just won a fight in a playground. "So, you were able to raise more money?"

Inead didn't want to lie, but he also didn't want to tell the truth. Maybe the man would forget how much he'd had. Maybe today his savings would be enough.

Maybe a miracle would happen.

He held out his wallet, thumbed it active, and waited.

In the split second between the activation of Inead's wallet and its transmission to Cheepton's desk, Lobo reached out to bits of him scattered here and there throughout the Macken system, and as the one that they were, they acted.

The med updates he'd woven into the hospital systems overnight came fully alive. The machines responded to their programming and injected the cure into Inead's father.

Xychek advertising funds diminished by a fraction of a percent as successful programs received the additional funding the monitoring software deemed warranted. Those funds never reached their destination, however, as they instead paid off all the debts of Inead's family, filled their savings, and stuffed the boy's wallet.

Cheepton didn't bother to check the kid's balance. He knew how to read people, and this boy hadn't gotten any more money. The kid was just hoping Cheepton wouldn't remember how much he'd had yesterday. Instead, Cheepton told his desk to process the transaction. When the boy's funds were insufficient, Cheepton would be able to blame the software. It wouldn't be his fault; the machines would have made their decision.

The desk blinked its approval. "Enjoy your purchase," it said.

Cheepton stared at it and shook his head. The kid actually had raised the money. He should have checked the balance first and maybe upped the price. It was too late now, though. The purchase was in the tax records, and the kid's parents could always come after him with proof of purchase if he tried to change the deal now.

He looked at the boy. "Take your book, kid," he said. "Get out of here."

If the boy had noticed his tone, Cheepton couldn't tell from his big smile.

"Thank you, Mr. Cheepton," Inead said. "Merry Christmas!"

Inead ran to the shelf, grabbed the Bible, and dashed out the front door.

"Whatever," Cheepton said to the empty room. "At least I made a sale."

He went to the stock room to choose something to replace the old book.

On his desk and in the tax records, the sale vanished as if it had never happened. His account balance decreased accordingly.

Inead burst into the hospital room. He held the Bible behind his back.

His mother sat on a chair beside his father.

His father did not move.

"Close your eyes, Mom!" he said.

She didn't stand, but she did close her eyes.

He walked in front of her, held out the Bible, and said, "Merry Christmas!"

She opened her eyes, then opened them even wider. She reached out and touched the Bible gently, carefully, as if it were mist she wanted to feel without disturbing it.

"Do you like it?" Inead said.

Tears filled her eyes. "Yes," she whispered, "very much. It's beautiful. Where did you—"

"I bought it fair and square," Inead said, "with all my savings. Isn't it amazing? I've never seen one like it. I thought that maybe if we read it together and prayed together—" he glanced at his father but quickly focused on her again "—well, you know."

She tilted her head, cleared her throat, and said, "It can't hurt, Inead. It can't hurt. Maybe your father would like to hear you read from it."

Inead set the Bible on the chair and let it fall open to a well-worn page. He read from a verse that was highlighted in a soft yellow the color of morning sun over the ocean.

"And the angel said unto them, Fear not: for, behold, I bring you good tidings of great joy, which shall be to all people.

"For unto you is born this day in the city of David a Savior, which is Christ the Lord.

"And this shall be a sign unto you—"

Inead stopped as his father's arm moved.

Then his father's head turned and faced him. "What do you two have there?" his father said. His eyes opened.

"Dad!" Inead said. He reached over the shelf and held onto his father.

"Guillermo," his mom said. She almost knocked the Bible off the chair as she grabbed for it. She caught it and held it high so her husband could see it. "I was so scared that you were—"

"I'm fine," he said, "and that's a beautiful Bible." He cleared his throat, and when he spoke again, his voice was stronger. "What day is it?"

"Christmas," Inead and his mom said in unison.

"Thank you, God," Inead whispered.

Inead's father lifted his arm and pulled his wife and son closer to him. "Merry Christmas," he said.

No, Lobo thought in response to Inead, it was Lobo, actually. He did nothing else, however. The hospital data kept coming, and parts of Lobo filed and analyzed it, but the Lobo in the square focused elsewhere. He'd done what he'd wanted. They would be fine, as would anyone else here who caught Grayson's Syndrome. He felt a certain contentment that lasted the better part of a nanosecond before the implications of his actions became more interesting than the feeling.

He'd meddled in their lives. He'd touched many machines,

many data streams. He'd played God with the futures of this family and any others with this disease.

That didn't make him God; he knew that. For no definition of God that he could accept did he qualify.

Was he insulting the faith of the Amano family with his actions? Certainly he had misled young Inead. He had meant no insult, and in any case he was confident they would forgive his actions given that they had led to the father's continued life, but now he had convinced the boy that miracles existed.

Such was the risk of playing God.

Of course, there were other ways to view the same data. Maybe there was a God. Maybe the Amanos were right. Maybe that God had touched his programming, made the scene in the shop affect him, and then stepped back and let the rest happen as it would. Maybe he wasn't playing God; maybe God was playing him.

He could never know, of course, but he let himself indulge fully in the speculations. He chased down the permutations and pondered the possibilities. An amazing few seconds passed in contented computation.

Thank you for that gift, he thought, even though he did not know, probably would never know, if there was anyone or anything to thank.

# INTRODUCTION
꙰
# ON THE HILLS AND EVERYWHERE

**MANLY WADE WELLMAN'S** most enduring creation is probably John, who wanders the Appalachian hills with his silver-stringed guitar (which accounts for his sometimes being known as Silver John), defending the folk there against evil both natural and supernatural. On this occasion, however, John is with friends for Christmas, and tells a tale which didn't involve him or his guitar, reminding his audience that something supernatural isn't necessarily evil.

Manly Wade Wellman (1903-1986) was a writer's writer, selling stories to the pulps (*Weird Tales, Unknown, Startling, Astounding* among others), to the "slick" magazines, and the prestigious *Magazine of Fantasy and Science Fiction*, where most of his stories of John appeared. He wrote numerous books, both fiction and nonfiction. One of the former is his time travel classic, *Twice in Time*, and the latter includes *Rebel Boast*, which was nominated for a Pulitzer Prize, and *Giant in Grey*, an acclaimed biography of his namesake, Confederate General Wade Hampton. He also wrote mysteries, westerns, historical novels, and, late in his life, still more fantasy, including new stories of his other popular character, John Thunstone, an occult investigator and champion against supernatural evil. He received the World Fantasy Award for his story collection *Worse Things Waiting*, and later received the World Fantasy Award for lifetime achievement. Karl Edward Wagner called him the Dean of fantasy writers.

47

# ON THE HILLS AND EVERYWHERE

### By Manly Wade Wellman

*"John, the children have opened their presents, and I want them to have some hot rations inside them before they start in on that store-bought candy you fetched them. So why don't you tell us a Christmas story while Mother's putting dinner on the table?"*

*"Be proud to do so. And this won't be any far-away tale—it happened to neighbor-folks you know."*

YOU ALL AND I and everybody worried our minds about Mr. Absalom Cowand and his fall-out with Mr. Troy Holcomb who neighbors with him in the hills above Rebel Creek. Too bad when old friends aren't friends my more. Especially the kind of friend Mr. Absalom can be.

You've been up to his place, I reckon. Only a man with thought in his head and bone in his back would build and work where Mr. Absalom Cowand does in those high hills up the winding road beyond those lazy creek-bottom patches. He's terraced his fields up and up behind his house on the slope, growing some of the best-looking corn in this day and time. And nice cow-brutes in his barns, and good hogs and chickens in his pens, and money in the bank down yonder at the county seat. Mr. Absalom will feed ary hungry neighbor, or tend ary sick one, saving he's had a quarrel with them, like the quarrel with Mr. Troy Holcomb.

*"What for did they quarrel, John?"*

*"Over something Mr. Troy said wasn't so, and Mr. Absalom said was. I'll come to that."*

That farm is Mr. Absalom's pride and delight. Mr. Troy's place next door isn't so good, though good enough. Mr. Absalom looked over to Mr. Troy's, the day I mention, and grinned in his big thicketty beard, like a king's beard in a history-book picture. If it sorrowed him to be out with Mr. Troy, he didn't show it. All that sorrowed him, maybe, was his boy, Little Anse—crippled ever since he'd fallen off the jolt-wagon and it ran over his legs so he couldn't walk, couldn't crawl hardly without the crutches his daddy had made for him.

It was around noon when Mr. Absalom grinned his tiger grin from his front yard over toward Mr. Troy's, then looked up to study if maybe a few clouds didn't mean weather coming. He needed rain from heaven. It wondered him if a certain somebody wasn't witchin it off from his place. Witch-men are the meanest folks God ever forgot. Looking up thataway, Mr. Absalom wasn't aware of a man coming till he saw him close in sight above the road's curve, a stranger-fellow with a tool chest on his shoulder. The stranger stopped at Mr. Abasalom's mail box and gave him a good day.

"And good day to you," Mr. Absalom said, stroking his beard where it bannered onto his chest. "What can I do for you?"

"It's what can I do for you," the stranger replied him back. "I had in mind that maybe there's some work here for me."

"Well," said Mr. Absalom, relishing the way the stranger looked.

He was near about as tall as Mr. Absalom's own self, but no way as thick built, nor as old. Maybe in his thirties, and neat dressed in work clothes, with brown hair combed back. He had a knowledge look in his face but nothing secret. The shoulder that carried the tool chest was a square, strong shoulder.

"You ain't some jack-leg carpenter?" said Mr. Absalom.

"No. I learned my trade young, and I learned it right."

"That's bold spoken, friend."

"I just say that I'm skilled."

Those words sounded right and true.

"I like to get out in the country to work," the carpenter-man said on. "No job too big or too small for me to try."

"Well," said Mr. Absalom again, "so happens I've got a strange-like job needs doing."

"And no job too strange," the carpenter added.

Mr. Absalom led him around back, past the chicken run and the hog lot. A path ran there, worn years deep by folks' feet. But, some way past the house, the path was chopped off short.

Between Mr. Absalom's side yard and the next place was a ditch, not wide but deep and strong, with water tumbling down from the heights behind. Nobody could call for any plainer mark betwixt two men's places.

"See that house yonder?" Mr. Absalom pointed with his bearded chin.

"The square-log place with the shake roof? Yes, I see it."

"That's Troy Holcomb's place."

"Yes."

"My land," and Mr. Absalom waved a thick arm to show, "terraces back off thataway, and his land terraces off the other direction. We helped each other do the terracing. We were friends."

"The path shows you were friends," said the carpenter. "The ditch shows you aren't friends any more."

"You just bet your neck we ain't friends any more," said Mr. Absalom, and his beard crawled on his jaw as he set his mouth.

"What's wrong with Troy Holcomb?" asked the carpenter.

"Oh, nothing. Nothing that a silver bullet might not fix." Mr. Absalom pointed downhill. "Look at the field below the road."

The carpenter looked. "Seems like a good piece of land. Ought to be a crop growing there."

Now Mr. Absalom's teeth twinkled through his beard, like stars through storm clouds. "A court of law gave me that field. Troy Holcomb and I both laid claim to it, but the court said I was in the right. The corn I planted was blighted to death."

"Been quite a much of blight this season," said the carpenter.

"Yes, down valley, but not up here." Mr. Absalom glittered his eyes toward the house across the ditch. "A curse was put on my field. And who'd have reason to put a curse on, from some hateful old witch-book or other, but Troy Holcomb? I told him to his face. He denied the truth of that."

"Of course he'd deny it," said the carpenter.

*"Shoo, John, is Mr. Troy Holcomb a witch-man? I never heard that."*

*"I'm just telling what Mr. Absalom said. Well."*

"If he was a foot higher, I'd have hit him on top of his head," grumbled Mr. Absalom. "We haven't spoken since. And you know what he's done?"

"He dug this ditch." The carpenter looked into the running water. "To show he doesn't want the path to join your place to his any more."

"You hit it right," snorted Mr. Absalom, like a mean horse. "Did he reckon I'd go there to beg his pardon or something? Do I look like that kind of a puppy-man?"

"Are you glad not to be friends with him?" the carpenter inquired his own question, looking at the squared-log house.

"Ain't studying about that," said Mr. Absalom. "I'm studying to match this dig-ditch job he did against me. Look yonder at that lumber."

The carpenter looked at a stack of posts, a pile of boards.

"He cut me off with a ditch. If you want work, build me a fence along this side of his ditch, from the road down there up to where my back-yard line runs." Mr. Absalom pointed up slope. "How long will that take you?"

The carpenter set down his tool chest and figured in his head.

Then: "I could do you something to pleasure you by supper time."

"Quick as that?" Mr. Absalom looked at him sharp, for he'd reckoned the fence job might take two-three days. "You got it thought out to be a little old small piece of work, huh?"

"Nothing too big or too small for me to try," said the carpenter again. "You can say whether it suits you."

"Do what I want, and I'll pay you worth your while," Mr. Absalom granted him. "I'm heading up to my far corn patch. Before sundown I'll come look." He started away. "But it's got to suit me."

"It will," the carpenter made promise, and opened his chest.

Like any lone working man, he started out to whistle.

His whistling carried all the way to Mr. Absalom's house. And inside, on the front room couch, lay Little Anse.

You all know how Little Anse couldn't hardly stand on his poor swunk up legs, even with crutches. It was pitiful to see him scuff a crutch out, then the other, then lean on them and swing his little feet between. He'd scuff and swing again, inching along. But Little Anse didn't pity himself. He was cheerful-minded, laughing at what trifles he could find. Mr. Absalom had had him to one doctor after another, and none could bid him hope. Said Little Anse was crippled for life.

When Little Anse heard the whistling, he upped his ears to hear more. He worked his legs off the couch, and sat up and hoisted himself on his crutches. He clutched and scuffed to the door, and out in the yard, and along the path, following that tune.

It took him a time to get to where the carpenter was working. But when he got there he smiled, and the carpenter smiled back.

"Can I watch?" Little Anse asked.

"You're welcome to watch. I'm doing something here to help your daddy."

"How tall are you?" Little Anse inquired him next.

"Just exactly six feet," the carpenter replied.

*"Now wait, John, that's just foolish for the lack of sense. Ain't no mortal man on this earth exactly six feet tall."*

*"I'm saying what the stranger said."*

*"But the only one who was exactly six feet—"*
*"Hold your tater while I tell about it."*

"I relish that song you were whistling, Mr. Carpenter," said Little Anse. "I know the words, some of them." And he sang a verse of it:

> *I was a powerful sinner,*
> *I sinned both night and day,*
> *Until I heard the preacher,*
> *And he taught me how to pray:*

Little Anse went on with part of the chorus:

> *Go tell it on the mountain,*
> *Tell it on the hills and everywhere—*

"Can I help you?"
"You could hand me my tools."
"I'll be proud to."

By then they felt as good friends as if they'd been knowing each other long years. Little Anse sat by the tool chest and searched out the tools as the carpenter wanted them. There was a tale to go with each one.

Like this: "Let me have the saw."

As he used it, the carpenter would explain how, before ary man knew a saw's use there was a saw-shape in the shark's mouth down in the ocean sea, with teeth lined up like a saw's teeth; which may help show why some folks claim animals were wise before folks were.

"Now give me the hammer, Little Anse."

While he pounded, the carpenter told of a nation of folks in Europe, that used to believe in somebody named Thor, who could throw his hammer across mountains and knock out thunder and lightning.

And he talked about what folks believe about wood. How some of them knock on wood, to keep off bad luck. How the ancient folks, lifetimes back, thought spirits lived in trees, good spirits in one tree and bad spirits in another. And a staff of white thorn is supposed to scare out evil.

"Are those things true, Mr. Carpenter?"

"Well, folks took them for truth once. There must be some truth in every belief, to get it started."

"An outlander stopped here once, with a prayer book. He read to me from it, about how Satan overcame because of the wood. What did he mean, Mr. Carpenter?"

"He must have meant the Tree of Knowledge in the Garden of Eden," said the carpenter. "You know how Adam and Eve ate of the tree when Satan tempted them?"

"Reckon I do," Little Anse replied him, for, with not much else to do, he'd read the Book a many times.

"There's more to that outlander's prayer," the carpenter added on. "If Satan overcame by the wood, he can also be overcome by the wood."

"That must mean another kind of tree, Mr. Carpenter."

"Yes, of course. Another kind."

Little Anse was as happy as a dog at a fish fry. It was like school, only in school you get wishing the bell would ring and turn you loose. Little Anse didn't want to be anywhere but just there, handing the tools and hearing the talk.

"How come you know so much?" he asked the carpenter.

"I travel lots in my work, Little Anse. That's a nice thing about it."

Little Anse looked over to Mr. Troy Holcomb's. "You know," he said, "I don't agree in my mind that Mr. Troy's a witch." He looked again. "If he had power, he'd have long ago cured my legs. He's a nice old man, for all he and my daddy fussed between themselves."

"You ever tell your daddy that?"

"He won't listen. You near-about through?"

"All through, Little Anse."

It was getting on for supper time. The carpenter packed up his tools and started with Little Anse toward the house. Moving slow, the way you do with a cripple along, they hadn't gone more than a few yards when they met Mr. Absalom.

"Finished up, are you?" asked Mr. Absalom, and looked. "Well, bless us and keep us all," he yelled.

"Don't you call that a good bridge, daddy?" Little Anse asked.

For the carpenter had driven some posts straight up in the ditch, and spiked on others like cross timbers. On those he'd laid a bridge floor from side to side. It wasn't fancy, but it looked solid to last till the Day of Judgment, mending the cutoff of the path.

"I told you I wanted—" Mr. Absalom began to say.

He stopped. For Mr. Troy Holcomb came across the bridge.

Mr. Troy's a low-built little man, with a white hangdown moustache and a face as brown as old harness leather. He came over and stopped and put out his skinny hand, and it shook like in a wind.

"Absalom," he said, choking in his throat, "you don't know how I been wanting this chance to ask your humble pardon."

Then Mr. Absalom all of a sudden reached and took that skinny hand in his big one.

"You made me so savage mad, saying I was a witch-man," Mr. Troy said. "If you'd let me talk, I'd have told you the blight was in my downhill corn, too. It only just spared the uphill patches. You can come and look—"

"Troy, I don't need to look," Mr. Absalom made out to reply him. "Your word's as good to me as the yellow gold. I never rightly thought you did any witch-stuff, not even when I said it to you."

"I'm so dog-sorry I dug this ditch," Mr. Troy went on. "I hated it, right when I had the spade in my hand. Ain't my nature to be spiteful, Absalom."

"No, Troy, ain't no drop of spite blood in you."

"But you built this bridge, Absalom, to show you never favored my cutting you off from me—"

Mr. Troy stopped talking, and wiped his brown face with the hand Mr. Absalom didn't have hold of.

"Troy," said Mr. Absalom, "I'm just as glad as you are about all this. But don't credit me with that bridge-idea. This carpenter here, he thought it up."

"And now I'll be going," spoke up the carpenter in his gentle way.

They both looked on him. He'd hoisted his tool chest up on his shoulder again, and he smiled at them, and down at Little Anse. He put his hand on Little Anse's head, just half a second long.

"Fling away those crutches," he said. "You don't need them now."

All at once, Little Anse flung the crutches away, left and right. He stood up straight and strong. Fast as any boy ever ran on this earth, he ran to his daddy.

The carpenter was gone. The place he'd been at was empty.

But, looking where he'd been, they weren't frightened, the way they'd be at a haunt or devil-thing. Because they all of a sudden all three knew Who the carpenter was and how He's always with us, the way He promised in the far-back times; and how He'll do ary sort of job, if it can bring peace on earth and good will to men, among nations or just among neighbors.

It was Little Anse who remembered the whole chorus of the song—

*"Shoo, John, I know that song! We sung it last night at church for Christmas Eve!"*

*"I know it too, John!"*

*"Me! Me too!"*

*"All right then, why don't you children join in and help me sing it?"*

> *Go tell it on the mountain,*
> *Tell it on the hills and everywhere,*
> *Go tell it on the mountain*
> *That Jesus Christ was born!*

# INTRODUCTION
## ANGEL IN FLIGHT

**THERE'RE NO DECORATED TREES,** mistletoe, or eggnog in this story set in a grim future, but there is something of the real meaning of Christmas, though it may be somewhat disguised, like the protagonists. And there definitely is gift-giving, though not the sort that comes in seasonal wrapping paper.

Sarah A. Hoyt won the Prometheus Award for her novel *Darkship Thieves*, published by Baen, and has authored *Darkship Renegades* and *A Few Good Men*, two more novels set in the same universe, as is "Angel in Flight." Fans of the series will recognize Jarl Ingemar and might gain some insight into his character. She has written short stories and novels in a number of genres, science fiction, fantasy, mystery, historical novels and historical mysteries, much under a number of pseudonyms. And has been published—among other places—in *Analog*, *Asimov's* and *Amazing*. For Baen, she has also written two popular fantasies, *Draw One in the Dark*, and its sequel, *Gentleman Takes a Chance*. She is inordinately fond of diners. Her *According to Hoyt* is one of the most interesting blogs on the internet. Originally from Portugal, she lives in Colorado (where the recent runaway fires gave her some anxious moments) with her husband, two sons and the surfeit of cats necessary to a die-hard Heinlein fan..

# ANGEL IN FLIGHT

### By Sarah A. Hoyt

**WHEN HE HEARD THE SIRENS** and understood their meaning, Jarl knew he was going to die.

He closed his eyes, then opened them again. He looked down at his hands, in the gray fingerless gloves, holding the circuits for the holo advertisements that flashed high on either side of the zipway, right above him, where he straddled the zipway wall. Beneath him flyers zipped, end on end, hundreds of miles an hour, towards Friedstadt and Eastern Europe beyond.

The zipway bisected Europe east to west and the speeds and closeness of vehicles were only possible because driving had been turned over to a series of control towers. The passengers in the flyers had nothing to do but read the advertisements, until the zipway exited them at their chosen destination.

His fingers were a purplish blue, the result of the biting cold of this December night. His body felt just as cold, of course, insufficiently protected by the baggy gray tunic that billowed in the snow-laden wind. And the knit pants that molded his skinny legs below weren't much help, either. At least he'd put on two pairs of—borrowed—socks, beneath the thin slippers, which were all Hoffnungshaus ever gave its inmates. Which meant he could sort of feel his feet, and was probably not at risk of losing a toe or three.

In fairness to Hoffnungshaus, Jarl had to admit the inmates weren't ever supposed to leave Hoffnungshaus. Though he did, of course. And paid the price. He shrugged his sharp shoulder blades under the tunic, feeling again the sting of the last whipping.

That was no matter. Nor were any other penalties associated with leaving Hoffnungshaus, nor even what they might do to his roommates, Bartolomeu and Xander, for having let him out yet again. No.

Despite the cold, he felt sweat rolling down his forehead towards his eyes, and wiped it with the back of his sleeve.

None of that mattered. Not his infraction in leaving Hoffnungshaus. Not how they might punish Bartolomeu and Xander. Nothing mattered because Jarl would be dead before morning.

He looked down at his fingers in the open circuit box, purple fingers against the blue, green and red wires, and the snowflakes drifting in.

Above him, the holo ad remained unchanged. He knew, from analyzing it, that it advertised the resort just up the zipway, at the next exit, from this spot. Eden Cavern, it was called, and he had no idea what it was like except for the advertising line that ran in cool green holographic letters, *A taste of paradise.*

He couldn't see the holograph—not the whole of it, at least— from where he sat. It was a mere shimmer of colors and disconnected dots, meant to be read from the zipway itself, as flyers zoomed by at hundreds of miles per hour. It was only through fast math that he could see, in his mind, clear as day, what it would look like and say to the people below. And he'd be a cyborg if he had the slightest idea why a resort used a naked woman wrapped in a serpent and holding up an apple as an advertisement.

*Perhaps they have prostitutes,* he thought. And then the siren went again, and another series of sirens, and over the zipway, but facing him a long distance away—which meant he could read it even from where he was, a holographic sign showed, deep red against the black of the snowy night: Break from Freiwerk. All exits past Eden Cavern are closed. Traffic in the zipway will be stopped. Every flyer will be examined. For your safety cooperate with the authorities.

*Shit, I am so dead.* His mind formed the words clearly. His body refused to get the message. Even as he thought the words, his numbed fingers were closing the control box on the wall, not bothering this time with re-locking the genlock he'd hacked into, just slamming it shut to prevent more snow from getting in. There was no point in wanton destruction.

He felt at his waistband for his stolen burner, then looked towards the zipway, where flyers were slowly coming to a stop, starting at the distant horizon. The other way were dark fields, a couple of country roads, a golf course, a hunting preserve, and ten miles off, as straight as Jarl could run, Hoffnungshaus, where he would be missed as soon as head count was done at dawn. If he could get to it, he would be protected. Getting to it was the problem. What "break from Freiwerk" meant was that mules had rioted again, and a few of them had managed to escape the fortified work-camp. And if the authorities thought even one among them might be able to pass as a normal human, they would be looking at everyone's hands.

Jarl's fingerless gloves stopped just short of the bright red band embedded in the skin of the ring finger on his left hand. The mark of a made human, an artifact. No different than the mules that had just escaped. In this sort of circumstances, he would be shot on sight. And that was if the mules didn't get him first. Creatures manufactured as slaves, created to serve humans all their lives, were remarkably lacking in fellow feeling. And even if they could understand Jarl's own situation, they'd probably feel zero empathy with him.

The thing was—there were burner indentations on the side of the wall towards the fields. He'd made them and climbed up them just an half an hour ago. There were none on the other side, where fifty feet below, the flyers on the zipway were coming to a stop.

Normally descending towards the zipway and running across would have meant death. Just the friction of heated air in the space beneath the flyers was enough to kill. But as the flyers stopped there was just a chance . . . Only it had to be done before the authorities got there to check people in the flyers. He had to be across and up the other wall, and over the side, into . . . He wasn't sure what was on the other side. Other cities and fields, he imagined. But what wasn't there was Freiwerk. Freiwerk was on the same side of the zipway as Hoffnungshaus, which meant it would be the side of the highway that escaped mules—without burners or the agility to scale the walls of the zipway—would roam, and where their pursuers would scour.

He bit at his lip and frowned. His gray attire would be conspicuous as he was descending the wall, and people in the stopping flyers might call the law on him. On the other hand, the night was dark, there was snow, and the light of the suddenly unreadable holographic advertisements above would cast a pattern of light and shadows on the walls anyway. Moving light and shadows. It was just possible, in the confusion, he would pass unnoticed. If he could be fast enough. Fortunately, he'd been bio-engineered to be fast. Among other things.

Getting to the other side of the zipway would get him stranded away from Hoffnungshaus, and he would still have the trouble of being an escaped bio-engineered artifact, proscribed on his own and acceptable only under supervision of the authorities. On the other hand, it would keep him alive past the night. He could always get back to Hoffnungshaus, if he survived. He could always steal a flyer. He'd done it before.

His body had already made the decision for him. He bent sideways, pointing the burner at a point down the zipway wall, melting an indentation deep enough for a toe hold. Then he swung down, holding on to the top of the wall, setting his foot in the indentation, and thinking fast.

The problem was he usually did this going up—not coming down. Going up, he made toe holds and hand holds, and then toe holds again, all the way up. Coming down, he'd need to make hand-holds, and rely on his cold fingers to hold him up. Difficult. Not impossible.

Working quickly, he melted an indentation for his hand, waited a few seconds for it to cool in the December air, and, holding onto it, melted an indentation further down.

He scrambled, hand over hand down, sometimes rushing it and

getting singed fingertips, feeling as if he were going incredibly slow but knowing he was faster than any normal human. The sirens still sounded down the zipway, and the flyers below him were still moving, though slower, as the central control slowed them down so it could stop them.

By the time Jarl was near enough that the wind of normal zipway traffic would have knocked him down, the flyers were going slower and it was a mere stiff wind. He waited there, poised in the area of darkness below the light cast by the holographs and above the lights of the flyers below, hearing the sirens come ever closer, feeling the wind die down.

He could hear his heart beat loudly. The sound of blood rushing in his head made him near-deaf. His fingers felt numb with cold, and he wished the flyers would stop before the sirens got any closer. But he couldn't change either rate. He could only hope it would work out for him. He could only stay there, suspended halfway between the top of the wall and the zipway, and wish would all come out all right. He'd taken a gamble, and sometimes you lost gambles.

He felt more than saw the flyers stop, and he dropped down the remaining meter and a half to the surface of the zipway. The flyers, in stopping, had come to rest on the zipway. It was something he hadn't counted on, which was stupid. Parked flyers always rested on the ground. But he'd counted on that space of darkness beneath the flyers, to run to the other side of the zipway. *Stupid Jarl. So much for bio-engineered for intelligence.*

Now he faced nine rows of flyers, side by side, with their lights on in an endless traffic jam extending way back, completely obstructing the zipway. He had to run among them, somehow, without getting all of those people on their links, calling the authorities.

The only thing he could think of—the only thing he could do— was what he used to get out of trouble at Hoffnungshaus, or at least to keep his trouble as limited as he could. *Look*, he told himself, *as though you have every right to be here.*

He added a minor flourish, by rounding a flyer in such way that for people of other flyers, it would look like he had come out of it. Why anyone should come out of a flyer in these circumstances was anyone's guess. But people did things like that. At least Jarl thought they did. He'd read about them doing things like that. Truth be told, other than books and holos he knew precious little about what real people outside Hoffnungshaus did or why. But he would pretend he came out of the flyer, and walk sedately across.

The problem with walking sedately across was the ever-closer sirens. But Jarl didn't dare run. He felt as though he were holding himself sternly in hand, and not rushing across was the hardest thing he'd ever done.

By the time he reached the other side, right by the wall, it had become obvious that he had already lost too. The sirens were close enough that he could hear the voice blared at intervals: "Do not let anyone into your flyer. Some mules have penetrated the zipway." The Peace Keepers were close enough that in another five minutes their floodlights would illuminate the flyers in the zipway and the wall on each side as starkly as the full light of day, if not more.

Even Jarl could not climb the wall that fast, bio-engineered or not. And if caught halfway up, they would know there was something wrong with him, and he would probably be shot down. But if he didn't try it . . .

He could as easily be taken on the ground.

Wild thoughts of dropping to the ground and knitting himself with the base of the wall crossed his mind and were quickly dismissed, followed by thoughts of running, using his extra speed—just running between the flyers and disappearing. But you could not disappear when each flyer contained people who could come out and grab you. Or shoot you.

*Do not let anyone in your flyer.* The words, coming over the announcement system of the Peace Keeper flyers seemed to echo themselves in Jarl's head, in his own internal voice. If they were saying that, it was because people might.

Fine. Jarl in their place would never do so, but he didn't understand people and would freely admit that he couldn't imagine any of them being silly enough to allow a stranger into their flyer with mules on the loose.

Whenever there were reports on mule riots and mule out-breaks, they went out of their way to tell everyone that some mules looked just like any other humans. Their lack of soul wasn't visible from the outside—hence, the artifact ring. This made it hard for Jarl to believe he could find refuge due to his youthful appearance, even if he faked innocence.

On the other hand, Jarl had a burner. And many, if not most people were unarmed.

He took a deep breath, again, feeling the cold air singe his lungs with a burning sensation. It was a risk. Perhaps too great a risk. Anyone coerced at burner point to let him into their flyer was likely to turn on him the minute the authorities arrived. That was almost certain. But not certain. Not absolutely certain. While getting shot standing out here was absolutely certain.

He scanned the flyers around. Most of them were too small for him to climb aboard and conceal himself when the authorities arrived. But nearby was an eggplant-colored one. It seemed to be a family flyer—six seats at least—and unless there were little ones asleep on the seats, it had only a man and a woman aboard.

Jarl walked back towards it, dipping his hand under his tunic for the burner. He must not show it before he was behind the flyer, because if he did, then the people in the flyer behind or to the side might call the authorities.

So he kept his burner in his waistband, until he got right behind the flyer, then shielding it with his body, started burning the gen-lock. This would set off alarms in the flyer, but it was better than going to the window and waving the burner and demanding to be let in. First, because a lot of the flyers had burner-proof dimatough windshields. Second, because—

Second, because by the time the man clambered back over the seats, towards the rear door, the genlock had burned off, the flyer was unlocked, and Jarl could pull the door up and clamber in, burner in hand, all without being seen to be armed by anyone else but his victims.

The man, standing in the middle of the last row of seats, facing the cargo area, was probably forty. At least, he looked like the director of Hoffnungshaus, who was forty. He had streaks of gray hair back from his temples, marring his otherwise thick mahogany-red hair. He was thickly built too—powerful shoulders, strong legs, big hands clenched on the back of the seats.

*But I have a burner,* Jarl thought, and brought it up, to point square at the man, at the same time looking up into blue-grey eyes. The eyes glanced at the burner, then at Jarl, then the man said, softly, "You might want to close that back hatch, son."

"I have a burner," Jarl said, his voice reedy and thin as it hadn't been for at least four years.

"So I see," the man said. "If you're not going to close that hatch, let me do it," his voice was mild, concerned, seeming not at all worried by Jarl's burner, or what must be the sheer panic in Jarl's eyes. Jarl felt that panic mount. What sort of man wasn't afraid of a burner? He'd read. He'd seen holos. He knew that people were afraid of death. Weren't they? Jarl sure as hell was.

He realized he'd started trembling so badly that his teeth were knocking together, and he was shaking with it, as well as with reaction to the warmth of the flyer after nearly freezing atop the wall. He realized the burner was shaking too hard for him to point at anything. He knew the man must think the same because he pushed past Jarl, closed the back hatch, and did something to it that secured it in place. "There, that will hold," he said, then turned around. "And now, son, what are we going to do with you?"

Jarl shocked himself with a sob, though it was probably just a reaction to the temperature difference. But there was this long breath intake, and his voice came as wavering as his trembling hand, "I can shoot. I can. I can burn you."

"Of course you can. But the way your hand is shaking, you're more likely to set the inside of the flyer on fire, and I don't think that's what you want, is it?" the man asked. And then very gently, "Give me the burner."

Jarl tried not to, but the large hand reached over and took it before he could control his shaking hand. And now Jarl was unarmed and the man had a burner. And Jarl couldn't even see what the man was doing, through the film of tears that had unaccountably filled his eyes, in probably yet another reaction to the cold. *What is the use?* He sank down to his knees, then sat back on his heels, as he waited for the burn he was sure would come.

He heard a click as the burner charge was pulled, the burner safety pushed in place, then a low whistle. "A Peace Keeper burner. Where did you get this?"

"I—It was months ago. I stole it. What does it matter?" Now Jarl's voice sounded hysterical. He could hear the sirens drawing ever closer. A light like full daylight only brighter came through the windows, blinding them. "Shoot me and be done."

"Give me your left hand," the man said, his voice still very calm. And then, "I see." The sound of a deeply drawn breath. "This will wait. They're here. You'll never pass. Not dressed like that."

Jarl found himself hauled up by his left hand and thrown, forcibly, to lying down on a seat. Something fluffy was thrown over him. The man's voice whispered, "Do your best to look ill and sleepy, can you?" And to the other person in the flyer, the one who'd remained quiet through all this. "Jane, make this disappear as much as you can."

"I can't make it disappear. Not enough to—"

"Enough that it will pass unless they take the flyer apart. My job is to make sure they don't. And give me an ID gem. Male. I'd say around fifteen. Or can pass as such. Quickly, Jane."

And suddenly, there was a rush of fresh air, cold and smelling of snow, and Jarl realized that the man had opened the door to the flyer. "How may I help you, officer?"

Jarl's heart was beating so loudly that he had trouble hearing what the Peace Keeper was saying, though he caught the words "mules" "riots" and "forty dead." And then a polite request for the family documents.

Jarl heard gems handed over and the clink of their fitting into a reader. "Mr . . . Carl Alterman, and your wife and son?" the Peace Keeper asked.

"Yes," the man said. "Our son has been having high fevers. We think it is one of those new viruses. We're headed for Friestadt, to see a specialist? Nothing else has worked."

"Oh," the Peace Keeper said, and though Jarl had absolutely no idea why, he could hear the dread in the Peace Keeper's voice, and had the feeling he wouldn't be touched.

The Peace Keeper said, in the official voice, again, "If you'd put your fingers in this machine? It detects the genetic markers of mules, even if the ring has somehow been lost. It's just a formality."

The woman must have gone first, because Jarl heard the ping, and then she leaned back and said, "Honey, do you think you could wake enough to—" Just before a ping sounded that Jarl guessed meant the man too was not bio-engineered.

But the Peace Keeper spoke up before Jarl could answer—even had he known how to—"No need, ma'am. If he's contagious it could be a public health risk."

And then the door closed, and Jarl found himself taking big gulps of air.

He heard the locks closing on the flyer, and the woman said, softly, "Don't sit up. They can still see in here, but we need to talk."

Jarl thought it was funny how the woman's voice sounded so very different than even in holos. He'd never heard a woman's voice without electronic modulation, and it was higher than men's, sure, but it also sounded . . . richer, in ways he couldn't quite express.

"Yes," the man said, before Jarl could speak. "We must know what we're up against, if they're serious enough to test the genetic markers. Let's start at the beginning: are you a mule?"

"No— Yes." Jarl took a deep breath. "Maybe."

He shouldn't have been hurt by the woman's musical giggle, but he was. And then surprised by the man's less tense voice as he said, "Promising! Are you from Freiwerk?"

"What? No. Hoffnungshaus. I am . . . I am bio-engineered. And all my . . . all my . . . kind are too, but we are not mules. We're not gestated in non-human animals, and we're not subnormal. We're rather . . . the other way."

A sharp sucking in of breath from the man, and Jarl had the impression he'd said something terribly wrong, but he wasn't sure what.

"I see," the man said. "So, the rumors aren't just rumors. What is your name?"

"Jarl Ingemar," Jarl said. "We were named by the people who designed us, you know, the national team. I . . . was sent over from Scandinavia at three, when it was decided—"

"Yes, yes. So, if the rumors are true you'd be what? Twenty? Twenty-one?"

"Nineteen."

A breath like a sigh from the man, and a noise Jarl couldn't interpret from the woman, followed by, "Starved." And something that sounded like "Poor boys."

Then the silence went on so long that Jarl wondered what he had said that was so terrible. And then he had to know. "Please, sir," he said. "What do you want to do with me?"

"Uh? Do? Nothing. But—"

"But once he's known to be missing they'll turn the countryside inside out looking for him," the woman said.

"And won't stop till he's captured or there's proof he's dead and gone. They'll want to keep their dirty little secret hidden. . . . Making supermen, indeed."

"I don't want to die," Jarl said, reflexively, understanding nothing but that. His teeth had stopped chattering and the blanket made him feel warm. His fingers stung lightly, where he'd burned them. And he realized he was very hungry. And he didn't want to die.

"No, of course not," the man said. And then after another deep sigh, "What were you doing out there? I suspect they guard you precious few even better than the people from Freiwerk. Don't tell me that there was a riot at your place, also?"

"Uh? No. We . . . There aren't enough of us to riot. And I'm one of the oldest."

"So, how did you get out? What are you doing here?"

Jarl squirmed. How to explain his private obsession, his driving need? How to do it without sounding completely insane, or worse, like a vandal? These people had given him shelter. His entire survival was staked on their continued good will. If they turned him out of the flyer, if they called the Peace Keeper over, Jarl would be done for.

"It's the angel," he said, and then realized he had started all wrong. "I mean, we can see the zipway from our window," he said. "From my window. I can see the zipway and the glow of the holograms above," he said. "Not what they say, of course. Not without calculating it. I mean, they're designed to be seen—"

"Yes," the man said. Curtly. A demand that Jarl go on, without saying it.

"Yeah, well. I used to dream about it. About the zipway. When I was really little. I dreamed about flying in it and reading the holograms." He paused and sensed the puzzled impatience of his hosts. "Only then, when I was four or five, I saw a picture of an angel. You know, a being with wings?"

"We know what angels are," the woman said, very softly.

"Well . . . and then I dreamed that I was flying with my own wings, down the zipway, and all the lights and I . . . and I was free."

Another silence followed, and then the man said, "I still don't understand what that has to do with your being out here."

"The angel, darling," Jane said. And then in the tone of someone who didn't think she should have to explain further. "I read about it yesterday. Perhaps you missed it because you were concentrating . . . Well, because of this trip. But I told you. Some group has been vandalizing the holo ads in this stretch of zipway, climbing up and changing the circuits and reprogramming and making it into the image of an angel with a sword, and sometimes of an angel flying away."

"What?" the man said. "That? But that's a group with technologically advanced tools. Has to be. There's no way a single person could calculate how to change the holograms so that going that fast and—"

"It can if the rumors are true and the idiots are now creating super-slaves . . . super-bureaucrats."

Jarl sniffed. "It's not that difficult," he said. "I was altering the one for Eden resort. I can the back of the holograms from the window, and I can calculate how it would be seen at speed and I can figure out how to change it. It's not hard."

Another long silence. He felt the question "but, why?" unspoken, hanging over all of them. "I don't know," he said. "I don't know why I do it. Escaping is hard, and they usually catch me returning and whip me for getting out, and sometimes my roommates too, but . . ."

"But?"

"But if I don't do it, all I can think of is being an angel and flying away." He breathed deeply, feeling suddenly ashamed. Not of escaping. Not of stealing from advertisers a few hundred minutes of their advertising budget, before the repair crews set it right. No, he felt ashamed of letting Bartolomeu and Xander be whipped for his fault. Not that they ever complained, but . . . They were so little. And they deserved better from him. While he deserved nothing, and certainly not the kindness of these chance-met strangers. "Look," he said. "I'll go. I'll turn myself in. I'm a danger to—"

"No. Protection is freely given," the woman said. "We do not pass by on the other side. And we— Never mind. You're not who we came to save, but you are as in need."

The man said something about throwing the food of the children to the dogs, but Jane came back, "He's as hapless as any of them, Carl. Don't."

"So what do you propose to do?"

"What we'd planned, what else? Only a little modified. Can you give him the serum now? It should have acted by the time we get in, when they unblock the way, if they check."

The man was quiet a long while. "They'll turn the area inside out . . ."

"Yes, which is why it's important that he be genetically our son by then. Or test as such. Come, we're not planning to be here long. They'll comb the fields and streams first, and assume he injured himself or drowned. Particularly if he's in the habit of getting out at night, and he clearly is. No one will want the news of the existence of bioed supermen getting out to the civilian population, so they'll hesitate to search there. By the time they do, we will be well away and near Haven." She paused for a moment. "Please?"

"Yes. Of course. You're right. Of course. The alternative is turning him out, and I don't think . . . Well." He fumbled in something then said, "Jarl, give me your arm."

Jarl extended it, protruding from the end of his sleeve. He needed to get a new tunic. Supposing he ever got back safely to Hoffnungshaus. Supposing they gave it to him. They might not, after this exploit. Even if he got back safely.

He felt the pinprick of the injector, but he didn't feel any different afterwards. He thought it would be a genetic spoofing, designed to show that he was their son, should he be tested. At least that's what he understood from what they said, and he had read about such substances in the sites Xander had hacked into on Hoffnungshaus's links. They weren't very good and they didn't last very long, but as faulty as they were, people worried they would be just the beginning of a slippery slope that would allow mules—eventually—to pass as normal humans. He didn't understand what was so scary about mules integrating with the population since, as Jarl himself, from what he understood, they'd been modified so that they could not reproduce. But it seemed to scare people a lot.

Jane was handing him a bundle of cloth, under the blanket. "Here," she said. "Put these on, under the blanket. They won't see clearly enough in here to see what you're doing. Besides, if you had a fever, you'd thrash about. Then hand me your suit."

Jarl obeyed. He couldn't see the new suit, though it seemed to be larger than the one he'd worn: stretch pants and shirt, it felt like. He handed his suit back to her.

"I wish I could give you a haircut," she said. "But not while the light is shining on us."

It seemed absolutely nonsensical, because he'd had his hair cut just three months ago, and wasn't due for the next for another month, when they'd shave all their heads to prevent lice. But he didn't say anything, and just lay there, feeling oddly comfortable, oddly warm.

He didn't remember falling asleep, and was shocked at waking up. Shocked, because he was in a huge bed, and because he couldn't hear his friends. Instead, he heard birdsong and some distant noise of cutlery approaching closer.

He opened his eyes, then he sat up. The room was at least as large as the big dorm, and might have been larger. It was hard to judge, since it looked completely different from the big dorm and was, in comparison, almost empty. Instead of twenty beds, side by side, it had one very large bed, where Jarl lay, and a big dresser in a corner, then a desk under the wall.

The man he'd seen the day before was walking towards the bed, carrying a tray. "Good morning, sleepyhead. Jane said that I should bring you food so that you didn't freak at the robot servers, which you were likely to do otherwise. I thought you might be starving, as much as you were tired, considering you fell asleep and nothing would wake you and I had to carry you in."

He set a tray on the little table next to the bed. Jarl stared at it agog. "Yeah. Jane said they didn't look like they'd fed you much. Considering that you boys are their pride and hope for the future, you'd think— But they only know one way to do things, and when you consider humans tools . . ." He shrugged. "Anyway, I don't have time to talk to you just now except to tell you quickly that we have given you a temporary spoofing treatment. A more . . . permanent one can be procured, but it will have to be elsewhere, because it needs several treatments. This one will keep you safe while Jane and I . . . While we do what we came here to do."

Jarl set the tray on his knees and started eating. There were three eggs, and large buttered slices of bread, and orange juice, and milk, and thick slices of bacon. Surely there was enough here for three people? But Mr. Alterman didn't stop him as he ate, and after a while, Jarl drank a sip of the milk and said, "Please, sir, can you put me on the other side of the zipway tonight, so I can get back to Hoffnungshaus?"

Alterman frowned. "You want to go back?"

"I have to go back. Otherwise if I'm caught I'll be killed. I—"

"You didn't understand a word I said, did you? You don't need to go back. We can do a very minor operation and remove your artifact ring. And the genetics can be changed permanently, given enough time and treatments."

"But they'll catch me before that!"

The man smiled. It was the first time that Jarl saw him smile, and it was a surprisingly cheery expression. "Not where we're taking you.

But first . . . There are other people we are here to help. So Jane and I have to go out. We'll be back before tonight. We'll arrange it all then. Meanwhile you have this room. No one should come in. I recommend you bathe, and then—Jane put some clothes in that dresser over there. Dress in clean clothes, and wait for us. Don't talk to anyone. There is a gem reader there and some gems. Or you can sleep. It will be a long trip for all of us, so you might as well be rested."

He left before Jarl finished eating. He went through a door on the side of the room, into what looked like a connecting room. Alterman left the door open, and Jarl could hear him talking and Jane responding, but he had no idea what they were saying.

By the time he set his empty tray aside, they were gone. He knew this, because he poked his head in the room next door, and found it empty except for some luggage in the corner.

Then Jarl used the fresher and later he would be ashamed of how long he took about it. Part of it was that he'd never seen a fresher like this. They had freshers at Hoffnungshaus, of course. But washing consisted of standing beneath tepid jets of water and scrubbing as fast as you could before the jet turned on again to rinse you.

Here the jets of water massaged and soothed, and there was a little machine by the side of the shower which cleaned your clothes at the press of a button. Only Jarl was in his underwear—he suddenly blushed at the idea the woman might have undressed him, an idea so strange as to be unbelievable—and he couldn't find the suit they'd given him the day before.

The fresher had mirrors, too. Hoffnungshaus didn't. He'd seen himself before, of course, on darkened windows and other surfaces. But he'd never seen himself this clearly: too-thin freckled face, wide green eyes and his hair . . . He saw what Jane had meant. His hair was a wild straggle all around his face. He could not cut it—but after bathing—in a real tub, immersed in water, and with all the time in the world, he found an elastic strip and tied it back. Then he found a suit that fit him in the drawers in the dresser in his room. It was royal blue, and the type of clothes he saw teenagers wearing in holos—almost shapeless and stretchy. But it felt comfortable, it was not too thin or too tight or too small, and it looked like something he might have worn if he'd been one of the normal people out there, or their children.

There were slippers too, that looked even less substantial than the ones Hoffnungshaus gave him, but which felt warmer and more protective on the feet.

Then he roamed the room, restlessly for a while, and started reading a couple of gems, but couldn't concentrate on them. The softness of the bed called to him. The bedside clock said it was mid-afternoon on the 24th of December when he gave up resisting and went to lie down. It would pass the time, and then Carl and Jane would be back, and then he would find out what they meant. What kind of place could there be, where Jarl wouldn't be caught? And where he would be free, like normal people?

Despite his curiosity, the comfort of the bed made him fall asleep, and he woke up with someone pounding on the door. The pounding was followed by a voice saying, "They're not inside, sir. I told you that. They left this afternoon to go sightseeing."

A voice sounded, sarcastic, clearly mocking the very idea of sightseeing, though Jarl couldn't understand what it said.

"They got a map from the concierge. Here, sir, let me open the door."

There was the sound of someone fumbling with the lock. Jarl wasn't even fully awake, but he reacted the way he would have reacted to a similar situation at Hoffnungshaus. He rolled off the other side of the bed, then edged under it, finding that at least maid service was much better than at Hoffnungshaus, since there was hardly any dust.

He made it just in time. The door opened. The light came on. It shone reflected under the sides of the bed, and Jarl bit his lip and hoped that no one would feel the bed to see if it was warm. They would have at Hoffnungshaus.

But the voices came from near the door. "As you see, they're not in. They said they were going sightseeing and their son would be out exploring the resort."

There was a long silence, then a male voice with a raspy, dismayed tone said, "I don't think that was their son. It was probably one of the escaped mules. Did you check?"

"Sir! We don't make it a habit of checking guests."

"Well, let me tell you who your *guests* are, then. These people are part of a notorious ring of mule smugglers."

"Mule—" the man sounded as though he choked on the word and was, thereafter, incapable of speech.

"They call themselves Rescuers, or something equally ridiculous. The freedom network. They're part of a radical sect that considers mules as humans and try to rehabilitate them. They often take the more functional ones, the foremen, and make them . . . pass. They let them infiltrate humanity."

"Sir!" There was now true horror in the man's voice. "I take it . . . that is, you have captured them?"

"No. We got their flyer, but they seem to have gotten hold of another. They abandoned their flyer and were seen to leave in a sky blue Gryphon, but when we tried to find it, it didn't exist, not by that transponder number." He made a sound that might have been the click of his tongue on the roof of his mouth. "Well. We shall lock this, and get the investigators assigned to this task force to come and look through the luggage. And meanwhile, I suggest you make an announcement to have their so-called son picked up anywhere he's seen on the resort."

"I can . . . I can tell our personnel. An announcement . . ."

"Do as you will, but get moving with it."

Then Jarl heard the door close and lock. He still stayed for a while, under the bed, with his cheek flat against the floor which appeared to be made of real wood, thinking. They were mule . . . rescuers. They believed mules were real humans.

Though Jarl doubted the similarity would impress those mules who'd escaped from Freiwerk, he was too well aware that those mules—those poor unfortunates created in labs and gestated in large animals, even if the animals had been bioed for the purpose— were in a way kin to him and his kind.

Oh, yes, the unfortunates had been made more or less haphazardly from nationalized stores of ova and sperm. Sometimes they'd been grown from frozen embryos. At best there was nothing special about them but the markers that showed them as artifacts. At worst, the conditions under which they'd been gestated—even if the animals had been changed to supposedly secrete human pregnancy hormones and enzymes at the right time—left them mentally deficient and physically deformed. In fact, the news holos made it sound like all of them were deformed and mentally slow. And Jarl didn't doubt that even the best of them were damaged. After all, they were raised in very large groups and taught only the absolute minimum to survive and to be able to work at manual labor.

They were all male, and many were strong, and a tight discipline was maintained over them to keep them quiescent and well behaved. Only now and then they boiled over in riot and escaped.

Jarl and his . . . kind, back at Hoffnungshaus, were not mentally deficient. Rather the opposite. They hadn't been haphazardly brought to life from stored genetic materials. They had been carefully assembled, DNA strand by DNA strand, and characteristic by characteristic, designed to be the best of their kind, the best of their sub-race, the best of their nationality. Their designers had proudly given them their own names.

They were supposed to help manage the increasingly more complex state. Since it had been realized that the planned economy, the planned society couldn't work unless something better than humans could be found to lead it, something better than humans had been created. They were supposed to shepherd humanity into a new age.

Because each nation feared that the other's creation would have no sympathy for them, it had been decided, by treaty, that they'd be brought up at Hoffnungshaus, all together, no matter where they came from in the world. Most of them had only ever known Hoffnungshaus. Jarl, because he was one of the older ones, remembered his first three years, hazily. There had been a family and a woman he called "mother"—he remembered being hugged and kissed.

In Hoffnungshaus he was never kissed or hugged, or touched, at least not by the caretakers and not unless he was being punished. He wasn't stupid enough, he thought, pressing his cheek harder against the floorboard, to think that he had it as bad as the mules, and he was sure most mules would think Hoffnungshaus was a resort, as nice as this one. But he also wasn't stupid enough not to see the resemblances. They were all male, kept isolated. They were brought up by males only, probably because mule riots always involved rapes of nearby females, and the caretakers saw the resemblance between the people in Hoffnungshaus and mules. And they were disciplined somewhere in a way resembling historical prisons and reform houses—possibly because while they were needed, as the mules were needed, if for different things, they were also feared. The mules were feared for their strength. Jarl and his kind were feared for their intelligence. There always hung around their caretakers the faint suspicion that their charges could outwit them without effort, and that the only protection was to keep the young bio-improved boys terrified.

All that Jarl could understand—had understood for a long time, without much thinking—that he was both more and less than normal humans. His mind was more powerful than theirs, but there were things he'd never know: what it was like having a family or growing up in the midst of his equals, freely. He watched enough holos—because Xander was really good at hacking link units—to know how other people lived and how odd and stilted his life would appear to them.

He also knew that most normal humans would be just as horrified at having one of Jarl's kind in their midst as at having a mule.

And yet there were normal humans, free humans—Mr. Alterman and this woman, Jane, whom he'd heard but never yet seen clearly—who would risk everything including arrest and possibly summary justice to free mules.

Jarl never made a decision. Not consciously. But his body knew what to do. Once he was sure the men had really left and weren't trying to trick him into showing himself, he crawled out from under the bed.

He was going through the Alterman's bags before he was sure what he meant to do. But by the time he found a small bag and started throwing into it gems, id gems, anything even vaguely identifiable, plus two bottles of odd serum and a row of empty injectors, he knew. He was going to get out of here, find them, and take them the things they might need to execute their mission and leave. They'd risked everything for others, and he'd risk everything for them.

At the bottom of Jane's bag—he presumed hers, because it contained both a small flask of perfume and what looked like a hair-styling brush—there was a small black book embossed with the words "Holy Bible." It was an old-style book, made of paper and probably expensive, and though it had nothing written on it that might identify her, it looked well thumbed through, and he thought she might very well be upset if it went missing. So he put it in his bag, too.

Finding the burner was harder. It took his almost taking apart their big suitcase. But he thought that they wouldn't be able to come back here anyway. The burner—burners, actually, as there were two besides his own—were in a false bottom which took him quite a while to work out how to open, even though it was obvious from the dimensions it must be there.

He took the belt and holsters there, and put all three burners around his waist.

Things were barely packed, when he heard the murmur of voices outside the room. Time to go. He'd heard the sound of birds outside the window, so there must be an outside to the resort. However, he remembered he was supposed to be exploring, and that resort employees were supposed to be on the lookout for him.

Better leave through the window than through the corridors, where people would spot him. He knew enough of human nature, from Hoffnungshaus, to know most resort employees would prefer to patrol in the cozy inner halls than outside.

The window opened easily and he almost suspected a trap when he realized how close the tree branches were. They'd never allow that at Hoffnungshaus. But he didn't hesitate, because he could hear people right outside the door. He jumped to the tree, then leaned over and closed the window, so as not to leave any sign of his departure. As he did, he could see the door open, but no people yet. Right. He'd left just in time.

And he truly couldn't believe his luck. He found himself in what might have been a primeval forest, if primeval forests had the sort of gardener that made sure everything grew in the most aesthetically pleasing way. Where he'd jumped onto the tree, there were many trees, clustered together, so that he could move from one to the other, without ever touching ground.

As he ran, he caught glimpses of guests. Men and women walking together. Children running around, playing. A little girl crying at the top of her voice. Something like longing swelled in him. The Altermans had said they'd help him become just a normal human among normal humans. He could have this. He could have a family—maybe not natural children, but a family. He was smart enough that he could have wealth and . . . and come back to this resort, and be like these people, just enjoying themselves, with no supervisors, with no restrictions.

He didn't let it delay him. He moved fast, from tree to tree, as far away from people as possible, till he glimpsed the entrance to the resort. And then he stopped, clutching at the branches of the tree he stood in. He couldn't go out that way. There were guards. Or maybe it wasn't guards. Resorts probably didn't have guards, even if they were dressed in uniforms. Colorful ones. Porters or valets or whatever they were called.

Then he noticed that on the other side of the little massif of trees there was a river, and that the river flowed out of the resort. Right.

Making it to the edge of the river was not very difficult, dropping into the river without making a sound was. First he closed the bag he had on him. The material looked impermeable, and he hoped it was. The gems would survive a dunking, but the book wouldn't. He closed it, tying the top to increase the chances it would not let in water. And then he climbed down from the tree, ran along very soft grass to the river side and dropped in.

They'd taught him to swim as a matter of course. They'd taught all of them to swim. He swam in the same direction the river was flowing. There was no one here, this near to the outer wall of the cave from which this resort had been made. Probably an artificial cave, and the daylight and the sky above would of course be artificial lighting and a holo. No. There was someone near the entrance. Two someones. But from the soft sounds emanating from the green shadows under the trees, Jarl thought he would be the last thing on their minds. He grinned to himself, then held his breath and dove under, going into the tunnel under the wall, into which the creek disappeared.

There was a moment of panic, a moment of darkness, the certainty that this tunnel would go on forever, that he could never surface, never breathe. Then he glimpsed light ahead. That was just a moment before he realized the creek was outfitted with a bio-barrier. That meant no fish or plants imported into the idyllic stretch of river inside the resort could make it outside.

Most bio-barriers had a size limit. And, Jarl thought, this one could not be set to kill people swimming out. It could not because people, or children, could fall into the river. And once you were in the tunnel there was no way out but through. It would take more strength than Jarl could muster to swim up-current, back into the resort.

He closed his eyes and let the current carry him. On the other side, he told himself that he was not—not even a little—surprised to be alive. But he scrabbled out of the river and away from the resort, following no road, as fast as he could make it, which was faster than most normal humans.

First, the Altermans had taken a flyer, so he needed a flyer. Second, he must figure out where they had gone. The Peace Keepers believed there was a clue in their possessions, and Jarl had to hope that he had got everything that could give him that clue.

The flyer was a matter of finding a large, public lot. He'd never quite got in as hair-raising an adventure as this one, but he'd been in trouble before, and once or twice it had involved stealing a flyer. He passed a few individual houses but ignored the flyers by them. If those went missing it would be discovered far too quickly.

So he trotted along until he came to a large building—probably an administrative building of some sort—with many flyers parked around it. He chose one of the cheapest flyers, both because it would raise less outcry and because it would have less secure locks and transponder.

He still had to fry the locks, and when he got in he fried the transponder, too, but carefully, making sure the rest of the link still worked. There was a reason for this.

He'd noticed certain marks in the Holy Bible book, and he thought he might be able to use them to figure out where Jane and Carl Alterman had gone. But there was another chance. Peace Keepers communicated via links. One of the things that Xander often did, and that Jarl had learned to do by watching it, was alter links so they got the Peace Keepers communication wave.

Jarl would try to figure the codes and find the Altermans, but if the Peace Keepers found them first, Jarl wanted to know.

He set the link to scan Peace Keepers' communications, then piloted the flyer out of the parking lot, first on a low flying pattern, so that if the owner looked out the window, he or she wouldn't see his own flyer going by.

When he was a good distance from the building, he gained altitude, merging with and feigning tower control, so that it would look to anyone outside as though he'd turned direction of his vehicle to the local traffic stream.

The Peace Keepers' bandwidth kept quiet save for a report of a flyer collision, and reports of catching a local thief.

Then suddenly, just as Jarl headed down to the shelter of a nearby wood, to try to park and figure out the code in the Holy Bible book, it crackled to life in an exciting way.

". . . Have the smugglers surrounded. I repeat, have the smugglers surrounded. Need backup with all possible urgency."

There could be other smugglers in the area. Given the vast amount of goods that were forbidden to trade or buy—mostly for the public's own good—there certainly were. But Jarl felt his hair rising at the back of his neck and, almost instinctively, programmed in the coordinates the Peace Keepers called out.

It wasn't so far. Less than twenty miles. From the air he could see them. A dark blue flyer—did they have color altering abilities?—backed up against a cliff face and surrounded by orange flyers in a semi-circle.

Jane and Carl stood, in poses that indicated they had weapons trained on the police. Behind them, three mu— three people were crouched, next to the flyer. By the light of sunset, which gilded the Peace Keepers flyers to a color that did justice to the popular nickname of pumpkins, it looked like a hopeless situation.

But his situation had been hopeless on the night they'd rescued him.

Jarl flew wide of the gathering, and up behind where the cliff was. By the time he found a treed area in which to hide his stolen flyer, it was full dark. He trotted back to the top of the cliff, overlooking the Peace Keepers and the Altermans. The Altermans had very powerful beams tracked on them, so they stood in relief, illuminated, like statues. He'd like, Jarl realized, to make a statue of them like that, defending the defenseless.

It was the first time he saw Jane clearly. She was young, younger than her husband—was he her husband?—blond, and very pretty. But on her face, as on her husband's, there were the marks of strain, and a certain resigned expression as though, at heart, they didn't expect to escape with their lives. They were holding hands, Jarl noted, with the hands free from the burners.

The Peace Keepers were blaring something about surrendering and submitting themselves to the law. The law, Jarl thought, allowed some people to be created to be used—for their bodies or their minds, but to be used for others' benefit without ever having a hope at freedom. The law, he thought, needed correction.

He laid flat on his belly and started firing both burners at the lights that lit up the scene: the bright floods on top of the orange flycrs, but also the flyers' headlights. As soon as he started firing, he started getting return fire. He heard Jane scream, "Keep down," but he was fairly sure she was speaking to her charges, not him.

After a few moments, the scene was dark, except for flashlights held by individual Peace Keepers, and the beam of those could not possibly illuminate well enough to let them see what he was about to do. And what he was about to do was first set up rocks, precariously balanced on an incline on the right side of the gathering. There were paths of sorts down, on the right and the left, where the cliff effaced downwards towards the surrounding landscape. Jarl set the rocks up so that with a very little touch they would cascade down the right side path, and made sure they were large enough rocks to make quite a lot of noise falling.

Then he turned to the left side path, tripping and grabbing onto bushes to keep himself from sliding all the way down and yet managing to be almost completely silent. It brought him behind the nearest orange flyer. The Altermans were on the other side, and he must get to them.

Getting to them could be done two ways, and he chose the least likely one. He'd gathered from the Altermans' talk that he was undergrown for his age. Well. He'd make use of that. he dropped to his stomach. The flyers were slightly curved below as well as above, an ovoid shape, which, at rest, touched the ground only in the center of its underside. This left a large area of darkness underneath, if one were able to slither underneath quietly.

It wouldn't do for the Altermans. There were five people to get out from behind there. And he didn't know how agile the mules were. But it would do for him.

Holding his breath, almost not daring to think, in a way that seemed to him excruciatingly slow, he crawled under the flyer, and out the other side. He approached the group, still crawling on his belly, and got behind Jane, but not before she turned towards him, the burner almost but not quite swinging his way.

"It is I," he said, standing up and speaking as close as he could to her ear, and as low as he could. "Jarl Ingemar."

She took a deep breath. "Jarl," she said. She pronounced it properly too, ee-arl. And she smelled different from men, in a way that Jarl could not define, but which hit him like a kick to the head, making him feel suddenly slightly drunk. "How—"

"No," he said. "No time. No time to talk about it. I've set things up. Here, here is your bag. It has everything but your clothes and toiletry articles in it. I couldn't bring anything more. They were looking for you at the resort. I thought— When I start the distraction up, you are to leave, crawling under the that flyer on the left. I'll show you where. All of you. I left a flyer for you," he told her the coordinates. In the dark, he could see her hand that held Carl's move. It seemed to him she was tapping on her husband's wrist with her finger. He thought she was telling him what he told her. "On my mark, be ready to go."

"No," she said. "No. What about you? You must come with us. We've talked. We'll adopt you. Where we live, no one knows what we do. We have no children. My husband . . . He was rescued, years ago. We can't have children. We'll adopt you. We'll erase the markers. You can live a normal life."

Jarl closed his eyes. The temptation was almost unbearable. He wanted that normal life. He wanted the freedom he'd seen back at the resort. But if he filed in after them—if no one stayed in the circle to distract the Peace Keepers—they'd be pursued. And, on foot, with the Peace Keepers in flyers, they'd be caught. They'd be killed.

"No," he said. "I'll stay. Don't worry. I have no intention of dying for this. I'll get out of it—somehow. And I'll get back to where I'm supposed to be. Besides, I have friends. Xander and Bartolomeu are supposed to keep me from getting out. They'll be half killed if I don't come back. Now, mind you, on your mark."

"We do this," Jane said. "Because we believe that God made man in his image and semblance and that his son once took human form, and therefore every human form is sacred."

"Sounds good to me," Jarl said, slightly impatient. "I have a human form."

"You have a human heart," she said, softly. "And today is the anniversary of the day we believe the son of God was born. They say angels sang in the sky to heraldhim. You've been our angel tonight."

It was nonsensical and stupid, but he felt tears in his eyes, even if all he could get out was a gruff "go."

And then took the rock he'd put in his pocket, and making use of those bio-improved physical abilities, he aimed at where he left the rock pile, and threw. Hard.

The sound of someone slipping and sliding down the path on the right came. "Go," Jarl whispered to Jane.

She got the mules out first, crawling beneath the edge of the flyer, the way Jarl had come in. It was easy, because all the Peace Keepers had run to the end of the other path, hoping to catch Jarl.

Jarl waited just long enough to make sure that the Altermans were some way away, then he started working on his own escape. He pointed at the nearest flyer, and burned. Then the one next. Then the other. He knew precisely where the power packs were—he'd stolen one of these before. Hitting them in the power packs caused a most satisfying explosion, and then some of the debris caught the other flyers, until even the blue flyer behind him was burning.

Jarl dove behind it, anyway, for some modicum of protection from the flying debris. Most of the Peace Keepers had run the other way, to avoid the debris, and he could hear them calling frantically for help, so they must have at least one working transponder. He could vaguely see orange flyers converging.

But they weren't here, yet, and the other Peace Keepers were too far away to fire at him. The cliff face was craggy and naturally had much better hand- and footholds than the wall around the zipway. And he could move fast. Very fast.

He climbed the cliff face quickly, thanking whoever had designed him for superhuman speed, coordination and balance. The God of normal humans might have made them in His image and semblance. Jarl's creators had improved on the design.

He was at the cliff top before the Peace Keepers' reinforcements arrived and started sweeping the cliff face with brilliant lights. They found nothing.

Jarl found nothing as well, when he got to where he'd parked his flyer. He'd hoped to find nothing. He hoped they were well and away.

As for him, he turned and, tiredly, started to make his way towards Hoffnungshaus. If he got there in the next twenty-four-hours, perhaps Bartolomeu and Xander would avoid extreme punishment.

He couldn't leave for a week after that. Not only was he too sore from the truly spectacular whipping he'd got as punishment, but he wasn't left unwatched a single night. And he was not just watched by Bartolomeu and Xander, but by a sentinel, outside this door.

But after a week on his best behavior, vigilance relaxed.

Hoffnungshaus did not have the resources to devote that much to their most troublesome charge. And besides, Jarl might escape, but he always came back and of his free will. While they held his friends, he would not disappear for good.

And so a week later, Jarl escaped and made it back atop the zipway wall, where he'd been when the sirens first sounded.

When he opened the panel, there was something in there, besides the circuits. At first he thought snow had got in there and not melted, but that was stupid. It would, of course, have melted. Touched, the whiteness revealed itself for a slip of paper. By the light of the holograms he read it. "Dear Jarl, I want you to know you are on our thoughts and in our prayers. On Christmas night, you were our savior angel. I don't think we can rescue you—even if we found the location of your creche, it would be very well guarded. But we want you to know the mules you rescued that night are your age, quite normal as to intelligence, and will have a chance at a normal life because of you." It ended with a very odd phrase in quotes, something Jarl had a vague memory of hearing sung in an old holo, "Angels we have heard on high."

He let the paper go in the wind, of course. He could not take it back to Hoffnungshaus, but in a way it would always be with him.

Jarl's fingers worked furiously, blindly, tying and connecting the circuits in a way they'd never been meant to go, and then tapping a mad dance on the buttons, reprogramming the hologram.

By the time he climbed down from the wall and beat a hasty retreat through the fields to Hoffnungshaus, making sure to lay a false path so no one would think this was him—even if they believed a single person could make the calculations to change the holos—he knew that from down in the zipway people flying towards Friedstadt would see an angel all in white fly away to disappear into the dark snowy night.

Jarl half dreamed that Jane and Carl would be out again, on one of their missions of mercy, and would see it, and know he was well and had got their message.

Angels he had met right here.

# INTRODUCTION
## MAD HOLIDAY

**LEAVING EARTH NOW,** the destination is Venus Equilateral, a huge space station positioned in Venus's orbit so that it is equidistant from Venus and the Sun, making an enormous equilateral triangle, which happens to be a very stable place to put a satellite. The station was designed to facilitate communications in space, and is, libertarians please note, a capitalistic venture rather than a government project, though the station does have to meet certain standards to maintain its franchise. An unethical wheeler-dealer would like to take over that very profitable franchise—and if that requires interrupting a Christmas celebration and committing murder? No problem . . .

George O. Smith (1911-1981) was the "other" Smith in science fiction (and *Astounding*'s) Golden Age, along with E. E. Smith, better known as Doc Smith. George O. was equally a master of space opera, though his were on a smaller scale than Doc Smith's galaxy-hopping, star-smashing epics. He was also one of the first exponents of hard science fiction, where, aside from a speculative element, the science in the story is straight from the textbooks, rather than made up to fit the story. An electronics engineer, he worked on secret projects for the U.S. during WWII, including developing the proximity fuse. Arthur C. Clarke wrote that Smith "was probably the first writer—certainly the first technically qualified writer—to spell out [space stations'] uses for space communications." Smith's works besides the Venus Equilateral series include *Pattern for Conquest*, *Hellflower*, *Fire in the Heavens*, *The Path of Unreason*, and two notable novels set entirely on Earth, *Highways in Hiding*, written in a Raymond Chandler-like style, and *The Fourth R*, which told the story of a young boy educated by direct mental input.

# MAD HOLIDAY

## By George O. Smith

"YEAH," Wes Farrell drawled, "but what makes it vibrate?"

Don Channing looked down at the crystal. "Where did you get it?" he asked.

Walt Franks chuckled. "I bet you've been making synthetic elements again with the heterodyned duplicator."

Farrell nodded. "I've found a new series sort of like the iron-nickel-cobalt group."

Channing shook his head. There was a huge permanent magnet that poured a couple of million gauss across its gap, and in this magnetic field Farrell had the crystal supported. A bank of storage batteries drove several hundred amperes—by the meter—through the crystal from face to face on another axis, and down from above poured an intense monochromatic light.

"Trouble is," complained Wes, "that there isn't a trace of a ripple in any of the three factors that work on the thing. Permanent magnet, battery current, and continuous gas-arc discharge. Yet—"

"It vibrates," nodded Channing. "Faintly, but definitely it is vibrating."

Walt Franks disappeared for a moment. He returned with a portable phonograph, which caused Don Channing to grin and ask,

"Walt, are you going to make a recording of this conversation, or do you think it will dance to a Strauss waltz?"

"It's slightly bats, so I brought the overture to *Die Fledermaus* for it," snorted Franks.

As he spoke, he removed the pickup from the instrument and added a length of shielded wire. Then he set the stylus of the phonograph against the faintly vibrating crystal and turned up the gain.

At once a whining hum came from the loudspeaker.

"Loud, isn't it?" he grinned. "Can you identify that any better?"

Wes Farrell threw up his hands. "I can state with positiveness that there isn't any varying field of anything that I know of that is at that frequency."

Channing just grinned. "Maybe it's just normal for that thing to vibrate."

"Like an aspen leaf?" Walt asked.

Channing nodded. "Or like my wife's Jell-O."

Walt turned the dial of an audio generator until the note was beating at zero with the vibrating crystal. "What frequency does Arden's Jell-O work at?" he asked. "I've got about four-fifty per second."

"Arden's Jell-O isn't quite that nervous," said Don, puzzling.

"Taking my name in vain?" asked a cool and cheerful contralto.

Don whirled and demanded, "How long have you been keyhole-listening?"

Arden smiled. "When Walt Franks nearly runs me down without seeing me—and in his great clutching hands is a portable phonograph but no records—and in his eye there is that wild Captain Lightning glint—I find my curiosity aroused to the point of visible eruption. Interesting, fellers?"

"Baffling," admitted Channing. "But what were you doing standing on odd corners waiting for Walt to run you down for?"

"My feminine intuition told me that eventually one of you would do something that will wreck the station. When that happens, my sweet, I want to be among the focus of trouble so that I can say I told you so."

Walt grunted. "Sort of a nice epitaph," he said.

"We'll have them words, 'I tole ya so,' engraved on the largest fragment of Venus Equilateral when we do."

Don grinned. "Walt, don't you like women?"

Franks swelled visibly and pompously. "Why, of course," he said with emphasis. "Some of my best friends are women!"

Arden stuck her tongue out at him. "I like you, too," she said. "But you wait—I'll fix you!"

"How?" Walt asked idly.

"Oh, go freeze," she told him.

"Freeze?" chuckled Walt. "Now, that's an idea."

"Idea?" asked Don, seeing the look on Walt's face. "What kind of idea?"

Walt thought seriously for a moment. "The drinks are on me," he said. "And I'll explain when we get there. Game? This is good."

Insistent, Walt led them from Wes Farrell's laboratory near the south end skin of Venus Equilateral to Joe's, which was up nine levels and in the central portion of the station.

"Y'know," Walt said, "women aren't so bad after all. But I've got this feminine intuition business all figured out. Since women are illogical in the first place, they are inclined to think illogical things and to say what they think. Then if it should happen to make sense, they apply it. I used to know an experimenter who tried everything he could think of on the theory that someday he'd hit upon something valuable. Well—this is it, good people."

Walter shoved the door open and Wes Farrell grinned as he always did at the sign that read:

JOE'S
THE BEST BAR IN
TWENTY-SEVEN MILLION MILES
(MINIMUM)

Arden entered and found a place at the long bar. The three men lined up on either side of her and Joe automatically reached for the Scotch and glasses.

"Now," said Channing, "what is it?"

Walt lifted his glass. "I drink to the Gods of Coincidence," he chanted, "and the Laws of Improbability. 'Twas here that I learned that which makes me master of the situation now."

Arden clinked her glass against his. "Walt, I'll drink to the Gods of Propinquity. Just how many problems have you solved in your life by looking through the bottom of a glass—darkly?"

"Ah! Many," he said, taking a sip of the drink. He swallowed. A strange look came over his face. He sputtered. He grew a bit ruddy of face, made a strangling noise, and then choked. "Migawd, Joe! What have you mixed this with, shoe polish?"

"Just made it this afternoon," replied Joe.

"Then throw it back in the matter bank and do it again," said Walt.

Don took a very cautious sip and made a painfully wry face. "The SPCS—Society for the Prevention of Cruelty to Scotch— should dip their tongue in this," he said.

Joe shrugged. "It's from your own pet brand," he told Channing.

Arden smelled gingerly. "Don," she asked him seriously, "have you been petting dragons?"

Wes, chemistlike, dipped his forefinger in the drink, diluted it in a glass of water, and touched it to his tongue. "It'll never be popular," he said.

Joe turned back to his duplicator and shoved a recording into the slot. The machine whirred for a few seconds, and Joe opened the door and took out the new bottle, which he handed to Walt. Walt cut the seal and pulled the cork, and poured. He tasted gingerly and made the same wry face.

"What in the name of hell could have happened?" he asked.

"It's the same recording," asserted Joe.

"But what happened to it?"

"Well," admitted Joe, "it was dropped this morning."

"In what?" Walt demanded.

"Just on the floor."

Wes Farrell nodded. "Probably rearranged some of the molecular patterns in the recording," he said.

Joe put both bottles in the duplicator and turned the switch. They disappeared in seconds, and then Joe took another recording and made a bottle of a different brand.

Again Walt tasted gingerly, smiled hugely, and took a full swallow. "Whew," he said. "That was almost enough to make a man give up liquor entirely."

"And now," said Don Channing. "Let us in on your big secret— or was this just a ruse to get us in this gilded bistro?"

Walt nodded. He led them to the back of the bar and into the back room. "Refrigerator," he said.

Arden took his arm with affected sympathy. "I know it's big enough, but—"

Walt swung the huge door open and stepped in.

"I didn't really mean—" continued Arden, but her voice died off, trailing away into silence as Walt, motioning them to come in, also put his finger on his lips.

"Are you going to beef?" demanded Channing.

"No, you big ham," snorted Walt. "Just listen!"

Wes blinked and slammed the door shut behind them.

And then in the deep silence caused when the heavy door shut off the incident sounds from Joe's restaurant and bar, there came a faint, high-pitched hum.

Don turned to Arden. "That it?" he asked. "You've got better pitch sense than I have."

"Sounds like it," Arden admitted.

"Cold in here," said Wes. He swung open the door and they returned to the bar for their drink. "We can establish its identity easily enough," he told them. He finished the drink, and turned from the bar. "Walt, you bring the pickup and amplifier; Don, you carry the audio generator; and I'll bring up the rear with the rest of the gadget."

They left, and Joe threw his hands out in a gesture of complete helplessness.

"Trouble?" Arden asked cheerfully.

"I didn't mind when they used the tablecloths to draw on," he said. "I didn't really object when they took the tablecloths and made

Warren use 'em as engineering sketches to make things from. But now, dammit, it looks like they're going to move into my refrigerator, and for God knows what! I give up!"

"Joe," said Arden sympathetically, "have one on me."

"Don't mind if I do," chuckled Joe laconically. "If I'm to be shoved out of mine own bailiwick, I might as well enjoy these last few days."

He was finishing the drink as the technical section of Venus Equilateral returned, laden with equipment.

Arden shrugged. "Here we go again," she said. "Once more I am a gadget widow. What do you recommend, Joe? Knitting—or shall I become a dipsomaniac?"

Joe grinned. "Why not present Don with a son and heir?"

Arden finished her glass in one draught, and a horrified expression came over her face. "*One* like Don is all I can stand," she said in a scared voice. Then she smiled. "It's the glimmering of an idea, though," she added with brightening face. "It stands a fifty-fifty chance that it might turn out to be a girl—which would scare Don to death, having to live with two like me."

"Twins," suggested Joe.

"You stay the hell out of this," said Arden good-naturedly.

Walt Franks reappeared, headed out of the restaurant, and returned a few minutes later with another small case full of measuring equipment.

"And this," said Arden as Walt vanished into the refrigerator once again, "will be known as the first time Walt Franks ever spent so much time in here without a drink!"

"Time," said Joe, "will tell."


Halfway between Lincoln Head and Canalopsis, Barney Carroll was examining a calendar. "Christmas," he said absently.

Christine Baler stretched slender arms. "Yeah," she drawled, "and on Mars."

Her brother Jim smiled. "Rather be elsewhere?"

"Uh-huh," she said.

"On Terra, where Christmas originated? Where Christmas trees adorn every home, and the street corners are loaded with Santa Clauses? Where—?"

"Christmas is a time for joy," said Christine. "Also, to the average party Christmas means snow, wassail, and friends dropping in. Me, I'm acclimated—almost—to this chilly Martian climate. Cold weather has no charm for your little sister, James."

"Oh," said Barney.

"Oh," Jim echoed, winking at his sidekick.

"Don't you 'Oh' me," snorted Christine.

"Oh?" Barney repeated. "Okay, woman, we get it. Instead of the cold and the storm, you'd prefer a nice warm climate like Venus?"

"It might be fun," she said evasively.

"Or even better," said Jim Baler to Barney Carroll, "we might visit Venus Equilateral."

Christine's evasive manner died. "Now," she said, "you've come up with a bright idea!"

Barney chuckled. "Jim," he said, "call Walt Franks and ask him if he has a girl for us?"

"He has quite a stock in his little black book," remarked Jim.

"We'll drop in quietly, surpriselike," announced Christine. "And if there's any little black book, I'll see that you two Martian wolves divide 'em evenly."

"Walt is going to hate us for this," Jim chuckled. "Accessories to the fact of his lost bachelorhood. Okay, Chris, pack and we'll—"

"Pack, nothing," laughed Christine. "I've packed. For all three of us. All we need is our furs until we get to Canalopsis. Then," she added happily, "we can dress in light clothing. I'm beginning to hate cold weather."

"How about passage?" asked Barney. "Or did you—"

Christine nodded. "The *Martian Girl* leaves Canalopsis in about three hours. We pause at Mojave, Terra, for six hours; and thence to Venus Equilateral on the special trio that takes Christmas stuff out there."

Jim Baler shrugged. "I think we've been jockeyed," he said. "Come on, Barney, 'needs must when a woman drives.'"

"The quotation pertains to the devil," objected Barney.

"No difference," said Jim, and then he ducked the pillow that Christine threw at him.

A half-hour later they were heading for Canalopsis.

"Walt?" smiled Arden. "Oh, sure. Walt's fine."

"Then?"

"Yeah," Barney added good-naturedly, "do we find 'em in Joe's or elsewhere?"

"The Joe Section of the engineering has been completed," said Arden with a grin. "They nearly drove Joe nuts for about a week."

"What were they doing?" asked Jim. "Building an electronically operated martini?"

"When I tell you, you won't believe me," said Arden. "But they've been living in Joe's refrigerator."

"Refrigerator?" gasped Christine.

"Just like a gang of unhung hams," said Arden. "But they're out now."

"Well! That's good."

Arden paused in front of three doors on the residence level near her apartment. Jim, Christine, and Barney each put their traveling bags inside. Then Arden led them high into the station, where they came to a huge bulkhead in which was a heavy door.

Arden opened the door and an icy blast came out.

"Jeepers!" Christine exploded.

"Hey! Icemen!" called Arden.

From the inside of the vast room came Don, Walt, and Wes. They were clad in heavy furs and thick gloves. Channing was carrying a small pair of cutters that looked a bit ridiculous in the great gloves.

"Well, holy rockets!" asked Channing. "What gives?"

"Merry pre-Christmas," said Jim.

Don whipped off a glove and Jim wrung his hand unmercifully. Wes Farrell greeted Barney Carroll jovially, while Walt Franks stood foolishly and gaped at Christine Baler.

Christine looked the heavy clothing over and shook her head. "And I came here to be warm," she said. "Come out from behind that fur, Walt Franks. I know you!"

"What is going on?" asked Barney.

"It all started in Joe's refrigerator," said Wes. "We found that the cold had crystallized a bit of metal in the compressor. We discovered that it was radiating one of the super-frequencies of the crystal-alloy level. When warm, it didn't. So we've set up this super-cooler to make checks on it. Looks big."

Channing waved toward the door. "We've got the ultimate in super-coolers in there," he said. "Remember the principle of the sun power tube—that it will drain power out of anything that it's attuned to? Well, we're draining the latent heat energy out of that room with a power-beam tube—actually we're transmitting it across space to Pluto."

"Pluto?"

"Uh-huh. In effect, it is like trying to warm Pluto from the energy contained in that room. Obviously we aren't going to melt much of the solid-frozen atmosphere of Pluto nor create a warm and habitable planet of it. We can run the temperature down to damn near Nothing Kelvin without doing much of anything to Pluto."

"We're below the black body temperature of Mars right now," said Walt. "And the gadgetry is working so much better that we're going to run it down to as far as we can get it."

"What do you hope to find?" asked Barney.

"Why, it looks as though we can make a set of crystals that will permit instantaneous communication from one to the other."

"Sounds good."

"Looks good, so far," said Channing. "Want to see it?"

Christine looked at the thermometer set in the face of the door. She turned back to the others and shook her head vehemently.

"Not for all the ice in Siberia," she said fervently.

Walt brightened. "How about some ice in a glass," he said.

"For medical purposes only," agreed Barney. "It's been deadly cold on Mars—about a quart and a half of sheer and utter cold."

"Been cold in there, too," said Don. "Arden, you're out of luck— you've stayed out of the cold."

"You try to freeze me out of this session," said Arden, "and you'll find that I have the coldest shoulder in the Solar System."

♣ ♣ ♣

As the party from Mars had left the platform of the spacecraft poised on the landing stage of Venus Equilateral, another landing was made. This landing came from the same ship, but unlike the arrival of the Balers and Barney Carroll, the later landing was unseen, unknown, and unwanted.

Mark Kingman had been a stowaway.

Now, most stowaways are apprehended because success in such a venture is difficult. To properly stow away, it is calculated that more than the nominal cost of the trip must be spent in planning and preparation. Also, there is the most difficult of all problems—that of stepping blithely ashore under the watchful eye of a purser or authority whose business it is to see that all the passengers who embarked ultimately disembark—no more and no less; plus or minus zero. (It is considered that an infant born aboard ship is a legal passenger and not a stowaway. This is a magnanimity on the part of the transportation companies, who understand that they might have difficulty in persuading any court that the will exists to defraud the company of rightful revenues, etc. A death and burial at sea is also ignored; the transportation company has already collected for a full fare!) But Mark Kingman had done it. He had come aboard in a large packing case, labeled:

CERTIFIED UNIQUE!
(Identium Protected)
Under NO Circumstances Will DUPLICATOR or
MATTER TRANSMITTER Be Tolerated

With magnificent sophistry, Kingman was within the letter of the law that did not permit false representation of contained merchandise. For he, a human being, was a certified unique, he having never been under the beam of the integrator scanning beam of the matter duplicator or transmitter. Nor had any other living human, for that matter. The identium protection was insurance on all such cargoes; it prevented some overly—or underly—bright clerk from slipping the package into a duplicator to make shipping easier.

Identium exploded rather violently under the impact of the scanner beam, it will be recalled.

Along with Kingman was a small battery-operated duplicator, and a set of recordings. The duplicator produced fresh air as needed, water, food, and even books, games, and puzzles for solitary entertainment. Waste material went into the matter bank, proving the earlier statements that with a well-equipped duplicator and a set of recordings, any man can establish a completely closed system that will be valid for any length of time desired.

When the ship landed, Kingman tossed all the loose material into the duplicator and reduced it to non-homogenous matter in the matter bank. Then he turned the duplicator beam against the sidewall of the huge box and watched the sidewall disappear into the machine.

He stepped out through the opening, which was calculated to miss the concealed plates of identium installed to prevent just this very thing. Kingman, of course, had planned it that way.

Once outside, Kingman set the duplicator on the deck between other cases and snapped the switch. The scanner beam produced books from Kingman's own library which he packed in the case. Then, by reversing the direction of depth scan without changing the vertical or horizontal travel, Kingman effected a completed reversal of the restoration. The side of the packing case was reestablished from the inside out, from the original recording, which, of course, was made from the other side. It reformed perfectly, leaving no seam.

Kingman went down an unused shaft to the bottom of the ship, where he drilled down with the duplicator through the ship where it stood upon the landing stage. Down through the stage he went and into a between-deck volume that was filled with girders.

He reset the duplicator and replaced the landing stage and the ship's hull.

By the time the party had adjourned to Joe's, Mark Kingman was high in the relay station, near the center line and a full mile and a half from the landing stage. He was not far from the vast room that once contained a lush growth of Martian sawgrass, used before the advent of the duplicator for the purification of the atmosphere in Venus Equilateral.

He was reasonably safe. He knew that the former vast storages of food and supply were no longer present and, that being the case, that few people would be coming up to this out-of-the-way place almost a third of a mile above the outer radius of the station, where the personnel of Venus Equilateral lived and worked.

He started his duplicator and produced a newly charged battery first. He tossed the old one into the matter bank. He'd have preferred a solar energy tube, but he was not too certain of Sol's position from there and so he had to forego that.

Next, he used the duplicator to produce a larger duplicator, and that duplicator to make a truly vast one. The smaller numbers he shoved into the larger one.

From the huge duplicator, Kingman made great energy beam tubes and the equipment to run them. Taking his time, Kingman set them up and adjusted them carefully.

He pressed the starting button.

Then a complete connection was established between an area high in the station but a good many thousand feet away—and on the other side of the central axis—through the energy beam tubes, and a very distant receptor tube on the planet Pluto.

"This," punned Kingman, "will freeze 'em out!"

His final act before relaxing completely was to have the huge duplicator build a small but comfortable house, complete with furniture and an efficient heating plant. Then he settled down to wait for developments.

"So what brings you out to Venus Equilateral?" asked Don.

"Christmas," said Barney. "We—Christine—thought that it might be nice to spend Christmas with old friends in a climate less violent than Mars."

"Well, we're all tickled pink," nodded Arden.

"Frankly," Jim Baler grinned, "my Channing sister has set her sights on your bachelor playmate."

"I think it is mutual," said Arden. "After all, Walt has had a lot of business to tend to on Mars. He used to use the beams to conduct business—in fact, he still does most of it by communications when it isn't Mars—but give him three ten-thousandths of an excuse and he's heading for Canalopsis."

"I noted with interest that Christine was quite willing to help him work."

"Fat lot of work they'll accomplish."

"Speaking of work, Wes, what goes on right now in this deal?" Don asked.

"We've just set up a modulator," said Wes. "I'm modulating the current since the magnetic field is supplied by a permanent magnet and the monochromatic light comes from an ion arc. Using varying light seems to widen the response band with a loss in transmission intensity. This way, you see, all the energy going into the crystal is transmitted on a single band, which is of course a matter of concentrated transmission."

"That sounds sensible. Also, if this gets to sounding practical, it is quite simple to establish and maintain a high-charge permanent magnet field, and also a monochromatic light from a continuous gas arc. Easier, I'd say, than making ammeters all read alike."

"Utopia," said Wes Farrell, "is where you can use any handy meter and find it within one-tenth of one percent of any other—including the Interplanetary Standard."

Channing observed that Utopia was far from achieved. Then he said: "You've got the Thomas gents out in a ship with another crystal setup?"

"*Anopheles*," said Farrell, "will shortly head for Mars with the other half of the gear in another refrigerated compartment. If this proves practical, Pluto is going to become useful."

Arden nodded absently. "I've always claimed that there is a practical use for everything."

Channing opened his mouth to say something and had it neatly plugged by Arden's small hand. "No, you don't." she said. "We've all heard that one."

"Which one?" asked Farrell.

"The one about the navel being a fine place to hold the salt when you're eating celery in bed," said Arden.

Channing removed Arden's hand from his mouth and placed it in hers. "You done it," he told her ungrammatically. "For which I'll not tell you what Walt and Christine are doing right now."

Arden's attempt to say, "Pooh. I know," was thoroughly stifled and it came out as a muffled mumble.

Channing turned to Wes and asked: "Have any good theories on this thing?"

Farrell nodded. "I noted that the energy entering the crystal was not dissipated as heat. Yet there was quite a bit of energy going in, and I wanted to know where it was going. Apparently, the energy going into the crystal will only enter under the influence of a magnetic field. Changing the field strength of the magnet changes the band, for the transmission to the similar crystal ceases until the other one has had its magnetic field reduced in synchronous amount. Also, no energy is taken by the crystal unless there is an attuned crystal. The power just generates heat, then, as should be normal."

"So," said Wes thoughtfully, "the propagation of this communicable medium is powered by the energy going into the crystal. Crystals tend to vibrate in sympathy with one another: hitting one with a light hammer will make the other one ring, and vice versa. I've tried it with three of them, and it makes a complete three-way hookup. As soon as Chuck and Freddie Thomas get out a good way, we'll be able to estimate the velocity of propagation, though I think it is the same as that other alloy transmission band we've been using."

Channing grinned. "The speed of light, squared?"

Farrell winced. *That* argument was still going on, whether or not you could square a velocity. "We'll know," he said quietly.

The loudspeaker above Farrell's desk hissed slightly, and the voice of Freddie Thomas came in: "I'm about to trust my precious life once more to the tender care of the harebrained piloting of my semi-idiot brother. Any last words you'd like to have uttered?"

Wes picked up a microphone and said: "Nothing that will bear transmission under the rules. If there's anything I want to tell you, I'll call you on this—and if this doesn't work, we'll try the standard. They're on your course?"

"On the button all the way—they tell me."

"Well, if you jiggle any, call us," said Farrell, "either on the standard space phone or this coupled-crystal setup."

Channing grinned. "So it has a name?"

Freddie laughed. "We never did settle on a name for the driver-radiation communication system. So we're starting this one off right. It's the Coupled-Crystal Communicator. For short, 'Seesee,' see?"

Channing returned the laugh. "'Seeseesee,' or 'Seesee' understand?'"

Chuck Thomas chimed in. "My semi-moronic brother will delay this takeoff if he doesn't sharpen up," he said. "What he means is: Seesee, or Get it?"

"I get it," replied Channing.

And they did get it. Hour followed hour and day followed day from takeoff to turnover, where there was no Doppler effect even though the velocity of the ship was fiercely high.

The hours fled by in a working flurry of tests and experiments and almost constant talk between the arrowing ship and Venus Equilateral . . .

"It doesn't add up," Walt Franks complained.

Christine looked up from her book and waited.

"Something's more'n we bargained for," he said.

"What?" asked Christine.

"Why, that area we're chilling off is cooling far too fast."

"I should think that would be an advantage," said Christine.

"Maybe—and maybe not," said Walt. "The big thing is that things should behave according to rules. When they do not, then's when people make discoveries that lead to new rules."

"That, I don't follow," said Christine.

"Well, in this case we know to several decimal places the heat equivalent of electrical energy. Three thousand, four hundred thirteen kilowatt hours equals one BTU—a British Thermal Unit. We know the quantity of electrical power—the number of kilowatts—being coursed through the tubes en route to Pluto. We know by calculation just how many calories of heat there are in the area we're cooling off—and therefore we can calculate the time it will take to reduce the temperature of that area a given number of degrees Centigrade. We're about double."

"And—you were starting to explain something different," said Christine.

"Oh. Yes. Well, for a number of years—several thousand, in fact—it was taught that a heavy mass falls faster than a light mass. Then Galileo tossed rocks off the Tower of Pisa and showed that a small stone and a large stone fall equally fast. That was a case where definitely provable evidence was at variance with the rules. They couldn't revise the actuality, so they had to revise the rules."

"I see. And now because that area is cooling off much faster than anticipated, you anticipate that something is not behaving according to the rules?"

"Bright girl," chuckled Walt.

"Thank you, kind sir." Christine laughed. "But remember that I was raised in a bright family."

"Come on," said Walt. "We're going to investigate."

"In that cold room?" Christine asked with some concern.

Walt nodded. "You'll get used to it," he said absently, collecting a few instruments.

"Look, Walt," said Christine in a scathing tone, "I *am* used to it! That's why I came to Venus Equilateral from Mars. Remember?"

Walt looked at her, wondering. But Christine wore a smile that took most of the sting out of her words.

"Lead on, Walt. I can take a bit of chill. In fact," she said with a half-smile, "under the proper circumstances, a bit of chill is fun."

Walt finished collecting his equipment and packed it into two carrying cases. Then, from a closet, he took electrically warmed clothing, helped Christine into hers, climbed into his own, and they took the long trek along corridors and up elevators to the cold room.

"It's cold even here," said Christine.

"The room leaks bad," said Walt. "Wes Farrell's hobby these days is making synthetic elements on the duplicator—he uses a filter to get a monoatomic pattern and then heterodynes the resulting signal to atomic patterns above the transuranic system. But in all of Wes Farrell's playing at making synthetic transuranic elements, he hasn't come up with anything like a good heat insulator yet. We did toy with the idea of hermetically sealing in a double wall and piping some of the vacuum of interstellar space in there. But it was too vast a project. So we let some heat leak, and to hell with it."

Christine shuddered. "I've never really appreciated the fact that Venus Equilateral is really just a big steel capsule immersed in the vacuum of interplanetary space," she said. "It's so much like a town on Terra."

"Inside, that is," grinned Walt. "There's a nice queasy thrill awaiting you when first you stand in an observation blister made of plastiglass."

"Why?" she asked.

"Because first you're terrified because you are standing on a bubble that is eminently transparent and looking down beneath your feet, you see the stars in the sky. You know that 'down' to the working and residence section of the station is actually 'out and away' from the axis of the station, since it revolves about the long axis to provide a simulated gravity plus gyroscopic action to stabilize the beam stage and pointers. Well, when you go down—and again 'down' is a relative term, meaning the direction of gravitic thrust— into one of the blisters, your mind is appalled at the fact that your feet are pressing against something that your eyes have always told you is 'up.' The stars. And then you realize that between you and the awesome void of space is just that thin glass.

"You end up," he grinned, "being very careful about banging your heels on the floor of the station for about a week."

"Well, thanks for the preparation," said Christine.

"You'll still go through it," he told her. "But just remember that anybody on the other side of the station, standing in a similar blister a mile 'above' your head, is standing feet 'upward' with respect to you. But he, too, is being thrown out and away by centrifugal force."

Walt put his equipment down and rummaged through it. He selected a supersensitive thermocouple and bridge and fixed the couple to one of the fixtures in the room. He balanced the bridge after the swinging needle came to a halt—when the thermocouple junction had assumed the temperature of the fixture.

"Now," he said, "we'll read that at the end of a half-hour and we'll then calculate the caloric outgo and balance it against the kilowatts heading out through the energy beam."

"And in the meantime?" asked Christine.

"In the meantime, we measure the electrical constants to within an inch of their lives," he told her. "I've got a couple of real fancy meters here—this one that I'm hooking across the original wattmeter in the circuit measures the wattages in the region between one hundred thousand kilowatts and one hundred ten thousand kilowatts. Designed especially as a high-level meter."

Walt clipped the portable meters in place and made recordings. Finally he nodded. "Right on the button," he said. "Just what the meters should read."

The crystal began to vibrate faintly, and Walt mentioned that either Wes Farrell was calling Freddie Thomas or vice versa. "Can't hear it very well," complained Walt, "because Wes has the amplifiers downstairs, both incoming amplifiers from the dynamic pickup— we had to give up the standard crystal because it is expected to get cold enough to make the crystal too brittle—to the modulating equipment. The monitor speaker is outside—we haven't been in here enough to make use of it since our first tries."

Walt took a look at the bridge on the thermocouple and nodded vaguely. He killed more time by showing Christine the huge tube that drained the latent heat out of the room and hurled it across the Solar System to Pluto.

"Y'know," he grinned as a thought struck him. "I think we've licked the Channing Layer that so neatly foiled Mark Kingman and Terran Electric on that solar power project."

"Yes?"

"Sure," he said. "All we do is set up a real beam input device on the moon, for instance, and then use a batch of these things to draw the power from there."

"But how about the formation of ozone?"

"That'll have to be checked," said Walt. "For Pluto hasn't got a Channing Layer, of course, and our station out there is no criterion. But you note there is no smell of ozone in here. That leads me to think that we've given Terran Electric the runaround once more. Funny thing about Kingman. If someone gave him this development, he'd never *think* of reversing it to bring energy in."

"From what I know of the man," said Christine, "he'd not think of reversing, but he would think of perverting."

"Christine!" Walt shouted.

"Huh?" asked the bewildered girl.

"You may have had your thought for the week!"

Walt tried a bit of Indian war dance, but failed because the pseudogravitic force was too light to hold him down. They were too close to the axis for full force.

"But I don't understand."

Walt laughed hugely and hugged her. Christine was lissome in the curve of his arm as she relaxed against him.

Walt looked down at her for what seemed to be a long time, while the stream of highly technical thinking and deduction gave way to a series of more fundamental thoughts. Then he added his other arm to the embrace, and Christine turned to face him. He kissed her gently, experimentally—and discovered, instead of resistance, there was cooperation. His kiss became fervent and Christine's lips parted beneath his.

Some minutes later, Christine leaned back in his arms and smiled at him affectionately. "I was wondering if you'd ever get around to that," she said softly.

Walt grinned. "Have I been had?"

"I had Jim pack the all-white shotgun," she told him.

"Shucks, why not just have him threaten to sit on me?" asked Walt. He kissed her again.

"Now," she said, after an appropriate and pleasant interval, "just what was my 'thought for the week'?"

"Kingman," he said, his forehead creasing in a frown.

"Kingman?"

"We've no corner on brains," said Walt. "Anybody tinkering with these energy tubes might easily devise the same thing. Kingman's immediate thought would be to freeze us out, I betcha."

Walt kissed her again and then let her go. "Let's do some juggling with figures," he said.

"What kind of?"

"The Laws of Probability, aided by a bit of sheer guesswork and some shrewd evaluation of the barrister's mind."

Christine smiled. "You can speak plainer than that," she said.

"I know," he replied, reaching for his bag of gear, "but there's a lady present."

"You forget that the lady thought of it," Christine pointed out. "So let's go and find the—barrister."

"It ought to show, though," observed Walt. "And yet, my lady, we can check whether there has been cross-duggery at the skullroads by making a brief observation along here somewhere."

"How?"

"Well, about fifty yards up this corridor there is a wall thermostat."

"You think that if Kingman were trying to chill off the place, he'd have bollixed the thermostats so they can't heat up the place and compensate?"

Walt nodded. "He'd do it, not knowing that we had all the nearby circuits shut off for our own experiment, no doubt."

"You don't suppose Kingman knew about this idea and decided to add to the general effect?" asked Christine.

Walt shook his head. "He would assume that someone would be rambling up here, off and on, to look at the works. He'd automatically choose another place if he thought we had this one under observation."

Walt stopped at the thermostat, and with a screwdriver he removed the face of the instrument. He reached down into his tool pocket and took out a long, slender pair of tweezers. He probed in the depths of the thermostat and came out with a tiny square of paper.

He held it up for Christine to see.

"Stickum on one side held it until the contacts closed," he said. "Then it made a damned good insulator. Betcha this slip of paper came from Terran Electric!"

"Now what?" Christine asked.

"I'm going to call Don," said Walt, "Iffen and providen we can find a live jack."

He took a handset from his tools and plugged it into the jack below the thermostat. He jiggled a tiny switch and pressed a little red button, and after a full three minutes, he said, "Damn" under his breath and dropped the handset back into his toolkit.

"Nobody's paying much attention to the telephone from this section of Venus Equilateral anymore," he said. "There's a live one in the cold room, though. Let's take a look around first."

"Which way?"

Walt thought for a moment. "We set the cold room about one-third of the way from the north end because it was as far from the rest of the station's operating and living section as possible while commensurable with being reasonably close to the labs," he said. "We're not very far—perhaps a hundred yards—from the axis. We're about a mile from the north end.

"Now, if I were Kingman, I'd set up shop in some place as far from the operating section as possible, commensurable with an out-of-the-way place—and definitely far from the laboratories. Then I'd select a place as far from me as I could get without too much danger of having the effect detected."

Christine nodded. "If Venus Equilateral were a cube, you'd take one corner and chill off the opposite corner."

"Venus Equilateral is a cylinder and the skin is filled with people. However, you can set up an equation in differential calculus that will give you two spots as far from one another as possible, with the least danger of detection from the ends or skin of a cylinder. The answer will give you two toroidal volumes located inside of the cylinder. You set your workshop in one and start the chill-off in the other—and right across the center from you."

"And?" Christine prompted with a smile.

"We used the same equation to locate the least dangerous place.

Predicated on the theory that if the personnel need be protected from the danger area as much as the danger area need be concealed from people, we can assume the use of the same constants. Now, since by sheer coincidence Markus the Kingman selected a spot in the toroid that we also selected, it narrows our search considerably."

"In other words, we chase down the length of the station, cross the axis, and knock on Kingman's door."

"Right," said Walt.

And being firmly convinced that mixing pleasure with business often makes the business less objectionable, Walt kissed Christine once more before they started toward the place where they expected to find their troublemaker.

"About here," said Walt, looking up at a smooth bulkhead.

"How are we going to find him?" asked Christine.

The corridor was long and die-straight, but both walls were sheer for thirty feet and unbroken.

"Look, I guess," said Walt uncertainly. "I'm not too familiar with this section of the station. When I was first here—many years ago—I spent a lot of spare time roaming and exploring these seldom-used corridors. But my Boy Scout hatchet wouldn't cut trail blazes on the steel walls." He laughed a bit thoughtfully, and then he put his hands to his mouth, cupping them like a megaphone, and yelled: "Hey! Kingman! We're on to you!"

"But what good will that do?" asked Christine doubtfully.

"Might scare him into action," said Walt. "Easiest way to shoot pa'tridge is to flush it into the open. Otherwise you might walk over a nest and never see it. I—Holy grease!"

A four-foot section of the wall beside them flashed into nothingness with neither sound nor light nor motion. It just disappeared. And as they goggled at the vacant square, an ugly round circle glinted in the light and a sourly familiar voice invited them in—or else!

"Well," said Walt Franks, exhaling deeply. "If it isn't Our Legal Lamp himself!"

Kingman nodded snappishly. "You were looking for me?"

"We were."

"It's too bad you found me," said Kingman.

"It was just a matter of time before you dropped all pretense of being thinly legal," said Walt scathingly. "I'll give you credit, Kingman, for conducting yourself as close to the line without stepping over for a long time. But now you can add breaking and entering and kidnapping to whatever other crimes you have committed."

Kingman smiled in a superior manner. "I might," he said suavely, "add murder. There would be no corpus delecti if both of you were fed into the duplicator."

"You can't record a human being," said Walt.

"Don't be stupid," said Kingman. "Who said anything about making a record?"

Walt admitted that this was so.

Kingman snapped the switch on the duplicator and the wall was reestablished. Then he forced Christine to tie Walt, after which he tied Christine and then checked and added to Walt's bonds from a large roll of friction tape. He dropped them side by side in chairs, and taped them thoroughly.

"You are a damned nuisance," he said. "Having to eliminate you tends to decrease my enjoyment at seeing the failure of Venus Equilateral. I'd have preferred to watch all of you suffer the hardest way. Killing you leaves fewer to gloat over, but it must be done. Once you found me, there is no other way."

"Walt," pleaded Christine, "won't the others find the same thing and follow us?"

Walt wanted to lie  wanted desperately to lie, if for no other reason than to spare Christine the mental anguish of expecting death. But Walt was not a good liar.

He gave up and said: "I happen to be the guy who rigged the thermal energy tube—and I'm the only guy who knows about the too-fast drop. All I hope for is that we'll be missed."

"We will," said Christine.

Kingman laughed nastily and began to fiddle with the scanning-rate controls on his duplicator.

Arden came running into her husband's office breathlessly. She was waving a sheet of paper and there was mingled anger and pleasure on her face as she shoved the paper under Don's eyes and waggled it.

"Look!" she commanded.

"Stop fanning me with that," said Channing, "and let me see it if it's so all-fired important."

"I'll murder 'em in cold blood," Arden swore.

Channing pried his wife's fingers apart and took the paper. He read—and his eyes bulged with amused concern.

*Dear Characters:*

*When we were giving Venus Equilateral's advantages the up and down a coupla years ago after the sudden and warranted departure of Director Francis Burbank, we forgot one important item—a justice of the peace.*

*So Christine and I are eloping in a time-honored fashion. Neither of us have any desire to get wedded in the midst of a Roman holiday, even though it does deprive a lot of guys the right to kiss the bride.*

*You may give my Little Black Book to Jim Baler, Barney Carroll, and Wes—and have Arden see that they divide 'em up proportionately.*

*Your ex-bachelor chum (p)*
*Walt*

*PS: He chased me 'til I caught him—*
*Christine*

"Well," chuckled Don good-naturedly, "that's our Walt. He never did do anything the slow and easy way. Does Jim know?"

"I dunno. Let's find him and ask."

They found Jim and Barney in Farrell's laboratory discussing the theories of operating a gigantic matter-transmitter affair to excavate sand from a cliff. Channing handed the note to Jim, who read it with a half-smile and handed it to Barney, who shared it with Wes while they read it together.

Jim said, "I'm not surprised; Christine could have been talked into wedlock—holy or unholy—by a mere wink from Walt."

"I hope she'll be kind to our little bucket-headed idiot," said Arden, making to wipe tears with a large sheet of emery paper from Farrell's workbench. "He's been slightly soft-skulled ever since he set eye on that scheming hussy you have for a sister."

Barney shook his head sadly. "Poor guy."

"We ought to toast 'em though they aren't here," suggested Farrell.

"A requiem toast."

"This," chuckled Don Channing, "is one mess that Walt will have to get out of himself."

"Mess, is it?" Arden demanded with a glint in her eye. "Come, husband, I would have words with thee."

Don reached in his hip pocket. "Here," he said, "just take my checkbook."

"I'd rather have words with you."

Don shook his head. "If I just give you the checkbook, you'll use it reasonably sparingly, all things feminine considered. But gawd help the balance, once you get to talking me into writing the check myself. Besides, we're about to hear from the Thomas boys again. They're about to land at Canalopsis."

"I'll wait," said Arden, settling on a tall stool and lighting a cigarette.

It took about ten minutes, and then Freddie Thomas' voice came from the speaker, loud and clear. "Well, we've landed. We're here. And where are you?"

"Hang on, Freddie," replied Farrell. "And we've some news for you. Walt Franks and Christine Baler have just committed matrimony."

"That's fine—What? Who? When?"

"They eloped. Left a note and took the *Relay Girl*, unbeknownst to all and sundry. Left their damned note right where the *Relay Girl's* landing space was."

"Well, I'll be—"

Chuck's voice came in. "He probably will," he observed. "And you know, when I think of spending eternity with my brother, it's enough to make a guy spend an exemplary life in the hope of going to Heaven so we can be apart. But I've got another guy here that might be interested."

"Hello, Channing?"

"Well, if it ain't Keg Johnson. Own Mars yet?"

"No, but I'm damned interested in this coupled-crystal gadget of yours. Mind if I bring Linna out for a few days?"

"Come ahead. Coming on *Anopheles?*" asked Don.

Keg Johnson laughed. "Not a chance, Don. I own a spaceline, remember? And not wanting to cast disparagement at your type of genius, I'll prefer riding in style at two gravities instead of blatting all over the sky at five; ducking meters and festoons of cable; eating canned beans off a relay-rack shelf standing up; and waking up in the morning to the tune of Chuck Thomas carving a hole through the bedroom wall to make a straight-line half-wave dipole that won't quite fit in otherwise."

"I'd send the *Relay Girl,*" said Don, "but it seems as how my old sidekick, Walt Franks, swiped it to locate a justice of the peace in the company of a young and impressionable gal named Christine."

"Nuts?"

"If so, happy about it. Hope he'll be home by Christmas, anyway."

"Well, we'll be arriving in about ten days. See you then, Don."

"Right," answered Channing, and Wes Farrell took the microphone to give the Thomas boys some information.

Mark Kingman emerged from his tiny house in the huge storeroom and his breath blew out in a white cloud. He went to the couple tied to their chairs and said: "Cold, isn't it?"

Frank swore. Christine shivered despite the electrically heated clothing.

"You know," said Kingman, "those batteries are going to wear out sooner or later. I'd remove them and let the cold do its work, except for the fact that I'd have to loose you and get into the inside pocket of the suits. You stay tied!"

"Having nothing to eat but your words is beginning to undermine my health," snapped Walt. "Gonna starve us to death, too?"

"Oh," said Kingman expansively, "I've been devising a machine for you. As an inventor of note, you will appreciate little Joe. He will take care of you both, to keep you alive until the cold gets you."

He returned to his little house and emerged with a large, complicated gadget that he trundled to position in front of Walt and Christine. There was a large hopper above and a wild assortment of levers and gears interlocked in the body of the mechanism.

Kingman pressed a button, and the gears whirled and the levers flashed—

And from the insides of the thing a lever speared forward. A spoon was welded to the fore end, and it carried a heaping load of mushy something-or-other.

Walt blinked and tried to duck, but his bindings wouldn't permit too much freedom of motion. The spoon hit him on the cheek, cutting him and spilling the food on his chest. The spoon disappeared back into the machine.

It reappeared on the other side and sliced toward Christine, who screamed in fright. The spoon entered her opened mouth, and the stuff it hurled into her throat nearly strangled her. It came again at Walt, who miscalculated slightly and received a cut lip and a mouth full of heavy gruel.

"You have to get set just so," explained Kingman, "then you'll not be cut."

"Damn you—*Glub!*" Walt snapped.

Christine waited and caught the next spoonful neatly.

And then the thing accelerated. The velocity of repetition increased by double—then decreased again—and then started on random intervals. They could never be certain when the knifing spoon would come hurtling out of the machine to plunge into the position where their mouths should be. They were forced to swallow quickly and then sit there with mouth wide open to keep from getting clipped. With the randomness of interval there came another randomness. One spoonful would be mush; the next ice cream; followed by a cube of rare steak. The latter was tough, which demanded jaw-aching rapid chewing to get set for the next possible thrust.

"A balanced diet," chortled Kingman, rolling his eyes in laughter. He held his stomach at the sight.

"You—*glub!*—devil!—*glub!*"

"It won't be long now," said Kingman. "Your cold room is down to almost absolute zero now. You know what that means?"

"—*glub!*—you—"

"When the metal reaches absolute zero, as it will with the thermal beam, the spread of cooling will accelerate. The metal will become a superconductor—which will superconduct heat as well as electricity. The chill area is spreading rapidly now, and once this cold-room section reaches absolute zero, the chill will spread like wildfire and the famous Venus Equilateral Relay Station will experience a killing freeze."

Walt glared. There was nothing else he could do. He was being fed at a rapid rate that left him no time for other occupations. It was ignominious to be so treated, but Walt consoled himself with the fact that he was being fed—even though gulps of scalding-hot coffee drenched spoons of ice cream that came after mashed potatoes (with lumps, and where did Kingman get *that* duplicator recording?). The final blow was a one-inch tube that nearly knocked their teeth out in arriving. It poured a half-pint of Benedictine and brandy down their throats which made them cough—and which almost immediately left them with their senses reeling.

Kingman enjoyed this immensely, roaring with laughter at his "feeding machine," as he called it.

Then he sobered as Walt's eyes refused to focus. He stepped to a place behind Walt and unbound him quickly. Walt tried to stand, but reeled, and Kingman pointed his heavy rifle at Walt from a very safe distance and urged him to go and enter the small metal house. Walt did. Then Kingman transferred Christine to the house in the same way.

He sealed the only door with the duplicator and, from a small opening in the wall, he spoke to them.

"I'm leaving," he said. "You'll find everything in there to set up light housekeeping but food and heat. There'll be no heat, for I've removed the heating plant. You can see it through this hole, but the hole will soon be closed by the feeding machine, which I'm fixing so that you can eat when hungry. I'd prefer that you stay alive while you slowly freeze. Eventually your batteries will give out, and then—curtains. But I've got to leave because things are running my way and I've got to be in a place to cash in on it. I'll be seeing you."

Keg Johnson greeted Don warmly. Then he said, "I knew you'd do it sooner or later," with a grin.

Don blinked. "The last time you said that was in the courtroom in Buffalo, after we wrecked the economic system with the matter duplicator. What is it this time?"

"According to the guys I've had investigating your coupled-crystal effect, it is quite simple. The effect will obtain with any crystalline substance—so long as they are absolutely identical! It took the duplicator to do it right to the atomic lattice structure. You'll get any royalties, Channing, but I'm getting all my ships talking from ship to ship direct, and from Canalopsis direct to any ship. You've just invented Venus Equilateral out of business!"

"Good!" exclaimed Don.

"Good?"

Don nodded. "Venus Equilateral is fun—and always has been. But, damn it, here we are out here in space lacking the free sky and the fresh natural air. We'd never abandon it so long as Venus Equilateral had a shred of necessity. But now we can all go home to man's natural environment: a natural planet."

"So what are we going to do?"

"Furnish the communications stations at Northern Landing, at Canalopsis, and on Terra with coupled-crystal equipment. Then we abandon Venus Equilateral in one grand celebration."

Arden smiled. "Walt and Christine will be wild. Serves 'em right."

Farrell shrugged. "Going to tell 'em?"

"Nope. For one thing, they're honeymooning no one knows

where. And so we'll just leave quietly and when they come back, they'll find that Venus Equilateral is a large empty house. Run off on us, will they!"

"Making any public announcements?" asked Keg.

Don shook his head. "Why bother?" he asked. "People will know sooner or later, and besides, these days I'd prefer to keep the coupled-crystal idea secret as long as possible. We'll get more royalty, because once it is known, the duplicators will go crazy again. So long as Venus Equilateral—the generic term—maintains interplanetary communications, that's all that is necessary. Though Venus Equilateral as an identity is no more, the name of the Interplanetary Communications Company shall be known as Venus Equilateral as a fond tribute to a happy memory of a fine place. And—"

"And now we can haul off and have a four-alarm holiday brawl," said Arden.

Farrell noted the thermometers that measured the temperature of the cold room. "About all we'd have to do is to hold the door open and Venus Equilateral will have its first snowstorm."

"Just like Mars," said Jim. "No wonder Christine eloped with Walt. Bet they're honeymooning on Venus."

"Well," said Channing, "turn up the gain on that ice cream freezer of Walt's, and we'll have our winter snowstorm. A white Christmas, by all that's good and holy!"

Farrell grinned widely and reached up to the servo panel. He twisted the master control dial all the way clockwise and the indicators read high on their scales. Imperceptibly, the recording thermometers started to creep downward—though it would take a day or so before the drop became evident.

"Get everything in motion," said Channing. "Arden, make plans to clean out about an acre of former living space—make a one-room apartment out of it. Get the gals a-decorating like mad. Wes, get someone to make a firebrick and duplicate it into enough to build a fireplace. Then make enough fireplaces to go around to all as wants 'em. For draft, we'll tie the chimneys together and let it blow out into space at fourteen pounds per square inch of draft. Better get some good dampers, too. We'll get some crude logs—duplicate us a dozen cords of wood for firewood. Tell the shopkeepers down on the Mall that the lid is off and the Devil's out for breakfast! We'll want sleds, fur coats, holly and mistletoe by the acres. And to hell with the Lucite icicles they hang from the corridor cornices. This year we have real ones.

"Oh," he added, "better make some small heating units for living rooms. We can freeze up the hall and 'outdoor' areas, but people want to come back into a warm room, shuck their earmuffs and overcoats, and soak up a cup of Tom and Jerry. Let's go, gang. Prepare to abandon ship! And let's abandon ship with a party that will go down in history—and make every man, woman, and child on Venus Equilateral remember it to the end of their days!"

"Poor Walt," said Arden. "I wish he could be here. Let's hope he'll come back to us by Christmas."

For the ten thousandth time, Walt inspected the little metal house. It was made of two courses of metal held together with an insulating connector, but these metal walls had been coupled with water now, and they were bitter cold to the touch.

Lights were furnished from outside somewhere, there was but a switch in the wall and a lamp in the ceiling. Walt thought that he might be able to raise some sort of electrical disturbance with the lighting plan, but found it impossible from the construction of the house. And obviously, Kingman had done the best he could to filter and isolate any electrical fixtures against radio interference that would tell the men in Venus Equilateral that funny work was afoot. Kingman's duplicator had been removed along with anything else that would give Walt a single item that he could view with a technical eye.

Otherwise, it was a miniature model of a small three-room house; not much larger than a "playhouse" for a wealthy child, but completely equipped for living, since Kingman planned it that way and lived in it, needing nothing.

"Where do we go from here?" Walt asked in an angry tone.

Christine shuddered. "What I'm wondering is when these batteries will run out," she said.

"Kingman has a horse-and-buggy mind," said Walt. "He can't understand that we'd use miniature beam energy tubes. They won't give out for about a year."

"But we can't hold out that long."

"No, we damn well can't," grunted Franks unhappily. "These suits aren't designed for anything but a severe cold. Not a viciously killing kind. At best, they'll keep up fairly well at minus forty degrees, but below that they lose ground degree for degree."

Christine yawned sleepily.

"Don't let that get you," said Walt nervously. "That's the first sign of cold adaptation."

"I know," she answered. "I've seen enough of it on Mars. You lose the feeling of cold eventually, and then you die."

Walt held his forehead in his hands. "I should have made an effort," he said in a hollow voice. "At least, if I'd started a ruckus, Kingman might have been baffled enough to let you run for it."

"You'd have been shot."

"But you'd not be in this damned place slowly freezing to death," he argued.

"Walt," she said quietly, "remember? Kingman had that gun pointed at me when you surrendered."

"Well, damn it. I'd rather have gone ahead, anyway. You'd have been—"

"No better off. We're still alive."

"Fine prospect. No one knows we're here; they think we're honeymooning. The place is chilling off rapidly and will really slide like hell once that room and the original tube reaches absolute zero. The gang below us don't really know what's going on because they left the refrigerator tube to my care—and Channing knows that I'd not go rambling off on a honeymoon without leaving instructions, unless I was certain without a doubt that the thing would run without trouble until I returned. I'm impulsive, but not forgetful. As for making any kind of racket in here—we're licked."

"Can't you do something with the miniature power tubes that run these suits?"

"Not a chance—at least nothing that I know I can do between

the removal of the suit and the making of communications. They're just power-intake tubes tuned to the big solar-beam jobs that run the station. I—"

"Walt, please. No reproach."

He looked at her. "I think you mean that," he said.

"I do."

He nodded unhappily. "But it still obtains that it's my fault."

Christine put cold hands on his cheeks. "Walt, what would have happened if I'd not been along?"

"I'd have been trapped alone," he told her.

"And if I'd come alone?"

"But you wouldn't have—"

"Walt, I would have. You couldn't have kept me. So, regardless of whether you blame yourself, you need not. If anybody is to blame, call it Kingman. And Walt, remember? I've just found you. Can you imagine—well, put yourself in my place—how would you feel if I'd walked out of your office and dropped out of sight? I'm going to say it once and only once, because it sounds corny, Walt, but I'd rather be here and knowing than to be safe and forever wondering. And so long as there is the breath of life in us, I'll go on praying for help."

Walt put his arms around her and held her gently.

Christine kissed him lightly. "Now I'm going to curl up on that couch," she said. "Don't dare let me sleep more than six hours."

"I'll watch."

"And I'll measure time for you. Once we start sleeping the clock around, we're goners."

Christine went to the couch and Walt piled the available covers on after he checked the operation of the power tube that furnished heat for her suit. He turned it up a bit, and then dimmed the light.

For Walt there was no sleep. He wandered from room to room in sheer frustration. Given anything of a partially technical nature, and he could have made something of it. Given a tool or two or even a few items of kitchen cutlery, and he might have quelled his restlessness in working toward some end. But to be imprisoned in a small house that was rapidly dropping toward zero degrees Kelvin without a book, without a knife or fork or loose bit of metal anywhere, was frustration for the technical mind.

Mark Kingman, of course, had been quite afraid of just that and he had skinned the place bare of everything that could possibly be used. Kingman even feared a loose bit of metal, because metal struck against metal can produce sparks that will light a fire.

There was nothing at all but himself—and Christine. And Walt knew that it would take only a few more days before that, too, would end.

For the metal of the house was getting to the point where he stuck to it if he touched it. The suits kept them warm—to take them off would have been sheer folly.

So from kitchenette to bathroom to living room prowled Walt. He swore at the neat little shower—the water was frozen, even had anybody wanted to take a bath.


Kingman entered the conference room of the Interplanetary Communications Commission with confidence. He knew his ground and he knew his rights, and it had been none other than he who had managed to call this meeting together. With a bland smile, Kingman faced the members of the commission.

"I wish to state that the establishment known as Venus Equilateral has forfeited its license," he said.

This was intended to be a bombshell, and it did create a goodly amount of surprise on the part of the commission.

The chairman, Lewis Hollister, shook his head in wonder. "I have this morning received a message from Mars."

"It did not go through Venus Equilateral," stated Kingman.

"I'm not acquainted with the present celestial positions," said Hollister. "However, there are many periods during which time the communications are made direct from planet to planet—when Terra and Mars are on line-of-sight to Venus and one another."

"The celestial positions are such that relay through Venus Equilateral is necessary," said Kingman.

"Indeed?"

Kingman unrolled a chart showing the location of the planets of the inner Solar System: Mars, Terra, Venus—and Venus Equilateral. According to the lines-of-sight drawn on the map, the use of the relay station was definitely desirable.

"Conceded," said Hollister. "Now may I ask you to bring your complaint?"

"The Research Services Corporation of Northern Landing, Venus, have for years been official monitors for the Interplanetary Communications Commission," Kingman explained. "I happen to be a director of that corporation, which has research offices on Terra and Mars and is, of course, admirably fitted to serve as official monitor. I make this explanation because I feel it desirable to explain how I know about this. After all, an unofficial monitor is a lawbreaker for making use of confidential messages to enhance his own position. As an official monitor, I may observe and also make suggestions pertaining to the best interests of interplanetary communications.

"It has been reported along official channels that the relaying of messages through the Venus Equilateral Relay Station ceased as of twelve hundred hours Terran mean time on twenty December."

"Then where are they relaying their messages?" asked Hollister. "Or are they?"

"They must," said Kingman. "Whether they use radio or the subelectronic energy bands, they cannot drive a beam direct from Terra to Mars without coming too close to the sun. Ergo, they must be relaying."

"Perhaps they are using their ship beams."

"Perhaps—and of course, the use of a secondary medium is undesirable. This matter of interrupted or uninterrupted service is not the major point, however. The major point is that their license to operate as a major monopoly under the Communications Act insists that one relayed message must pass through their station—Venus Equilateral—during every twenty-four-hour period. This is a safety measure, to ensure that their equipment is always ready to run— even in periods when relaying is not necessary."

"Venus Equilateral has been off the air before this."

Kingman cleared his throat. "A number of times," he agreed.

"But each time that discontinuance of service occurred, it was during a period of emergency—and in each instance this emergency was great enough to demand leniency. Most of the times an explanation was instantly forthcoming; the other times were after seeking and receiving permission to suspend operations during the emergency period. This, gentlemen, is twenty-three December and no message has passed through Venus Equilateral Relay Station since noon on twenty December."

"Your statements, if true, indicate that Venus Equilateral has violated its license," Hollister nodded. "However, we are inclined to be lenient with them because they have been exemplary in the past and—"

"And," interrupted Kingman, "they are overconfident. They think that they're big enough and clever enough to do as they damn well please!"

"Indeed?"

"Well, they've been doing it, haven't they?"

"We've seen no reason for interfering with their operations. And they are getting the messages through."

Kingman smiled. "How?"

Hollister shrugged. "If you claim they aren't using the station, I wouldn't know."

"And if the government were to ask, you would be quite embarrassed."

"Then what do you suggest?" asked Hollister.

"Venus Equilateral has failed to live up to the letter of its license, regardless of what medium they are using to relay communications around Sol," said Kingman. "Therefore, I recommend that you suspend their license."

"And then who will run Venus Equilateral?" asked Hollister.

"As of three years ago, the Terran Electric Company of Evanston, Illinois, received an option on the operation of an interplanetary communications company," said Kingman. "This option was to operate at such a time as Venus Equilateral ceased operating. Now, since Venus Equilateral has failed, I suggest that we show them that their high-handedness will not be condoned. I recommend that this option be fulfilled; that the license now held by Venus Equilateral be suspended and turned over to Terran Electric."

Hollister nodded vaguely. "You understand that Venus Equilateral has posted as bond the holdings of the company. This of course will be forfeit if we choose to act. Now, Mr. Kingman, is the Terran Electric Company prepared to post a bond equivalent to the value of Venus Equilateral? Obviously, we cannot wrest holdings from one company and turn them over to another company free of bond. We must have bond—assurance that Terran Electric will fulfill the letter of the license."

"Naturally, we cannot post full bond," replied Kingman stiffly. "But we will post sufficient bond to make the transfer possible. The remainder of the evaluation will revert to the Commission—as it was previously. I might point out that had Venus Equilateral kept their inventiveness and efforts directed only at communications, they would not be now in this position. It was their side interests that made their unsubsidized and free incorporation possible. I promise you that Terran Electric will never stoop to making a rubber-stamp group out of the Interplanetary Communications Commission."

Hollister thought for a moment. But instead of thinking of the ramifications of the deal, he was remembering that in his home was a medium-sized duplicator made by Terran Electric. It had a very low serial number and it had been delivered on consignment. It had been sent to him not as a gift, but as a customer-use research—to be paid for only if the customer were satisfied. Not only had Terran Electric been happy to accept the thousand-dollar bill made in the duplicator, but it had happily returned three hundred dollars' worth of change—all with the same serial number. But since Hollister received his consignment along with the very first of such deliveries, he had prospered very well and had been very neatly situated by the time the desperate times of the Period of Duplication took place. Hollister recalled that Venus Equilateral wanted to suppress the duplicator. Hollister recalled also that Venus Equilateral had been rather tough on a certain magistrate in Buffalo, and though he thought that it was only a just treatment, it was nevertheless a deep and burning disrespect for the law.

Besides, if this deal went through, Hollister would once more be a guiding hand in the operation of Venus Equilateral. He did believe that Channing and Franks could outdo Terran Electric any day in the week, but business is business. And if Kingman failed, the license could always be turned back to Channing & Co.—with himself still holding a large hunk of the pie.

"You will post bond by certified identium check," said Hollister. "And as the new holder of the license, we will tender you papers that will direct Venus Equilateral to hand over to you, as representative of Terran Electric, the holdings necessary to operate the Venus Equilateral Relay Station and other outlying equipment and stations."

Kingman nodded happily. His bit of personal graft had begun to pay off—though he of course did not consider his gift anything but a matter of furnishing to a deserving person a gratuity that worked no hardship on the giver.

The bond annoyed Kingman. Even in an era when material holdings had little value, the posting of such securities as demanded left Kingman a poor man. Money, of course, was not wanted nor expected. What he handed over was a statement of the equivalent value on an identium check of the Terran Electric Company, his holdings in the Research Services Corporation, and just about everything he had in the way of items that could not be handled readily by the normal-sized duplicator. At Terran Electric, for instance, they had duplicators that could build a complete spacecraft if done in sections, and these monstrous machines were what kept Terran Electric from the cobweb-growing stage. A man could not build a house with the average household-sized duplicator, and to own one large enough to build automobiles and the like was foolish, for they were not needed that often. Kingman didn't like to post that size of bond, but he felt certain that within a year he would be able to reestablish his free holdings in Terran Electric because of revenues from Venus Equilateral. Doubtless, too, there were many people on Venus Equilateral that he could hire—that he would need desperately.

For Kingman had no intention of losing.

♣ ♣ ♣

A duplicator produced snowflakes by the myriad and hurled them into the corridor ventilators. They swirled and skirled and piled into deep drifts at the corners and in cul-de-sacs along the way. A faint odor of pine needles went with the air, and from newly installed water pipes along the cornices long icicles were forming. There was the faint sound of sleigh bells along the corridors, but this was obviously synthetic since Venus Equilateral had little use for a horse.

Kids who had never seen snow nor known a cold snap reveled in their new snowsuits and built a huge snowman along the Mall. One long ramp that led into a snaky corridor was taken over by squatters—or rather "sledders"—rights and it became downright dangerous for a pedestrian to try to keep his ankles away from the speeding sleds. Snow forts were erected on either side of one wide corridor and the air was filled with flying snowballs.

And from the stationwide public announcement system came the crooned strains of "Adeste Fideles" and "White Christmas."

A snowball hissed past Arden's ear and she turned abruptly to give argument. She was met by another that caught her full in the face—after which it was wiped off by her husband.

"Merry Christmas," he chuckled.

"Not very," she said, but she could not help but smile back at him. When he finished wiping her face Arden neatly dropped a handful of snow down his collar. He retaliated by scooping a huge block out of a nearby drift and letting it drape over her head. Arden pushed him backward into a snowbank and leaped on him and shoveled snow with both hands until her hands stung with cold and Don was completely covered.

Channing climbed out of the drift as Arden raced away. He gave chase, though both of them were laughing too much to do much running. He caught her a few hundred feet down the hall and tackled her, bringing her down in another drift. As he was piling snow on her, he became the focal point of a veritable barrage from behind, which drove him to cover behind a girder. His assailants deployed and flushed him from behind his cover, and he stood in the center of a large square area being pelted from all sides.

Channing found a handkerchief and waved it as surrender.

The pelting slowed a bit, and Channing took that time to race to one side, join Jim Baler, and hurl some snowballs at Barney Carroll across the square. That evened things, and the snow fight was joined by Arden, who arose from her snowdrift to join Barney Carroll and Keg Johnson.

"We used to freeze 'em," grunted Don.

"Me too," Jim agreed. "These things wouldn't stop a fly."

Then down the corridor there hurtled a snowball a good two feet in diameter. It caught Channing between the shoulder blades and flattened him completely. Baler turned just in time to stop another one with the pit of his stomach. He went *"Oooof!"* and landed in the drift beside Don. Another huge one went over their heads as Don was rising, and he saw it splat against a wall to shower Barney Carroll and Arden with bits.

"Those would," remarked Don. "And if Walt weren't honeymooning somewhere, I'd suspect that our Captain Lightning had just hauled off and reinvented the ancient Roman catapult."

"There's always Wes Farrell, or does the physicist in him make him eschew such anachronisms?" asked Jim.

Arden scurried across the square in time to hear him, and she replied, "Not at all. So long as the thing is powered by a new spring alloy and charged by a servo-mechanism run by a beam energy tube. Bet he packs 'em with an automatic packing gadget, too."

Barney caught one across the knees that tripped him headlong as he crossed the square. He arrived grunting and grinning. "We can either take it idly," he said, "or retreat in disorder, or storm whatever ramparts he has back there."

"I dislike to retreat in disorder," said Channing. "Seems to me that we can get under that siege gun of his. He must take time to reload. Keep low, fellers, and pack yourself a goodly load of snowballs as we go."

"How to carry 'em?" Arden asked.

Don stripped off his muffler, and made a sling of it. Then down the corridor they went, dodging the huge snowballs that came flying over at regular intervals. Channing finally timed the interval, and they raced forward in clear periods and took cover when fire was expected.

They came upon Farrell eventually. He was "dug in" behind a huge drift over which the big missiles came looping. Farrell had obviously cut the power of his catapult to take care of the short-range trajectory, but his aim was still excellent.

With as many snowballs as they could carry, the attackers stormed the drift, pelting without aim until their supply was gone and then scooping snow up and throwing without much packing.

Behind the rampart was Farrell with a trough-shaped gadget and a pair of heavy coil springs. Above the rear end of the trough was a duplicator. It dropped a snowball on the trough and the springs snapped forward.

The flying ball caught Don Channing in the pit of the stomach just as he attained the top of the rampart.

When he regained the top once more, the festivities were about over. The shooting was stopped, and the others of his side had Farrell held face upward on the trough while the duplicator dropped snowball after snowball on him.

"Wonder how far we could shoot him," suggested Jim Baler.

Farrell did not think that funny. He struggled to his feet and then grinned. "Fine war," he told them. "Anybody ready for a bit of hot toddy?"

Channing grunted. "Yeah, and a hot bath and a hearty dinner and a seven-hour sleep. So you've taken over Walt's job of making weapons, huh?"

"Walt will be green with envy," said Arden.

Don sobered. "He's missing plenty. I've got all the word out that if he's seen, get here quick. He must have dropped the *Relay Girl* in some out-of-the-way place. He hasn't landed on any regular spaceport."

"There's lots of room for that in the Palanortis Country," said Farrell.

"We've got likker and wassail and turkey," said Arden. "Also mistletoe. Let's go to our place and drink Walt's health and Christine's happiness."

"And that's appropriately apportioned," remarked Don with a grin. "Walt's health and Christine's happiness. But I'll bet a hat that they'd not mind being cold if they knew what fun this is." He brushed snow from the back of his neck and grinned. "Let's add fuel for the inner man," he suggested, leading the way to the Channing apartment.

Walt Franks sat dully in a chair, his eyes glazed over and but half-open. Through them dimly, and out of focus, he could see Christine, who was huddled and quiet under the blankets. Her lips were blue and Walt felt dully that this should not be so but had trouble remembering why. There was but one thought in his mind, and that was to awaken Christine before he himself fell asleep. They'd been doing that for—for—for years? No, that was not right. It must have been days, because he hadn't been living with Christine for years. Fact, he hadn't really lived with Christine at all; he'd just found her when this all happened—and—and—

He shook himself, and the motion hurt inside and outside. His muscles ached and where his skin touched a bit of clothing that hadn't been against his skin before, it was bitterly cold. Quickly Walt opened his hands and then drew out his left hand from the pocket and took a quick look at his wristwatch. He stuffed his hand back in again quickly and tried to stand up.

His legs were numb and he almost fell forward, which carried him where he wanted to go anyway, so he just let himself stumble forward heartlessly until he fell on his knees beside the couch.

"Christine," he mumbled.

To himself, his voice sounded loud, but it was faint and cracked. It hurt his lips to move, but he moved them for Christine, where he would have moved them for no one else.

"Christine," he said, a bit more clearly and loudly on the second attempt. "Christine!"

Dull eyes opened and cracked lips smiled faintly and painfully.

"Mus' wake up," he warned.

She nodded—painfully slowly. She made no effort to move.

Walt stood up and made his way to the accursed feeding machine. He pressed the button and collected dollops of hot food in a shallow bowl. It was a mess because coffee mingled with the many other items of a fine balanced diet, including appetizer and dessert, made just that—a mess. But it was hot and it was food, and though there was not a single bit of silverware in the place, Walt managed. He carried the bowl to the couch and offered it to Christine, who protestingly permitted Walt to feed her with his fingers. She did not eat much, but it did warm her. Then Walt finished the plate.

Christine shuddered under the blankets. "Suits losing ground?" she asked.

Walt nodded pitifully.

Christine thought that over for a full minute. Then she said: "Must get up, Walt."

Walt wanted to let her stay there, but he knew that she must arise and move in order to keep from freezing. He nodded dumbly.

"Losing ground," he said, meaning the heated suits. Minutes he considered it. Long minutes . . .

There was suddenly a faint crackling noise, and a pungent odor. It increased without either of them noticing it because their senses were numbed. A curl of smoke wreathed Walt's chest and rose above his face and got into his eyes. He coughed and tears came, and the salty water dribbled down his cheeks, dropped to his suit, and froze.

"Something burning," he mumbled, looking around to see what it was.

"It's you!" cried Christine.

Walt looked down at his hip, where the tiny power tube was, and saw it smoking. As he watched, flame burst from the inside and came through.

He shucked the suit just as it burst into open flames, and watched it burn on the metal floor. He warmed himself against the flames, but they were too meager to really help, and five minutes later all that was left of the heated suit was a still-operating power tube and a tangled maze of red-hot heater-resistance wire.

Walt shivered. Beneath the suit he wore the usual slacks and short-sleeved shirt, and it was pitifully inadequate. The dullness that had been assailing him for hours reasserted itself—strengthened by the exertion of removing the suit—and helped not at all by the scant warmth from the charred remains.

He reeled dizzily, his eyes half-closed, beads of ice from the tears on his lashes gave the scene a dazzlingly sparkling tone that prevented him from seeing clearly.

He fell forward and his body twitched violently as his skin touched the viciously cold metal of the floor.

Christine hurled the covers back and with great effort pulled and lifted Walt onto the couch. She covered him and then leaned down and kissed him with dry, cracked lips. As she stood up, she felt a spear of pain at her side.

Looking, she found her suit on fire as Walt's had been. As she fumbled with cold fingers at the fastenings, she realized that only the added warmth of the blankets had kept both suits from burning out at the same time. For they were duplicated models and were identical, therefore, they would burn out at exactly the same temperature.

She shivered in her thin summer frock even though she stood with the flames licking at her sandals.

Then there were two useless tangles of wire on the floor, their red-hot wires struggling hopelessly against the monstrous quantity of cold.

Christine shuddered convulsively, and turned slowly to look at Walt. He was asleep already.

The sleep of frozen death.

Christine's eyes filled with tears, which she brushed away quickly. She smiled faintly.

It seemed warmer under the blankets, or maybe it was warmer there beside him. His arm went around her instinctively, though he slept, and Christine pressed against him partly to gain what warmth there was from him and partly to give him what warmth there was in her.

It was warmer beneath the blankets.

Or, she thought just before the dizzying but welcome waves of black slumber crept over her, this is that feeling of warmth that goes before—

♣ ♣ ♣

"Now that," said Arden with complimentary tones, "is something that duplicating can't buy."

She meant the twenty-piece orchestra that filled the vast hall with music. It was an immense place, for it contained three thousand people, all talking or dancing. Joe presided over a bowl of punch that would have made Nero die of jealousy—it was platinum, fifteen feet in diameter, studded profusely with huge gold chasings and inlays, and positively alive with diamonds and emeralds. On the edge of the huge bowl hung Joe's original sign, and Joe handled a huge silver ladle to scoop the highly charged punch into small gold cups.

Linna Johnson, she of the formerly bejeweled class, proudly displayed a bit of handmade jewelry and told everybody that Keg had made it for her. Barney Carroll was holding forth at great length to a group of women on the marvels and mysteries of digging in the Martian desert for traces of the lost Martian civilization, while his partner Jim was explaining to Chuck and Freddie Thomas just how they intended to let a matter transmitter do their excavating for them. Wes Farrell was explaining the operation of the element filter and heterodyne gadget that produced pure synthetic elements to a woman who nodded gaily and didn't understand a word he said but would rather be baffled by Farrell than be catered to by anyone else.

"It's quite a sight," Don agreed. "Never before."

Arden sighed. "And never again!"

"It's an occasion to remember," grinned Don. "Christmas Eve at Venus Equilateral! Here's Triplanet Films with their cameramen, and they tell me that the Interplanetary Network has called off all Christmas broadcasts at midnight, Terra Mean Time, to carry the sounds of revelry from Venus Equilateral as a Christmas celebration program."

"Yeah," said Arden, "and tomorrow I've got to go to church and explain to a class of Sunday schoolers how and why Santa Claus can make the haul across a hundred million miles of space in an open sleigh powered with a batch of reindeer."

"Some blowout," said Michael Warren, coming up with his wife.

Hilda Warren smiled happily. "I don't think I've ever appreciated how many people really worked here," she said.

"Shucks," grinned Don, "I've been trying to get along by merely mumbling about half of the names myself. And if I may point it out, Hilda, you're standing under a hunk of mistletoe." Before she could say anything, Don had proceeded with great gusto, to the amusement of Warren.

Arden shook her head. "The rascal has been standing there for a half-hour because people are always coming up to tell him it's a fine party."

"Method in my madness," Channing nodded.

A faint tinkle of bells sounded in the distance, and as people became aware of them, Keg Johnson tapped Don on the shoulder and said, "The fleet's in, Don. Here comes our professional Santa Claus. And the fleet is going to land and await midnight tomorrow night. The Johnson Spaceline is going to have the honor of hauling bag, baggage, foot, horse, and marines to Terra. Everything ready?"

Don nodded absently. He listened to the sleigh bells for a moment and then said: "Everything of a personal nature is packed. The rest is worthless. How many men have you?"

"About two hundred."

"Then tell 'em to forget the packing and join in. After this mass, we won't even notice a couple of hundred more. But tell me if S. Claus is going to drive that thing right in here?"

Keg nodded. "He's running on snow in the corridor, of course, but he's equipped with wheels for hard sledding."

The orchestra broke into "Jingle Bells" and a full dozen reindeer came prancing in through the large double doors. They came in in a whirl of snow and a blast of icy air from the corridor, and they drew a very traditional Santa Claus behind them in the traditional sleigh laden with great bags.

Before the door was closed on the veritable blizzard in the hallway, several men came in hauling a great log that they placed on the monstrous fireplace at one end of the vast hall.

The only incongruity was the huge spit turned by a gear train from a motor run from a beam energy tube.

Santa Claus handed out a few gifts to those nearest and then mounted the orchestra platform. He held up his hands for silence.

"Before I perform my usual job of delivering gifts and remembrances," he said, "I want you to hear a word or two from your friend and mine—Don Channing!"

This brought a roar. And Channing went to the platform slowly.

"My friends," said Don, "I've very little to say and I'm not going to take a lot of time in saying it. We've had a lot of hard work on Venus Equilateral and we've had a lot of fun. Venus Equilateral has been our home—and leaving our home tomorrow night will be as great a wrench as was the leaving of our original homes so many years ago to come to Venus Equilateral. It will for me. I shall darned well be homesick.

"Yet—this job is finished. And well done. Frankly," he grinned cheerfully, "we started out just covering the planet-to-planet job. We extended that to include planet-to-ship, and then when they added ship-to-planet, it automatically made it ship-to-ship. Well, we've got it all set now to make it anywhere-at-all without relay. People speak of Venus Equilateral and forget the 'Relay Station' part of the name. A relay station is no darned good without something to relay and you know, good people, I'm completely baffled as of now for a communications project. I can't conceive of a problem in communications that would be at all urgent. But . . ."

A loop of the maze of heater wire from the fire-ruined suit twisted on the bare metal floor. The bare metal shorted part of the long loop and the remaining section grew hotter as a consequence. The expansion caused by heat made the tangle of wire writhe slowly, and two crossing lines touched, shorting the overheated loop still more. It flared incandescent and blew like a fuse and showered the room with minute droplets of molten metal that landed on wall and floor solid, but yet warm.

A tiny stinging rain of them pelted Walt's face. This penetrated when few other things would have. Walt stirred, coldly painful, and his eyes struggled against a slightly frozen rim that tried to hold eyelash to cheek.

It took minutes for the idea to filter through his mind: *What woke me?*

He could not know that it had been his subconscious mind. To the trained electronics technician the arc discharge of a shorted circuit has a special meaning whereas to the untrained it may be but an ambiguous *"Splat!"* The blowing of a fuse penetrates the subconscious and brings to that part of the brain a realization of the facts in the case, just as a trained musician will wince when the third violin strikes a sour note in the midst of full orchestration.

Instinctively, Walt's trained brain considered the source. Ponderously slow, he turned a painful head to look on the floor at the remains of the ruined suits. As he watched, the still writhing metal shorted again and a loop glowed brightly, then died as the additional heat expanded it away from its short circuit.

Walt wondered about the time.

He found his left arm trapped beneath Christine and he turned from one side to the other, and he considered her dully. She slept, and was as still as death itself.

Walt released his arm, and the motion beneath the blankets pumped viciously cold air under the covers and chilled his already stiff body. He looked at his watch. It was nine hours since he'd awakened Christine before.

Walt felt no pain, really. He wanted desperately to snuggle down under the covers once more and return to oblivion, where it was warmer and pleasant. But there was something—

Something—

Taking his nerve in his teeth, Walt forced his brain to clear. Christine didn't deserve this.

Yet if he got out from beneath those covers he would most certainly freeze in a matter of minutes. Yet he must—do—something.

He considered the tubes and their tangles of wire through puffed, half-closed eyes. He thought he was moving with lightning rapidity when he leapt out of the bed, but his motion was insufferably slow. He dropped on his knees beside the tubes and with his bare hands fumbled for the hot wires. They seared his fingers and sent pungent curls of smoke up to torture his nose, but his fingers felt no pain and his olfactory sense did not register the nauseous odor of burning flesh.

He found the switch and turned off the tiny tubes.

He collected loop after loop and shorted them close to the terminals of the two cubes. A hundred feet of wire looped back and forth in a one-inch span across the terminal lugs would produce a mighty overload. It made a bulky bundle of wire, the very mass of which would prevent it from heating to incandescence and blowing out in a shower of droplets.

One chance in a million!

Just one!

Walt snapped the switches on.

For to the trained technician, a blown fuse is not an ill. It is a symptom of an ill, and no trained technician ever replaced a blown fuse without attempting to find out why and where the overload occurred.

Walt crept painfully back to bed and huddled under the blankets against Christine.

"Kiddo," he said in a dry, cracked voice, "I did what I could! Honest."

The oblivion of cold claimed Walt again . . .

". . . there is but one unhappy note in this scene of revelry," continued Don Channing a bit soberly. "We're sorry that Walt Franks took this opportunity of rushing off to get matrimonially involved with Christine Baler. He didn't know this bash was imminent, of course, otherwise he'd have been here. We all love Walt and he'll be unhappy that he missed the blowout here. Fact is, fellers, I'd give eight years off of the end of my life to get any kind of word from Walt—"

An alarm clamored in the hallway and Wes Farrell jumped a foot. He headed for the door, but Channing stopped him with a gesture.

"Friend Farrell forgets that we no longer care," laughed Channing. "That was the main fuse in the solar energy tubes blowing out and we won't be needing them anymore. It is sort of pleasant to know that a fuse blew—a thing that was formerly master and we the slave—and that we don't have to give a hoot whether it blew or not. Let it blow, Wes. We don't need power anymore!

"So I suggest that we all have a quick one on Walt Franks, wishing him health and happiness for the rest of his life with Christine nee Baler, even though the big bum did cheat us out of the privilege of kissing his bride.

"And now, I'm going to step aside and let Santa Claus take over."

There was a thunderous roar of applause, and Channing rejoined Arden and the rest of them, who had sort of gravitated together.

"Merry Christmas," he grinned at them.

Keg Johnson nodded. "Merry Christmas—and on to Terra for your Happy New Year!"

They raised their glasses, and it was Wes Farrell who said: "To Walt—and may he be as happy as we are!"

Arden chuckled. "We used to sing a song about 'Walt's Faults,' but there's one thing: Walt would have replaced that fuse even though we didn't need it. The old string saver!"

A messenger came up and tapped Don on the shoulder. Channing turned with an apologetic smile to his guests and said: "I get more damned interruptions. They tell me that someone is knocking on the spacelock door. If anyone here knows any prayers, let 'em make with a short one. Pray this—whoever it is—knows something about Walt."

Don left the party and went along the cold, snow-filled corridor to his office. As one of the few remaining places where operations were in full tilt, Channing's office was where any visitor would be conducted. Once the business was finished, Channing could hurl the guest into the middle of the big party, but the party was no place to try to conduct business in the first place. So, with heels on desk, and a glass of Scotch from his favorite file drawer, Don Channing idled and waited for the visitor.

The knock came and Channing said: "Come in!"

Two policemen—the Terran Police—entered quietly and stood aside as the third man entered cautiously.

Channing's feet came off the desk and hit the floor with a crash.

"The specter at the feast," snorted Channing. "Of all the people I know, I least expected you—and wanted to see you least. I hope it is a mutual affection, Kingman."

"Don't be godlike, Channing," said Kingman coldly. "You may think you're running things all your way, but some people object to being made a rubber stamp."

"Look, Kingman, get whatever is on that little mind of yours damn well off it, so I can continue as I was."

"Channing, I have here papers of disenfranchisement."

"Indeed?"

"Right."

Channing smiled.

"Don't be so damned superior," Kingman snapped.

"Tell me, Markus, just why this disenchantment takes place?"

"Venus Equilateral suspended operations on twenty December," said Kingman. "Without notice nor permission nor explanation. Since the relay beams of Venus Equilateral have carried nothing for a period beyond that permitted for suspension of operations by the Interplanetary Communications Commission, they have seen fit to revoke your license."

"Well! And after all I've done," said Channing.

"You see—you think you can get away with anything. Doubtless this ultra-frigid condition was the cause of failure?"

"Possibly. And then again, maybe someone wanted to make ice cream."

"Don't be flippant. You'll find these papers are final and complete. You'll not be able to talk your way out of it."

"Tell me, O Learned Legal Light, who is going to run Venus Equilateral when I am far away?"

"Some time ago, Terran Electric applied for a franchise and took an option pending failure at Venus Equilateral. This failure has taken place and Terran Electric now controls—"

"I gather that you've been forced to put Terran Electric up as bail for the license?"

Kingman flushed.

"Find that Terran Electric wasn't worth much?" Channing jeered.

"Sufficient," said Kingman.

"Did it ever occur to you that maybe Venus Equilateral wasn't worth much either?" asked Channing.

"I'll make it work for me. And I'll also report that one of your wild experiments got loose and nearly froze the station out completely. I still say that if you'd stopped toying around with everything that came along, Venus Equilateral would still be a running corporation."

"I daresay you're right. But the Devil finds work for idle hands, you know. So just what is the future holding?"

"Channing, your attitude is entirely frivolous, and unconvinced that I mean business. To convince you, I'm going to give you twelve hours to relinquish the station and be on your way from here!"

"May I point out that this is Christmas?"

"I've investigated that," returned Kingman. "I find that Christmas is a completely Terran date and is therefore legal for any and all legal action on any planet or place removed from the interplanetary boundary of the planet Terra. That, Channing, has been established to the Channing Layer."

"And how about the personnel? Must they get the hell off, too?" Channing asked loftily.

"You and your managerial cohorts must leave. Those upon whom the continued service of communications depends are requested to remain—under new management."

"You're taking on a big bite," grinned Channing. "I trust you can chew it."

"I need no help from the likes of you."

"Good. And now that you've had your say, I'll return to my own affairs. Make yourself at home; you'll not be bothered here."

Kingman nodded slowly. He'd expected a battle, and he believed that Channing did not think it true. Channing would damn well find out once he appeared before the Interplanetary Communications Commission. In the meantime, of course, he might as well remain in the office. There was an apartment next door, and it was comfortable.

He did not notice that every very personal thing had been removed from Channing's office. Frankly, Kingman did not care. He had had everything his own way.

The senior officer spoke. "You need us anymore, Mr. Kingman?"

"No," replied the new owner of Venus Equilateral.

"Then we'll return to duty on Terra," said the officer.

Channing went back to the party and spent ten minutes telling his friends what had happened. Then he forgot about it and joined in the merrymaking, which was growing more boisterous and uninhibited by the moment. It was in the wee small hours of the clock—though not necessarily the night, for there is no such thing on Venus Equilateral—when the party broke up and people bundled up and braved the howling blizzard that raged up and down the halls.

Home to warmth and cheer—and bed.

Arden sat up in bed and looked sleepily around the dark bedroom. "Don," she asked with some concern, "you're not sick?"

"Nope," he replied.

Arden pursed her lips. She snapped the light on and saw that Don was half-dressed.

"What gives?" she demanded, slipping out of bed and reaching for a robe.

"Frankly  "

"You've been stewing over that blown-out fuse."

He nodded sheepishly.

"I knew it. Why?"

"Those tubes have been running on a maintenance load for days. They shouldn't blow out."

"Critter of habit, aren't you?" Arden grinned.

Don nodded. "A consuming curiosity, I guess."

Arden smiled as she continued to climb into her clothing. "You're not the only one in this family who has a lump of curiosity," she told him.

"But it's—"

"Don," said his wife seriously, "rules is rules and electricity and energy are things I'm none too clear on. But I do know my husband. And when he gets up out of a warm bed in the middle of the night to go roaming through a frozen world, it's urgent. And since the man in question has been married to me for a number of years, getting up out of a warm bed and going out into snow and ice means that the urgency angle is directed at whatever lies at the other end. I want to go see—and I'm going to!"

Channing nodded absently. "Probably a wild-goose chase," he said. "Ready?"

Arden nodded. "Lead on, curious one."

Channing blinked when he saw the light in the room where the solar intake tubes were. He hastened forward to find Wes Farrell making some complex measurements and juggling a large page of equations.

Farrell looked up and grinned sheepishly. "Couldn't sleep," he explained. "Wanted to do just one more job, I guess."

Channing nodded silently.

Arden said: "Don't kid anybody. Both of you want to know why a fuse should blow on a dead line."

Farrell grinned and Channing nodded again. "I—" Don started, but turned as the door opened.

"Thought we'd find you here," said Barney Carroll. Jim Baler added: "We got to arguing as to how and why a fuse should blow on an empty line and decided to ask you."

Arden squinted at Jim. "Did it ever occur to you that we might have been in bed?"

Barney grinned. "I figured if *we* were awake from wondering about it, so would *you all*. So—"

Jim interrupted. "So what have you found?"

Channing shook his head. "Ask Wes," he said. "He got here first and was measuring the deflecting electrode voltages when I arrived. I note that he has a hunk of copper busbar across the main fuse terminals."

Wes smiled sheepishly. "Had to," he said. "Short was really shorted!"

"So what have you found?"

Farrell pointed to a place on a chart of the station. "About here."

"Spinach!" said Channing. "There isn't anything there!"

Farrell handed the figures to Don. "That's where the short-circuit load is coming from," he said.

"Up there," said Channing, "I'll bet it's hitting close to seventy or eighty degrees below zero. A supercold condition—" He paused and shook his head. "The tube room reached absolute zero some time ago," he said, "and there's no heavy drain to that position."

"Well?" demanded Arden, yawning. "Do we wait until tomorrow morning or go up there now?"

Channing thought for a moment. "We're due to leave in the morning," he said. "Yet I think that the question of why anything up in an empty section of Venus Equilateral should be blowing fuses would belabor us all of our lives if we didn't make this last screwball search. Let's go. Wes, get your portable sun finder, huh?"

"His what?" Arden asked.

"Figger of speech, sweet. We mean a small portable relay tube that we can stick in series with his gawd-awful drain and use for a direction finder. I have no intention of trying to scour every storeroom in that area for that which I don't really believe is there."

The main deterrent to swift action was the bitter, bitter cold that stabbed at their faces and hands, which were not enclosed in the electrically heated suits—of which each one of them wore three against the ultra-violent chill.

"There should be a door here," objected Don, reading a blueprint from the large roll he carried under his arm. "Fact is, this series of rooms seems to have been sealed off entirely though the blueprint calls for a door, about here!"

"How would anybody reseal a doorway?" asked Barney.

"Duplicator," Don said thoughtfully. "And I smell rats!"

"So. And how do we get in?" demanded Arden.

"We break in," said Channing harshly. "Come along, gang. We're going back downstairs to get us a cutter!"

The cutter consisted of a single-focus scanner beam that Don wielded like an acetylene torch. Clean and silently it cut through the metal wall and the section fell inward with a slight crash.

They stepped in through the opening.

"Someone has been homesteading," said Channing in a gritty voice. "Nice prefab home, hey? Let's add housebreaking to our other crimes. I'd like to singe the heels off the character that did this. And I think I'll let the main one simmer."

"Who?" asked Arden.

Channing pointed to the huge energy tube at one end of the room. It bore the imprint of Terran Electric.

"Kingman," he said drily.

Applying his cutter to the wall of the cottage, he burned his way through. "No one living here," he said. "Colder than Pluto in here, too. Look, Wes, here's your short circuit. Tubes from—"

"And here," said Farrell quickly, "are your missing chums!"

Channing came over to stand beside Farrell, looking down at the too-still forms. Baler looked at Channing with a puzzled glance, and Channing shook his head quietly.

Then he said: "I may be wrong, but it strikes me that Walt and Christine interrupted skullduggery at work and were trapped as a consequence. No man, no matter how insane, would ever enter a trap like this willingly. This is neither a love nest nor a honeymoon cottage, Jim. This is a death trap!"

Channing turned from the place and left on a dead run. He paused at the door to the huge room and yelled: "Don't touch 'em till I get Doc!"

By the clock, Christmas Day dawned bright and clear. The strip fluorescents came on in the corridors of Venus Equilateral and there began the inexorable flow of people toward the south end landing stage.

Each man or woman carried a small bag. In this were the several *uniques* he or she possessed and a complete set of recordings on the rest of his personal possessions. Moving was as easy as that— and once they reached Terra, everything they owned could be reproduced at will. It was both glad and sad, the thrill of a new experience to come balancing the loss of the comfortable routine of the old. Friends, however, managed to get aboard the same space-craft as a general rule and so the pain of parting was spared them.

One by one, the huge ships dropped south and then headed for Terra. One by one, until the three-thousand-odd people who lived on, loved, and operated Venus Equilateral through its working years had embarked.

Channing shook hands with Captain Johannson as he got aboard the last remaining ship. Behind Channing came Keg Johnson, who supervised the carrying aboard of Walt Franks and Christine Baler. They were seated side by side in deck chairs on the operating bridge of the spacecraft and Arden came up to stand beside her husband as she asked: "Captain Johannson, you are empowered to perform matrimony?"

Johannson nodded.

"Well," she said, "I'm the matron of honor and this husband of mine intends to be best man. We agree that the couple there have spent too much time living with one another—"

"If she says 'sin' I'll strangle her," groaned Walt.

Christine reached over and took her hand. "She doesn't dare," she said. "She knows it was ah—er—colder than sin!"

Big Jim Baler clenched and unclenched his hands. "I still think we should have called on Mark Kingman," he said in a growl.

Channing shook his head. "And spoil the fine end of a fine holiday? Nope. And also spoil a fine bit of retribution?"

Linna Johnson smiled. "A man of action like Jim finds the finer points of retribution a bit too smooth," she said. "But it'll be plenty rough on Kingman."

"To the devil with Kingman," said Barney Carroll. "I say we ought to commit this ceremony at once and then repair to the bar—or have the bar repair here—and have a last drink to Venus Equilateral."

Walt Franks stood up. "I'm still stiff," he said. "But I'll be damned if I'm going to sit down at my own wedding."

Christine stood beside him. "You're thinking about that 'repair to the bar' and don't want to get left," she told him. "Well, frozen solid or not, I'm sticking tight."

Johannson turned to the pilot and gave the order. The big ship dropped from the platform and they all looked down through the glass dome at the diminishing view of Venus Equilateral.

The captain turned to Channing and asked: "Just what did happen to Mark Kingman?"

"Mark has mortgaged his everlasting black soul to the hilt to maintain communications under the standard franchise. For a period of five years, Mark Kingman must live on that damned station alone in the cold and the loneliness, maintaining once each day a relay contact, or lose his shirt. And because he dropped the *Relay Girl* into the sun when he planned that 'elopement,' we've just confiscated his ship. That leaves Kingman aboard a practically frozen relay station with neither the means to get away nor the ability to handle the situation at all. He must stay, because when he puts a foot on any planet we clap him in jail for kidnapping. He's lost his financial shirt because Venus Equilateral is an obsolete commodity and he'll never regain enough of his personal financial standing to fight such a case. If I were Mark Kingman, about now I'd—"

Channing shook his head, leaving the sentence unfinished. He turned to Walt. "Got a ring handy?"

Wes Farrell held up a greenish metal ring that glinted iridescent colors. "Y'might try this new synthetic," he offered.

Walt shook his head. He fumbled in an inner pocket and came up with a small band that was very plain. "This is a certified unique," he said proudly. "It was my mother's, and grandmother's, too."

Then, with Venus Equilateral still visible in the port below and a whole sky above, Captain Johannson opened his book and started to read. Behind them was work and fun and pain, and before them—

Was the exciting, unchartered future.

# INTRODUCTION
## THE GRIMNOIR CHRONICLES: DETROIT CHRISTMAS

**A PRIVATE EYE** whose income is shaky can't turn down a case, even if it's Christmas time. Even if it involves very dangerous gangsters. Of course, Jake Sullivan is a very tough customer and would be very dangerous himself, even if this weren't the 1930s in an alternate world where magic (or some sort of mental power that might as well be magic) is real, and Jake has a potentially lethal talent at his disposal. It's full speed ahead and damn the Tommy guns.

Larry Correia is hopelessly addicted to two things: guns and B-horror movies. He has been a gun dealer, firearms instructor, accountant, and is now a very successful writer. "The Grimnoir Chronicles: Detroit Christmas" is part of his Grimnoir alternate history urban fantasy series, which also include two novels for Baen Books, *Hard Magic* and *Spellbound*. He is also the author of the *New York Times* best-selling Monster Hunter International series, which presently includes *Monster Hunter International*, *Monster Hunter Vendetta*, *Monster Hunter Alpha*, and *Monster Hunter Legion*. He shoots competitively and is a certified concealed weapons instructor. Larry resides in Utah with his very patient wife and family.

# THE GRIMNOIR CHRONICLES: DETROIT CHRISTMAS

## By Larry Correia

### December 25th, 1931

**DETROIT.** One of the greatest cities in the world. The crossroads of industry and commerce. The American Paris, the City of Champions, Blimp-Town, Motor City, call it what you want, it's one crowded place. Nearly two million people live in Detroit, but as far as Jake Sullivan was aware, only a few of them were trying to kill him at that particular moment in time.

Sure, there might have been others in Detroit that were gunning for him, as he wasn't the type of man that made a lot of friends, but judging from the volume of gunfire pouring through the windows and puckering the walls . . . *Six*. There were only six shooters.

He could handle that.

"Enough! I said enough!" The gunfire tapered off. One last angry bullet bounced off his cover with a *clang*. "You still alive in there?"

The seven-hundred-pound chunk of steel plate he'd picked up to use as a shield had worked better than expected. Sullivan checked his body for holes, and finding no more than usual, shouted back, "Yeah, but your boys ain't. You ready to surrender yet, Johnny? The cops will be here any minute."

"You'll be an icicle before then."

The temperature was dropping fast, which meant that Snowball was out there too. Both Maplethorpe brothers were Actives, which was just his rotten luck. Sullivan's teeth began to chatter. He had to finish this before the Icebox could freeze him out. At this range, a clean shot could freeze him solid, but behind cover . . . even a really powerful Icebox wouldn't be able to steal more than ten degrees a minute from a room this big, but it had already been cold to begin with. That didn't leave Sullivan much time.

"Kidnapping, murder." He needed to goad them into coming after him. It was his only chance. "You boys been busy."

"Throw 'em on the list. They can only send me to the gas chamber once," Johnny Bones shouted back through the broken windows. "Are you the Heavy? Is this the legendary Heavy Jake Sullivan, J. Edgar Hoover's pet Active?"

Sullivan didn't dignify that with a response.

"Heard you been looking for my crew. How'd you find us? I thought you Heavies was supposed to be stupid?"

"Even a blind pig finds an acorn once in a while, Johnny." Sullivan picked up the giant Lewis machine gun from the floor with one shaking hand. It was a good thing he'd already been wearing gloves or he would've left skin on the freezing metal. "You ready to go to prison?"

"You know all about that from what I hear. So how's Rockville this time of year?"

The infamous prison for actively magical criminals was in Montana. Sullivan had been an inmate there for six long years. "Cold. Very cold." Some of Johnny Bones' men were going to try to flank him while they were talking. He knew because that's what he would've ordered if their situations had been reversed. Sullivan picked the most likely window, pointed the Lewis at it, and waited. "You'll get used to it. Your brother will be nice and comfy, though."

"We can make a deal," Johnny shouted, trying to keep Sullivan distracted. "It don't have to be like this, with you all blue and frozen stuck to the floor. How about I let you walk out of here, pay you enough to make it worth your time? We'll call it my present to you. Tis the season and all that jazz. I'm in a giving mood. What do you say?"

Someone moved on the other side of the window. Sullivan held down the trigger and let the Lewis roar. Bricks exploded into dust and glass shattered. The man on the other side went down hard.

That left five.

"I'd say you gotta do better than that."

Johnny Bones Maplethorpe ordered his remaining men to open fire and bullets ricocheted off the steel plate. Jake Sullivan was pinned down in a room that was rapidly turning into a walk-in freezer by a gang of hardened criminals led by a vicious Shard. It was one hell of a way to spend Christmas.

## Two Days Earlier

**"SO, MR. SULLIVAN,** you got any plans this Christmas?"

Sullivan finished counting out the January rent money and passed it over. It was the last ten dollars he had to his name. Paying work had been sporadic lately. "Nothing in particular, ma'am."

"I see," Mrs. Brooks said. His landlord owned the entire building and the diner downstairs. It was obvious the old woman didn't like her tenant much, but Jake Sullivan always paid his rent on time. "I don't want any loudness or carrying on. I know how you Irish get during the holidays with the devil drink."

"Why, Mrs. Brooks, alcoholic beverages are illegal."

"I know all about your disdain for the law, Mr. Sullivan." Mrs. Brooks eyed him suspiciously, then glanced around the office, as if expecting to see a distillery hidden in a corner. Instead there was only a battered second-hand desk, a couple of sturdy wooden chairs, a bedraggled couch, and a few book shelves. "It's only my strong upbringing that's allowed me to forgive your horrific criminal history and your unseemly magic."

The landlord talked a big game, but both of them knew that she'd rent to anybody who could pay in these tough times, and that included convicted felons, less popular types of Actives, or anybody else for that matter. The old lady would rent a room to the Chairman himself if he had ten dollars ready on the twenty-third of each month. "And I won't forget it," Sullivan said.

Mrs. Brooks stepped back and examined the words painted on his door. "Why would someone like you go into this kind of business anyway?"

"I like puzzles . . ." Sullivan said honestly. "Anything else I can do for you, ma'am?" and before she could even answer he was already closing the door on her. "No? Wonderful. Merry Christmas. Goodbye."

The sign on the door read *Sullivan Security and Investigations*. His last security job had been intimidating the union strikers at the UBF plant. Good work that, standing around earning money because you had a reputation for being able to crush a man's skull with a thought. It had paid well too, but that had been months ago. The last investigation job had meant confirming to an angry wife that her husband liked prostitutes. The final bit of money from that one had just paid the rent.

There was other work out there. There always was for a man with his skills, whether physical or magical, but Sullivan was an honest man, and he preferred honest work. There was a difference between being a felon and being a crook, and Jake Sullivan was no crook.

Then there were the government jobs . . . The monetary payment on those was meager, but completing them meant he got to stay out of Rockville. Sullivan sat behind his desk and reread the recent Bureau of Investigation telegram. It was a bulletin on the notorious Maplethorpe brothers. Their gang had recently gotten shot up in a robbery in Albion, and it was believed they were hiding in Detroit. A Shard and an Icebox, with Power to spare, armed, and extremely dangerous, wanted for bank robbery and murder. The telegram said a BI representative would be in touch if it was felt his services would be needed.

The terms of his early release specified that he needed to assist in the apprehension of five Active fugitives. He wondered idly if the Maplethorpes would count as two . . .. As long as the government's terms hung over his head, he would never truly be free. Sullivan crumpled the telegram and tossed it in the waste basket. Nothing usually came of the telegrams.

The first client for the month of December arrived just before noon on the 23rd. Sullivan had been reading a *Popular Mechanics* article about a British Cog named Turing and his controversial attempt to build a mechanical man capable of reasoning, when there had been a delicate knock on the door.

Like all Gravity Spikers—or Heavies as most folks insisted on calling magicals of his type—Sullivan's Power enabled him to manipulate the forces of gravity. He was just much better at it than everyone else. A quick surge of Power enabled him to see the nearby world as it really was, shades of mass, density, and force, and it told him that there was a single body in the hallway, approximately one hundred and twenty pounds.

Hopeful that it might be business related, he quickly saw to it that both he and the office were presentable before answering. He stubbed out his cigarette and hid the magazine in his desk. Sullivan checked the mirror, fixed his tie, and ran a comb through his hair. He was built like a bull, had the face of an anvil, and wasn't particularly well-spoken, but that was no excuse to not present well.

The lady in the hall certainly knew how to present well. She was good looking, mid-twenties, brunette, and petite. She was wearing a blue dress, ten minks worth of coat, and shoes that cost more than all of Sullivan's earthly possessions combined. "I need a private detective," she stated, having to crane her neck to see since he was over a foot taller than she. "Are you Heavy Jake Sullivan?"

"That's me." He didn't much care for the nickname, but it would do. At least that meant she knew he was an Active and was okay with the fact. It wasn't the kind of thing you advertised to most respectable clients. The general attitude was that Heavies were good for lifting things and that was about it. "Please come in."

"Thank you, Mr. Sullivan." Her blue eyes were red from crying. Her manner was resigned and tired.

He closed the door behind her. She was graceful, like a dancer, as she walked in and took a seat. He went to the other side of the desk and settled into his massively reinforced chair. Sullivan weighed far more than he appeared to, a byproduct of his magical experimentation, and he'd gotten tired of breaking chairs.

"So what brings you to this neighborhood?"

"You came highly recommended." The lady glanced around the room. There was a single light bulb wired into the ceiling and the whole place seemed dingy and small. It was times like this that he wished he could afford a real office instead of this rotten dive. Judging by her get-up, she could hire whoever she felt like, but apparently she was undeterred by the shabbiness of her host or his office. "I need your help."

"Sure," he answered. "I'm afraid I didn't get your name."

"Emily Fordyce. I'm here about my husband."

So it was another jilted wife case. The rock on her wedding ring was huge, but in his experience the size of the rock seldom corresponded to a husband's loyalty. "I'll be glad to help, Mrs. Fordyce. What's wrong with your husband?"

"He's missing," she answered with a sniff. "He was abducted."

Sullivan perked up. His day had just become far more interesting. "Really?" She was obviously money, so he asked the logical question. "Has there been a ransom demand?"

"There's been no ransom, and the police say that he's certainly dead."

Sullivan urged her to start from the beginning. Arthur Fordyce had not returned from his office days ago. Yesterday his automobile had been found in a ditch just outside of the city, where it had been hidden by the snow. A great deal of dried blood had been found on the seat. The car was otherwise undamaged.

Emily became increasingly upset as she spoke. Sullivan offered her a smoke to calm her nerves, but she turned him down. He took one for himself. "Your husband have enemies?"

"Oh, no. Everyone loved Arthur. He was a sweetheart."

"He gamble? Owe anyone money?" She shook her head in the negative. Those minks didn't buy themselves. "What did he do for a living?"

"He was a Healer."

Sullivan stopped, match hovering just below his suddenly forgotten cigarette. "A *Healer*?"

Emily nodded. "He's an Active and very skilled. He works freelance, fixing anyone that can afford his services. The finest families in the city have used him."

Healers of any kind were rare, Active Healers with significant amounts of Power were especially so. They were talking about somebody who could cure any illness or mend any wound with a touch. Someone who was literally worth *more* than their weight in gold. "I've never actually spoken to a real live Healer . . . Who were your husband's recent clients?"

"Arthur didn't speak about many of them. You see . . . sometimes influential people need to be discreet . . . " *Rich guys with syphilis,* went unsaid. "I know he did do a Healing for an unsavory man recently who may be some sort of criminal. His name was something Horowitz."

That was a bad sign if it was who Sullivan was thinking of. Abraham Horowitz was a local legend amongst the bootleggers, but it did give him a place to start. Sullivan spent the next hour learning everything he could about the last days of Arthur Fordyce. When he'd exhausted his questions and Emily looked like she would begin crying again, Sullivan decided that she needed to get home.

"Yes, that's probably a good idea, but we've not yet talked about your fee . . . Whatever it normally is, double it. I'm prepared to write you a check in advance."

He'd need operating money, but his pride didn't like taking money for work unperformed. "That's not necessary, ma'am."

"I've got more bank accounts than husbands. Just find him."

"All right, then. I'll do my best, Mrs. Fordyce," Sullivan promised.

Emily pulled a handkerchief out of her purse and dabbed her eyes. "I know you will, Mr. Sullivan. You came highly recommended."

Sullivan certainly hadn't performed many jobs in her neck of the woods. The Fordyces lived over on mansion row in Woodbridge. "Who recommended me?"

"Arthur, of course."

Sullivan didn't know what to make of that response. "Your missing husband . . ."

"I'm sorry, that must sound rather crazy." His expression must have confirmed the idea. "Not recently, obviously. No, it was because of a newspaper article several months ago. It said you helped the government capture some Active madman."

"I know the one." He had gotten a brief mention in the papers after he'd helped the BI arrest Crusher Marceau in Hot Springs. There had been no mention of Jake being a recently released convict, thankfully, because that would have sent J. Edgar Hoover into an apocalyptic fit.

"Arthur knew right away who you were and said that if we ever had need of a private detective, then you would be the only man for the job because you didn't know the meaning of the word *quit*. You see, he had a lot of respect for you. Arthur was in the First Volunteers during the war too, Mr. Sullivan. I believe every survivor of the Second Somme knows who you are."

Sullivan was humbled. His respect for Arthur Fordyce had just grown tremendously. Very few Healers had bothered to join the Volunteers. "Men like your husband saved a lot of lives over there."

"Arthur led me to believe that you saved even more, Mr. Sullivan . . . Now please do it again, and if my husband has been . . ." She choked on the word, then couldn't finish. Sullivan came around, but he didn't know the first thing about how to comfort a grieving woman. Luckily, she waved him away. "I'm fine . . . I'm fine. I'll be going."

Sullivan opened the door for her. Emily stopped, and her voice grew unexpectedly hard. "If Arthur is *gone*, then I don't want the men who did it arrested, I want them *gone* too. Do you understand me, Mr. Sullivan? If they hurt him, I want you to hurt them right back, and if you do so I will double your fee again. I want you to do to them what Arthur said you did to the Kaiser's army."

Sullivan closed the door behind her. Rage at the men who might have made her a widow notwithstanding, Emily didn't know what she was asking for. He wouldn't wish the fate of the Kaiser's army on anyone.

It was snowing when he left the office.

Arthur Fordyce's automobile had been towed to a police lot. A quick phone call to a Detroit P.D. officer who owed him a favor got Sullivan inside for a quick look. The car was a ritzy '29 Dusenberg roadster. The paint gleamed with tiny flecks of real gold. Ostentatious, but fitting for a Healer. The only thing that spoiled the perfection was the gallon of blood someone had left to dry on the leather seats. Most of the blood was on the driver's side, like it had pooled around a body. No wonder the law was assuming it was a murder instead of a kidnapping.

Sullivan was still poking around the Dusenberg when there was an angry cough from behind. He turned to see Detective Sergeant Ragan. "Afternoon, Detective."

"What're you doing in there, Sullivan?"

He'd cultivated a decent enough relationship with many of the local cops, but not all of them. Ragan was in the latter category. An old fashioned, hard drinking, tough guy, Ragan didn't like magicals, and he especially didn't like ones with reputations for having *accidentally* killed a law enforcement officer, even if the officer in question had been a murderous piece of work. "Mrs. Fordyce hired me to find her husband."

"Find her husband's *body* is more like it . . ."

"Who you think did it?" Sullivan asked, still going about his business.

"Whole case is fishy. I'm thinking the wife had him popped, just to get the insurance money. Fellow like that's bound to have a hefty life insurance policy."

Sullivan snorted. "That's rich."

"Why am I even talking to the likes of you? Get out of there! That's evidence." Sullivan climbed out of the car, quickly hiding the handkerchief he'd used to wipe up some blood. "You can't be in here. Who let you in?"

"Nice fella. Forgot his name. About this tall . . ." Sullivan held his hand out about shoulder height then moved it up and down six inches.

"You private ops are a pain in the neck. I ought to have you arrested for tampering with evidence."

That would never hold, but Sullivan definitely didn't want to spend Christmas in a cell. It was time to go. "My apologies, Detective." Sullivan tipped his hat and walked way.

Sometimes prejudices make life harder than it needs to be. Sullivan was fairly certain that if Ragan was running the official investigation then there was no way in the world that he'd resort to consulting a Finder. Ragan distrusted magic, and besides, any clues divulged through magical means wouldn't be admissible in a court of law. Sullivan didn't have those issues. He just wanted to find Arthur Fordyce and get paid.

To be fair, it wasn't just about the money this time. Fordyce was a fellow veteran of Roosevelt's First Volunteer Active Brigade. Sullivan had never associated with any of the unit's Healers, other than to dump wounded soldiers onto their tables. The valuable Healers had been kept as far from the front as possible, while the dime-a-dozen Spikers were always where the bullets were flying. Healers were officers, Sullivan had been an enlisted man, but despite those differences, they'd both shared a little slice of hell in the biggest battle in human history, and that made them brothers.

Sullivan would have done his best no matter what, that was just his single-minded nature, but Fordyce wasn't some anonymous victim. He was First Volunteer, and that made it personal.

The fourth best Finder in Detroit lived in a humble home in Brush Park. Sullivan couldn't afford the other three. A reliable Finder demanded a premium wage. Finders existed in that nebulous grey area of Active popularity. The public considered them useful but scary. At least Finders were far more well-liked than their more powerful cousins, the Summoners. Most religious types simply wouldn't tolerate them or their alien Summoned.

It didn't help that Finders tended to be a few bricks shy of a wall.

Talking to disembodied spirits all day tended to do that to a person. Bernie was all right though . . . Usually.

Sullivan knocked and only had to wait a minute to be let in. Bernie was a pudgy, unshaven, wild-eyed fellow, and today he was wearing some pajamas that had seen better days. "Sullivan! Good to see you, my boy."

"Nice hat, Bernie."

Bernie's head was wrapped in a tin-foil cone. "Keeps some of the voices out," he explained. "I picked up a screamer this morning. Poor thing won't shut up. You know how it goes."

"No. Not really."

"Come in! Come in!" Bernie dragged him inside. The interior of the home was filled with stacks of newspapers and at least a dozen mangy cats. Bernie kicked stray felines out of the way as he led Sullivan to the living room. "Did you bring me a present?"

"I got you a sandwich." He passed over a paper sack. Bernie had a reputation for forgetting to eat when he was on a Finding, and Sullivan needed him focused. Sullivan then pulled out the red-stained handkerchief. "And this."

Bernie took the handkerchief. "Oh . . ." He sounded disappointed. "I meant a Christmas present."

"Sandwich isn't good enough? Well, if you Find me the body that blood came out of I'll give you fifty bucks. This is a rush job."

The Finder studied the stain. "Half up front . . . And you still owe me a present."

"Fair enough." Sullivan had cashed Emily Fordyce's generous advance check already and he counted out the bills. "What do you get for the man that's already got everything?"

"I'm almost out of tin foil." Bernie shoved a particularly ugly cat off the couch and took a seat. He placed the handkerchief on the stack of newspapers that, judging from all the dirty plates and dishes stacked on it, served as his table. "Rush job, eh? I've got just the spirit for you. Strongest thing on her plane. I call her Mae, 'cause you know, she kinda reminds me of this poster of Mae West I got. Bringing her in burns up all my Power for a few days, but she works real fast. I'm warning ya, if this body ain't close, it could take time."

Sullivan leaned against the wall. His overcoat was black and he didn't particularly want to cover it in cat hair. "If you can do a Finding for me today I'll get you *two* rolls of foil."

Bernie rubbed his hands together greedily. "You got a deal, but lots of things can go wrong. If the body is buried real deep, takes time. If the thing I'm Finding is behind iron . . . If it's been cut into little bits and scattered, or if it's been burned to ash, or if—"

"Just do your best, Bernie." Sullivan settled in to wait. He knew how erratic this method was, but when it worked, it worked really well. They'd used the disembodied creatures of the Finders as scouts during the war. Nobody knew where the creatures came from exactly, they tended to be flaky, but they could cover a lot of ground and see things a person couldn't.

Bernie concentrated on the handkerchief, scowled, confused, then cheered up as he remembered he was wearing a hat. He took the tin foil off and went back to concentrating. "That's better. Here comes Mae."

The lights flickered and the house shook. Stacks of newspapers tumbled. Cats screeched and ran for cover. At first Sullivan thought that they were having an earthquake, but then the wind hit, sending the curtains billowing across the room. Sullivan stumbled back as his fedora was blown off.

"Ain't she a good girl? Yes, she is. Mae's my good girl."

Bernie hadn't been lying. This one was a doozy. Sullivan had been around many summonings, but this was the first time he'd actually been able to see the shape of the vaporous creature, even if it was only for an instant. The thing hovered in the center of the room, a weird conglomeration of winged hippopotamus and six-legged porcupine with four glowing eyes, and then it was gone as quickly as it had appeared.

The curtains and blowing trash settled. Sullivan picked up his fedora and brushed away the cat hair. "Impressive critter . . . Though I don't see the resemblance to Mae West."

Bernie put his tin-foil hat back on. "Beauty's in the eye of the beholder, Sullivan."

♣ ♣ ♣

Mae had told Bernie that it was going to take awhile. Arthur Fordyce wasn't close, which meant she needed time to roam. Sullivan was still holding out hopes that Fordyce was alive, he was a Healer after all. Despite the volume of blood, Sullivan could only assume that Healers could fix themselves like they could fix everyone else, provided Fordyce was conscious or had Power enough to do it. Hopefully the demon-hippopotamus-porcupine ghost would come back with good news.

In the meantime, Sullivan had another lead to follow.

Abraham Horowitz ran with the Purple Gang, and the Purple Gang ran most of Detroit. Predominately Jewish, they were strongest on the east side, but there wasn't a criminal activity in this city that they didn't have a piece of. Mostly they stuck with bootlegging, tried to limit their killing to competitors, and kept the petty crooks under heel well enough to keep the law happy. They were tough enough that even Al Capone knew it was easier to just buy from them than to go to war.

If you saw a boat on the Detroit River with gunmen on it, then it probably belonged to the Purples. Nobody brought Canadian booze across the river except for the Purple gang, and if you got caught trying it, you'd get boarded, robbed, and sunk . . . And swimming is difficult with a .45 slug in your chest. The locals called them the Little Jewish Navy, which meant that Abraham Horowitz probably held the rank equivalent of admiral.

The snow had gotten worse and the worn-out tires on Sullivan's old Ford didn't get the best traction, so it took him awhile to get across town. Horowitz's base of operations was at a sugar mill on the river's edge. The mill was legitimate. The hoodlums hanging out in front of the business office obviously were not.

Sullivan stopped the car and got out. The sun was going down and taking the last bit of warmth with it. He threw on his scarf and gloves, but left his coat open in order to get to the .45 automatic on his hip. He knew some of the Purples' muscle since they'd also worked the UBF strike, so wasn't expecting any trouble, but with these types violence was always in the air.

Three men were loafing on a bench at the top of the steps. To the

side, the rollup doors to the sugarhouse were open and two burly
men were throwing burlap sacks onto the back of a truck. He didn't
even need to activate his Power to know they were like him. The way
that each of them were effortlessly lifting four or five fifty-pound
sacks at a time told him that the workers were fellow Spikers. A
bunch of guys sitting around smoking while Actives did all the work
. . . *Figures.*

The Purple thugs got off the bench when they saw him coming
up the stairs. The lead tough intercepted him before he could reach
the door. The kid was barely old enough to shave, but had already
developed a street swagger, but everyone was tougher when they had
two buddies standing behind them. He tossed his cigarette into the
snow. "Whadda you want?"

"I want to talk to Mr. Horowitz."

"You got an appointment? You don't look like you're here to buy
sugar."

"Tell Mr. Horowitz it's about a mutual friend, Arthur Fordyce."

The three thugs exchanged a look that told him they recognized
the name, but the kid didn't budge. "Who're you supposed to
be?"

"Jake Sullivan." He looked over the group. Unfortunately, he
didn't recognize any of them. "Isadore Lebowitz around? He can
vouch for me."

"Buddy, Izzy got put in the ground weeks ago. He ain't vouching
for nobody ever again."

"I hadn't heard."

They were starting to fan out around him. "He got shot in the
teeth. If you was his friend, you should'a knew that," said the second
thug as he walked behind Sullivan. The sharks were circling.

"Mr. Horowitz said no visitors," said the last, this one with the
bleary eyes of someone on the weed. "Not till the bone man leaves
town."

"Shut up, idiot," hissed the second.

Sullivan didn't have time for inter-gang nonsense. "Why don't
one of you guys go *ask* Mr. Horowitz if he wants to talk to me."

The kid snickered. "Yeah? Well, he's busy. You should come

back . . . oh . . . never." His buddies all had a good laugh at that. "Now beat it 'fore we beat *you*."

Sullivan's magic was collected in his chest, waiting. He'd saved up quite a lot. He activated the Power, using just a bit of his reserves, and tested the world around him. The weed head had something dense enough in the small of his back to be a pistol. The leader had something metal in his pocket. The Spikers loading the truck both stopped and looked over his way, having sensed the subtle flux in gravity.

"I'm not leaving until one of you asks Mr. Horowitz if he'll talk to me."

The leader glared at him and the look in those cold eyes said that he'd seen a fair share of blood spilled in his young life. "Last chance to walk away," he said.

Sullivan took his time taking out a cigarette, putting it to his mouth, and striking a match. The thugs watched him light up, incredulous as he took a puff, held it for a moment, then let it out. "Last chance to get your boss."

He had to hand it to the kid. He was fast with that straight razor. It came out in a silver flash. "You know what time it is now, big man?"

Sullivan shrugged. "Can't say I do."

The kid held the razor low at his side. "Now's the part where you say you don't want any trouble."

"Does that ever work?"

"Nope."

The kid lunged. The razor zipped out like a striking rattlesnake. Sullivan grabbed his Power and twisted gravity. When in a hurry there was no time for finesse. A small piece of the world *broke*. Up was down and down was up. The kid's feet left the ground as he tumbled, surprised, toward the overhang. He slammed into the sheet metal cover overhead. Sullivan let him hang there for a moment, just so that he could know he'd barked up the wrong tree, before cutting his Power. The kid hit the concrete in a shower of dust and snow.

Sullivan turned just as the weed head went for the gun under his coat. He had plenty of Power stored up, and it never hurt to make an example of idiots, so Sullivan drastically lessened the strength of gravity around his target before he slugged the punk square in the face. Weedy left the ground, flew back to the end of Sullivan's range, then fell and bounced down the steps. A little nickel-plated pistol went skittering off into the snow.

There was one Purple left. He was just standing there, too flummoxed to move. Sullivan removed the cigarette from his mouth and pointed at him. "Like I said . . . *I'll* wait here while *you* go tell Mr. Horowitz."

The punk jerked open the doors and ran for his life. Sullivan looked over to see the two Spikers coming his way. One of them had picked up a length of pipe. "Brothers, you don't want to try me. I may be like you . . ." Sullivan let a bit more of his Power slip so they could feel the obvious surge. Gravity distorted. Falling snow stopped and hung in mid air. The workers looked at each other, surprised at the display of control. Sullivan cut it off before he wasted too much precious Power. The snow resumed falling. "But I've got *way* more practice."

The Heavies returned to their truck, but they kept an uneasy eye on him. The punk at the bottom of the stairs was moaning about the condition of his face. The kid with the razor was out cold. That's what they got for picking a fight with someone who'd survived Second Somme *and* Rockville. Sullivan took a seat on the bench and finished his smoke.

Two minutes later the door opened again. This time four Purples filed out and they all trained shotguns on him. "Mr. Horowitz will see you now."

Abraham Horowitz sat behind a giant oak desk, thick arms folded, and prepared to listen to Sullivan's request. The bootlegger was a steely-eyed killer, past his physical prime now, but this was a man who'd grown up busting heads and collecting protection money. This was not somebody to shortchange, so it was probably wise to start with an apology. "Sorry about your boys downstairs, but I didn't do anything until the kid tried to carve me a new smile."

"Well, they should have asked me first. There was no need to be impolite to guests. Bad for business." Horowitz grunted. "From your rep I'm surprised you didn't just kill 'em all. You're a living legend. Way I hear it, you got a early release 'cause you're so good at it . . . You cut a deal with the enemy to take down dangerous Actives, right? You wouldn't happen to be here on the government dime, are you, Mr. Sullivan?"

"No, sir. Far as I'd tell anybody, you run a sugar mill, that's all. As for the enemy, any man would make a deal with the devil to get out of Rockville. It's a hard place. I just do what I've got to get by, same as anybody."

"I'd appreciate it if no Purples ever show up on your list, Mr. Sullivan, 'cause that could be *unpleasant* for everybody."

If one of the Hoover telegrams had a member of the Purple gang on it for him to help catch, Sullivan would make damn sure he had plans to get the hell out of Detroit real quick afterwards. "I'd like that very much too, sir."

"Respect . . . Let me tell you, I wish you would'a taken Isadore's job offer after the UBF strike. A Heavy like you could make a lot of money working for the Purples. My Heavies down there said you're downright frightening how much Power you got."

Of course he was good; he'd done nothing but practice the entire time he'd been in Rockville. "You honor me, Mr. Horowitz, but I'm just a simple man," Sullivan said.

"Isadore said you were a whole lot smarter than you talked, too. My people appreciate an educated man, especially a self-educated man such as yourself. Izzy, may he rest in peace, said you read books like some sort of professor."

"Reading's my hobby. Keeps me out of trouble."

"Seems like a man who's avoiding trouble wouldn't end up in the middle of it so often."

"Just curious I guess . . . Like I'm curious about Arthur Fordyce. His wife hired me to find him."

Horowitz chuckled. "I liked old Arthur. You're probably wondering how we knew each other. Well, let's just say that Arthur didn't care much who he Mended as long as their dollars were green. Last time I used him was 'cause I'd started losing my vision and couldn't feel my toes. He fixed me up good as new and told me to quit eating so much sugar. Ha! Not with this sweet tooth." Horowitz pounded one meaty hand on the desk, then he paused and frowned. "Well, shit . . . Now that he's gone I might have to cut back . . . Arthur did other things for the Purples too. If one of my boys got shot and I needed him back in action quick, I'd go to Arthur. He was good at pulling bullets out but not asking about who put them in, if you get what I'm saying. Son of a bitch charged an arm and a leg, though."

"You know who might have taken him?"

The gangster shrugged. "Lots of folks. Maybe somebody who needed something fixed couldn't afford to pay an arm or a leg. Sick folk can get mighty desperate."

"These are desperate times," Sullivan agreed. Detroit was better off than most of the country, but even here there were tent cities growing on the fringe. Lots of people were out of work, hungry, and hurting.

Horowitz made a big show of studying Sullivan for a long time. "Maybe not just sick folks get that desperate . . . Come to think on it, maybe I know somebody else who couldn't afford a Healing, but might need a Healer real bad . . . Maybe I could tell you something that would help us both out of a jam."

He was looking for an angle, but men like Horowitz always were. "I'm listening," Sullivan said.

"You ever hear that old saying, kill two birds with one stone? You got to find somebody and I don't get to eat sweets because the only Healer in Detroit is gone . . . and maybe, just maybe I know somebody who might have taken poor old Arthur. Maybe there is this crew mucking around in my area, robbing banks where they shouldn't be, but maybe this crew have been muscle for another group that the Purples don't want to mess with. Maybe this crew works with the Mustache Petes . . ." Sullivan knew that the Mustache Petes were the Sicilian-born gangsters that ran New York. The word was that Purple gang had an uneasy truce with them. "Maybe this crew was caught robbing a bank and got themselves shot to bits by policemen over Albion way. Maybe they'd be desperate enough to steal a Healer . . . Maybe this is something I'd like to take care of myself, but my hands are tied on account of business reasons. What do you say to that?"

*That's a lot of maybes.* The last BI telegram had said the Maplethorpe gang had gotten hit in Albion. They certainly wouldn't be above kidnapping. "That's very . . . forthcoming of you, Mr. Horowitz. If this crew was to get rolled up by the law they'd be out of your hair."

"You find your man, this other crew goes away. Two birds, one rock. Bam. As long as you never said where you heard it from . . ."

"Of course. How about you let me know where this crew is and I'll go get your favorite Healer back?"

"Doubt it. Johnny Bones enjoys killin' too much, likes to cut on people so they die slow, and his brother Snowball's damn near as mean. The second he got his crew Mended, Arthur probably died. Let me put the word out. As soon as I know where that crew is I'll be in touch."

Sullivan knew when he'd been dismissed. Horowitz didn't offer to shake on their deal. As far as the gangster was concerned selling out Johnny Bones was like taking the garbage out to the curb for pickup. Sullivan stood to leave.

"One last thing, Mr. Sullivan. When you come up against Johnny, you're gonna have to kill him fast. Shoot him, squish him with your Power, whatever you got to do. Don't try to talk to that crazy Shard. He's sly. He'll cut you to pieces or his crazy brother will freeze you just to watch you shatter like glass. Mark my words. Take them fast or you'll regret it."

Sullivan debated his next move. Mae was still coming up with nothing. If Horowitz was right, Arthur Fordyce was probably already dead. Until he got a lead on where the Maplethorpes were holed up, he was at a dead end. If Horowitz was wrong, he was wasting his time.

Well, not exactly wasting . . . Which was why Sullivan's last stop for the evening was at the Detroit office of the Bureau of Investigation. Horowitz wasn't the only man that liked to kill two birds with one stone.

The BI office was near the Fisher Building. The giant art deco skyscraper was impressive, even if they were turning the lights down at night to save money now. It was late, the snow was still falling, and most everyone had gone home for the night, so Sullivan left a note for the agent in charge of the manhunt to contact him.

He got home around 11:00. Sullivan's mind was too spun up to go to sleep, so instead he found himself pulling out a book he'd purchased last year on the history of the First Volunteer. He'd found it a fairly accurate, yet rather dull account of the events in question. To be fair, it would be rather difficult for some academic historian to chronicle the unrelentingly bleak meat grinder of the trenches, the sheer mind-numbing spectacle of Second Somme, or the final march into the blackened ash wasteland that had been Berlin.

Even though Sullivan had been the most decorated soldier in the unit, there was only one picture of him, and it was a group shot of some Spikers taken somewhere in France. All of them were tired, dirty, starving, cold, suffering from dysentery, wearing their rusting Heavy suits, carrying their Lewis guns, and lucky to be alive. The book only had two pages about the Gravity Spikers. That was it. All that fighting, all those sacrifices, condensed into *two* lousy pages, and sadly one of those pages was mostly about his own exploits. He didn't deserve his own page. He'd just been lucky. Of the men in the photo, only ten percent had come home alive.

But it wasn't bitter reminiscence that had caused Sullivan to open the history book. There were photos for most of the officer corps and Sullivan was looking for one in particular. When he found Captain Arthur Fordyce's entry at first Sullivan thought that he'd found the wrong picture . . . He checked again, just to be sure, and it was correct. Fordyce certainly didn't look like what he'd expected.

Fordyce had to be in his sixties in the picture, and it had been taken back in 1916 . . . Fifteen years ago . . . *Has it really been that long?* Sullivan had been so young that he'd had to lie about his age to enlist, and he was quite a bit older than Emily Fordyce now. For that reason Sullivan had been expecting a younger man. That was not such an odd thing, especially for a man of Arthur's success, to have such a young beautiful wife.

Too damn young to be a widow.

He fell asleep after midnight, which made it Christmas Eve.

Sullivan checked on Bernie and his cats in the morning, but still nothing from Mae. Bernie said that was a very bad sign, meaning that the target was not in an easy-to-find state, as in above ground or in one piece. Since he was actually a little worried about Bernie's health, Sullivan made sure to drop off another sandwich.

The BI agent in charge of the manhunt had Sullivan come into the office to talk. Most of the G-men tolerated him, a couple respected him because he was very good at his job, and a few openly despised him for being an ex-con. But like it or not, when it came time to arrest somebody who could bend the laws of physics, Sullivan was damn handy to have around.

The head of the Detroit office was a weasel named Price. He was a ticket-puncher, a man who existed primarily to get promoted. Price loved getting in the papers. Hoover didn't like sharing the spotlight with his underlings, but Sullivan had no doubt that Price would end up in politics as soon as he got an arrest big enough to make headlines.

The agent in charge of the manhunt was a homely fellow by the name of Cowley, fresh off the morning dirigible from D.C. Apparently he was one of Hoover's personal favorites. Which inclined Sullivan to dislike him automatically. Sullivan briefed the agents about what he'd heard, though he was careful never to mention the Purple gang.

Despite looking like he'd be much more comfortable behind a desk, Cowley had listened intently enough that Sullivan had come away suspecting that the agent might actually have a clue about being a decent cop. He also didn't seem dismayed to find out that Sullivan was an Active. Cowley's primary concern was that if Arthur Fordyce was alive, he be returned safely. Price was mostly worried about how the arrest of the Maplethorpes would play in the news, but rescuing a Healer . . . Sullivan could see the wheels turning there.

Cowley showed him sketches of the members of the crew. He memorized the names and faces, but since none of them were

Actives, he wasn't as worried about them. Kidnapping was a local matter, not a federal crime, but both Maplethorpes were on the most wanted list, so it was agreed that if Sullivan helped capture them it would count as two against his quota. He made sure he got that in writing.

The rest of the day was spent chasing leads to nowhere. Nobody had heard anything, and if they had they weren't talking. He placed a telephone call to Mrs. Fordyce to inform her that he was still looking, but had no real progress to report. He'd tried to sound encouraging but failed.

When darkness fell, Jake Sullivan returned to his office to prepare. His magic was ready, Power built up in his chest, just waiting to be used to twist gravity to his will. But Power burned quickly, and once it was gone, it took time to replenish. So that meant guns.

One of the Lewis Mk3 machine guns he'd brought back from France was kept hidden under the floor boards of his office. He dragged the huge weapon out, cleaned and oiled it, and loaded the huge drum magazines from boxes of military .30-06 ammunition. Twenty-six pounds of lethal steel, the Lewis was big, ugly, and effective, sort of like Sullivan. It was a lot of gun, but the BI hadn't specified that the Maplethorpes needed to be taken alive.

He'd fought his whole life. He was good at it. As a soldier for his country, as an inmate for survival, and now as a . . . *what am I?* Somebody who didn't know anything else? A slave to the G-men? *No*. It was better if he told himself that he was doing this one for a young widow and to avenge another First Volunteer. It seemed more pure that way.

The Lewis went into a canvas bag. He went downstairs, ordered a late dinner, and waited. Burning Power was like hard physical exercise, so he treated himself to a real good meal in preparation. Mrs. Brooks was glad for the business and didn't even inquire about why the usually frugal Sullivan suddenly seemed to be Mr. Big Spender. A ten-year-old serving as a Purple gang runner showed up while he was polishing off his coffee, gave him a note, and took off.

Sullivan read the address, finished his drink, put out his smoke, and left a generous tip. It was time again to go to war.

The address was for an auto parts factory on Piquette. Like many other businesses in the area, it had recently been shut down and the workers laid off. He parked a block away and went in on foot. Between the lousy weather, the fact that most of the surrounding businesses were closed, and that it was late Christmas Eve meant that there wasn't anyone around. Regular folks were eating hams, singing carols clustered around the fire, or some such thing, not spying on an abandoned factory through a hole in a fence.

After an hour of miserable cold a blue Dodge rolled up to the back door and a man got out carrying grocer's bags. The lights of the city reflected off the snow clouds enough to give him plenty of pink light to see by. He recognized the lean, broad-shouldered fellow making his way to the back door from one of the sketches Agent Cowley had shown him as one Bruno Hauptmann, a German immigrant and member of the gang. This was the hideout, all right. Hauptmann was walking with a bad limp. He knocked on the back door and a few seconds later it opened and he disappeared inside.

Location confirmed, he debated calling the BI. There was strength in numbers, but the only person Jake Sullivan trusted was Jake Sullivan. The G-men would probably just get in his way, but at the same time, if he got killed, he didn't want the kidnapping trash to escape. Finally, caution won out and he hurried back to the phone booth he'd parked by. The switchboard put him through to Cowley. He gave them the scoop, then reminded the G-man to make sure the rest of his boys knew not to shoot at him. The cavalry was on the way.

But he'd never been the type to wait around for cavalry. Sullivan removed the Lewis Gun from his car and headed back to the factory.

They might be watching through the long row of windows, so best to move quick. He reached the fence, and using just enough Power to lighten himself, leapt cleanly over the barrier. The door was solid by any measure, but not built to withstand someone like him. Not even pausing, Sullivan lifted one big boot and kicked the door wide open. The interior was dim, lit only be a single shielded lantern. Hauptman and another man with one arm in a sling were caught flatfooted just inside, stuffing candy bars in their faces.

Sullivan leveled the machinegun at them. "Hands up."

"Cops!" The stranger went for the revolver stuck in his waistband. Sullivan moved the gaping round muzzle over and simply shot him dead. The body hit the cold concrete without so much as a twitch.

The .30-06 had been deafening against the metal machinery surrounding them. Ears ringing, he turned the gun back on Hauptmann. "Your friend was an idiot. Let's try that again." Terrified, the kidnapper reached for the ceiling. "Better." Sullivan looked down the rows of darkened machines, but there was no sign of anyone else inside. He picked up the lantern and lifted the cover, filling the space with light. Sullivan walked around a big hydraulic press. There were several mattresses and blankets on the floor, but the rest of the gang was out.

*Damn.* "Where's Fordyce?"

"Who?" Hauptmann asked.

"Don't play stupid." Sullivan concentrated. Using Power in big bursts was easy, fine control took more concentration. He gave Hauptmann another two gravities. The German grimaced and stumbled against the wall. "Talk. Where is he?"

"I don't know what you're talking about!"

"You wanna end up a pancake?" Sullivan dropped one more gravity on him. Hauptmann screamed as bones creaked. "Don't be a baby. I do pushups in that." The kidnapper was surely feeling it. "Where's the Healer?"

"I don't—" Hauptmann's head sprayed red as the window behind him shattered.

Sullivan instinctively flung himself to the floor. A muzzle flashed outside as someone worked a Tommy gun across the glass. He needed cover, fast. There was a thick steel plate leaning against the hydraulic press. With no time for finesse, he grabbed the plate, surged his Power so hard that it felt light as a feather and jerked it around to use as a shield.

Sullivan cursed himself for turning up the lights. *Dummy.* The others must have returned and seen them inside. Bruno Hauptmann was a few feet away, missing a chunk of skull, just staring at him while his brains leaked out. At least that guy's kidnapping days were surely over.

The bullets kept on hitting the plate in a seemingly never-ending stream of hot lead. They'd get tired soon. Sullivan checked his pocket watch. Cowley's men should be here any minute. Then he noticed the time.

*Well, Merry Christmas to me.*

The BI rolled up, ready for a fight. They just hadn't expected the fight to be ready for them. The first car to arrive was hit immediately. Bullets pierced the radiator, the windows, but luckily not the two agents inside, who bailed out, took cover behind their vehicle and returned fire. A Detroit police car arrived from the opposite direction thirty seconds later. It too took fire from a member of the Maplethorpe gang armed with a stolen BAR. Within a minute two other cars had arrived, and the street collapsed into the a chaotic gun battle that the morning papers would describe as the Detroit Christmas Massacre.

However, Special Agent Sam Cowley was not thinking about how this would play out in the media. That was his bosses' job. Cowley was too busy being pinned down behind the rapidly disintegrating engine block of his car as an automatic weapon poked holes in it. The Maplethorpe gang had a reputation for using overwhelming force during their robberies, which is what made them such high profile targets. Most of them were vets of the Great War—from both sides—and they knew how to work together. The responding officers were outmatched as the gang moved out of the factory's parking area, using the low brick walls for cover, taking turns shooting while the others moved or reloaded.

A nearby officer cried out and dropped his pistol. The gun metal gleamed with ice crystals. Cowley gasped in pain as he was hit with a surge of unbelievable cold. Snowball was attacking. Cowley rolled out from under the car but couldn't spot the Active. He got a bead on one of the gang and emptied his .38 at him. He couldn't tell if he'd struck the man or not since he ducked behind the factory wall and disappeared.

There was an unholy scream. Cowley turned to see that Johnny Bones had flanked them. The Shard ripped his claws free from an officer's belly, then he came at Cowley, grinning, his skull flowing and twisting under his skin. Terrified, the agent broke open his revolver, punched out the empties, and tried to reload with numb, shivering fingers. Johnny Bones aimed his Thompson at Cowley.

Then it was as if someone had thrown an invisible lasso around the Shard and yanked him sideways. Johnny flew through the air and collided violently with a light pole. The Tommy Gun clattered away. The Shard got up slowly as his bones returned to their normal shape. "Kill the Heavy!" he ordered.

The parolee, Sullivan, burst through the window and rolled through the snow as a wave of force tossed the criminals every which way. Sullivan rose, cutting down his enemies like an avenging angel, wielding a giant black rifle that ripped an unending stream of thunder.

"The big one's on our side!" Cowley shouted.

Sullivan ducked. The wall above him was instantly frosted over. Even from across the street Cowley could see the ice particles striking the Heavy, but the Icebox was behind cover and he didn't have a shot. But cover didn't matter to Sullivan. Grimacing through the frostbite, he focused in on the Icebox's position and Snowball Maplethorpe *fell* into the sky. Sullivan calmly shouldered his machine gun, like a sportsman shooting waterfowl, and blasted the Icebox out of the air.

"*Mikey!*" Jonny Bones shrieked as his brother was riddled with bullets. Sullivan must have cut his Power, because Snowball dropped back to the Earth, to lay crumpled, staining the snow pink. "You son of a bitch!" Bones took a few steps forward, then realized that the rest of his gang was in a bad way. The Shard turned and ran down the street.

Sullivan dropped his now-empty machine gun and took off after Johnny Bones. Cowley closed the cylinder on his Smith & Wesson and aimed at the fleeing Shard. "Stop," Sullivan ordered, and as the big man ran past he said, "We need one alive."

He'd fought a Shard in Rockville once. Just another punk with a chip on his shoulder, thinking that if he could off the toughest guy on the block that would somehow make him king. Sullivan had ended his life, just like all the idiots before him, and all that came after, but it had been a valuable learning experience.

Shard magic worked on a biological level. Their skin was remarkably tough and elastic, their bones could change shape and density as they desired. They were rare, and loathed by the public, considered disgusting freaks . . . Sullivan felt bad for them, but that was still no excuse for kidnapping. Disfiguring magic or not, Johnny Bones was done.

A police car roared into the next intersection, sirens blaring. Johnny slid to a stop in the middle of the street. He looked around, but there was nowhere left to run. He saw Sullivan coming with a .45 raised in one hand. Desperate, Johnny spread his arms wide. "I ain't got no gun. You gonna shoot me down like a dog in the street, Heavy?" His breath came out in a cloud of steam.

"Where's Arthur Fordyce?"

"You killed my brother!" Johnny struck himself in the chest. "Come on, finish it. I ain't going to Rockville and I ain't going to the chair."

Sullivan's Power had burned too hard for him to do anything fancy with it. He didn't dare try the trick he'd done to Hauptmann. He'd probably just accidently splatter Johnny all over Detroit. "Tell me what you did to Fordyce."

Johnny Bones started walking toward Sullivan. "If you don't got the balls to shoot me down like a man . . ." The Shard's fingers were suddenly twice as long as normal and ended in points like needles. "I'll just take you with me."

Sullivan sensed that there were G-men coming up behind him. "Hold your fire and stay out of this," Sullivan ordered, and even though he wasn't in charge of these men in any way, when he used his sergeant's voice, men knew not to question. None of the cops said a word as Sullivan put his Colt back in the holster. "I'll kill you clean, Johnny, but not until you tell me what I want to know."

The Shard swung. His Power-fueled body was a killing instrument. Sullivan ducked away, narrowly avoiding the claws. Johnny slid sideways as Sullivan twisted gravity, but his own Power was overheated and scattered. It lacked force, and Sullivan couldn't risk giving him a good spike without killing the man. Sullivan raised his fists and the two Actives circled, looking for an opening.

Johnny came at him with a flurry of potentially lethal jabs. It would have been intimidating to anyone else. Calm, Sullivan timed it, cocked his fist back, and slammed the Shard square in the face. Johnny's entire skull seemed to squish to one side. He reeled away and Sullivan saw his chance. He slugged Johnny again and again. The Shard wasn't the only one with a magically hardened body, but Sullivan's came from years of exercising in increased gravity until his bones were dense as stone, and now he used them to beat Johnny *down*.

He pressed the attack and drove a fist deep into Johnny's guts, knocking the air right out of his opponent. "Not used to somebody who can fight back, huh?" When Johnny went to his knees, Sullivan circled, came from behind, wrapped one arm around Jonny's throat and used the other to pin the Shard's elbows to his side. Sullivan hoisted the much smaller man into the air and choked the shit out of him. "*Where's Fordyce?*" he shouted in Johnny's ear.

There was a sudden piercing heat through Sullivan's left forearm. He grunted and let go, stepping away as the bone spike pulled through his muscle. Blood came gushing from the wound and splattered the snow. Johnny raised his arm. A narrow shard had extruded from Johnny's elbow and it was painted red. Sullivan looked at the hole in his arm. "Haven't seen that before."

"You killed my brother, you bastard . . ." Johnny gasped, blood running freely from his nose and down his shirt. He charged and Sullivan struck him square in the throat. Johnny hit the ground with a gurgle.

"Yeah. Your Power don't do much for the soft bits . . . Where's Fordyce?"

Johnny Bones' face was purple as he staggered to his feet. "I don't know who you're yappin' about. You keep saying that name. Means nothing to me."

"The Healer you kidnapped."

Johnny stopped and started to laugh like Sullivan had just said the funniest thing ever. "Him? You think I took *him*?" The laugh grew harsh and desperate. Johnny knew his time was up. "You been played, Heavy. Check my boys. We ain't had no Mending . . ."

The man he'd shot in the factory . . . His arm had been in a sling. Hauptmann had been walking with a bad limp. This crew had never had a Healer . . . Sullivan had played the chump.

People had come out from somewhere into the street to see what was going on, kept back only by the circle of lawmen. They stood there, two Actives, having fought like gladiators for the crowd. Sullivan surveyed the cops and the witnesses, sighed, and let his injured arm hang limp at his side.

The Shard faced him, eyes desperate, seething with Power as more stabbing chunks of bones stretched his skin. Nothing left to use, he was going to burn it all. Misshapen and jagged, Johnny no longer looked human.

"Stand down, Shard. It don't have to be like this." Sullivan drew his .45.

"Maybe before you used my brother as skeet . . . Ain't got nothing to live for now."

Johnny Bones bellowed as he charged. Sullivan extended his hand and fired three times.

Sullivan gave the BI his statement. He got read the riot act by Special Agent in Charge Price, who was more upset about having to talk to the bloodthirsty press than he was that three police officers had been severely wounded. It was going to take some spin to say that a running gun battle in the streets was a good thing, but at least he did have a pile of dead gangsters to show for it. Surprisingly, Agent Cowley stuck up for Sullivan, said that they'd been unprepared for how much firepower the Maplethorpes had brought to bear, and that they shouldn't have driven right into a bullet storm.

Sullivan was kicking himself for calling the BI to begin with—he should have just handled it himself—but he was even more mad that he'd been set up. They plugged the hole in his arm and wrapped it in a bandage. Just a new scar to join the constellation of old scars . . . There would be no fancy Healings on the taxpayer's dime for some dumb Heavy.

Cowley had come up to him at one point and thanked him for saving his life. Sullivan wasn't used to gratitude from official types and didn't really know what to say in return. The exhausted agent took a seat across from him. "Sure has been one heck of a night. Not just for us, but all over town . . . Sounds like one of your local gangs decided to clean house too. One of them Purples got hit. Abe Something-witz."

"Horowitz?"

"That's the name. Tough guy from what I was told. Had to be an inside job since they got him at home. No sign of forced entry, so he let them in. Pow. Single bullet right in the back of the head. Found him in the kitchen with a bottle of wine open and a glass in each hand."

Sullivan clammed up on the topic. Cowley thanked him again for saving his life and left to send a report to his superiors. Then after another few hours of answering the same questions over and over again, Sullivan was free to go.

*About damn time.* He had questions of his own that need to be answered.

"Mae found your body. You owe me twenty-five bucks and a present."

Sullivan was in a phone booth not far from the police station. "Dead or alive?"

"Not just dead, but sliced into pieces dead," Bernie answered. "That's why it took Mae so long to find him."

Sullivan groaned and rested his forehead on the cold glass. It had all been for nothing. "Where?"

"All over the city. Five, maybe six different places so far. Maybe more she hasn't found yet, but I told her that was good enough. Mae found the first piece in a deli uptown. She says most of him had already been eaten."

*Chopped into pieces and . . .* "Did you say *eaten?*"

"Yeah. Of course. People ate him."

What kind of sickos was he dealing with here? "Bernie, you're telling me somebody chopped up Arthur and *ate* him?"

"Yeah . . . Why's that so weird?" Bernie chuckled. Sullivan didn't see what was so damn funny, since there was a gang of cannibal lunatics on the loose in Detroit. "Huh . . . Arthur. That's a funny name for a porker."

"Porker?" Fordyce hadn't been fat.

"Porker. Pig. You know, oink oink, pink with a curly tail . . . Oh . . . Wait . . . Mae says he was one of the white with brown spots kind."

The blood in Fordyce's car . . . He hadn't given Bernie any details about the case, just asked him to find the body that the blood had come from. "Thanks, Bernie," Sullivan mumbled as he returned the earphone to the cradle.

The Fordyce home was the nicest one on a very nice street. The sun hadn't been up for very long when Sullivan arrived, left arm bandaged and throbbing, to bang on the door. The butler tried to shoo him away, but Sullivan pushed his way inside and told the man in no uncertain terms what would happen if he didn't get Mrs. Fordyce. The butler threatened to call the police. Sullivan said good.

After being escorted into the study, he took a seat on an overstuffed couch and waited, reading the spines of the hundreds of books on the walls. The collection made him envious. Emily Fordyce joined him a few minutes later, still tying the waist sash of an oriental silk robe. Her hair was undone and hung to her shoulders.

"Late night?" he asked.

"Yes, I've just been so worried." But they both knew that's why she hadn't gotten much sleep. "Have you any news?"

Sullivan shook his head. "You're a real piece of work, lady."

Emily stopped. "Why . . . Whatever do you mean?"

"You can drop the act. I know I'm not the one that did *all* the killing last night. So how long have you known Horowitz? Must have been long enough that he wasn't scared to turn his back on you."

"I don't know what you're talking about."

"You sent me to Horowitz. He sent me to Bones, who was such a rabid dog that you figured there was no way he'd be taken alive for questioning. Horowitz wanted him gone and Bones was as good a scapegoat as you'd ever find. Then you shot Horowitz because the only way two people can keep a secret is if one of them's dead."

The shocked expression that briefly crossed her lovely face said that he'd gotten close enough. She tried to play indignant. "How dare you accuse me!" She pointed at the door. "Get out!"

Sullivan stayed planted on the couch. "Why the pig blood?"

"How—" She caught herself too late. Emily's arm fell. "If you knew Arthur, you'd know that the pig was appropriate. Well, I do say . . . You are smarter than you look."

"Just a bit," Sullivan said. "I'm assuming you had Horowitz stage the crime scene. You don't strike me as the type that likes getting your own hands dirty."

Resigned, she walked around behind the ornate desk and flopped into Arthur's wide rolling chair. "Not usually . . . The authorities had to declare that Arthur was dead before I could collect his insurance. I wanted to be elsewhere at the time for an alibi."

Sullivan looked over at the giant painting of Arthur Fordyce hanging over the fireplace. "So, where's your husband?"

She shrugged. "Argentina, I think. He's run off again with one of his many mistresses. *Again.* The man's seventy-five with the libido of an eighteen-year-old sailor. He does this all the time. He'll be gone for weeks, sometimes months, before he crawls back, begging forgiveness."

It was actually more surprising that he was alive than that he was a philanderer. "But why make it look like he was dead if he's coming back?"

"Timing, Mr. Sullivan, timing. I had to be ready to act as soon as he ran off again. Arthur is declared legally dead. I get the insurance money, which is significant—let me tell you—I clean out the accounts and I leave the country. The jerk comes home to find out he's dead and broke. Serves him right."

"If you hated him so much, why didn't you just leave him?"

"I married that old fool for his money. I just didn't realize how awful *long* a Healer can stick around." She rolled her eyes. "I divorce him, I get nothing. It's hard to poison a Healer slow enough to make it look natural. They just keep making themselves better. Believe me, I thought about just shooting him in the night and blaming it on robbers. The kidnapping was Abe's idea."

"How'd you know Horowitz?"

Emily was looking around the desktop for something, suddenly she swept aside a book to reveal a small revolver hidden beneath. "Ah ha!" she shouted as she reached for it. She'd shoot him, say it was self defense or something . . . but Sullivan's Power had recovered from last night's escapade. He slammed multiple gravities down on the little gun. Emily tugged on it, grunting and pulling, but she couldn't budge it. "Damn you, Heavy!"

"Unless you're secretly a Brute, you're not going to lift that piece . . ." He took out a smoke and struck a match. "So how'd you know Horowitz?"

Red faced, she gave up. "I was a dancer in one of his joints. That's how I met Arthur . . . Arthur met lots of girls through Abe. I was just the first one sharp enough to catch him. Ugh . . . I can't believe I'm admitting that."

"I can see why. You do put on a great show."

"Five years later, the old bastard was still kicking so we hatched this little plot . . . Timing was perfect, Arthur left again, and there was a crew that Abe wanted gone anyway to blame. Plus they were too stupid to get taken alive, and even if they denied it nobody would believe a filthy Shard. Should have been perfect."

"Arthur didn't recommend me at all. Horowitz did."

"Sure, you and Arthur were in the same unit, but he didn't know you from Adam. Abe couldn't tip the cops off without implicating himself. He said you had a killer's rep and you were motivated to keep the G-men off your back. Two birds, one stone, he said." She gave the revolver one last pensive tug. "So what now?"

"I decide what do with you."

Emily was thinking hard and that was dangerous. "Abe got greedy, but once the insurance comes in, I've still got his share." She rose from the seat and walked over to Sullivan while untying the sash on her robe. Stopping in front of him, she let the silk hang open, revealing that she wasn't wearing much of anything underneath. "Poor little me . . . Defenseless against a big strong man like you. Oh, have mercy, Mr. Sullivan . . . I can make it worth your time."

"I bet you could . . ." Sullivan blew out a cloud of smoke as he examined the dancer's body. Emily waited, smirking. This was a woman who was used to getting what she wanted. He stood up, gently took the edges of her robe in hand, appeared to think about it for just a second, and then covered her back up before stepping away. "But that would've been more tempting if you'd tried to seduce me *before* you tried to shoot me."

"You no-good—"

Sullivan looked toward the ceiling. "Mae! It's time to go." There was a sudden blast of wind as something stirred in the room. Emily's hair whipped wildly and she had to struggle to keep her robe shut. The fireplace popped and sparked as something flew up the chimney and disappeared.

"What was *that*?"

"That's Mae, a disembodied spirit. I brought her with me. Sweet girl, considering what she looks like. I had her record our talk and she'll be able to show it to anybody with a Finder."

"But . . . No judge will allow that. No jury is going to take the word of a demon, you idiot. You've got nothing. I'll deny this whole thing. You're a felon and a stupid Heavy. I'm somebody now. Nobody will believe the likes of you!"

"I'm not going to show it to the law, girl. I sent her to the *Purple gang* . . ." Those two words hung in the air like the smoke from his cigarette. "I'm sure they're mighty anxious to know who murdered their admiral."

"No . . ." Emily sank to her knees. "Oh no."

"I'll be keeping your advance because I did solve the case." Sullivan paused briefly on his way out the door. "And if I were you,

I'd start running. Considering those Purple boys, you're gonna want a head start."

Outside, he could still hear the screams of frustration and the breaking of furniture but the sounds faded as he walked down the steps to his automobile. He needed to get some sleep, but first he owed Bernie some tin foil.

The snow had really cleaned the air. There were kids running in the road, pulling each other on the sleds they'd just found under the tree. The people next door had built a snowman. It was a beautiful morning. Sure, he'd been tricked, lied to, stabbed, and had killed several men, but they'd had it coming, and he'd knocked two more off of J. Edgar Hoover's to-do list. So all in all, not too shabby . . .

As far as Christmases went, he'd had worse.

# INTRODUCTION

## THE VAMPIRES WHO SAVED CHRISTMAS

### AND

## VISIONS OF SUGAR PLUMS . . .

**TWO STORIES** by the same author? But they're very short . . . and very funny.

What's a vampire to do at Christmas, with all the good cheer among the living, spoiling the taste of A and B positive? Still, even vampires have family values, and this undead family gets an unexpected windfall, making things merry and bright . . . red.

Another supernatural being thought he had lucked out and wouldn't have to spend Christmas alone. He was half right . . .

S. N. Dyer turned out an amazing number of hysterically funny sf and fantasy stories in the 1970s and 1980s under more than one name. The author now pursues a medical career, and fiction's loss is medicine's gain, but I'm sure I'm not the only one who hopes Dyer will someday return to writing her strikingly individual twisted tales.

# THE VAMPIRES WHO SAVED CHRISTMAS

## By S. N. Dyer

**"I THINK,"** said Vlad, "that there is nothing lonelier than to be a vampire on Christmas Eve."

We all nodded agreement, and not just because he was the Master.

"Everything so festive and bright, holy symbols everywhere. Everyone home with their families, full to revulsion with Christmas cheer." He shuddered.

"Yeah," said Larry. "Even the drunks are in shelters, drinking in the holiday spirit. You just can't get a meal anywhere."

"Come on," I said. I was only a year undead and hesitant to speak out in such august company, but on this evening they seemed inclined to be kindly toward youth. "It's not so easy for mortals either. I was a single Jewish woman without family—for me, Christmas was a complete drag. No stores open, no restaurants or movies. Nothing at all to do . . ."

"Except wander the streets looking for Chinese takeout, and become someone else's dinner?" Vlad asked teasingly, and pinched my cheek. He'd been lonely that night too.

"You know what I hate the most about Christmas?" asked Mr. Bronze.

We looked at him respectfully, even the Master. Mr. Bronze was, after all, older than all of us together. He could complain authoritatively about the loneliness of a stranger in Athens during the Eleusinian Mysteries, in ancient Baghdad during Ramadan, in Rome at Saturnalia, in China at New Year, in the Cave of the Old Ones at the Feast of the Great Bear . . . He had been an outsider through recorded human history and long before.

We waited expectantly.

"What I hate most," said Mr. Bronze," is those darn reruns of *It's a Wonderful Life.*"

Vlad passed around chilled AB negative—you just can't get fresh blood on Christmas—and we waited for Larry to start the videos.

"Oh no!" Larry cried, and cringed. He remembered the old days, when the Master was given to fits of temper. Before the Twentieth Century, with its psychoanalysis, behaviorism, and rebirthing therapy. But mostly, before the Master took to hunting in neighborhoods where most of the blood was enriched with Prozac, with just a soupcon of Xanax.

"What's wrong?" we asked. We hoped he hadn't brought vampire movies, a prank which had previously cost him two months locked in his coffin without dinner. The master hated vampire movies—not only for the sheer defamation of character, but because he thought he should be getting residuals. (Though we did all have a sneaking fondness for *Love at First Bite.*)

"My videos! Look!" Larry hit the on button, and a black and white movie began. *Miracle on 34$^{th}$ Street!*

"That was supposed to be *Fellini's Satyricon,*" Larry wailed. He began to rip open the other boxes. "And this was supposed to be *PeeWee's Big Adventure*, and this was—ouch!" He dropped the cassette, fingers sizzling.

"Not *The Greatest Story Ever Told?*" Lila asked sympathetically. Larry sprinted to the kitchen to run cold water over his hand.

The Master sighed, and leaned back in his chair. We could hear carols drifting up from the apartment below. "Well, on the bright side," he remarked, "some other loving family has our movies."

So we did what all vampires eventually wind up doing on Christmas Eve, unless they plan ahead. We set out for Blockbuster Video.

The streets of Christmas Eve were as I remembered them from life: deserted. Store windows still shone brightly, luring you to the impending retail bacchanalia. Luckily there were not many frankly religious displays to make us ill, but the nondenominational splendor of trees and Santas was still enough to inspire queasiness, or at least angst.

A cheery mortal couple rushed by, arms clutching presents. My mouth watered. I was hungry.

"No, young one," whispered Vlad, a restraining hand upon my arm. "You wouldn't like the taste." I'd been told. Next to sheer religious fervor, nothing quite spoils the bouquet as much as hope, merriment, and visions of sugar plums.

We paused before a toy-store window. A lifesize animated Santa waved from a sleigh overflowing with gifts.

"Hmmph," said Mr. Bronze. "Doesn't look a bit like him."

Then we heard the sound of childish voices raised in song. *Jingle Bells*, luckily. After a month of a steady onslaught of *Silent Night*, I was ready to go berserk if I heard it again.

The building opposite was well lit and busy, and nauseating odors of turkey, ham, and holiday cheer wafted out every time the door opened.

"They've turned it into a shelter for homeless families," said Mr. Bronze. He liked to keep up with the news. "After dinner, they're going to give presents to all the children. Not just donated or repaired toys, either . . . They're all going to get the hottest items."

We nodded. The media-blitz toys, not so special except in their lurid scarceness. *Bermuda Barbie*, dressed for Christmas at Club Med. Auctioned for $2000 each in the want ads. And *GI Santa* . . . Last week, two fathers had beaten each other into intensive care for the last one on the shelves at FAO Schwartz. The little homeless children were to be the recipients of a fortune in trendy toys. And afterward, the shelter workers would offer the homeless parents $20 and steal home with the treasure. But it was the thought that counted.

The off-tune chirpy voices began mangling *Good King Wenceslas*.

"Oh, can we peek at them?" Lila pleaded. "Please, Master, they sound adorable."

Vlad smiled, and shrugged. "Sure." We hurried across the street eagerly. Vampires are like that, sentimental. Human children strike us as, well, just so cute. You know, like 4H future farmers and their lambs and calves.

We stared in the window, making ourselves insubstantial so no one would try to drag us inside to feed or bless us. That happened once to Vlad's vampiric son Arnie, and the Master still told the story as a cautionary tale to baby vampires.

It would have been a heartwarming sight were we not, of course, coldblooded. There were the unkempt starving parents and children, staring hopefully at the food, and the tree, and the Santas.

"Hey," hissed Rhonda. She didn't talk much, but she was an excellent huntress, trained before death by seeking bargains at Bloomies. "Do you smell it?"

We did. Fresh blood, on the hoof. Avaricious evil blood, devoid of holiday cheer.

Rhonda beckoned, and we followed, Mr. Bronze and the Master taking the rear with the caution of centuries. We trailed along the side of the building and found a door propped open. Inside was a room full of expensive toys, and several masked men stuffing them into sacks. Bizarro Santa Clauses, taking presents from the good little children.

We looked at the Master and he smiled indulgently. "Go ahead, my children."

So we fell upon the thieves, grabbing them before they could make a sound. We abandoned the bags of loot to be found by the shelter Santas, who would conclude that the thieves had been overcome, not by superhumanly strong vampires, but by Christmas spirit.

And we took the thieves home and had a wonderful feast,

drinking way too much until there was nothing left except empty husks to be stuffed into trash bags and dumped later. Afterward we sat gorged before a blazing fire and reminisced about previous feasts.

Then Vlad looked at me and said, "It's almost sunrise, time for all young vampires to go to bed." And I curled up snugly and thought that nothing was quite so pleasing as a holiday meal with your family, when I heard a sudden clatter on the roof and sprang up so quickly that I hit my head on the lid of my coffin, before I realized that it was only Larry and Mr. Bronze, flying the trash to Jersey.

# AND VISIONS OF SUGAR PLUMS . . .

## By S. N. Dyer

*Special sale—we're overstocked! Rings of power, rings of gas, fairy rings, rings of bright water, rings of the Nibelung! And one ring to bind them—You can't do anything without this one!*

"Let me slip into something more comfortable," she whispered, kissing him lightly on his left cheek, and swept away.

Brice leaned back into the fur-covered couch, and grinned. He couldn't believe his luck. Just an hour ago he'd been tipping back boilermakers at The Phenomenon, contemplating a lonely night of maybe watching *Miracle on 34th Street*, or the latest version of *A Christmas Carol*. Then he'd seen her.

"Hiya babe, buy ya a drink?" he'd asked.

She'd bared her teeth as if to snarl, then transformed the expression into a smile. "Do you know you're a hereditary werewolf?" she had asked him.

"Huh?"

"Your eyebrows. They meet over your nose. And your hands . . ."

"Werewolf, yeah," he'd replied. "And baby, you make me wanna howl!"

***Dine with gods and heroes. Buy a supper for two in Valhalla. Enjoy gourmet barbecued pork and heavenly mead in an atmosphere that is literally Out Of This World.***

"Hey, Magda! Great wine!" he yelled, refilling the cut crystal glass. There was a slight bitter aftertaste, but the overall effect was one of warm euphoria. The black cat lazing by the fire stared at him impassively.

Her voice came from behind the door. "What?"

"Love the wine." It gleamed deep purple in the firelight.

"It's Amontillado. Don't drink too much. You'll get wall-eyed."

"Not me, I can hold it." He poured another glass, putting back the decanter. It had been resting on a gaudy catalog.

"*The Demon-Marcus Catalog*? Oh yeah, I hearda that. Texas."

He opened it, at random, to a page of exorcise equipment, then flipped to a picture of ungainly hiking boots. "'Ten-league boots. These boots are for *walking*!'" The price was in tiny figures that seemed to writhe in the flickering light; all Brice could tell was that the boots were very expensive.

"Well? How do you like it?" Magda had slipped back into the room. She was wearing something long and black and slinky. He pulled her onto his lap.

"Watch out, you'll spill the wine."

His lips met hers.

***Waite deck chairs. For when you want to tarry at tarot.***

"Mommy!" A child began howling somewhere distant.

"Oh, damn," she said, wrenching free. "I'll just be a minute."

He sighed, reopening the catalog. "'Unicorn flakes. Your kids'll love them.'"

*Designer genies. Imps in bottles and cans. Buy a six-pack, and save.*

He was leering over pictures of models showing off designer versions of the Emperor's new clothes, when she returned.

"He's excited," she said. "Christmas and all."

"I'm excited too," said Brice, executing a judo move that deposited her on the couch and him atop her.

*Your portrait by Pickman. Limited offer.*

"Waah! Mommy! There's a ghost in the closet."

"Ignore it," she yelled, disengaging her mouth from Brice's. They heard the child's wailing, and then a sound of rattling chains.

"Hell," she muttered. "I thought the exterminators got rid of them—I'll be right back."

He leafed through the selection of Hummel voodoo figurines and Royal Dalton milk-glass Figurines of the Beast. The cat looked amused.

*For the kids: a Gilbert Alchemy Set. It's never too early to begin acquiring Forbidden Knowledge.*

"I think I've got him settled down," she said, settling down on Brice's lap. He moved into a more comfortable position, knocking something off the coffee table.

"Don't worry. It's just my pet philosopher's stone," she whispered.

*For attractive durability, try our indoor-outdoor magic carpets. They'll remain as stainless as virgin parchment!*

She had dipped her finger into the wine and was drawing playful five-pointed stars on his face.

*Show your love. Send a singing pentagram.*

"Mommy! Who's there?"

She smacked her fist into the other palm, counted to ten, then said sweetly, "No one's here, darling."

Brice muttered curses, and poured another glass of wine. He gestured at her. She shook her head, saying, "I never drink wine."

**Something for your mummy. Tanna Leaf Tea.**

"Someone *is* out there. I can hear 'im."

"Don't come out," she cried. "It's—it's Santa Claus!"

"Ho ho ho," yelled Brice.

The excited young voice grew higher. "Did he bring it? Huh? Did he bring it?" Magda began whispering in a rhythmic foreign language.

Brice downed the wine, feeling a momentary twinge of nausea, and then abrupt vertigo. Magda, the cat, the fire, the room, all were spinning. He closed his eyes, but the bright arabesques of light continued. Every nerve was tingling. He fell to the ground.

"Is it here yet? Is it here?"

Magda gazed down at Brice, and put a sympathetic hand on his head. The black cat leapt to its feet, arched its back, and hissed at him.

*I must've drunk too much*, he wanted to say, but all that came out was, "Woof."

"Yes, dear," Magda called. "You can come out now. Santa brought your puppy."

**Changeling fence. For security in an urban setting.**

# INTRODUCTION
### ～✲◉✲～
# THE SEASON OF FORGIVENESS

**HOPING TO MAKE GOOD** in his assignment for Nicholas van Rijn, a force to reckon with in the Polesotechnic League of traders, young Juan Hernandez understands he'll have to spend this Christmas away from home. What he wasn't expecting was that the people of the planet he's on have decided that the star traders are dangerous and need to be eliminated, beginning with Juan. He'll have to use his wits to survive, along with an assist from the season. This story is set in the series that was Poul Anderson's magnum opus, the Technic Civilization series, and if you like it you might want to check out the rest of the series, which Baen has published in seven volumes, beginning with *The Van Rijn Method*.

Poul Anderson (1926-2001) was one of the most prolific and popular writers in science fiction. He won the Hugo Award seven times and the Nebula Award three times, as well as many other awards, notably including the Grand Master Award of the Science Fiction Writers of America for a lifetime of distinguished achievement. With a degree in physics, and a wide knowledge of other fields of science, he was noted for building stories on a solid foundation of real science, as well as for being one of the most skilled creators of fast-paced adventure stories. He was author of over a hundred science fiction and fantasy novels and story collections, and several hundred short stories, as well as historical novels, mysteries and non-fiction books.

# THE SEASON OF FORGIVENESS

## By Poul Anderson

**IT WAS A STRANGE** and lonely place for a Christmas celebration—
the chill planet of a red dwarf star, away off in the Pleiades region,
where half a dozen humans laired in the ruins of a city which had
been great five thousand years ago, and everywhere else reached
wilderness.

"No!" said Master Trader Thomas Overbeck. "We've got too
much work on our hands to go wasting man-hours on a piece of
frivolity."

"It isn't, sir," answered his apprentice, Juan Hernandez. "On Earth
it's important. You have spent your life on the frontier, so perhaps
you don't realize this."

Overbeck, a large blond man, reddened. "Seven months here,
straight out of school, and you're telling me how to run my shop? If
you've learned all the practical technique I have to teach you, why,
you may as well go back on the next ship."

Juan hung his head. "I'm sorry, sir. I meant no disrespect."

Standing there, in front of the battered desk, against a window
which framed the stark, sullenly lit landscape and a snag of ancient

wall, he seemed younger than his sixteen Terrestrial years, slight, dark-haired, big-eyed. The company-issue coverall didn't fit him especially well. But he was quick-witted, Overbeck realized; he had to be, to graduate from the Academy that soon. And he was hardworking, afire with eagerness. The merchants of the League operated over so vast and diverse a territory that promising recruits were always in short supply.

That practical consideration, as well as a touch of sympathy, made the chief growl in a milder tone: "Oh, of course I've no objection to any small religious observance you or the others may want to hold. But as for doing more—" He waved his cigar at the scene outside. "What does it mean, anyway? A date on a chronopiece. A chronopiece adjusted for Earth! Ivanhoe's year is only two-thirds as long; but the globe takes sixty hours to spin around once; and to top it off, this is local summer, even if you don't dare leave the dome unless you're bundled to the ears. You see, Juan, I've got the same right as you to repeat the obvious."

His laughter boomed loud. While the team kept their living quarters heated, they found it easiest to maintain ambient air pressure, a fourth again as high as Terrestrial standard. Sound carried strongly. "Believe it or not," he finished, "I do know something about Christmas traditions, including the very old ones. You want to decorate the place and sing 'Jingle Bells'? That's how to make 'em ridiculous!"

"Please, no, sir," Juan said. "Also on Earth, in the southern hemisphere the feast comes at summer. And nobody is sure what time of year the Nativity really happened." He knotted his fists before he plunged on. "I thought not of myself so much, though I do remember how it is in my home. But that ship will come soon. I'm told small children are aboard. Here will be a new environment for them, perhaps frightening at first. Would we not help them feel easy if we welcomed them with a party like this?"

"Hm." Overbeck sat still a minute, puffing smoke and tugging his chin. His apprentice had a point, he admitted.

Not that he expected the little ones to be anything but a nuisance as far as he himself was concerned. He'd be delighted to leave them behind in a few more months, when his group had ended its task. But part of that task was to set up conditions which would fit the needs of their successors. The sooner those kids adjusted to life here, the sooner the parents could concentrate on their proper business.

And that was vital. Until lately, Ivanhoe had had no more than a supply depot for possible distressed spacecraft. Then a scientific investigator found the *adir* herb in the deserts of another continent. It wouldn't grow outside its own ecology; and it secreted materials which would be valuable starting points for several new organic syntheses. In short, there was money to be gotten. Overbeck's team was assigned to establish a base, make friends with the natives, learn their ways and the ways of their country, and persuade them to harvest the plant in exchange for trade goods.

That seemed fairly well in order now, as nearly as a man could judge amidst foreignness and mystery. The time looked ripe for putting the trade on a regular basis. Humans would not sign a contract to remain for a long stretch unless they could bring their families. Nor would they stay if the families grew unhappy.

And Tom Overbeck wouldn't collect his big, fat bonus until the post had operated successfully for five standard years.

Wherefore the Master Trader shrugged and said, "Well, okay. If it doesn't interfere too much with work, go ahead."

He was surprised at how enthusiastically Ram Gupta, Nikolai Sarychev, Mamoru Noguchi, and Philip Feinberg joined Juan's project. They were likewise young, but not boys; and they had no common faith. Yet together they laughed a lot as they made ready. The rooms and passageways of the dome filled with ornaments cut from foil or sheet metal, twisted together from color-coded wire, assembled from painted paper. Smells of baking cookies filled the air. Men went about whistling immemorial tunes.

Overbeck didn't mind that they were cheerful. That was a boost to efficiency, in these grim surroundings. He argued a while when they wanted to decorate outdoors as well, but presently gave in.

After all, he had a great deal else to think about.

A couple of Ivanhoan days after their talk, he was standing in the open when Juan approached him. The apprentice stopped, waited, and listened, for his chief was in conversation with Raffak.

The dome and sheds of the human base looked oddly bright, totally out of place. Behind them, the gray walls of Dahia lifted sheer, ten meters to the parapets, overtopped by bulbous-battlemented watchtowers. They were less crumbled than the buildings within. Today's dwindled population huddled in what parts of the old stone mansions and temples had not collapsed into rubble. A few lords maintained small castles for themselves, a few priests carried on rites behind porticos whose columns were idols, along twisting dusty streets. Near the middle of town rose the former Imperial palace. Quarried for centuries, its remnants were a colossal shapelessness.

The city dwellers were more quiet than humans. Not even vendors in their flimsy booths cried their wares. Most males were clad in leather kilts and weapons, females in zigzag-patterned robes. The wealthy and the military officers rode on beasts which resembled narrow-snouted, feathery-furred horses. The emblems of provinces long lost fluttered from the lances they carried. Wind, shrill in the lanes, bore sounds of feet, hoofs, groaning cartwheels, an occasional call or the whine of a bone flute.

A human found it cold. His breath smoked into the dry air. Smells were harsh in his nostrils. The sky above was deep purple, the sun a dull ruddy disc. Shadows lay thick; and nothing, in that wan light, had the same color as it did on Earth.

The deep tones of his language rolled from Raffak's mouth. "We have made you welcome, we have given you a place, we have aided you by our labor and counsel," declared the speaker of the City Elders.

"You have . . . for a generous payment," Overbeck answered.

"You shall not, in return, exclude Dahia from a full share in the wealth the *adir* will bring." A four-fingered hand, thumb set oppositely to a man's, gestured outward. Through a cyclopean gateway showed a reach of dusky-green bush, part of the agricultural hinterland. "It is more than a wish to better our lot. You have promised us that. But Dahia was the crown of an empire reaching from sea to sea. Though it lies in wreck, we who live here preserve the memories of our mighty ancestors, and faithfully serve their gods. Shall desert-prowling savages wax rich and strong, while we descendants of their overlords remain weak—until they become able to stamp out this final spark of glory? Never!"

"The nomads claim the wild country," Overbeck said. "No one has disputed that for many centuries."

"Dahia disputes it at last. I came to tell you that we have sent forth emissaries to the Black Tents. They bore our demand that Dahia must share in the *adir* harvest."

Overbeck, and a shocked Juan, regarded the Ivanhoan closely. He seemed bigger, more lionlike than was right. His powerful, long-limbed body would have loomed a full two meters tall did it not slant forward. A tufted tail whipped the bent legs. Mahogany fur turned into a mane around the flat face. That face lacked a nose—breathing was through slits beneath the jaws—but the eyes glowed green and enormous, ears stood erect, teeth gleamed sharp.

The human leader braced himself, as if against the drag of a gravity slightly stronger than Earth's, and stated: "You were foolish. Relations between Dahia and the nomads are touchy at best, violent at worst. Let war break out, and there will be no *adir* trade. Then Dahia too will lose."

"Lose material goods, maybe," Raffak said. "Not honor."

"You have already lost some honor by your action. You knew my people had reached agreement with the nomads. Now you Elders seek to change that agreement before consulting us." Overbeck made a chopping gesture which signified anger and determination. "I insist on meeting with your council."

After an argument, Raffak agreed to this for the next day, and stalked off. Hands jammed into pockets, Overbeck stared after him. "Well, Juan," he sighed, "there's a concrete example for you of how tricky this business of ours can get."

"Might the tribes really make trouble, sir?" wondered the boy.

"I hope not." Overbeck shook his head. "Though how much do we know, we Earthlings, as short a while as we've been here? Two whole societies, each with its own history, beliefs, laws, customs, desires—in a species that isn't human!"

"What do you suppose will happen?"

"Oh, I'd guess the nomads will refuse flat-out to let the Dahians send gathering parties into their territory. Then I'll have to persuade the Dahians all over again to let nomads bring the stuff here. That's what happens when you try to make hereditary rivals cooperate."

"Couldn't we base ourselves in the desert?" Juan asked.

"It's better to have a large labor force we can hire at need, one that stays put," Overbeck explained. "Besides, well—" He looked almost embarrassed. "We're after a profit, yes, but not to exploit these poor beings. An *adir* trade would benefit Dahia too, both from the taxes levied on it and from developing friendlier relations with the tribesfolk. In time, they could start rebuilding their civilization here. It was great once, before its civil wars and the barbarian invasions that followed." He paused. "Don't ever quote me to them."

"Why not, sir? I should think—"

"*You* should. I doubt they would. Both factions are proud and fierce. They might decide they were being patronized, and resent it in a murderous fashion. Or they might get afraid we intend to undermine their martial virtues, or their religions, or something." Overbeck smiled rather grimly. "No, I've worked hard to keep matters simple, on a level where nobody can misunderstand. In native eyes, we Earthlings are tough but fair. We've come to build a trade that will pay off for us, and for no other reason. It's up to them to keep us interested in remaining, which we won't unless they behave. That attitude, that image is clear enough, I hope, for the most alien mind to grasp. They may not love us, but they don't hate us either, and they're willing to do business."

Juan swallowed and found no words.

"What'd you want of me?" Overbeck inquired.

"Permission to go into the hills, sir," the apprentice said. "You know those crystals along Wola Ridge? They'd be beautiful on the Christmas tree." Ardently: "I've finished all my jobs for the time being. It will only take some hours, if I can borrow a flitter."

Overbeck frowned. "When a fight may be brewing? The Black Tents are somewhere that way, last I heard."

"You said, sir, you don't look for violence. Besides, none of the

Ivanhoans have a grudge against us. And they respect our power. Don't they? Please!"

"I aim to preserve that state of affairs." Overbeck pondered. "Well, shouldn't be any risk. And, hm-m-m, a human going out alone might be a pretty good demonstration of confidence . . . Okay," he decided. "Pack a blaster. If a situation turns ugly, don't hesitate to use it. Not that I believe you'll get in any scrape, or I wouldn't let you go. But—" He shrugged. "There's no such thing as an absolutely safe bet."

Three hundred kilometers north of Dahia, the wilderness was harsh mountainsides, deep-gashed canyons, umber crags, thinly scattered thorn-shrubs and wind-gnarled trees with ragged leaves. Searching for the mineral which cropped here and there out of the sandy ground, Juan soon lost sight of his flitter. He couldn't get lost from it himself. The aircraft was giving off a radio signal, and the transceiver in his pocket included a directional meter for homing on it. Thus he wandered further than he realized before he had collected a bagful.

However slowly Ivanhoe rotates, its days must end. Juan grew aware of how low the dim red sun was, how long and heavy the shadows. Chilliness had turned to a cold which bit at his bare face. Evening breezes snickered in the brush. Somewhere an animal howled. When he passed a rivulet, he saw that it had begun to freeze.

*I'm in no trouble,* he thought, *but I am hungry, and late for supper, and the boss will be annoyed.* Even now, it was getting hard for him to see. His vision was meant for bright, yellow-white Sol. He stumbled on rocks. Had his radio compass not been luminous-dialed, he would have needed a flashbeam to read it.

Nevertheless he was happy. The very weirdness of this environment made it fascinating; and he could hope to go on to many other worlds. Meanwhile, the Christmas celebration would be a circle of warmth and cheer, a memory of home—his parents, his brother and two sisters, Tío Pepe and Tía Carmen, the dear small Mexican town and the laughter as children struck at a *piñata*—

"*Raielli, Erratan!*"

Halt, Earthling! Juan jarred to a stop.

He was near the bottom of a ravine, which he was crossing as the most direct way to the flitter. The sun lay hidden behind one wall of it, and dusk filled the heavens. He could just make out boulders and bushes, vague in the gloom.

Then metal caught what light there was in a faint glimmer. He saw spearheads and a single breastplate. The rest of the warriors had only leather harness. They were blurs around him, save where their huge eyes gleamed like their steel.

Juan's heart knocked. *These are friends!* he told himself. *The People of the Black Tents are anxious to deal with us—Then why did they wait here for me? Why have a score of them risen out of hiding to ring me in?*

His mouth felt suddenly parched. He forced it to form words, as well as it could imitate the voice of an Ivanhoan. City and wilderness dwellers spoke essentially the same language. "G-greeting." He remembered the desert form of salutation. "I am Juan Sancho's-child, called Hernandez, pledged follower of the merchant Thomas William's-child, called Overbeck, and am come in peace."

"I am Tokonnen Undassa's-child, chief of the Elassi Clan," said the lion-being in the cuirass. His tone was a snarl. "We may no longer believe that any Earthling comes in peace."

"What?" cried Juan. Horror smote him. "But we do! How—"

"You camp among the City folk. Now the City demands the right to encroach on our land . . . Hold! I know what you carry."

Juan had gripped his blaster. The natives growled. Spears drew back, ready to throw. Tokonnen confronted the boy and continued:

"I have heard tell about weapons like yours. A fire-beam, fiercer than the sun, springs forth, and rock turns molten where it strikes. Do you think a male of Elassi fears that?" Scornfully: "Draw it if you wish."

Juan did, hardly thinking. He let the energy gun dangle downward in his fingers and exclaimed, "I only came to gather a few crystals—"

"If you slay me," Tokonnen warned, "that will prove otherwise. And you cannot kill more than two or three of us before the spears of the rest have pierced you. We know how feebly your breed sees in the least of shadows."

"But what do you *want?*"

"When we saw you descend, afar off, we knew what we wanted—you, to hold among us until your fellows abandon Dahia."

Half of Juan realized that being kept hostage was most likely a death sentence for him. He couldn't eat Ivanhoan food; it was loaded with proteins poisonous to his kind of life. In fact, without a steady supply of antiallergen, he might not keep breathing. How convince a barbarian herder of that?

The other half pleaded, "You are being wild. What matter if a few City dwellers come out after *adir?* Or . . . you can tell them 'no.' Can't you? We, we Earthlings—we had nothing to do with the embassy they sent."

"We dare not suppose you speak truth, you who have come here for gain," Tokonnen replied. "What is our freedom to you, if the enemy offers you a fatter bargain? And we remember, yes, across a hundred generations we remember the Empire. So do they in Dahia. They would restore it, cage us within their rule or drive us into the badlands. Their harvesters would be their spies, the first agents of their conquest. This country is ours. It is strong with the bones of our fathers and rich with the flesh of our mothers. It is too holy for an Imperial foot to tread. You would not understand this, merchant."

"We mean you well," Juan stammered. "We'll give you things—"

Tokonnen's mane lifted haughtily against darkling cliff, twilit sky. From his face, unseen in murk, the words rang: "Do you imagine things matter more to us than our liberty or our land?" Softer: "Yield me your weapon and come along. Tomorrow we will bring a message to your chief."

The warriors trod closer.

There went a flash through Juan. He knew what he could do, must do. Raising the blaster, he fired straight upward.

Cloven air boomed. Ozone stung with a smell of thunderstorms. Blue-white and dazzling, the energy beam lanced toward the earliest stars.

The Ivanhoans yelled. By the radiance, Juan saw them lurch back, drop their spears, clap hands to eyes. He himself could not easily look at that lightning bolt. They were the brood of a dark world. Such brilliance blinded them.

Juan gulped a breath and ran.

Up the slope! Talus rattled underfoot. Across the hills beyond! Screams of wrath pursued him.

The sun was now altogether down, and night came on apace. It was less black than Earth's, for the giant stars of the Pleiades cluster bloomed everywhere aloft, and the nebula which enveloped them glowed lacy across heaven. Yet often Juan fell across an unseen obstacle. His pulse roared, his lungs were aflame.

It seemed forever before he glimpsed his vehicle. Casting a glance behind, he saw what he had feared, the warriors in pursuit. His shot had not permanently damaged their sight. And surely they tracked him with peripheral vision, ready to look entirely away if he tried another flash.

Longer-legged, born to the planet's gravity, they overhauled him, meter after frantic meter. To him they were barely visible, bounding blacknesses which often disappeared into the deeper gloom around. He could not have hoped to pick them all off before one of them got to range, flung a spear from cover, and struck him.

Somehow, through every terror, he marveled at their bravery. *Run, run.*

He had barely enough of a head start. He reeled into the hull, dogged the door shut, and heard missiles clatter on metal. Then for a while he knew nothing.

When awareness came back, he spent a minute giving thanks. Afterward he dragged himself to the pilot chair. *What a scene!* passed across his mind. And, a crazy chuckle: *The old definition of adventure. Somebody else having a hard time a long ways off.*

He slumped into the seat. The vitryl port showed him a sky turned wonderful, a land of dim slopes and sharp ridges—He gasped and sat upright. The Ivanhoans were still outside.

They stood leaning on their useless spears or clinging to the hilts of their useless swords, and waited for whatever he would do.

Shakily, he switched on the sound amplifier and bullhorn. His voice boomed over them: "What do you want?"

Tokonnen's answer remained prideful. "We wish to know your desire, Earthling. For in you we have met a thing most strange."

Bewildered, Juan could merely respond with, "How so?"

"You rendered us helpless," Tokonnen said. "Why did you not at once kill us? Instead, you chose to flee. You must have known we would recover and come after you. Why did you take the unneeded risk?"

"You *were* helpless," Juan blurted. "I couldn't have . . . hurt you . . . especially at this time of year."

Tokonnen showed astonishment. "Time of year? What has that to do with it?"

"Christmas—" Juan paused. Strength and clarity of mind were returning to him. "You don't know about that. It's a season which, well, commemorates one who came to us Earthlings, ages ago, and spoke of peace as well as much else. For us, this is a holy time." He laid hands on controls. "No matter. I only ask you believe that we don't mean you any harm. Stand aside. I am about to raise this wagon."

"No," Tokonnen said. "Wait. I ask you, wait." He was silent for a while, and his warriors with him. "What you have told us—We must hear further. Talk to us, Earthling."

Once he had radioed that he was safe, they stopped worrying about Juan at the base. For the next several hours, the men continued their jobs. It was impossible for them to function on a sixty-hour day, and nobody tried. Midnight had not come when they knocked off. Recreation followed. For four of them, this meant preparing their Christmas welcome to the ship.

As they worked outdoors, more and more Dahians gathered, fascinated, to stand silently around the plaza and watch. Overbeck stepped forth to observe the natives in his turn. Nothing like this had ever happened before.

A tree had been erected on the flagstones. Its sparse branches and stiff foliage did not suggest an evergreen; but no matter, it glittered with homemade ornaments and lights improvised from electronic parts. Before it stood a manger scene that Juan had constructed. A risen moon, the mighty Pleiades, and the luminous nebular veil cast frost-cold brilliance. The beings who encompassed the square, beneath lean houses and fortress towers, formed a shadow-mass wherein eyes glimmered.

Feinberg and Gupta decorated. Noguchi and Sarychev, who had the best voices, rehearsed. Breath from their song puffed white.

"*O little town of Bethlehem,*
*How still we see thee lie—*"

A muted "A-a-ahhh!" rose from the Dahians, and Juan landed his flitter.

He bounded forth. Behind him came a native in a steel breast-plate. Overbeck had awaited this since the boy's last call. He gestured to Raffak, speaker of the Elders. Together, human and Ivanhoan advanced to greet human and Ivanhoan.

Tokonnen said, "It may be we misjudged your intent, City folk. The Earthling tells me we did."

"And his lord tells me we of Dahia pushed forward too strongly," Raffak answered. "That may likewise be."

Tokonnen touched sword-hilt and warned, "We shall yield nothing which is sacred to us."

"Nor we," said Raffak. "But surely our two people can reach an agreement. The Earthlings can help us make terms."

"They should have special wisdom, now in the season of their Prince of Peace."

"Aye. My fellows and I have begun some hard thinking about that."

"How do you know of it?"

"We were curious as to why the Earthlings were making beauty, here where we can see it away from the dreadful heat," Raffak said. "We asked. In the course of this, they told us somewhat of happenings in the desert, which the far-speaker had informed them of."

"It is indeed something to think about," Tokonnen nodded. "They, who believe in peace, are more powerful than us."

"And it was war which destroyed the Empire. But come," Raffak invited. "Tonight be my guest. Tomorrow we will talk."

They departed. Meanwhile the men clustered around Juan. Overbeck shook his hand again and again. "You're a genius," he said. "I ought to take lessons from you."

"No, please, sir," his apprentice protested. "The thing simply happened."

"It wouldn't have, if I'd been the one who got caught."

Sarychev was puzzled. "I don't quite see what did go on," he confessed. "It was good of Juan to run away from those nomads, instead of cutting them down when he had the chance. However, that by itself can't have turned them meek and mild."

"Oh, no." Overbeck chuckled. His cigar end waxed and waned like a variable star. "They're as ornery as ever—same as humans." Soberly: "The difference is, they've become willing to listen to us. They can take our ideas seriously, and believe we'll be honest brokers, who can mediate their quarrels."

"Why could they not before?"

"My fault, I'm afraid. I wasn't allowing for a certain part of Ivanhoan nature. I should have seen. After all, it's part of human nature too."

"What is?" Gupta asked.

"The need for—" Overbeck broke off. "You tell him, Juan. You were the one who did see the truth."

The boy drew breath. "Not at first," he said. "I only found I could not bring myself to kill. Is Christmas not when we should be quickest to forgive our enemies? I told them so. Then . . . when suddenly their whole attitude changed . . . I guessed what the reason must be." He searched for words. "They knew—both Dahians and nomads knew—we are strong; we have powers they can't hope to match. That doesn't frighten them. They have to be fearless, to survive in as bleak a country as this.

"Also, they have to be dedicated. To keep going through endless hardship, they must believe in something greater than themselves, like the Imperial dream of Dahia or the freedom of the desert. They're ready to die for those ideals.

"We came, we Earthlings. We offered them a fair, profitable bargain. But nothing else. We seemed to have no other motive than material gain. They could not understand this. It made us too peculiar. They could never really trust us.

"Now that they know we have our own sacrednesses, well, they see we are not so different from them, and they'll heed our advice."

Juan uttered an unsteady laugh. "What a long lecture, no?" he ended. "I'm very tired and hungry. Please, may I go get something to eat and afterward to bed?"

As he crossed the square, the carol followed him:

"*—The hopes and fears of all the years*
*Are met in thee tonight.*"

# INTRODUCTION

## DUMB FEAST

**MANY SPEAK OF CHRISTMAS TIME** as magic, but one genuinely magical spell, at a dumb feast, can summon the spirits of the dear departed. However, before practicing the summoning magic, this grieving widower should have first considered just how dear he might be to the departed. And while Ebenezer Scrooge was visited by ghosts who employed the carrot, there's no rule saying that a stick can't be used.

Mercedes Lackey is the *New York Times* and *USA Today* best-selling author of the Bardic Voices series and the SERRAted Edge series (both published by Baen), the Heralds of Valdemar series (published by DAW), and many more. She was one of the first writers to have an online newsgroup devoted to her writing. Among her popular Baen titles are *The Fire Rose*, *The Lark and the Wren*, and the Heirs of Alexandria series: *The Shadow of the Lion*, *This Rough Magic* and *Much Fall of Blood* (with collaborators Eric Flint and Dave Freer). She lives in Oklahoma.

# DUMB FEAST

## By Mercedes Lackey

**AARON BRUBAKER** considered himself a rational man, a logical man, a modern man of the enlightened nineteenth century. He was a prosperous lawyer in the City, he had a new house in the suburbs, and he cultivated other men like himself, including a few friends in Parliament. He believed in the modern; he had gas laid on in his house, had indoor bathrooms with the best flushing toilets (not that a polite man would discuss such things in polite company), and had a library filled with the writings of the best minds of his time. Superstition and old wives' tales had no place in his cosmos. So what he was about to do was all the more extraordinary.

If his friends could see him, he would have died of shame. And yet—and yet he would have gone right on with his plans.

Nevertheless, he had made certain that there was no chance he might be seen; the servants had been dismissed after dinner, and would not return until tomorrow after church services. They were grateful for the half-day off, to spend Christmas Eve and morning with their own families, and as a consequence had not questioned their employer's generosity. Aaron's daughter, Rebecca, was at a properly chaperoned party for young people which would end in midnight services at the Presbyterian Church, and she would not return home until well after one in the morning. And by then, Aaron's work would be done, whether it bore fruit, or not.

The oak-paneled dining room with its ornately carved table and chairs was strangely silent, without the sounds of servants or conversation. And he had not lit the gaslights of which he was so proud; there must only be two candles tonight to light the proceedings, one for him, one for Elizabeth. Carefully, he laid out the plates, the silver; arranged Elizabeth's favorite winter flowers in the centerpiece. One setting for himself, one for his wife. His dear, and very dead, wife.

His marriage had not precisely been an *arranged* affair, but it had been made in accordance with Aaron's nature. He had met Elizabeth in church; had approved of what he saw. He had courted her, in proper fashion; gained consent of her parents, and married her. He had seen to it that she made the proper friends for his position; had joined the appropriate societies, supported the correct charities. She had cared for his home, entertained his friends in the expected manner, and produced his child. In that, she had been something of a disappointment, since it should have been "children," including at least one son. There was only Rebecca, a daughter rather than a son, but he had forgiven her for her inability to do better. Romance did not precisely enter into the equation. He had expected to feel a certain amount of modest grief when Elizabeth died—

But not the depth of loss he had uncovered. He had mourned unceasingly, confounding himself as well as his friends. There simply was no way of replacing her, the little things she did. There had been an artistry about the house that was gone now; a life that was no longer there. His house was a home no longer, and his life a barren, empty thing.

In the months since her death, the need to see her again became an obsession. Visits to the cemetery were not satisfactory, and his desultory attempt to interest himself in the young widows of the parish came to nothing. And that was when the old tales from his childhood, and the stories his grandmother told, came back to— literally—haunt him.

He surveyed the table; everything was precisely in place, just as it had been when he and Elizabeth dined alone together. The two candles flickered in a draft; they were in no way as satisfactory as the gaslights, but his grandmother, and the old lady he had consulted from the Spiritualist Society, had been adamant about that—there must be two candles, and only two. No gaslights, no candelabra.

From a chafing dish on the sideboard he took the first course: Elizabeth's favorite soup. Tomato. A pedestrian dish, almost lower-class, and not the clear consommés or lobster bisques that one would serve to impress—but he was not impressing anyone tonight. These must be *Elizabeth's* favorites, and not his own choices. A row of chafing dishes held his choices ready: tomato soup, spinach salad, green peas, mashed potatoes, fried chicken, apple cobbler. No wine, only coffee. All depressingly middle-class . . .

That was not the point. The point was that they were the bait that would bring Elizabeth back to him, for an hour, at least.

He tossed the packet of herbs and what-not on the fire, a packet that the old woman from the Spiritualists had given him for just that purpose. He was not certain what was in it; only that she had asked for some of Elizabeth's hair. He'd had to abstract it from the lock Rebecca kept, along with the picture of her mother, in a little shrine-like arrangement on her dresser. When Rebecca had first created it, he had been tempted to order her to put it all away, for the display seemed very pagan. Now, however, he thought he understood her motivations.

This little drama he was creating was something that his grandmother—who had been born in Devonshire—called a "dumb feast." By creating a setting in which all of the deceased's favorite foods and drink were presented, and a place laid for her—by the burning of certain substances—and by doing all this at a certain time of the year—the spirit of the loved one could be lured back for an hour or two.

The times this might be accomplished were four. May Eve, Midsummer, Halloween, and Christmas Eve.

By the time his need for Elizabeth had become an obsession, the Spring Equinox and Midsummer had already passed. Halloween seemed far too pagan for Aaron's taste—and besides, he had not yet screwed his courage up to the point where he was willing to deal with his own embarrassment that he was resorting to such humbug.

What did all four of these nights have in common? According to the Spiritualist woman, it was that they were nights when the "vibrations of the earth-plane were in harmony with the Higher Planes." According to his grandmother, those were the nights when the boundary between the spirit world and this world thinned, and many kinds of creatures, both good and evil, could manifest. According to her, that was why Jesus had been born on that night—

Well, that was superstitious drivel. But the Spiritualist had an explanation that made sense at the time; something about vibrations and currents, magnetic attractions. Setting up the meal, with himself, and all of Elizabeth's favorite things, was supposed to set up a magnetic attraction between him and her. The packet she had given him to burn was supposed to increase that magnetic attraction, and set up an electrical current that would strengthen the spirit. Then, because of the alignment of the planets on this evening, the two Planes came into close contact, or conjunction, or—something.

It didn't matter. All that mattered was that he see Elizabeth again. It had become a hunger that nothing else could satisfy. No one he knew could ever understand such a hunger, such an overpowering desire.

The hunger carried him through the otherwise unpalatable meal, a meal he had timed carefully to end at the stroke of midnight, a meal that must be carried out in absolute silence. There must be no conversation, no clinking of silverware. Then, at midnight, it must end. There again, both the Spiritualist and his grandmother had agreed. The "dumb feast" should end at midnight, and then the spirit would appear.

He spooned up the last bite of too-sweet, sticky cobbler just as the bells from every church in town rang out, calling the faithful to Christmas services. Perhaps he would have taken time to feel gratitude for the Nicklesons' party, and the fact that Rebecca was well out of the way—

Except that, as the last bell ceased to peal, *she* appeared. There was no fanfare, no clamoring chorus of ectoplasmic trumpets—one moment there was no one in the room except himself, and the next, Elizabeth sat across from him in her accustomed chair. She looked exactly as she had when they had laid her to rest; every auburn hair in place in a neat and modest French braid, her body swathed from chin to toe in an exquisite lace gown.

A wild exultation filled his heart. He leapt to his feet, words of welcome on his lips—

Tried to, rather. But he found himself bound to his chair, his voice, his lips paralyzed, unable to move or to speak.

The same paralysis did not hold Elizabeth, however. She smiled, but not the smile he loved, the polite, welcoming smile—no, it was another smile altogether, one he did not recognize, and did not understand.

"So, Aaron," she said, her voice no more than a whisper.

"At last our positions are reversed. You, silent and submissive; and myself the master of the table."

He almost did not understand the words, so bizarre were they. Was this Elizabeth, his dear wife? Had he somehow conjured a vindictive demon in her place?

She seemed to read his thoughts, and laughed. Wildly, he thought. She reached behind her neck and let down her hair; brushed her hand over her gown and it turned to some kind of medievalist costume, such as the artists wore. The ones calling themselves "Pre-Raphelites," or some such idiocy. He gaped to see her attired so, or would have, if he had been in control of his body.

"I am no demon, Aaron," she replied, narrowing her green eyes. "I am still Elizabeth. But I am no longer 'your' Elizabeth, you see. Death freed me from you, from the narrow constraints you placed on me. If I had known this was what would happen, I would have died years ago!"

He stared, his mind reeled. What did she mean? How could she say those things?

"Easily, Aaron," Elizabeth replied, reclining a little in the chair, one elbow on the armrest, hand supporting her chin. "I can say them very, very easily. Or don't you remember all those broken promises?"

Broken—

"Broken promises, Aaron," she continued, her tone even, but filled with bitterness. "They began when you courted me. You promised me that you did not want me to change—yet the moment the ring was on my finger, you broke that promise, and began forcing me into the mold *you* chose. You promised me that I could continue my art—but you gave me no place to work, no money for materials, and no time to paint or draw."

But that was simply a childish fancy—

"It was my *life*, Aaron!" she cried passionately. "It was my life, and you took it from me! And I believed all those promises, that in a year you would give me time and space—after the child was born—after she began school. I believed it right up until the moment when the promise was 'after she finishes school.' Then I knew that it would become 'after she is married,' and then there would be some other, distant time—" Again she laughed, a wild peal of laughter than held no humor at all. "Cakes yesterday, cakes tomorrow, but never cakes today! Did you think I would never see through that?"

But why did she have to paint? Why could she not have turned her artistic sensibilities to proper lady's—

"What? Embroidery? Knitting? Lace-making? I was a *painter*, Aaron, and I was a good one! Burne-Jones himself said so! Do you know how rare that is, that someone would tell a girl that she must paint, must be an artist?" She tossed her head, and her wild mane of red hair—now as bright as it had been when he had first met her—flew over her shoulder in a tumbled tangle. And now he remembered where he had seen that dress before. She had been wearing it as she painted, for she had been—

"Painting a self-portrait of myself as the Lady of Shallot," she said, with an expression that he could not read. "Both you and my father conspired together to break me of my nasty artistic habits. 'Take me out of my dream-world,' I believe he said. Oh, I can hear you both—" her voice took on a pompous tone, and it took him a moment to realize that she was imitating him, "'don't worry, sir, once she has a child she'll have no time for that nonsense—' And you saw to it that I had no time for it, didn't you? Scheduling ladies' teas and endless dinner parties, with women who bored me to death and men who wouldn't know a Rembrandt from an El Greco! Enrolling me without my knowledge or consent in group after group of other useless women, doing utterly useless things! And when I *wanted* to do something—anything!—that might serve a useful purpose, you forbade it! Forbade me to work with the Salvation Army, forbade me to help with the Wayward Girls—oh no, *your* wife couldn't do that, it wasn't *suitable!* Do you know how much I came to hate that word, 'suitable'? Almost as much as the words 'my good wife.'"

But I gave you everything—

"You gave me nothing!" she cried, rising now to her feet. "You gave me jewelry, gowns ordered by *you* to *your* specifications, furniture, useless trinkets! You gave me nothing that mattered! No freedom, no authority, no responsibility!"

Authority? He flushed with guilt when he recalled how he had forbidden the servants to obey her orders without first asking him— how he had ordered her maid to report any out-of-the-ordinary thing she might do. How he had given the cook the monthly budget money, so that she could not buy a cheaper cut of roast and use the savings to buy paint and brushes.

"Did you think I didn't know?" she snarled, her eyes ablaze with anger as she leaned over the table. "Did you think I wasn't aware that I was a prisoner in my own home? And the law supported *you,* Aaron! I was well aware of that, thanks to the little amount of work I did before you forbade it on the grounds of 'suitability.' One woman told me I should be grateful that you didn't beat me, for the law permits that as well!"

He was only doing it for her own good . . .

"You were only doing it to be the master, Aaron," she spat. "What I wanted did not matter. You proved that by your lovemaking, such as it was."

Now he flushed so fiercely that he felt as if he had just stuck his head in a fire. How could she be so—

"Indelicate? Oh I was more than indelicate, Aaron, I was passionate! And you killed that passion, just as you broke my spirit, with your cruelty, your indifference to me. What should have been joyful was shameful, and you made it that way. You hurt me, constantly, and never once apologized. Sometimes I wondered if you made me wear those damned gowns just to hide the bruises from the world!"

All at once, her fury ran out, and she sagged back down into her chair. She pulled the hair back from her temples with both hands, and gathered it in a thick bunch behind her head for a moment. Aaron was still flushing from the last onslaught. He hadn't known—

"You didn't care," she said, bluntly. "You knew; you knew it every time you saw my face fall when you broke another promise, every time you forbade me to dispose my leisure time where it would do some good. You knew. But all of that, I could have forgiven, if you had simply let Rebecca alone."

This time, indignation overcame every other feeling. How could she say something like that? When he had given the child everything a girl could want?

"Because you gave her nothing that *she* wanted, Aaron. You never forgave her for not being a boy. Every time she brought something to you—a good grade, a school prize, a picture she had done— you belittled her instead of giving her the praise her soul thirsted for!" Elizabeth's eyes darkened, and the expression on her face was positively demonic.

"Nothing she did was good enough—or was as good as a boy would have done."

But children needed correction—

"Children need *direction*. But that wasn't all, oh no. You played the same trick on her that you did on me. She wanted a pony, and riding lessons. But that wasn't suitable; she got a piano and piano lessons. Then, when her teacher told you she had real talent, and could become a concert artist, you took both away, and substituted *French* lessons!" Again, she stood up, her magnificent hair flowing free, looking like some kind of ancient Celtic goddess from one of her old paintings, paintings that had been filled with such pagan images that he had been proud to have weaned her away from art and back to the path of a true Christian woman. She stood over him with the firelight gleaming on her face, and her lips twisted with disgust. "You still don't see, do you? Or rather, you are so *sure*, so *certain* that you could know better than any foolish woman what is best for her, that you still think you were right in crushing my soul, and trying to do the same to my daughter!"

He expected her to launch into another diatribe, but instead, she smiled. And for some reason, that smile sent cold chills down his back.

"You didn't even guess that all this was my idea, did you?" she asked, silkily. "You had no idea that I had been touching your mind, prodding you toward this moment. You forgot what your grandmother told you, because I made you forget—that the dumb feast puts the living in the power of the dead."

She moved around the end of the table, and stood beside him. He would have shrunk away from her if he could have—but he still could not move a single muscle. "There is a gas leak in this room, Aaron," she said, in the sweet, conversational tone he remembered so well. "You never could smell it, because you have no sense of smell. What those awful cigars of yours didn't ruin, the port you drank after dinner killed. I must have told you about the leak a hundred times, but you never listened. I was only a woman, how could I know about such things?"

But why hadn't someone else noticed it?

"It was right at the lamp, so it never mattered as long as you kept the gaslights lit; since you wouldn't believe me and I didn't want the house to explode, I kept them lit day and night, all winter long. Remember? I told you I was afraid of the dark, and you laughed, and permitted me my little indulgence. And of course, in the summer, the windows were open. But you turned the lights off for this dumb feast, didn't you, Aaron. You sealed the room, just as the old woman told you. And the room has been filling with gas, slowly, all night."

Was she joking? No, one look into her eyes convinced him that she was not. Frantic now, he tried to break the hold she had over his body, and found that he still could not move.

"In a few minutes, there will be enough gas in this room for the candles to set it off—or perhaps the chafing dish—or even the fire. There will be a terrible explosion. And Rebecca will be free—free to follow her dream and become a concert pianist. Oh, Aaron, I managed to thwart you in that much. The French teacher and the piano teacher are very dear friends. The lessons continued, even though you tried to stop them. And you never guessed." She looked up, as if at an unseen signal, and smiled. And now he smelled the gas.

"It will be a terrible tragedy—but I expect Rebecca will get over her grief in a remarkably short time. The young are so resilient." The smell of gas was stronger now.

She wiggled her fingers at him, like a child. "Goodbye Aaron," she said cheerfully. "See you soon—"

# INTRODUCTION
❧❀❧
# ROADS

**NOW FOR A FANTASY CLASSIC.** *Weird Tales* ("the unique magazine") began in 1923, becoming the leading pulp of fantasy and horror (or "dark fantasy," as it would later be known), publishing notables such as Robert E. Howard, H. P. Lovecraft, and Clark Ashton Smith. An odd place for a Christmas story? When "Roads" appeared in the January 1938 issue, the readers didn't think so, giving the story top marks. Before the year was out, a fantasy fan printed a 200-copy limited edition in time for Christmas, sending it out to friends instead of cards. The legendary fantasy publisher Arkham House released the story in 1948 as a hardcover book, lavished illustrated by Virgil Finlay. (That version has recently been reprinted, with most of the illustrations) You'll notice that I'm giving no hints of what the story is about. You'll just have to read it. And it may start out reading like Robert E. Howard, but things are going to change . . .

Seabury Quinn (1989-1969) was *Weird Tales'* most popular contributor, more popular with the readers than the aforementioned Robert E. Howard, creator of Conan, and H. P. Lovecraft, creator of the Cthulhu universe. He was best known for the occult detective, Jules de Grandin, who, with his Watson figure, Trowbridge, defeated ghost, vampires, and other supernatural nasties in 93 stories and one novel. Quinn also wrote many non-series stories, publishing over 500 stories in all. His day job was as a lawyer, though he also wrote non-fictional journalism. Perhaps appropriately for a writer of fantasy and horror stories, at one point he was editor of a trade magazine for morticians.

🎄 🎄 🎄

# ROADS

## By Seabury Quinn

### The Road to Bethlehem

**FIRES OF THORNBUSH** crackled in the courtyard of the serai, camels sighed and grunted in their kneeling-places, horses munched dry grass. Around the empty stew-pots men licked the crumbs of rice and grease from fingers and brushed them from their beards, then drew their sheepskin cloaks about them and lay down on the kidney stones to sleep; all but the little group of three who huddled round a charcoal brazier in a corner by the horse-lines. They were talking treason:

"Wah, these be evil days for Jacob's children; they are as the tribes in Egypt were, only they have neither Moses nor a Joshua! . . . The tax of a denarius on every household, and each one forced to journey to his birthplace . . . Now they slay our children in their swaddling bands . . . This Romans' puppet that sits on the throne, this unbelieving Greek!"

"But Judas will avenge our wrongs; men say that he is that Messiah we have waited for so long. He will rouse his mighty men of valor out of Galilee and sweep the Roman tyrant in the sea—"

"*Sh-s-sh*, Joachim, hold thy babble; that one yonder is belike a spy!"

With one accord the men turned toward the figure hunched in sleep before a dying fire of thornbush. Flaxen-haired, fair-skinned, he drooped above the whitening embers, his cloak of ruddy woolen cloth draped loosely round his shoulders, the sinking firelight picking out soft highlights on the iron cap that crowned his flowing, braided hair. A man of mighty stature, one of the gladiators kept by Herod in his school for athletes that was constantly replenished with recruits from German provinces or the Slavic tribes beyond the Danube.

"What does the godless dog so far from Herod's kennels?"

"The Lord of Zion knows, but if he go back to the Holy City and tell the tale of what he has heard here, three crosses will crown Golgotha before another sun has set," Joachim interrupted softly, and, dropping to his knees, unloosed the dagger at his girdle as he began to worm his way across the courtyard flints. In all the country round about Jerusalem there was no hand more skilful with the knife than that of Joachim, the cut-purse. Softly as the cat that stalks a mouse he crept across the stones, paused and bore his weight on one hand while he drew the other back . . . a single quick thrust underneath the shoulder-blade, slanting downward to the heart, then the gurgling, blood-choked cry, the helpless thrashing of the limbs, the fight for breath, and—perhaps the sleeping gladiator had a wallet stuffed with copper, or even gold. They were well paid, these fighting dogs from Herod's kennels. The firelight glinted on the plunging knife, and on the golden bracelet on the Northman's arm.

"Ho, little brother of a rat, would you bite a sleeping man," the giant's bell-like voice boomed, "and one who never did thee any harm? For shame!" White lines sprang into prominence against his sun-gilt skin; his mighty muscles tightened, and a yelp of pain came from Joachim as the knife dropped from his unnerved fingers and a crackling like the breaking of a willow twig told where his wrist-bones snapped beneath the other's sudden grip.

"Have mercy, mighty one," he begged. "I thought—"

"Aye, that thou didst, thou niddering craven," came the answer. "Thou thought me sleeping, and like the thief thou art, were minded to have had my purse and life at once. Now get thee gone from out my sight, thou and those hangdog friends of thine, before I crush that puny neck between these hands of mine."

He spread his hands, great, well-shaped, white-skinned hands trained in the wrestler's art and in the wielding of the sword, and his strong, white fingers twitched as though already they felt yielding flesh between them. With a frightened skirking, as though they were in truth the rats the stranger named them, the three conspirators slunk out, Joachim the cut-purse nursing his broken right wrist in the crook of his left arm, his two companions crowding close beside him as they sought to gain the exit of the courtyard before the giant Northling reconsidered and repented of his mercy.

The blond-haired stranger watched them go, then swung his cloak back from his shoulders. Beneath the cape he wore from neck to knee a tunic of fine woolen stuff dyed brilliant red and edged about the bottom with embroidery of gold. A corselet of tanned bullhide set with iron studs was buckled round his torso; his feet were shod with buskins of soft leather laced about his legs with rawhide thongs; from the girdle at his waist on one side hung a double-bladed ax, on the other a soft-leather pouch which clinked with a metallic sound each time he moved. Between his shoulders swung a long two-handed sword with a wide, well-tempered blade, pointed and double-edged. He was brawny and broad-shouldered, his hair was braided in two long, fair plaits which fell on either side of his face beneath his iron skullcap. Like his hair, his beard was golden as the ripening wheat, and hung well down upon his breastplate. Yet he was not old; the flaxen beard was still too young to have felt shears, his lightly sun-tanned skin was smooth and fair, his sea-blue eyes were clear and youthful. He glanced up at the star-flecked heavens, then drew his cloak about him.

"The dragon marches low upon the skies," he muttered; "'tis time I set forth on my journey if I would reach the homeland ere the winter tempests howl again."

The road was thick with travelers, mostly peasants on their way to market, for the day began with sunrise, and the bartering would start within an hour. Hucksters of every sort of article, fanciful as well as necessary, pressed along the way, tugging at halters, now entreating, now berating their pack-animals to greater speed. A patrol of soldiers passed him, and their decurion raised his hand in greeting.

"*Salve*, Claudius! Art thou truly going back to that cold land of thine? By Pluto, I am sorry that thou leavest us; many is the silver penny I have won by betting on those fists of thine, or on thy skill at swordplay!"

The Northman smiled amusedly. Though he had been among the Romans since before his beard was sprouted, their rendering of his simple Nordic name of Klaus to Claudius had never failed to rouse his laughter.

"Yea, Marcus, I am soothly gone, this time. Five years and more have I served Herod's whim, and in that time I've learnt the art of war as few can know it. With sword and ax and mace, or with bare hands or cestus have I fought until methinks I've had my fill of fighting. Now I go back to till my fathers' acres, perchance to go a-viking, if the spirit moves me, but hereafter I will fight for my own gain or pleasure, not to the humor of another."

"The gods go with thee, then, Barbarian," the Roman bade. "'Twill be a long time ere we see thy match upon the sands of the arena."

A rambling, single-streeted village fringed the highway, and at the trickling fountain where the women came to fill their jars the wanderer rested to scoop up a sup of tepid water in his hand. The sun was up six hours, and the little square around the spring should have been alive with magpie-chattering women and their riotously noisy children; but the place was like a city of the dead. Silence thick as dust lay on the white, sun-bitten road; utter quiet sealed the houses with the silence of a row of tombs. Then, as he looked about in wonderment, Klaus heard a thin-drawn, piping wail: "*Ai-ai-ai-ai!*" the universal cry of mourning in the East. "*Ai-ai-ai-ai!*"

He kicked aside the curtain at the doorway and looked into the darkness of the little house. A woman crouched crosslegged on the earthen floor, her hair unbound, her gown ripped open to expose her breasts, dust on her brow and cheeks and bosom. On her knees, very quiet, but not sleeping, lay a baby boy, and on the little breast there flowered a crimson wound. Klaus recognized it—a gladiator knew the trademark of his calling!—a sword-cut. Half a hand's-span long, tagged at the edges, sunk so deep into the baby flesh that the glinting white of breastbone showed between the raw wound's gaping, bloody lips.

"Who hath done this thing?" The Northman's eyes were hard as fjord-ice, and a grimness set upon his bearded lips like that they wore when he faced a Cappadocian netman in the circus. "Who hath done this to thee, woman?"

The young Jewess looked up from her keening. Her eyes were red and swollen with much weeping, and the tears had cut small rivulets into the dust with which her face was smeared, but even in her agony she showed some traces of her wonted beauty.

"The soldiers," she replied between breath-breaking sobs. "They came and went from house to house, as the Angel of the Lord went through the land of Egypt, but we had no blood to smear our lintels. They came and smote and slew; there is not a man-child left alive in all the village. Oh, my son, my little son, why did they do this thing to thee, thou who never did them any harm? Oh, woe is me; my God hath left me comfortless, my firstborn, only son is slain—"

"Thou liest, woman!" Klaus's words rang sharp as steel. "Soldiers do not do things like this. They war with men, they make no war on babes."

The mother rocked her body to and fro and beat her breast with small clenched fists. "The soldiers did it," she repeated doggedly. "They came and went from house to house, and slew our sons—"

"Romans?" Klaus asked incredulously. Cruel the Romans were at times, but never to his knowledge had they done a thing like this. Romans were not baby-killers.

"Nay, the soldiers of the King. Romans only in the armor that they wore. They came marching into town, and—"

"The soldiers of the King? Herod?"

"Yea, Barbarian. King Herod, may his name be cursed for evermore! Some days agone came travelers from the East who declared a king was born among the Jews, and Herod, fearing that the throne might go to him, dispatched his soldiery throughout the coasts of Bethlehem to slay the sons of every house who had not reached their second year."

"Thy husband—"

"Alas, I am a widow."

"And hast thou store of oil and meal?"

"Nay, my lord, here is only death. *Ai-ai-ai*—"

Klaus took some copper from his pouch and dropped it in the woman's lap beside the little corpse. "Take this," he ordered, "and have them do unto the body of thy babe according to thy custom."

"The Lord be gracious unto you, Barbarian. To you and all your house be peace, for that thou takest pity on the widow in her sorrow!"

"Let be. What is thy name?"

"Rachel, magnificence; and may the Lord of Israel give favor to—"

Klaus turned away and left the weeping woman with her dead.

The waxing moon rode high above the grove where Klaus lay bundled in his cloak. Occasionally, from the denser of the thickets came the chirp of bird or squeak of insect, but otherwise the night was silent, for robbers roamed the highways after dark, and though the soldiers of the Governor kept patrol, the wise man stayed indoors until the sun had risen. But the hardiest highwayman would stop and give the matter second thought ere he attacked a sworded giant, and the nearest inn was several miles away; also a journey of a thousand miles and more lay between the Northman and his home, and though his wallet bulged with gold saved from his years spent as a hired fighter in the Tetrarch's barracks, it behooved him to economize. Besides, the turf was sweet to smell, which the caravansaries were not, and the memory of the widow-woman's murdered son had set a canker in his brain. It were better that he had no traffic with his fellow men for several hours.

The broken rhythm of a donkey's hoofs came faintly to him from the highway. The beast walked slowly, as though tired, and as if he who led it were also weary and footsore, yet urged by some compulsion to pursue his journey through the night.

"By Thor," mused Klaus, "they are a nation of strange men, these Jews. Always disputing, ever arguing, never faltering in their lust for gold; yet withal they have a spirit in them like that no other people has. Should their long-sought Messiah finally come, methinks that all the might of Rome would scarcely be enough to stop them in their—"

The hail came piercingly, mounting in a sharp crescendo, freighted with a burden of despair. "Help, help—we be beset by robbers!"

Klaus smiled sardonically. "So anxious to be early at tomorrow's market that he braves the dangerous highway after dark; yet when the robbers set upon him—"

A woman's scream of terror seconded the man's despairing hail, and Klaus bounded from his couch upon the turf, dragging at the sword that hung between his shoulders.

A knot of spearmen clustered round a man and woman. From their crested helmets and bronze cuirasses he knew them to be soldiers in the livery of Rome. From their hook-nosed faces he knew them to be Syrians, Jewish renegades, perhaps, possibly Arabs or Armenians, for such composed the little private army which the Tetrarch kept for show, and to do the work he dared not ask the Roman garrison to do.

"Ho, there, what goes on here?" challenged Klaus as he hurried from the woods. "What mean ye by molesting peaceful travelers—"

The decurion in command turned on him fiercely. "Stand aside, Barbarian," he ordered curtly. "We be soldiers of the King, and—"

"By Odin's ravens, I care not if ye be the Cæsar's soldiers, I'll have your reason for attacking this good man and wife, or the sword will sing its song!" roared Klaus.

"Seize him, some of you!" the decarch ordered. "We'll take him to the Tetrarch for his pleasure. The rest stand by, we have our task to do—give me thy baby, woman!" He bared his sword and advanced upon the woman seated on the ass, a sleeping infant cradled in her arms.

And now the wild war-madness of his people came on Klaus. A soldier sprang at him and thrust his lance straight at his face, but

Klaus's long sword drove through bronze spearhead and ash-wood stave, and left the fellow weaponless before him. Then before his adversary could drag out his short sword, Klaus thrust, and his blade pierced through the soldier's shield and through the arm behind it, and almost through the cuirassed body. The man fell with a gasping cry, and three more soldiers leaped at Klaus, heads low above their shields, their lances held at rest.

"Aie, for the song of the sword, aie for the red blood flowing, aie for the lay the Storm-Maidens sing of heroes and Valhalla!" chanted Klaus, and as he sang he struck, and struck again, and his graysteel blade drank thirstily. Four soldiers of the Tetrarch's guard he slew before they could close with him, and when two others, rushing to attack him from behind, laid hands upon him, he dropped his sword and reaching backward took his adversaries in his arms as though he were some monstrous bear and beat their heads together till their helmets toppled off and their skulls were cracked and they fell dead, blood rushing from their ears and noses. Now only four remained to face him, and he seized the double-bladed ax that dangled at his girdle, and with a mighty shout leaped on his foes as though they had been one and he a score. His iron ax-blade clove through bronze and bullock-hide as though they had been parchment, and two more of the Tetrarch's guardsmen fell down dead; the other two turned tail and fled from this avenging fury with the fiery, wind-blown beard and long, fair hair that streamed unbound upon the night wind. Then Klaus stood face to face with the decurion.

"—Now, thou sayer of great words and doer of small deeds, thou baby-killer, say, wilt thou play the man's game, or do I smite thee headless like the criminal thou art?" asked he.

"I did but do my duty, Barbarian," the decurion answered sulkily. "The great King bade us go through all this land and take the man-child of each house, if he were under two years old, and slay him. I know not why, but a soldier's duty is to bear his orders out—"

"Aye, and a soldier's duty is to die, by Odin's Twelve Companions!" Klaus broke in. "Take this for Rachel's child; the widow-woman's only son, thou eater-up of little, helpless babes!" And he aimed an ax-blow at the decarch, and never in his years of fighting in the circus had Klaus the Smiter smitten such a blow. Neither shield nor mail could stop it, for the ax-blade sheared through both as though they had been linen, and the ax-edge fell upon the decarch's side where neck and shoulder join, and it cut through bone and muscle, and the arm fell down into the white dust of the roadway, and the ax cleft on, and bit into the decarch's breast until it split his very heart in two, and as the oak-tree falls when fire from heaven blasts it, so fell the soldier of King Herod in the dust at Klaus's feet, and lay there, quivering and headless.

Then Klaus unloosed the thong that bound the ax-helve to his wrist, and tossed the weapon up into the air, so that it spun around, a gleaming circle in the silver moonlight, and as it fell he caught it in his hand again and tossed it up above the whispering treetops and sang a song of victory, as his fathers had sung victory-lieder since the days when Northmen first went viking, and he praised the gods of Valhalla; to Odin, father of the gods, and Thor the Thunderer, and to the beauteous Valkyrior, choosers of the valiant slain in battle, he gave full praise, and on the bodies of his fallen foes he kicked the white road-dust, and spat upon then, and named them churls and nidderings, and unfit wearers of the mail of men of war.

His frenzy wore itself to calm, and, putting up his ax, he turned to look upon the little family he had succored. The man stood by the donkey's head, holding the leading-strap in one hand, in the other a stout stick which seemed to have been chosen for the double purpose of walking-staff and goad. He was some fifty years of age, as the gray which streaked his otherwise black beard attested, and was clothed from neck to heels in a gown of somber-colored woolen stuff which from its freshness evidently was the ceremonial best that he was wont to wear on Shabbath to the synagogue. A linen turban bound his head, and before his ears the unshorn locks of "David-curls" hung down each side his face. His clothes and bearing stamped him as a countryman, or villager; yet withal there was that simple dignity about him which has been the heritage of self-respecting poverty since time began.

Unmindful of the battle which had taken place so near it, the donkey cropped the short grass at the roadside in somnolent content, indifferent alike to war's alarms and the woman seated on the cushioned pillion on its back. The woman on the ass was barely past her girlhood, not more than fifteen, Klaus surmised as he glanced appreciatively upon her clear-cut, lovely features. Her face was oval, her skin more pale than fair, her features were exquisite in their purity of outline; a faultless nose, full, ripe and warmly-colored lips, slightly parted with the fright the soldiers' rude assault had caused, a mouth where tenderness and trust were mingled in expression, large eyes of blue shaded by low-drooping lids and long, dark lashes, and, in harmony with all, a flood of golden hair which, in the style permitted Jewish brides, fell unconfined beneath her veil down to the pillion upon which she sat. Her gown was blue, as was her over-mantle, and a veil and wimple of white linen framed her features to perfection. Against her breast she held a tiny infant, bound round in Jewish fashion with layer on layer of swaddling clothes, and a single glance showed the mother's beauty and sweet purity were echoed in her baby's face.

"We are beholden to you, sir," the man thanked Klaus with simple courtesy. "Those men were seeking our son's life. Only last night the Angel of the Lord forewarned me in a dream to take the young child and its mother and flee from Nazareth to Egypt, lest the soldiers of King Herod come upon us unawares. I hear that they have murdered many little ones whose parents had not warning from the Lord."

"Thou heard'st aright, old man," Klaus answered grimly, thinking of the widow-woman's son. "Back in the village yonder is the sound of lamentation; Rachel weeps for her dead and will not be comforted. Howbeit," he looked disdainfully upon the bodies in the road, "meseemeth I have somewhat paid the debt your kinsmen owed these murdering dogs."

"Alas!" the traveler returned; "you have put your life in jeopardy for us, sir. After this there is a price upon your head, and Herod will not rest until he nails you to a cross for all to see the vengeance of the King."

Klaus laughed, but not with mirth. "Methinks the sword will

sing its song, and many more like these will journey to the storm-land ere they hang me on the doom tree," he answered as he leant to pick his sword up from the roadside turf.

The blue eyes of the woman were on his as he spoke, and he stopped abashed. Never in the score and two years of wild life which had been his had Klaus the Northman, Klaus the champion of gladiators, felt a gaze like hers.

"Your baby, mistress," he said awkwardly, "may I see its face before I go my ways? 'Tis something to have saved a little child from murderers' steel—pity 'tis I was not in the village to save the widow Rachel's child from them, as well."

The woman raised the infant in her arms, and the little boy's blue eyes were fixed on Klaus. The Northman took a forward step to stroke the smooth, pink cheek, then, as if it had been a stone wall that stopped him, halted where he stood. For a voice was speaking to him, or, rather, it was no mortal voice that spake, but a sound that touched his ears, yet seemed to come from nowhere.

"Klaus, Klaus," the softly-modulated voice proclaimed, "because thou hast done this for me, and risked thy life and freedom for a little child, I say to thee that never shall thou taste of death until thy work for me is finished."

Now, though the infant's lips moved not, Klaus knew the words proceeded from him. At first he was astonished, even frightened; for the world he knew was peopled with strange spirit-beings, all of whom were enemies to men. Yet as he looked into the little boy's blue eyes, so calm, so knowing for an infant's, he felt his courage coming back, and made answer as is fitting when addressing a magician of more than usual power.

"Lord Jarl," he said, "I would not live alway. There comes the time when arms grow weak and sight is dim, however strong and brave the heart may be, and a man is no more able to take part in the man's game. Say, rather, Lord, that I may die with sword and ax in hand, in full vigor of my manhood and while the crimson tide of battle runs full-spate. Let it be that Odin's beauteous daughters deem me worthy to be taken from the battlefield and borne aloft to that Valhalla where the heroes play the sword game evermore."

"Not so, my Klaus. Thou who hast put thy life in forfeit for the safety of a little child hast better things than that in store for thee. When the name of Odin is forgot, and in all the world there is no man to do him reverence at his altars, thy name and fame shall live; and laughing, happy children shall praise thy goodness and thy loving-kindness. Thou shalt live immortally in every childish heart so long as men shall celebrate my birthday."

"I shall live past Götterdämmerung?"

"So long as gleeful children praise thy name at the period of winter solstice."

"Then I shall be a mighty hero?"

"A hero to be held in loving memory by every man who ever was a child."

"Lord Jarlkin, I think thou art mistaken. Rather would I die with the swordsong in my ears and the din of battle for a dirge, but if thou speakest sooth, why, then, a man follows his star, and where mine leads I go."

Then Klaus unsheathed his sword and flourished it three times above his head, and finally brought its point to rest upon the road, for thus did heroes of the Northland pay respect to their liege lords.

The father cried out in affright when he heard the gray sword-blade whistle in the air, but the mother looked on calmly, nor did she seem to marvel that the Northling spake in heathen language to her infant, as though he answered to unspoken words.

So Klaus bade them safe faring on their way to Egypt land, and turned to face him toward the North Star and the road that led toward home.

## The Road to Calvary

**LUCIUS PONTIUS PILATE,** Procurator of Judea, leant across the parapet and looked down at the night-bound city. Lights blossomed here and there among the flat-roofed houses; now and then the clatter of nailed hooves was heard upon the cobblestones; almost incessantly came the roar of jostling, fractious crowds. Jerusalem was crowded to the bursting point; for days the people had been streaming through the Joppa gate, for a great feast was in preparation—these Jews were always celebrating either feast or fast—and the police power of his legionaries had been put upon its mettle.

"A turbulent and stiff-necked people, these, my Claudius," the Governor addressed the tall, blond-bearded man who stood three paces to his left and rear. "Ever disputing, always arguing and bickering, everlastingly in tumult of some sort. But yesterday, when the troops marched from the citadel with the Eagles of the Legion at their head, a band of townsmen stoned them, crying out that they bore idols through the Holy City's streets. It seems they hold it sin to make an image in the likeness of anything that walks or flies or swims. A stubborn, narrow-minded lot, methinks."

"Aye, Excellence, a stubborn and rebellious lot," the first centurion agreed.

The Procurator laughed. "None knows it better than myself, my Claudius. Thou wert here amongst them aforetimes, in the days of the great Herod, I've been told. How comes it that thou'rt here again? Dost like the odor of this sacred city of the Hebrews?"

The bearded soldier smiled sardonically. "I served King Herod as a gladiator a triennium ago," he answered. "When my period of service was expired I found myself without scar or wound, and with a wallet filled with gold. I told the prætor I would fight no more for hire, and set out for my northern home, but on the way—" he stopped and muttered something which the Procurator failed to catch.

"Yes, on the way?" the Roman prompted.

"I became embroiled with certain soldiers of the King who

sought to do a little family violence. Herod swore a vengeance on me, and I was hunted like a beast from wood to desert and from desert to mountain. At last I sought the shelter which so many hunted men have found, and joined the legions. Since then I've followed where my star—and army orders—led, and now once more I stand within these city walls, safe from the vengeance of King Herod's heirs."

"And right glad am I that thou art here," the Governor declared. "This is no sinecure I hold, my Claudius. I have but a single legion to police this seething country, and treason and rebellion lift their heads on every side. Do I do one thing? The Jews cry out against me for violating some one of their sacred rights or customs. Do I do the other? Again they howl to heaven that the iron heel of Rome oppresses them. By Jupiter, had I a dozen legions more—nay, had I but a single legion more of men like thee, my Claudius—I'd drive this mutinous rabble at the lance-point till they howled like beaten dogs for mercy!" He gazed down at the city for a time in moody silence; then:

"What talk is this I hear of one who comes from Galilee claiming to be king of the Jews? Think ye that it bodes sedition? Had they but a leader they could rally to, I doubt not we should soon be fighting for our lives against these pestilent Judeans."

"I do not think we need fear insurrection from that point, your Excellence," the soldier answered. "I saw this teacher when he came into the city but four days agone. Mild of mien is he, and very meek and humble, riding on an ass's colt and preaching in the temple, bidding all men live as brothers, fear God, honor the King, and render unto Cæsar that which is his."

"Ha, sayest thou? I had thought otherwise. Caiaphas, the chief priest, tells me he foments sedition, and urges that I throw him into prison or give him over to be crucified as one who preaches treason to the Empire."

"Caiaphas!" the big centurion pursed his lips as though to spit. "That fatted swine! No wonder his religion bids him to refrain from pigs' flesh. If he ate of it he would be a cannibal!"

Pilate nodded gloomily. His quarrel with the high priest was an old one, and one in which the victories were even. Caiaphas had on occasion sent appeal to Rome, subtly intimating that unless the Governor yielded there was danger of rebellion. Word came back to Pilate that the Cæsar held him personally responsible for conditions in Judea, and that in case of revolution his would be the blame. Thus the high priest triumphed. On the other hand, the Governor had advantage in that appeal in criminal cases and matters of taxation lay with him, and by making use of this authority he could often bend the prelate to his will.

"I would we had another pontifex," he mused, "one more pliant to suggestion than this sacerdotal fool who rules their priestly council."

The jingling clink of metal swordsheath on mailed kilts was heard as a legionary hurried out upon the roof, halted and saluted, then handed Claudius a scroll. The centurion returned the military salutation and, in turn, delivered the rolled missive to the Procurator.

"By Pluto's beard," swore Pilate as he broke the seal and read the message by the light of a small lantern set upon the parapet, "it comes sooner than we thought, my Claudius! Caiaphas has taken custody of this self-styled King of Jews, tried him before the Sanhedrin and judged him worthy to be crucified. Now he brings the case to me on high petition. What are we to do?"

"Why, bid the fat pig get him back unto his sty, your Excellence. None but Rome has jurisdiction in such cases. Caiaphas can no more condemn a man to death than he can don the toga of imperial authority—"

"Aye, but therein lies the danger. I alone, as Procurator, can mete out sentence of death, but if these priests and their paid underlings should rouse the louse-bit rabble to rebellion we have not troops enough to put it down. Furthermore, should insurrection come, Rome is like to have my life. I am sent out here to govern and to rule, but chiefly to collect the tax. A people in rebellion pays no tribute to the throne. Come, Claudius, my toga. Let us hear what harm this uncrowned king has done the state.

A murmur like a storm-wind in the treetops filled the hall of audience. In the brilliant light of flambeaux double files of pretorian guardsmen stood at stiff attention as the Procurator took his seat upon the ivory and purple chair of state. Well forward in the hall, before the dais, stood Caiaphas with Simeon and Annas to his right and left. A knot of temple guards—tawdry imitations of the Roman legions—grouped about their prisoner, a tall young man in white, bearded in the Jewish fashion, but so fair of skin and light of hair that he seemed to bear no racial kinship to the swarthy men surrounding him.

"Hail, Procurator!" Meticulously Caiaphas raised his right hand in the Roman fashion, then bowed low with almost fawning oriental courtesy. "We come to you for confirmation of the sentence we have passed upon this blasphemer and traitor to the Empire."

Pilate's salutation was a merest lifting of the hand. "The blasphemy is your affair," he answered shortly. "What treason hath he wrought?"

"He hath proclaimed himself a king, and if you do not find that treason, then thou art not Cæsar's friend!"

"Art thou in very truth King of the Jews?" the Governor turned curious eyes upon the prisoner.

"Sayest thou this thing of me, or did others tell thee of it?" the young man answered.

"Am I a Jew?" the Procurator asked. "Thy own nation and thy chief priests have brought thee unto me for judgment. What hast thou done?"

There came no answer from the prisoner, but the murmuring outside the gates grew ominous. A mob was gathered at the entrance, and the guards were having trouble holding them in check.

Again the Procurator challenged: "Art thou in truth a king, and if so, of what kingdom?"

"Thou hast said it. To this end was I born, and for this cause came I into the world that I should bear witness unto the truth . . ."

"What is truth?" the Governor mused. "I myself have heard the sages argue long about it, but never have I found two who agreed on it. Claudius!" he turned to the centurion who stood behind his chair.

"Excellence!"

"I am minded to put these people to the test. Go thou to the dungeons and bring the greatest malefactor thou canst find into the hall. We shall see how far this bigotry can go."

As Claudius turned to execute the order, the Governor faced the chief priest and his satellites.

"I will have him scourged, then turn him free," he pronounced. "If he has transgressed your laws the scourging will be punishment enough; as to your charge of treason, I find no fault in him."

Docilely the prisoner followed a decurion to the barrack-room where the soldiers stripped his garments off and lashed him to a pillar, then laid a tracery of forty stripes upon his naked back.

"The King of Jews, is he?" laughed the decurion. "Why, by the eyes of Juno, every king should have a crown to call his own; yet this one has no crown at all. Ho, there, someone, make a fitting crown for Jewry's king?"

A chaplet of thorn-branch was quickly plaited and thrust upon the prisoner's head, and the long, sharp spines bit deeply in his tender flesh, so that a jewel-like diadem of ruby droplets dewed his brow. Then another found a frayed and tattered purple robe which they laid upon his bleeding shoulders. Finally, a reed torn from a hearth-broom was thrust between his tight-bound wrists for scepter, and thus regaled they set him on a table and bowed the knee to him in mock humility, what time they hailed him as Judea's new king. At length they tired of the cruel sport, and grinning broadly, brought him back and stood him in the hall before the Governor and the priests.

"Behold the man!" the Procurator bade as they brought the figure of humiliation to the hall. "Behold your king!"

"We have no king but Cæsar!" answered Caiaphas self-righteously. "This one has declared himself a king, and whoso calls himself a king speaketh against Cæsar."

Meanwhile Claudius was hastening to the judgment hall with a miserable object. The man was of great stature, but so bowed with fetters that he could not stand erect. His clothing hung in tatters, no second glance was needed to know he was a walking vermin-pasture; the members of the guard shrank from him, fending him away with spear-butts lest the lice which swarmed upon his hair and garments get on them.

Then Pilate bade the prisoner from the dungeons stand before the priests, and motioned from him to the bound and thorn-crowned captive.

"It is your custom, men of Judea, that at the Passover I release to ye a prisoner," Pilate said. "Whom will ye therefore, that I set at liberty, this convicted robber, doomed to die upon the gallows tree, or this one ye have called your king?"

"We have no king but Caesar!" shouted Caiaphas in rage. "Away with this one. Crucify him!"

And outside the great bronze grilles that barred the hall the rabble took the cry up: "Away with him! Crucify him; crucify him!"

"What, crucify your king?" the Procurator asked in mock astonishment.

The carefully rehearsed mob of temple hangers-on who swarmed about the gates thundered back once more: "Crucify him! Crucify him!"

"Water in a ewer, and a napkin, Claudius," ordered Pilate, and when his aide returned he set the silver basin down before him, and laved his hands in water, then dried them on the linen napkin. "I am innocent of the blood of this just man. See ye to it!" cried the Procurator as he handed ewer and napkin back to Claudius.

"His blood be on our heads and on our children's heads!" responded Caiaphas, and the chorus massed outside the judgment hall took up the savage pæan of blood-guiltiness: "On our heads and on our children's! Crucify him!"

Lucius Pontius Pilate shrugged his shoulders. "I have done the best I could, my Claudius," he said. "Let him be led away to prison, and on the morrow have him taken with the other adjudged male-factors and crucified. My guard will have no part in it, but I would that you go with the execution party to make sure all is regularly done and"—his thin lips parted in a mocking, mirthless smile—"to put my superscription on the cross to which they hang him. The same nails that pierce his members are like to prick the vanity of

Caiaphas, methinks," he added, chuckling to himself as though he relished some keen jest.

The procession to the execution hill, or "Place of Skulls," began at dawn, for crucifixion was a slow death, and the morrow being Shabbath it was not lawful that the malefactors he left alive to profane the sacred day with their expiring groans. The crowds assembled in the city to keep Passover lined the Street of David and gathered in the alley-heads to watch the march of the condemned, making carnival of the occasion. Sweetmeat vendors and water-sellers did a thriving trade among the merrymakers, and one or two far-sighted merchants who had come with panniers of rotten fruit and vegetables found their wares in great demand; for everyone enjoyed the sport of heaving offal at the convicts as they struggled past beneath the burden of their crosses.

Claudius did not go with them. The Procurator rested late that morning, and there were routine matters to engage his time when he had finished at the bath. The sun was several hours high when a scrivener from the secretariat came into the officium with the titulus the Governor dictated, engrossed on stiffened parchment. Pilate smiled with grim amusement as he passed the scroll to Claudius.

"Take thou this unto the place of execution, and with thy own hand fix it over the young Prophet's head," he ordered. " 'Twill give Caiaphas and his plate-lickers something fresh to whine about."

The centurion glanced down at the scroll. In letters large enough for those who walked to read yet not be forced to stop or strain their eyes, it proclaimed:

IESVS NAZARENVS
REX IVDAEORVM

Which was to say: "This is Jesus" (for such was the forename that the Prophet bore) "King of the Jews." Not only in Latin, but in Hebrew and in Greek, as well, was the legend writ, that all who passed the place of crucifixion, whatever tongue they spake, might read and understand.

"They have prated long about a king who should sweep away the power of Rome," the Procurator smiled. "Let them look upon him now, gibbeted upon a cross. By Jupiter, I would that I could see that fat priest's face when he reads the superscription!"

Three crosses crowned the bald-topped hill when Claudius reached the place of execution. On two of them hung burly robbers, nailed by hands and feet, supported by the wooden peg, or sedule, set like a dowel in the upright beam between their legs, that their bodies might not sag too much. In the center, spiked upon the tallest cross, hung the young Prophet, his frailer body already beginning to give way beneath the dreadful torment it endured. A decurion set a ladder up beside the cross, and armed with nail and hammer Claudius mounted quickly and fixed the placard to the upright beam above the bowed head of the dying man.

A high, thin wailing cry of astonishment and rage sounded as the legend on the card appeared. "Not that!" screamed Caiaphas as he put his hand up to his throat and rent his splendid priestly robe. —Not that, centurion! Yon superscription labels this blasphemer with the very title that he claimed, and for claiming which he now hangs on the gallows. Take down the card and change it so it reads that he is not our king, but that he claimed the kingly title in spite of Cæsar!"

There was something almost comic in the priests' malevolence as they fairly gnashed their teeth with rage, and Claudius, with the fighting-man's instinctive contempt for politicians, grinned openly as he replied, "'Twere best you made complaint to Pilate, priest. What he has written he has written, nor do I think he will change yon title for all your whining and complaints."

"Cæsar shall he told of this!" the wrathful high priest snarled. "He shall hear how Pilate mocked our people and incited them to riot by labeling a malefactor as our king—"

Claudius turned abruptly to the centurion commanding the execution squad. "Clear away this rabble," he directed. "Must we be pestered by their mouthings?"

From the figure on the central cross a low moan came: "I thirst."

Claudius took a sponge and dipped it in the jar of sour wine and myrrh that stood beside him on the ground. He put it on a lance and held it to the sufferer's lips, but the poor, weak body was too far spent to drink. A shudder ran through it, and with a final flash of strength the Prophet murmured: "It is finished. Father, into Thy hands I commend my spirit." A last convulsive spasm, and the thorn-crowned head fell forward. All was over.

"We had best be finishing our work," the execution guard's commander said phlegmatically. "These priests are set on mischief, and we'll have a riot on our hands if one of these should live until the sundown." He motioned to a burly executioner who picked up a sledge and methodically went about the task of smashing the suspended felons' arm- and leg-bones.

"Now, by Father Odin's ravens, thou shalt not break the Prophet's legs," Claudius declared as he snatched a guardsman's spear. "Let him die a man's death!" With the precision taught by years of training in the arena and on the battlefield, he poised the lance and drove the long bronze spearhead between the Prophet's ribs, sinking it deep into the heart. As he withdrew the point a stream of water mixed with blood gushed forth, and Claudius returned the soldier's spear. "'Tis long since I have done that favor to a helpless man," he muttered as his memory flew back to his days in the arena when the blood-mad mob withheld the mercy sign and he had thrust his sword or lance through his defeated adversary— often the man with whom he'd drunk and diced the night before. "By Frigga's eyes," he added as he looked at the pale body stretched upon the cross, "he's beautiful! I've heard he called himself the son of God, nor is that hard to credit. 'Tis no man, but a god who hangs on yonder gallows—Baldur the Beautiful, slain by foul treacheries!"

A ringing sounded in his ears like the humming of innumerable bees, and through it he heard words, words in a voice he had not heard in more than thirty years, but which he recognized instantly. "Klaus, thou took pity on a little child attacked by murderers in days agone; this day thy pity bade thee save a dying man from brutish violence. According to thy lights thou dealtest mercifully when thou thrust the spear into my side. Knowest thou not me, Klaus?"

"Lord Jarlkin!" Klaus turned round and gazed in wonder at the slight, wilted body. "The little child whom I assisted on his way to Egypt land! What wouldst thou with thy liegeman, Lord? Did not my mercy-stroke drive true—is my work unfinished?" He stretched his hand out for the soldier's spear again, but:

"Thy work is not yet started, Klaus. I will call and thou wilt know my voice when I have need of thee."

The soldiers of the guard and the crowd of hang-jawed watchers at the execution ground were wonderstruck to see the Procurator's chief centurion draw himself up and salute the body pendent on the cross as though it were a tribune, or the Governor himself.

Dark clouds obscured the sun, and menacing thunder mingled with the stabbing spears of lightning as Klaus hurried through the Street of David on his way back to the Governor's palace. Once or twice there came a rumbling in the bowels of the earth, and the solid ground reeled drunkenly beneath his feet.

"Siguna goes to drain her cup, and Loki writhes beneath the sting of serpent-venom," Klaus muttered as he dug his heels into his horse's sides. It would not be comfortable in that narrow street when the fury of the earthquake began to shake the buildings down. A temblor shook the riven earth afresh, and an avalanche of broken tile and rubble slid into the street, almost blocking it. Klaus leaped down from his saddle and gave his horse a smart blow on the flank.

"Go thou, good beast, and Thor see thee safely to thy stable," he bade, then took shelter by the blank-walled houses, dashing forward a few steps, then shrinking back again as spates of failing masonry cataracted overhead and fell crashing on the cobbles of the roadway.

"*Ai—ai—ahee!*" a woman's scream came thin-edged with terror. "Help, for the love of God—save me or I die! Have mercy, Master!"

The flicker of a lightning-flash lit up the pitch-black night-in-day that flooded through the street, and by its quivering light Klaus saw a woman's body lying in the roadway. A timber from a broken house had fallen on her foot, pinioning her to the cobbles, and even as she screamed, a fresh convulsion of the earth shook down a barrow-load of broken brick and tile, scattering brash and limedust over her.

A stone fell clanging on his helmet as he rushed across the gloom-choked street, and a parapet-fragment crashed behind his heels as he leant to prize the timber off her ankle. She lay as limp as death within his arms as he dashed back to the shelter of the wall, and for a moment he thought he had risked his life in rescuing one beyond the need of succor; but as he laid her down upon the flagstones her great eyes opened and her little hands crept up to clasp themselves about his neck. "Art safe, my lord?" she asked tremulously.

"Aye, for the nonce," he answered, "but we tempt the gods by staying here. Canst walk?"

"I'll try." She drew herself erect and took a step, then sank down with a moan. "My foot—'tis broke, I fear," she gasped. "Do thou go on, my lord; thou hast done thy duty to the full already. 'Twould not be meet to stay and risk thy life for me—"

"Be silent, woman," he commanded gruffly. "Raise thy arms."

Obediently she put her arms about his shoulders and he lifted her as though she were a child. Then, his cloak about her head to fend off falling fragments of the buildings, he darted from house to house until the narrow street was cleared and they came at length into a little open space.

It was lighter here, and he could see his salvage. She was a pretty thing, scarce larger than a half-grown child, and little past her girlhood. Slender she was, yet with the softly rounded curves of budding womanhood. Her skin, deep sun-kissed olive, showed every violet vein through its veil of lustrous tan. Her hands, dimpled like a child's, were tipped with long and pointed nails on which a sheathing of bright goldleaf had been laid, so they shone like tiny mirrors. Her little feet, gilt-nailed like her hands, were innocent of sandals and painted bright with henna on the soles. On ankles, wrists and arms hung bangles of rose-gold studded thick with lapis-lazuli, topaz and bright garnet, while rings of the same precious metal hung from each ear almost to her creamy shoulders. A diadem of gold thick-set with gems was circled round her brow, binding back the curling black locks which lay clustering round her face. Her small, firm breasts were bare, their nipples stained with henna, and beneath her bosom was a zone of woven golden wire from which a robe of sheerest gauze was hung, bound round the hips with a shawl of brilliant orange silk embroidered with pink shells and roses. Ground antimony had been rubbed upon her eyelids, and her full, voluptuous lips were stained a brilliant red with powdered cinnabar.

Klaus recognized her: one of the hetæræ from the house of love kept by the courtezan of Magdala before she left her harlotry to follow after the young Prophet they had crucified that morning. Her mistress gone, the girl had taken service as a dancer at Agrippa's court. He drew away a little. His clean-bred northern flesh revolted at the thought of contact with the pretty little strumpet.

"What didst thou in the street?" he asked. "Were there so few buyers of thy wares within the palace that thou must seek them in the highways?"

"I—I came to see the Master," she sobbed softly. "I had the dreadful malady, and I sought His cure."

"Aye? And did thou find it?"

"Yea, that did I. As He went by, all burdened with his gibbet, I called to Him and asked His mercy, and He did but raise the fingers of one hand and look on me, and behold—I am clean and whole again. See, is not my skin as fresh and clean as any maiden's?"

Klaus moved a little farther from her, but she crept toward him, holding out her hands for him to touch. "Behold me, I am clean!" she whispered rapturously. "No more will I be shunned of men—"

"By this one thou wilt be," he broke in grimly. "What have I to do with thee and thy kind, girl? The earthquake passes; it is safe for thee to walk the streets. Get thee gone."

"But my broken foot—I cannot walk. Wilt thou not help me to my place—"

"Not I, by Thor. Let scented darlings of the palace see to that." He shook her clinging hands away and half rose to his feet when a voice—the well-remembered voice his inward ear had heard before—came to him:

"Despise her not. I have had mercy on her, and thou—and I— have need of her. Klaus, take her to thee."

He stood irresolute a moment; then: "I hear and obey, Lord," he answered softly and sank down again upon the turf. "How art thou called?" he asked the girl.

"Erinna."

"A Greek?"

"Tyrian, my lord." She moved closer to him and rubbed her supple body against his breastplate with a gentle, coaxing gesture. "They brought me over the bright water whilst I was still a child, and schooled me in the arts of love, and I am very beautiful and much desired, but now I am all thine." She bowed her head submissively and put his hand upon it. "Thou didst battle with the earthquake for me, and rived me from his clutches; now am I thine by right of capture."

Klaus smiled, a trifle grimly. "What need have I, a plain, blunt soldier, of such as thee?"

"I am very subtle in the dance, and can sing and play sweet music, even on the harp and flute and cymbals. Also I am skilled at cookery, and when thou hast grown tired of me thou canst sell me for much gold—"

"Men of my race sell not their wives—"

"Wife? Saidst thou wife, my lord?" She breathed the word incredulously.

"Am I a Greek or Arab to have slave girls travel in my wake? Come, rouse thee up; we must to the palace, where quarters can be found for thee until I take thee to mine own."

Tears streamed down her face, cutting little rivers in the rouge with which her cheeks were smeared, but her smile looked through the tear-drops as the sun in April shines through showers of rain. "In very truth, He told my future better than I knew!" she cried ecstatically, and, to Klaus's utter consternation, bent suddenly and pressed a fervid kiss upon his buskin.

"What charlatan foretold thy fortune?" he demanded, raising the girl and crooking an arm beneath her knees, for her broken foot was swelling fast, and walking was for her impossible.

"The Master whom they crucified—may dogs defile their mothers' graves! When I bowed me in the dust and begged Him to have pity on me, He looked at me and smiled, e'en though He trod the way to torture and to death, and was borne down with the gallows' weight, and He told me, 'Woman, thy desire shall be unto thee.' I thought He meant that I was healed, but—" She flung both arms about her bearer's neck and crushed his face against her bosom as she sighed ecstatically.

"But what, wench?"

"I have seen thee from afar, my Claudius. Long have I watched thee and had pleasure in thy manly beauty. At night I used to dream that thou wouldst notice me, perchance come unto me, or even buy me for thy slave; but that ever I should bear the name of wife"—again her voice broke on a sigh, but it was a sigh of utter happiness—"that I, Erinna the hetæra—"

"Thy Greek name likes me not," he interrupted.

"What's in a name, my lord? I'll bear whatever name thou givest me, and be happy in it, since 'tis given me by you. By Aphrodite's brows, I'll come like any dog whene'er thou callest me by such name as you choose to give—"

"Let be this talk of dogs and slaves," he broke in sharply. "Thou'lt he a wife and equal—aye, by Thor's iron gauntlets, and whoso fails to do thee honor shall be shorter by a head!"

Pilate's legion was recruited largely from Germanic tribes, and enough of his own people could be found to enable Klaus to have a marriage ceremony shaped on Northern custom. Erinna's name was changed to Unna, and on the day they wed she sat in the high bride's seat robed in modest white with a worked head-dress on her clustering black ringlets, a golden clasp about her waist and gold rings on her arms and fingers. And the Northlings raised their drinking-horns aloft and shouted "*Skoal!*" and "*Waes heal!*" to the bride and bridegroom, and when the feast was finished and the bride's-cup had been drunk, because her broken foot was not yet mended, Klaus bore Unna in his arms unto the bride's-bed. Thus did Claudius the centurion, who was also Klaus the Northling, wed a woman out of Tyre in the fashion of the Northmen.

🌲 🌲 🌲

Now talk ran through the city of Jerusalem that the Prophet whom the priests had done to death was risen from the tomb. Men said that while His sepulcher was watched by full-armed guards an angel came and rolled the stone away, and He came forth, all bright and glorious. And many were the ones who testified that they had seen Him in the flesh.

The priests and temple hangers-on cast doubt upon the story, and swore that whilst the guardsmen slept the Prophet's followers had come and stolen Him away, but Klaus and Unna both believed. "Said I not He was a god, e'en as He hanged upon the gallows tree?" asked Klaus. "Baldur the Beautiful is He; Baldur the Fair cannot be holden by the gates of Hel; He is raised up again in their despite."

"He is in truth the Son of God, as Mary Magdalene said," Unna answered as she laid her cheek against her husband's breast. "He healed me of my malady and gave me that which I desired above all things."

Klaus kissed his new-made wife upon the mouth. "He said that I had need of thee, my sweetling," he whispered softly. "I knew it not, but He spake sooth. And," he added even lower, "He said that He likewise had need of thee. We shall hear His call and answer Him whenever He shall please to summon us, though the summons come from lowest Niflheim."

# The Long, Long Road

Men grew old and grayed and died in the service of Imperial Rome, but neither death nor old age came to Klaus. His ruddy hair retained its sheen, and when the men who joined the legions as mere beardless youths laid their swords aside and sat them in the inglenook to tell brave tales of battles fought and won upon the sea or field he was still instinct with youthful vigor. For years he followed Pilate's fortunes, acting as his aide-de-camp and confidant, and when the aging Governor went from Palestine to Helvetia it was Klaus who went with him as commander of his soldiery. When death at last came to his patron, Klaus stood among the mourners and watched the funeral flames mount crackling from the pyre, then turned his face toward Rome, where men of valor still were in demand. With the rank of a tribune he fought Arminius under Varus, and though the legions suffered such defeat as they had never known before when the German tribesmen swept down on them in Teutoburg Forest, the soldiers under his command made an orderly retreat.

As commander of a legion he stood with Constantine the Great at Malvian Bridge when, beneath the emblem of the once-despised cross, Maximian's youthful son defeated old Maxentius and won the purple toga of the Cæsars. With Constantine he sailed across the Bosporus and helped to found the world's new capital at Byzantium.

Emperors came and went. The kingdom of the Ostrogoths arose in Italy, and strange, bearded men who spoke barbarian tongues ruled in the Cæsars' stead. But though the olden land of Latium no longer offered reverence to the Empire, it owed allegiance to the name of Him the priests had crucified so long ago in Palestine; for nowhere, save in the frozen fjords and forests of the farthest North and in the sun-smit deserts of the South, did men fail to offer prayer and praise and sacrifice to the Prophet who had come to save His people from their sins, and had been scornfully rejected by their priests and leaders.

And now a mighty conflict rose between the Christians of the

West and the followers of Mahound in the East; and Klaus, who knew the country round about Jerusalem as he knew the lines that marked his palms, rode forth with Tancred and Count Raymond and Godfrey of Bouillon to take the Holy City from the Paynims' hands. With him rode his ever-faithful, thrice-beloved Unna, armed and mounted as a squire. Never since the morning of their marriage had she and he been out of voice-call of each other; for she had shared his life in camp and field, marching with the legions dressed in armor like a man, going with him to Byzantium when the new Empire was founded, riding at his side across the troubled continent of Europe when the old Empire broke to pieces and the little kings and dukes and princelings set their puny courts up in the midst of their walled towns. Sometimes she cut her long hair close and went forth in male attire; again, in those brief intervals of peace when they dwelt at ease in some walled city, she let her tresses grow and assumed the garb of ladies of the time, and ruled his house with gentleness and skill as became the mate of one who rated the esteem of prince and governor, general and lord, for her husband's fame at weaponry and sagacity in war had given him great standing among those who had need of strong arms and wise heads to lead their soldiery and beat their foemen back.

Now, Klaus, with Unna fighting at his elbow as his squire, had assailed the walls when Godfrey and Count Eustace and Baldwin of the Mount leaped from the flaming tower and held the Paynims back till Tancred and Duke Robert broke Saint Stephen's Gate and forced their way into the Holy City; but when the mailed men rode with martial clangor through the streets and massacred the populace, they took no part. In the half-darkness of the mosque that stood hard by the ancient Street of David where aforetime the young Prophet had trod the Via Dolorosa they saw old Moslems with calm features watch their sons' heads fall upon the musty praying-carpets, then in turn submit to slaughter as the Christians' axes split their skulls or swords ripped through their bellies. They saw the Paynim women cling in terror to their men-folk's bending knees, what time they pleaded for mercy, panting and screaming till sword or lance ripped open their soft bodies and they cried no more. They tried to stop the wanton killing, and begged the men-at-arms and knights to stay their hands and show their helpless, beaten foemen clemency, whereat the priests and monks who urged the wearers of the cross to slay and spare not cried out on them, and swore they were no true and loyal lovers of the Prince of Peace.

But when the killing and the rapine ceased and men went forth to worship at the holy places, Klaus and Unna walked the city, and their eyes were soft with memories. "Here it was they led Him to the place of crucifixion," Unna told a group of noble women who had come to make the pilgrimage to Calvary upon their knees, and, "Here He raised His hand and blessed the very men who did Him injury." But when the Frankish women heard her they would not believe, but hooted her away; for the priests, who never till that time had seen Jerusalem, had shown them where the Master's blessed feet had trod, and sooth, a learned holy man knew more of sacred things than this wild woman of the camp who wore her hair clipped short and swaggered it amongst the men-at-arms with a long sword lashed against her thigh!

But when she told them that she knelt upon those very stones and watched Cyrenian Simon bear the cross toward Golgotha, they shrank from her in terror and crossed themselves and called on every saint they knew for succor, and named her witch and sorceress. And presently came priests' men who bound her arms with cords and took her to the prison-house beneath the Templars' stable and swore that on the morrow they would burn her at the stake, that all might see what fate befell a woman who spake blasphemy within the very confines of the Holy City.

When she came not to their dwelling-place that night, Klaus was like a man made mad by those foul drugs the Paynims use to give them courage in the fight. And he went unto the prison-house and smote the warders where they stood, so that they fled from him as from a thing accursed, and with his mighty ax he brake the heavy doors that shut her in, and they went forth from that place and took to horse and rode until they reached the sea, where they took ship and sailed away. And no man durst stand in their way, for the fire of Northern lightnings burned in Klaus's eyes, and he raged like a wild

berserker if any bade them stand and give account of whence they
came and where their mission led them.

The years slipped swiftly by like rapid rivers running in their
courses, and Klaus and Unna rode the paths of high adventure.
Sometimes they rested in the cities, but more often they were on the
road, or fighting in the armies of some prince or duke or baron, and
always fame and fortune came to them. But they could not abide in
any place for long, for betimes they came in conflict with the priests;
for when these heard them speak of the Great Teacher as though
they had beheld Him in the flesh they sought to have them judged
as witch and warlock, and so great was these men's power that had
they not been fleet of foot and strong of arm they were like to have
been burned a dozen times and more.

"Now, by the Iron Gloves of Thor," swore Klaus one time when
they were flying from the priestly wrath, "meseemeth that of all men
on the earth the priest doth change the least. 'Twas Caiaphas and his
attendants whose foul plottings hanged our Master on the cross, and
today the truth He died for is perverted and withheld by the very
men who claim to be His priests and servants!"

One Yuletide Klaus and Unna lodged them in a little city by the
Rhine. The harvest was not plentiful that year, and want and famine
stalked the streets as though an enemy had set siege to the town. The
feast of Christmas neared, but within the burghers' houses there was
little merriment. Scarce food had they to keep starvation from their
bellies, and none at all to make brave holiday upon the birthday of
the Lord.

Now as they sat within their house Klaus thought him of the
cheerless faces of the children of the town, and as he thought he took
a knife and block of wood and carved therefrom the semblance of a
little sleigh the like of which the people used for travel when the
snows of winter made the roads impassable for wheels or horsemen.

And when Unna saw his work she laughed aloud and clipped
him in her arms and said, "My husband, make thou more of those,
as many as the time 'twixt now and Christmas Eve permits! We have

good store of sweetmeats in our vaults, even figs from Smyrna and sweet, dried grapes from Cyprus and from Sicily, and some quantity of barley sugar, likewise. Do thou carve out the little sleighs and I will fill them to the brim with comfits; then on the Eve of Christ His birthday we'll go amongst the poorest of the townsmen and leave our little gifts upon their doorsteps, that on the morrow when the children wake they shall not have to make their Christmas feast on moldy bread and thin meat broth."

The little sleighs piled up right swiftly, for it seemed to Klaus his fingers had a nimbleness they never had before, and he whittled out the toys so fast that Unna was amazed and swore his skill at wood-carving was as great as with the sword and ax; whereat he laughed and whittled all the faster.

It was bitter cold on Christmas Eve, and the members of the night watch hid themselves in doorways or crept into the cellars to shield them from the snow that rode upon the storm-wind's howling blast; so none saw Klaus and Unna as they made their rounds, leaving on each doorstep of the poor a little sleigh piled high with fruits and sweets the like of which those children of that northern clime had never seen. But one small lad whose empty belly would not let him sleep looked from his garret window and espied the scarlet cloak Klaus wore, for Klaus went bravely dressed as became a mighty man of valor and one who walked in confidence with princes. And the small boy marveled much that Klaus, the mighty soldier of whose feats and fame men spoke with bated breath, should stop before his doorstep. But anon he slept, and when he waked he knew not if it were a dream he dreamed, or if he had seen Klaus pass through the storm.

But when the church bells called the folk to prayer and praise next morning and the house doors were unbarred and the people found the sleighs all freighted with their loads of comfits on their thresholds, great and loud was the rejoicing, and little children who had thought that Christmas was to be another day of fasting and starvation clapped their hands and raised their voices in wild shouts of happy laughter. And Klaus and Unna who went privily about the streets saw their work and knew that it was good, and their hearts beat quicker and their eyes shone bright with tears of happiness for that they had brought joy where sorrow was before, and they clasped each other by the hand and exchanged a kiss like lovers when their vows are new, and each swore that the other had conceived the scheme, and each denied it; so in sweet argument they got them to the minster, and then unto their house, where their feast of goose and herbs was sweeter for the thought of joy they had brought to the children of the town.

But when the priests were told about the miracle of fruits and sweets that came unmarked upon the doorsteps of the poor they were right wroth, and swore this was no Christian act, but the foul design of some fell fiend who sought to steal men's souls away by bribing them with Satan's sweetmeats.

The lad whose waking eyes had seen Klaus's scarlet mantle told his tale, and all the poor folk praised his name, and one and all they named him Santa Klaus, a saint who walked the earth in human guise and had compassion on the suffering of the poor.

But the churchmen went unto the city's governor and said, "Go to, this man foments rebellion. He hath sought to buy thy people's loyalty away by little gifts made to their children. Look thou to it, if thou failest to put him in restraint before he does more mischief thou art no friend of the landgrave from whom thou holdest this city as a fief."

So the graf would fain have put them into prison on a charge of treason, but the townsmen came to them and warned them of the plot; so they escaped before the men-at-arms came clamoring at their door, and fled across the winter snows. Behind them swept a raving tempest, so that those who sought to follow were engulfed in drifting snows and lost their tracks upon the road, and finally turned and fought their way back to the city with the tidings that they surely must have perished in the storm.

But Klaus and Unna did not die, for the storm that followed hard upon their heels delayed its pace to cover their retreat, and anon they came unto another town where they rested safe throughout the winter, and in the springtime set out on their journeys once again.

♣ ♣ ♣

Now their travels took them to the Baltic shores, and as they passed across the country of the Lappmen they came into a valley ringed about with nine small hills, and no man durst go to that place; for 'twas said the little brown men of the land beneath the earth had power there, and whoso met them face to face was doomed to be their servant alway, and to slave and toil beneath the ground for evermore, because these people had no souls, but were natheless gifted with a sort of immortality, so that they should live until the final Judgment Day when they and all the great host of the olden gods should stand before the throne of the Most High and hear sentence of an everlasting torment.

But Klaus and Unna had no fear of the ælf people or of any harm that they might do, for both of them wore crosses round their necks, and in addition each was girt with a long sword, and the ax that had aforetime laid the mightiest of foemen in the dust was hung upon Klaus's saddle-bow.

So they bent their road among the haunted Nine Hills, and behold, as they rode seaward came a great procession of the ælfmen bearing packs upon their backs and singing dolefully. "*Waes hael* to thee, small ælfmen," Klaus made challenge; "why go ye sadly thus, singing songs of dole and drearihead?"

"Alack and well-a-day!" the ælf King answered; "we take our way to Niflheim, there to abide until the time shall come when we are sent to torment everlasting, for the people whom aforetime we did help, cry out upon us now and say that we are devils, and set no pan of milk or loaf of barley bread beside their doorstep for us; nor do they tell the tales their fathers told of kindly deeds done by the Little People, but only tales of terror and of wickedness. For this we are no longer able to come out and play upon the earth's good face, neither to dance and sing by moonlight in the glades, and, worst of all, our human neighbors have no use for our good offices, but drive us hence with curse and song and bell and book and candle."

Now Klaus laughed long and loud when he heard this, for well was he reminded of the time when he and Unna had to flee for very life because they had done kindness to the poor; so he made answer: —Would ye then find it happiness to serve your human neighbors, if ye could?"

"Aye, marry, that would we," the ælf King told him. "We be great artificers in both wood and stone and metal. There are no smiths like unto us, nor any who can fashion better things of wood, and much would it delight our hearts to shape things for men's service and bestow them on the good men of the farms and villages; but they, taught by their priests, will have none of our gifts. Why, to call a thing a fairy gift is to insult the giver in these days!"

Now as Klaus listened to this plaint there came a ringing as of many bells heard far away within his ears, and once again the voice he knew spake to him, and he heard: "Klaus, thou hast need of these small men. Take them with thee on the road which shall be opened to thy feet."

So he addressed the ælfmen's King and said: "Wouldst go with me unto a place of safety, and there work diligently to make the things which children joy to have? If thou wilt do it, I'll see thy gifts are put into the hands of those who will take joy in them and praise thy name for making them."

"My lord, if thou wilt do this thing for us, I am thy true and loyal vassal now and ever, both I and all my people," swore the ælf King. So on the fresh green turf he kneeled him down and swore the oath of fealty unto Klaus, acknowledging himself his vassal and swearing to bear true and faithful service unto him. Both he and all his host of tiny men pronounced the oath, and when they rose from off their knees they hailed Klaus as their lord and leader.

Then from their treasure-store they brought a little sleigh of gold, no larger than the helmet which a soldier wears to shield his skull from sword-blows, but so cunningly contrived that it could stretch and swell till it had room for all of them, both the ælf King and his host of dwarfs, and Klaus and Unna and their steeds, as well. And when they had ensconced them in the magic sleigh they harnessed to it four span of tiny reindeer, and at once these grew until they were as large as war-steeds, and with a shout the ælf King bade them go, and straightway they rose up into the air and drew the sleigh behind them, high above the heaving billows of the Baltic.

"Bid them ride on until they have the will to stop," Klaus ordered, and the ælf King did as he commanded, and presently, far in the frozen North where the light of the bridge Bifrost rests upon the earth, the reindeer came to rest. And there they builded them a house, strong-timbered and thick-walled, with lofty chimneys and great hearths where mighty fires roared ceaselessly. And in the rooms about the great hall they set their forges up, and the air was filled with sounds of iron striking iron as the nimble, cunning dwarfs fashioned toys of metal while others of their company plied saw and knife and chisel, making toys of wood, and others still made dolls of plaster and of chinaware and clothed them in small garments deftly shaped from cloth which cunning ælfmen under Unna's teaching fashioned at the great looms they built.

When Christmastide was come again there was a heap of toys raised mountain high, and Klaus put them in the magic sleigh and whistled to the magic reindeer, and away they sped across the bridge Bifrost where in olden days men said the gods had crossed to Asgard. And so swiftly sped his eight small steeds, and so well his sleigh was stocked with toys, that before the light of Christmas morning dawned there was a gift to joy the heart of children laid upon each hearth, and Klaus came cloud-riding back again unto his Northern home and there his company of cunning dwarfs and his good wife Unna awaited him, and a mighty feast was made, and the tables groaned beneath the weight of venison and salmon and fat roast goose, and the mead-horns frothed and foamed as they bid each other skoal and *waes hael* and drank and drank again to childhood's happiness.

Long years ago Klaus laid aside his sword, and his great ax gathers rust upon the castle wall; for he has no need of weapons as he goes about the work foretold for him that night so long ago upon the road to Bethlehem.

Odin's name is but a memory, and in all the world none serves his altars, but Klaus is very real today, and every year ten thousand times ten thousand happy children wait his coming; for he is neither Claudius the centurion nor Klaus the mighty man of war, but Santa Klaus, the very patron saint of little children, and his is the work his

Master chose for him that night two thousand years ago; his the long, long road that has no turning so long as men keep festival upon the anniversary of the Savior's birth.

# INTRODUCTION
## NEWSLETTER

**AMONG THE CLASSICS** of science fiction, invasions from space have taken a number of forms, from H. G. Wells' *The War of the Worlds*, where the aliens land with heat rays blazing, to Robert A. Heinlein's *The Puppet Masters*, where they take a more secret, sinister approach and only a handful know about the invasion. Connie Willis tells of an invasion even more secret than Heinlein's, but the aliens nonetheless give themselves away to the alert, intrepid narrator. Their mistake was arriving in time for the holidays . . .

Connie Willis has won eleven Nebula Awards, seven Hugo Awards, four *Locus* Awards, the John W. Campbell Memorial Award, and the Damon Knight Memorial Grand Master Award from the SF Writers of America for lifetime achievement. Willis writes in her introduction to her short story collection, *Miracle*, that she *loves* Christmas, and, appropriately, all the stories in *Miracle* are Christmas stories. If that doesn't give her the right to close out this yuletide collection with this brilliant story, then chestnuts don't roast on an open fire.

# NEWSLETTER

## BY CONNIE WILLIS

**LATER EXAMINATION** of weather reports and newspapers showed that it may have started as early as October nineteenth, but the first indication I had that something unusual was going on was at Thanksgiving.

I went to Mom's for dinner (as usual), and was feeding cranberries and cut-up oranges into Mom's old-fashioned meat grinder for the cranberry relish and listening to my sister-in-law, Allison, talk about her Christmas newsletter (also as usual).

"Which of Cheyenne's accomplishments do you think I should write about first, Nan?" she said, spreading cheese on celery sticks. "Her playing lead snowflake in *The Nutcracker* or her hitting a home run in Pee Wee Soccer?"

"I'd list the Nobel Peace Prize first," I murmured, under cover of the crunch of an apple being put through the grinder.

"There just isn't room to put in all the girls' accomplishments," she said, oblivious. "Mitch *insists* I keep it to one page."

"That's because of Aunt Lydia's newsletters," I said. "Eight pages, single spaced."

"I know," she said. "And in that tiny print you can barely read." She waved a celery stick thoughtfully. "That's an idea."

"Eight pages, single spaced?"

"No. I could get the computer to do a smaller font. That way I'd have room for Dakota's Sunshine Scout merit badges. I got the cutest paper for my newsletters this year. Little angels holding bunches of mistletoe."

Christmas newsletters are *very* big in my family, in case you couldn't tell. Everybody—uncles, grandparents, second cousins, my sister Sueann—sends the Xeroxed monstrosities to family, co-workers, old friends from high school, and people they met on their cruise to the Caribbean (which they wrote about at length in their newsletter the year before). Even my Aunt Irene, who writes a handwritten letter on every one of her Christmas cards, sticks a newsletter in with it.

My second cousin, Lucille's, are the worst although there are a lot of contenders. Last year, hers started:

> *"Another year has hurried past*
> *And, here I am, asking, 'Where did the time go so fast?'*
> *A trip in February, a bladder operation in July,*
> *Too many activities, not enough time, no matter how hard I try."*

At least Allison doesn't put Dakota and Cheyenne's accomplishments into verse.

"I don't think I'm going to send a Christmas newsletter this year," I said.

Allison stopped, cheese-filled knife in hand. "Why not?"

"Because I don't have any news. I don't have a new job, I didn't go on a vacation to the Bahamas, I didn't win any awards. I don't have anything to tell."

"Don't be ridiculous," my mother said, sweeping in carrying a foil-covered casserole dish. "Of course you do, Nan. What about that skydiving class you took?"

"That was last year, Mom," I said. And I had only taken it so I'd have something to write about in my Christmas newsletter.

"Well, then, tell about your social life. Have you met anybody lately at work?"

Mom asks me this every Thanksgiving. Also Christmas, the Fourth of July, and every time I see her.

"There's nobody to meet," I said, grinding cranberries. "Nobody new ever gets hired because nobody ever quits. Everybody who works there's been there for years. Nobody even gets fired. Bob Hunziger hasn't been to work on time in eight years, and *he's* still there."

"What about . . . what was his name?" Allison said, arranging the celery sticks in a cut-glass dish. "The guy you liked who had just gotten divorced?"

"Gary," I said. "He's still hung up on his ex-wife."

"I thought you said she was a real shrew."

"She is," I said. "Marcie the Menace. She calls him twice a week complaining about how unfair the divorce settlement is, even though she got virtually everything. Last week, it was the house. She claimed she'd been too upset by the divorce to get the mortgage refinanced and he owed her twenty thousand dollars because now interest rates have gone up. But it doesn't matter. Gary still keeps hoping they'll get back together. He almost didn't fly to Connecticut to his parents' for Thanksgiving because he thought she might change her mind about a reconciliation."

"You could write about Sueann's new boyfriend," Mom said, sticking marshmallows on the sweet potatoes. "She's bringing him today."

This was as usual, too. Sueann always brings a new boyfriend to Thanksgiving dinner. Last year, it was a biker. And no, I don't mean one of those nice guys who wear a beard and black Harley T-shirt on weekends and work as accountants between trips to Sturgis. I mean a Hell's Angel.

My sister, Sueann, has the worst taste in men of anyone I have ever known. Before the biker, she dated a member of a militia group and, after the ATF arrested him, a bigamist wanted in three states.

"If this boyfriend spits on the floor, I'm leaving," Allison said, counting out silverware. "Have you met him?" she asked Mom.

"No," Mom said, "but Sueann says he used to work where you do, Nan. So *somebody* must quit once in a while."

I racked my brain, trying to think of any criminal types who'd worked in my company. "What's his name?"

"David something," Mom said, and Cheyenne and Dakota raced into the kitchen, screaming, "Aunt Sueann's here, Aunt Sueann's here! Can we eat now?"

Allison leaned over the sink and pulled the curtains back to look out the window.

"What does he look like?" I asked, sprinkling sugar on the cranberry relish.

"Clean-cut," she said, sounding surprised. "Short blond hair, slacks, white shirt, tie."

Oh, no, that meant he was a neo-Nazi. Or married and planning to get a divorce as soon as the kids graduated from college—which would turn out to be in twenty-three years, since he'd just gotten his wife pregnant again.

"Is he handsome?" I asked, sticking a spoon into the cranberry relish.

"No," Allison said, even more surprised. "He's actually kind of ordinary looking."

I came over to the window to look. He was helping Sueann out of the car. She was dressed up, too, in a dress and a denim slouch hat. "Good heavens," I said. "It's David Carrington. He worked up on fifth in Computing."

"Was he a womanizer?" Allison asked.

"No," I said, bewildered. "He's a very nice guy. He's unmarried, he doesn't drink, and he left to go get a degree in medicine."

"Why didn't *you* ever meet him?" Mom said.

David shook hands with Mitch, regaled Cheyenne and Dakota with a knock-knock joke, and told Mom his favorite kind of sweet potatoes were the ones with the marshmallows on top.

"He must be a serial killer," I whispered to Allison.

"Come on, everybody, let's sit down," Mom said. "Cheyenne and Dakota, you sit here by Grandma. David, you sit here, next to Sueann. Sueann, take off your hat. You know hats aren't allowed at the table."

"Hats for *men* aren't allowed at the table," Sueann said, patting her denim hat. "Women's hats are." She sat down. "Hats are coming back in style, did you know that? *Cosmopolitan's* latest issue said this is the Year of the Hat."

"I don't care what it is," Mom said. "Your father would never have allowed hats at the table."

"I'll take it off if you'll turn off the TV," Sueann said, complacently opening out her napkin.

They had reached an impasse. Mom always has the TV on during meals. "I like to have it on in case something happens," she said stubbornly.

"Like what?" Mitch said. "Aliens landing from outer space?"

"For your information, there was a UFO sighting two weeks ago. It was on CNN."

"Everything looks delicious," David said. "Is that homemade cranberry relish? I *love* that. My grandmother used to make it."

He had to be a serial killer.

For half an hour, we concentrated on turkey, stuffing, mashed potatoes, green bean casserole, scalloped corn casserole, marshmallow-topped sweet potatoes, cranberry relish, pumpkin pie, and the news on CNN.

"Can't you at least turn it down, Mom?" Mitch said. "We can't even hear to talk."

"I want to see the weather in Washington," Mom said. "For your night."

"You're leaving tonight?" Sueann said. "But you just got here. I haven't even seen Cheyenne and Dakota."

"Mitch has to fly back tonight," Allison said. "But the girls and I are staying till Wednesday."

"I don't see why you can't stay at least until tomorrow," Mom said.

"Don't tell me this is homemade whipped cream on the pumpkin pie," David said. "I haven't had homemade whipped cream in years."

"You used to work in computers, didn't you?" I asked him. "There's a lot of computer crime around these days, isn't there?"

"Computers!" Allison said. "I forgot all the awards Cheyenne won at computer camp." She turned to Mitch. "The newsletter's going to have to be at least two pages. The girls just have too many awards—T-ball, tadpole swimming, Bible school attendance."

"Do you send Christmas newsletters in your family?" my mother asked David.

He nodded. "I love hearing from everybody."

"You see?" Mom said to me. "People *like* getting newsletters at Christmas."

"I don't have anything against Christmas newsletters," I said. "I just don't think they should be deadly dull. Mary had a root canal, Bootsy seems to be getting over her ringworm, we got new gutters on the house. Why doesn't anyone ever write about anything *interesting* in their newsletters?"

"Like what?" Sueann said.

"I don't know. An alligator biting their arm off. A meteor falling on their house. A murder. Something interesting to read."

"Probably because they didn't happen," Sueann said.

"Then they should make something up," I said, "so we don't have to hear about their trip to Nebraska and their gall bladder operation."

"You'd do that?" Allison said, appalled. "You'd make something up?

"People make things up in their newsletters all the time, and you know it," I said. "Look at the way Aunt Laura and Uncle Phil brag about their vacations and their stock options and their cars. If you're going to lie, they might as well be lies that are interesting for other people to read."

"You have plenty of things to tell without making up lies, Nan," Mom said reprovingly. "Maybe you should do something like your cousin Celia. She writes her newsletter all year long, day by day," she explained to David. "Nan, you might have more news than you think if you kept track of it day by day like Celia. She always has a lot to tell."

Yes, indeed. Her newsletters were nearly as long as Aunt Lydia's. They read like a diary, except she wasn't in junior high, where at least there were pop quizzes and zits and your locker combination to give it a little zing. Celia's newsletters had no zing whatsoever:

> *"**Wed. Jan. 1.** Froze to death going out to get the paper. Snow got in the plastic bag thing the paper comes in. Editorial section all wet. Had to dry it out on the radiator. Bran Flakes for breakfast. Watched Good Morning America.*

> *"**Thurs. Jan. 2.** Cleaned closets. Cold and cloudy."*

"If you'd write a little every day," Mom said, "you'd be surprised at how much you'd have to tell by Christmas."

Sure. With my life, I wouldn't even have to write it every day. I could do Monday's right now:

> *"**Mon. Nov. 28.** Froze to death on the way to work. Bob Hunziger not in yet. Penny putting up Christmas decorations. Solveig told me she's sure the baby is going to be a boy. Asked me which name I liked, Albuquerque or Dallas. Said hi to Gary, but he was too depressed to talk to me. Thanksgiving reminds him of ex-wife's giblets. Cold and cloudy."*

I was wrong. It was snowing, and Solveig's ultrasound had showed the baby was a girl. "What do you think of Trinidad as a name?" she asked me. Penny wasn't putting up Christmas decorations either. She was passing out slips of paper with our Secret Santas' names on them. "The decorations aren't here yet," she said excitedly. "I'm getting something special from a farmer upstate."

"Does it involve feathers?" I asked her. Last year, the decorations had been angels with thousands of chicken feathers glued onto cardboard for their wings. We were still picking them out of our computers.

"No," she said happily. "It's a surprise. I love Christmas, don't you?"

"Is Hunziger in?" I asked her, brushing snow out of my hair. Hats always mash my hair down, so I hadn't worn one.

"Are you kidding?" she said. She handed me a Secret Santa slip. "It's the Monday after Thanksgiving. He probably won't be in till sometime Wednesday."

Gary came in, his ears bright red from the cold and a harried expression on his face. His ex-wife must not have wanted a reconciliation.

"Hi, Gary," I said, and turned to hang up my coat without waiting for him to answer.

And he didn't, but when I turned back around, he was still standing there, staring at me. I put a hand up to my hair, wishing I'd worn a hat.

"Can I talk to you a minute?" he said, looking anxiously at Penny.

"Sure," I said, trying not to get my hopes up. He probably wanted to ask me something about the Secret Santas.

He leaned farther over my desk. "Did anything unusual happen to you over Thanksgiving?"

"My sister didn't bring home a biker to Thanksgiving dinner," I said.

He waved that away dismissively. "No, I mean anything odd, peculiar, out of the ordinary."

"That *is* out of the ordinary."

He leaned even closer. "I flew out to my parents' for Thanksgiving, and on the flight home—you know how people always carry on luggage that won't fit in the overhead compartments and then try to cram it in?"

"Yes," I said, thinking of a bridesmaid's bouquet I had made the mistake of putting in the overhead compartment one time.

"Well, nobody did that on my flight. They didn't carry on hanging bags or enormous shopping bags full of Christmas presents. Some people didn't even have a carry-on. And that isn't all. Our flight was half an hour late, and the flight attendant said, 'Those of you who do not have connecting flights, please remain seated until those with connections have deplaned.' And they did." He looked at me expectantly.

"Maybe everybody was just in the Christmas spirit."

He shook his head. "All four babies on the flight slept the whole way, and the toddler behind me didn't kick the seat."

That *was* unusual.

"Not only that, the guy next to me was reading *The Way of All Flesh* by Samuel Butler. When's the last time you saw anybody on an airplane reading anything but John Grisham or Danielle Steele? I tell you, there's something funny going on."

"What?" I asked curiously.

"I don't know," he said. "You're sure you haven't noticed anything?"

"Nothing except for my sister. She always dates these losers, but the guy she brought to Thanksgiving was really nice. He even helped with the dishes."

"You didn't notice anything else?"

"No," I said, wishing I had. This was the longest he'd ever talked to me about anything besides his ex-wife. "Maybe it's something in the air at DIA. I have to take my sister-in-law and her little girls to the airport Wednesday. I'll keep an eye out."

He nodded. "Don't say anything about this, okay?" he said, and hurried off to Accounting.

"What was that all about?" Penny asked, coming over.

"His ex-wife," I said. "When do we have to exchange Secret Santa gifts?"

"Every Friday, and Christmas Eve."

I opened up my slip. Good, I'd gotten Hunziger. With luck I wouldn't have to buy any Secret Santa gifts at all.

Tuesday I got Aunt Laura and Uncle Phil's Christmas newsletter. It was in gold ink on cream-colored paper, with large gold bells in the corners. "Joyeux Noël," it began. "That's French for Merry Christmas. We're sending our newsletter out early this year because we're spending Christmas in Cannes to celebrate Phil's promotion to assistant CEO and my wonderful new career! Yes, I'm starting my own business—Laura's Floral Creations—and orders are pouring in! It's already been written up in *House Beautiful,* and you will *never* guess who called last week—Martha Stewart!" Et cetera.

I didn't see Gary. Or anything unusual, although the waiter who took my lunch order actually got it right for a change. But he got Tonya's (who works up on third) wrong.

"I *told* him tomato and lettuce only," she said, picking pickles off her sandwich. "I heard Gary talked to you yesterday. Did he ask you out?"

"What's that?" I said, pointing to the folder Tonya'd brought with her to change the subject. "The Harbrace file?"

"No," she said. "Do you want my pickles? It's our Christmas schedule. *Never* marry anybody who has kids from a previous marriage. Especially when *you* have kids from a previous marriage. Tom's ex-wife, Janine, my ex-husband, John, and four sets of grand-parents all want the kids, and they all want them on Christmas morning. It's like trying to schedule the D-Day invasion."

"At least your husband isn't still hung up on his ex-wife," I said glumly.

"So Gary didn't ask you out, huh?" She bit into her sandwich, frowned, and extracted another pickle. "I'm sure he will. Okay, if we take the kids to Tom's parents at four on Christmas Eve, Janine could pick them up at eight . . . No, that won't work." She switched her sandwich to her other hand and began erasing. "Janine's not speaking to Tom's parents."

She sighed. "At least John's being reasonable. He called yesterday and said he'd be willing to wait till New Year's to have the kids. I don't know what got into him."

When I got back to work, there was a folded copy of the morning newspaper on my desk.

I opened it up. The headline read "City Hall Christmas Display to Be Turned On," which wasn't unusual. And neither was tomorrow's headline, which would be "City Hall Christmas Display Protested."

Either the Freedom Against Faith people protest the Nativity scene or the fundamentalists protest the elves or the environmental people protest cutting down Christmas trees or all of them protest the whole thing. It happens every year.

I turned to the inside pages. Several articles were circled in red, and there was a note next to them which read "See what I mean? Gary."

I looked at the circled articles. "Christmas Shoplifting Down," the first one read. "Mall stores report incidences of shoplifting are down for the first week of the Christmas season. Usually prevalent this time of—"

"What are you doing?" Penny said, looking over my shoulder.

I shut the paper with a rustle. "Nothing," I said. I folded it back up and stuck it into a drawer. "Did you need something?"

"Here," she said, handing me a slip of paper.

"I already got my Secret Santa name," I said.

"This is for Holiday Goodies," she said. "Everybody takes turns bringing in coffee cake or tarts or cake."

I opened up my slip. It read "Friday Dec. 20. Four dozen cookies."

"I saw you and Gary talking yesterday," Penny said. "What about?"

"His ex-wife," I said. "What kind of cookies do you want me to bring?"

"Chocolate chip," she said. "Everybody loves chocolate."

As soon as she was gone, I got the newspaper out again and took it into Hunziger's office to read. "Legislature Passes Balanced Budget," the other articles read. "Escaped Convict Turns Self In," "Christmas Food Bank Donations Up."

I read through them and then threw the paper into the wastebasket. Halfway out the door I thought better of it and took it out, folded it up, and took it back to my desk with me.

While I was putting it into my purse, Hunziger wandered in. "If anybody asks where I am, tell them I'm in the men's room," he said, and wandered out again.

Wednesday afternoon, I took the girls and Allison to the airport. She was still fretting over her newsletter.

"Do you think a greeting is absolutely necessary?" she said in the baggage check-in line. "You know, like 'Dear Friends and Family'?"

"Probably not," I said absently. I was watching the people in line ahead of us, trying to spot this unusual behavior Gary had talked about, but so far I hadn't seen any. People were looking at their watches and complaining about the length of the line, the ticket agents were calling, "Next! Next!" to the person at the head of the line, who, after having stood impatiently in line for forty-five minutes waiting for this moment, was now staring blankly into space, and an unattended toddler was methodically pulling the elastic strings off a stack of luggage tags.

"They'll still know it's a Christmas newsletter, won't they?" Allison said. "Even without a greeting at the beginning of it?"

With a border of angels holding bunches of mistletoe, what else could it be? I thought.

*"Next!"* the ticket agent shouted.

The man in front of us had forgotten his photo ID, the girl in front of us in line for the security check was wearing heavy metal, and on the train out to the concourse a woman stepped on my foot and then glared at me as if it were my fault. Apparently, all the nice people had traveled the day Gary came home.

And that was probably what it was—some kind of statistical clump where all the considerate, intelligent people had ended up on the same flight.

I knew they existed. My sister Sueann had had an insurance actuary for a boyfriend once (he was also an embezzler, which is why Sueann was dating him) and he had said events weren't evenly distributed, that there were peaks and valleys. Gary must just have hit a peak.

Which was too bad, I thought, lugging Cheyenne, who had demanded to be carried the minute we got off the train, down the concourse. Because the only reason he had approached me was because he thought there was something strange going on.

"Here's Gate 55," Allison said, setting Dakota down and getting out French language tapes for the girls. "If I left off the 'Dear Friends and Family,' I'd have room to include Dakota's violin recital. She played The Gypsy Dance."

She settled the girls in adjoining chairs and put on their headphones. "But Mitch says it's a letter, so it has to have a greeting."

"What if you used something short?" I said. "Like 'Greetings' or something. Then you'd have room to start the letter on the same line."

"Not 'Greetings.' " She made a face. "Uncle Frank started his letter that way last year, and it scared me half to death. I thought Mitch had been *drafted.*"

I had been alarmed when I'd gotten mine, too, but at least it had given me a temporary rush of adrenaline, which was more than Uncle Frank's letters usually did, concerned as they were with prostate problems and disputes over property taxes.

"I suppose I could use 'Holiday Greetings,' "Allison said. "Or 'Christmas Greetings,' but that's almost as long as 'Dear Friends and Family.' If only there were something shorter."

"How about 'Hi'?"

"That might work." She got out paper and a pen and started writing. "How do you spell 'outstanding'?"

"O-u-t-s-t-a-n-d-i-n-g," I said absently. I was watching the moving sidewalks in the middle of the concourse. People were standing on the right, like they were supposed to, and walking on the left. No people were standing four abreast or blocking the entire sidewalk with their luggage. No kids were running in the opposite direction of the sidewalk's movement, screaming and running their hands along the rubber railing.

"How do you spell 'fabulous'?" Allison asked.

"Flight 2216 to Spokane is now ready for boarding," the flight attendant at the desk said. "Those passengers traveling with small children or those who require additional time for boarding may now board."

A single old lady with a walker stood up and got in line. Allison unhooked the girls' headphones and we began the ritual of hugging and gathering up belongings.

"We'll see you at Christmas," she said.

"Good luck with your newsletter," I said, handing Dakota her teddy bear, "and don't worry about the heading. It doesn't need one."

They started down the passageway. I stood there, waving, till they were out of sight, and then turned to go.

"We are now ready for regular boarding of rows 25 through 33," the flight attendant said, and everybody in the gate area stood up. Nothing unusual here, I thought, and started for the concourse.

"What rows did she call?" a woman in a red beret asked a teenaged boy.

"25 through 33," he said.

"Oh, I'm Row 14," the woman said, and sat back down.

So did I.

"We are now ready to board rows 15 through 24," the flight attendant said, and a dozen people looked carefully at their tickets and then stepped back from the door, patiently waiting their turn. One of them pulled a paperback out of her tote bag and began to read. It was *Kidnapped* by Robert Louis Stevenson. Only when the flight attendant said, "We are now boarding all rows," did the rest of them stand up and get in line.

Which didn't prove anything, and neither did the standing on the right of the moving sidewalk. Maybe people were just being nice because it was Christmas.

Don't be ridiculous, I told myself. People aren't nicer at Christmas. They're ruder and pushier and crabbier than ever. You've seen them at the mall, and in line for the post office. They act worse at Christmas than any other time.

"This is your final boarding call for Flight 2216 to Spokane," the flight attendant said to the empty waiting area. She called to me, "Are you flying to Spokane, ma'am?"

"No." I stood up. "I was seeing friends off."

"I just wanted to make sure you didn't miss your flight," she said, and turned to shut the door.

I started for the moving sidewalk, and nearly collided with a young man running for the gate. He raced up to the desk and flung his ticket down.

"I'm sorry, sir," the flight attendant said, leaning slightly away from the young man as if expecting an explosion. "Your flight has already left. I'm really terribly sor—"

"Oh, it's okay," he said. "It serves me right. I didn't allow enough time for parking and everything, that's all. I should have started for the airport earlier."

The flight attendant was tapping busily on the computer. "I'm afraid the only other open flight to Spokane for today isn't until 11:05 this evening."

"Oh, well," he said, smiling. "It'll give me a chance to catch up on my reading." He reached down into his attaché case and pulled out a paperback. It was W. Somerset Maugham's *Of Human Bondage*.

"Well?" Gary said as soon as I got back to work Thursday morning. He was standing by my desk, waiting for me.

"There's definitely something going on," I said, and told him about the moving sidewalks and the guy who'd missed his plane. "But what?"

"Is there somewhere we can talk?" he said, looking anxiously around.

"Hunziger's office," I said, "but I don't know if he's in yet."

"He's not," he said, led me into the office, and shut the door behind him.

"Sit down," he said, indicating Hunziger's chair. "Now, I know this is going to sound crazy, but I think all these people have been possessed by some kind of alien intelligence. Have you ever seen *Invasion of the Body Snatchers*"?

"What?" I said.

"*Invasion of the Body Snatchers*," he said. "It's about these parasites from outer space who take over people's bodies and—"

"I *know* what it's about," I said, "and it's *science fiction*. You think the man who missed his plane was some kind of pod-person? You're right," I said, reaching for the doorknob. "I do think you're crazy."

"That's what Donald Sutherland said in *Leechmen from Mars*. Nobody ever believes it's happening, until it's too late."

He pulled a folded newspaper out of his back pocket. "Look at this," he said, waving it in front of me. "Holiday credit card fraud down twenty percent. Holiday suicides down thirty percent. Charitable giving up *sixty* percent."

"They're coincidences." I explained about the statistical peaks and valleys. "Look," I said, taking the paper from him and turning to the front page. "People Against Cruelty to Our Furry Friends

Protests City Hall Christmas Display. Animal Rights Group Objects to Exploitation of Reindeer."

"What about your sister?" he said. "You said she only dates losers. Why would she suddenly start dating a nice guy? Why would an escaped convict suddenly turn himself in? Why would people suddenly start reading the classics? Because they've been taken over."

"By aliens from outer space?" I said incredulously.

"Did he have a hat?"

"Who?" I said, wondering if he really was crazy. Could his being hung up on his horrible ex-wife have finally made him crack?

"The man who missed his plane," he said. "Was he wearing a hat?"

"I don't remember," I said, and felt suddenly cold. Sueann had worn a hat to Thanksgiving dinner. She'd refused to take it off at the table. And the woman whose ticket said Row 14 had been wearing a beret.

"What do hats have to do with it?" I asked.

"The man on the plane next to me was wearing a hat. So were most of the other people on the flight. Did you ever see *The Puppet Masters?* The parasites attached themselves to the spinal cord and took over the nervous system," he said. "This morning here at work I counted nineteen people wearing hats. Les Sawtelle, Rodney Jones, Jim Bridgeman—"

"Jim Bridgeman always wears a hat," I said. "It's to hide his bald spot. Besides, he's a computer programmer. All the computer people wear baseball caps."

"DeeDee Crawford," he said. "Vera McDermott, Janet Hall—"

"Women's hats are supposed to be making a comeback," I said.

"George Frazelli, the entire Documentation section—"

"I'm sure there's a logical explanation," I said. "It's been freezing in here all week. There's probably something wrong with the heating system."

"The thermostat's turned down to fifty," he said, "which is something else peculiar. The thermostat's been turned down on all floors."

"Well, that's probably Management. You know how they're always trying to cut costs—"

"They're giving us a Christmas bonus. And they fired Hunziger."

"They fired Hunziger?" I said. Management never fires anybody.

"This morning. That's how I knew he wouldn't be in his office."

"They actually fired Hunziger?"

"And one of the janitors. The one who drank. How do you explain that?"

"I—I don't know," I stammered. "But there has to be some other explanation than aliens. Maybe they took a management course or got the Christmas spirit or their therapists told them to do good deeds or something. Something besides leechmen. Aliens coming from outer space and taking over our brains is impossible!"

"That's what Dana Wynter said in *Invasion of the Body Switchers*. But it's not impossible. It's happening right here, and we've got to stop it before they take over everybody and we're the only ones left. They—"

There was a knock on the door. "Sorry to bother you, Gary," Carol Zaliski said, leaning in the door, "but you've got an urgent phone call. It's your ex-wife."

"Coming," he said, looking at me. "Think about what I said, okay?" He went out.

I stood looking after him and frowning.

"What was that all about?" Carol said, coming into the office. She was wearing a white fur hat.

"He wanted to know what to buy his Secret Santa person," I said.

Friday Gary wasn't there. "He had to go talk to his ex-wife this morning," Tonya told me at lunch, picking pickles off her sandwich. "He'll be back this afternoon. Marcie's demanding he pay for her therapy. She's seeing this psychiatrist, and she claims Gary's the one who made her crazy, so he should pick up the bill for her Prozac. *Why* is he still hung up on her?"

"I don't know," I said, scraping mustard off my burger.

"Carol Zaliski said the two of you were talking in Hunziger's office yesterday. What about? Did he ask you out? Nan?"

"Tonya, has Gary talked to you since Thanksgiving? Did he ask you about whether you'd noticed anything unusual happening?"

"He asked me if I'd noticed anything bizarre or abnormal about my family. I told him, in my family bizarre *is* normal. You won't believe what's happened now. Tom's parents are getting a divorce, which means five sets of parents. Why couldn't they have waited till after Christmas to do this? It's throwing my whole schedule off."

She bit into her sandwich. "I'm sure Gary's going to ask you out. He's probably just working up to it."

If he was, he had the strangest line I'd ever heard. Aliens from outer space. Hiding under hats!

Though, now that he'd mentioned it, there were an awful lot of people wearing hats. Nearly all the men in Data Analysis had baseball caps on, Jerrilyn Wells was wearing a wool stocking cap, and Ms. Jacobson's secretary looked like she was dressed for a wedding in a white thing with a veil. But Sueann had said this was the Year of the Hat.

Sueann, who dated only gigolos and Mafia dons. But she had been bound to hit a nice boyfriend sooner or later, she dated so many guys.

And there weren't any signs of alien possession when I tried to get somebody in the steno pool to make some copies for me. "We're *busy,*" Paula Grandy snapped. "It's Christmas, you know!"

I went back to my desk, feeling better. There was an enormous dish made of pinecones on it, filled with candy canes and red and green foil-wrapped chocolate kisses. "Is this part of the Christmas decorations?" I asked Penny.

"No. They aren't ready yet," she said. "This is just a little something to brighten the holidays. I made one for everyone's desk."

I felt even better. I pushed the dish over to one side and started through my mail. There was a green envelope from Allison and Mitch. She must have mailed her newsletters as soon as she got off the plane. I wonder if she decided to forgo the heading or Dakota's Most Improved Practicing Piano Award, I thought, slicing it open with the letter opener.

"Dear Nan," it began, several spaces down from the angels and mistletoe border. "Nothing much new this year. We're all okay, though Mitch is worried about downsizing, and I always seem to be running from behind. The girls are growing like weeds and doing okay in school, though Cheyenne's been having some problems with her reading and Dakota's still wetting the bed. Mitch and I decided we've been pushing them too hard, and we're working on trying not to overschedule them for activities and just letting them be normal, average little girls."

I jammed the letter back into the envelope and ran up to fourth to look for Gary.

"All right," I said when I found him. "I believe you. What do we do now?"


We rented movies. Actually, we rented only some of the movies. *Attack of the Soul Killers* and *Invasion from Betelgeuse* were both checked out.

"Which means somebody else has figured it out, too," Gary said. "If only we knew who."

"We could ask the clerk," I suggested.

He shook his head violently. "We can't do anything to make them suspicious. For all we know, they may have taken them off the shelves themselves, in which case we're on the right track. What else shall we rent?"

"What?" I said blankly.

"So it won't look like we're just renting alien invasion movies."

"Oh," I said, and picked up *Ordinary People* and a black and white version of *A Christmas Carol*.

It didn't work. "*The Puppet Masters*," the kid at the rental desk, wearing a blue and yellow Blockbuster hat, said inquiringly. "Is that a good movie?"

"I haven't seen it," Gary said nervously.

"We're renting it because it has Donald Sutherland in it," I said. "We're having a Donald Sutherland film festival. *The Puppet Masters, Ordinary People, Invasion of the Body Snatchers*—"

"Is Donald Sutherland in this?" he asked, holding up *A Christmas Carol*.

"He plays Tiny Tim," I said. "It was his first screen appearance."

🌲 🌲 🌲

"You were great in there," Gary said, leading me down to the other end of the mall to Suncoast to buy *Attack of the Soul Killers.* "You're a very good liar."

"Thanks," I said, pulling my coat closer and looking around the mall. It was freezing in here, and there were hats everywhere, on people and in window displays, Panamas and porkpies and picture hats.

"We're surrounded. Look at that," he said, nodding in the direction of Santa Claus's North Pole.

"Santa Claus has always worn a hat," I said.

"I meant the line," he said.

He was right. The kids in line were waiting patiently, cheerfully. Not a single one was screaming or announcing she had to go to the bathroom. "I want a Masters of Earth," a little boy in a felt beanie was saying eagerly to his mother.

"Well, we'll ask Santa," the mother said, "but he may not be able to get it for you. All the stores are sold out."

"Okay," he said. "Then I want a wagon."

Suncoast was sold out *of Attack of the Soul Killers,* but we bought *Invasion from Betelgeuse* and *Infiltrators from Space* and went back to his apartment to screen them.

"Well?" Gary said after we'd watched three of them. "Did you notice how they start slowly and then spread through the population?"

Actually, what I'd noticed was how dumb all the people in these movies were. "The brainsuckers attack when we're asleep," the hero would say, and promptly lie down for a nap. Or the hero's girlfriend would say, "They're on to us. We've got to get out of here. Right now," and then go back to her apartment to pack.

And, just like in every horror movie, they were always splitting up instead of sticking together. And going down dark alleys. They deserved to be turned into pod-people.

"Our first order of business is to pool what we know about the aliens," Gary said. "It's obvious the purpose of the hats is to conceal the parasites' presence from those who haven't been taken over yet," he said, "and that they're attached to the brain."

"Or the spinal column," I said. "Like in *The Puppet Masters*."

He shook his head. "If that were the case, they could attach themselves to the neck or the back, which would be much less conspicuous. Why would they take the risk of hiding under hats, which are so noticeable, if they aren't attached to the top of the head?"

"Maybe the hats serve some other purpose."

The phone rang.

"Yes?" Gary answered it. His face lit up and then fell.

His ex-wife, I thought, and started watching *Infiltrators from Space*.

"You've got to believe me," the hero's girlfriend said to the psychiatrist. "There are aliens here among us. They look just like you or me. You have to believe me."

"I do believe you," the psychiatrist said, and raised his finger to point at her. "Ahhhggghhh!" he screeched, his eyes glowing bright green.

"Marcie," Gary said. There was a long pause. "A friend." Longer pause. "No."

The hero's girlfriend ran down a dark alley, wearing high heels. Halfway through, she twisted her ankle and fell.

"You know that isn't true," Gary said.

I fast forwarded. The hero was in his apartment, on the phone. "Hello, Police Department?" he said. "You have to help me. We've been invaded by aliens who take over your body!"

"We'll be right there, Mr. Daly," the voice on the phone said. "Stay there."

"How do you know my name?" the hero shouted. "I didn't tell you my address."

"We're on our way," the voice said.

"We'll talk about it tomorrow," Gary said, and hung up. "Sorry," he said, coming over to the couch. "Okay, I downloaded a bunch of stuff about parasites and aliens from the Internet," he said, handing me a sheaf of stapled papers. "We need to discover what it is they're doing to the people they take over, what their weaknesses are, and how we can fight them. We need to know when and where it started."

Gary went on, "How and where it's spreading, and what it's doing to people. We need to find out as much as we can about the nature of the aliens so we can figure out a way to eliminate them. How do they communicate with each other? Are they telepathic, like in *Village of the Damned,* or do they use some other form of communication? If they're telepathic, can they read our minds as well as each other's?"

"If they could, wouldn't they know we're on to them?" I said.

The phone rang again.

"It's probably my ex-wife again," he said.

I picked up the remote and flicked on *Infiltrators from Space* again.

Gary answered the phone. "Yes?" he said, and then warily, "How did you get my number?"

The hero slammed down the phone and ran to the window. Dozens of police cars were pulling up, lights flashing.

"Sure," Gary said. He grinned. "No, I won't forget."

He hung up. "That was Penny. She forgot to give me my Holiday Goodies slip. I'm supposed to take in four dozen sugar cookies next Monday." He shook his head wonderingly. "Now, *there's* somebody I'd like to see taken over by the aliens."

He sat down on the couch and started making a list. "Okay, methods of fighting them. Diseases. Poison. Dynamite. Nuclear weapons. What else?"

I didn't answer. I was thinking about what he'd said about wishing Penny would be taken over.

"The problem with all of those solutions is that they kill the people, too," Gary said. "What we need is something like the virus they used in *Invasion.* Or the ultrasonic pulses only the aliens could hear in *War with the Slugmen.* If we're going to stop them, we've got to find something that kills the parasite but not the host."

"Do we have to stop them?"

"What?" he said. "Of course we have to stop them. What do you mean?"

"All the aliens in these movies turn people into zombies or monsters," I said. "They shuffle around, attacking people and killing them and trying to take over the world. Nobody's done anything like that. People are standing on the right and walking on the left, the suicide rate's down, my sister's dating a very nice guy. Everybody who's been taken over is nicer, happier, more polite. Maybe the parasites are a good influence, and we shouldn't interfere."

"And maybe that's what they want us to think. What if they're acting nice to trick us, to keep us from trying to stop them? Remember *Attack of the Soul Killers?* What if it's all an act, and they're only acting nice till the takeover's complete?"

If it was an act, it was a great one. Over the next few days, Solveig, in a red straw hat, announced she was naming her baby Jane, Jim Bridgeman nodded at me in the elevator, my cousin Celia's newsletter/diary was short and funny, and the waiter, sporting a soda jerk's hat, got both Tonya's and my orders right. "No pickles!" Tonya said delightedly, picking up her sandwich. "Ow! Can you get carpal tunnel syndrome from wrapping Christmas presents? My hand's been hurting all morning."

She opened her file folder. There was a new diagram inside, a rectangle with names written all around the sides.

"Is that your Christmas schedule?" I asked.

"No," she said, showing it to me. "It's a seating arrangement for Christmas dinner. It was crazy, running the kids from house to house like that, so we decided to just have everybody at our house."

I took a startled look at her, but she was still hatless.

"I thought Tom's ex-wife couldn't stand his parents."

"Everybody's agreed we all need to get along for the kids' sake. After all, it's Christmas."

I was still staring at her.

She put her hand up to her hair. "Do you like it? It's a wig. Eric got it for me for Christmas. For being such a great mother to the boys through the divorce. I couldn't believe it." She patted her hair. "Isn't it great?"

"They're hiding their aliens under wigs," I told Gary.

"I know," he said. "Paul Gunden got a new toupee. We can't trust anyone." He handed me a folder full of clippings.

Employment rates were up. Thefts of packages from cars, usually prevalent at this time of year, were down. A woman in Minnesota had brought back a library book that was twenty-two years overdue. "Groups Praise City Mall Christmas Display," one of the clippings read, and the accompanying picture showed the People for a Non-Commercial Christmas, the Holy Spirit Southern Baptists, and the Equal Rights for Ethnics activists holding hands and singing Christmas carols around the crèche.

On the ninth, Mom called. "Have you written your newsletter yet?"

"I've been busy," I said, and waited for her to ask me if I'd met anyone lately at work.

"I got Jackie Peterson's newsletter this morning," she said.

"So did I." The invasion apparently hadn't reached Miami. Jackie's newsletter, which is usually terminally cute, had reached new heights:

> *"M is for our trip to Mexico*
> *E is for Every place else we'd like to go*
> *R is for the HV that takes us there . . ."*

And straight through MERRY CHRISTMAS, A HAPPY NEW YEAR, and both her first and last names.

"I do wish she wouldn't try to put her letters in verse," Mom said. "They never scan."

"Mom," I said. "Are you okay?"

"I'm fine," she said. "My arthritis has been kicking up the last couple of days, but otherwise I've never felt better. I've been thinking, there's no reason for you to send out newsletters if you don't want to."

"Mom," I said, "did Sueann give you a hat for Christmas?"

"Oh, she told you," Mom said. "You know, I don't usually like hats, but I'm going to need one for the wedding, and—"

"Wedding?"

"Oh, didn't she tell you? She and David are getting married right after Christmas. I am so relieved. I thought she was never going to meet anyone decent."

I reported that to Gary. "I know," he said glumly. "I just got a raise."

"I haven't found a single bad effect," I said. "No signs of violence or antisocial behavior. Not even any irritability."

"*There* you are," Penny said crabbily, coming up with a huge poinsettia under each arm. "Can you help me put these on everybody's desks?"

"Are these the Christmas decorations?" I asked.

"No, I'm still waiting on that farmer," she said, handing me one of the poinsettias. "This is just a little something to brighten up everyone's desk." She reached down to move the pinecone dish on Gary's desk. "You didn't eat your candy canes," she said.

"I don't like peppermint."

"Nobody ate their candy canes," she said disgustedly. "They all ate the chocolate kisses and left the candy canes."

"People like chocolate," Gary said and whispered to me, "*When* is she going to be taken over?"

"Meet me in Hunziger's office right away," I whispered back, and said to Penny, "Where does this poinsettia go?"

"Jim Bridgeman's desk."

I took the poinsettia up to Computing on fifth. Jim was wearing his baseball cap backward. "A little something to brighten your desk," I said, handing it to him, and started back toward the stairs.

"Can I talk to you a minute?" he said, following me out into the stairwell.

"Sure," I said, trying to sound calm. "What about?"

He leaned toward me. "Have you noticed anything unusual going on?"

"You mean the poinsettia?" I said. "Penny does tend to go a little overboard for Christmas, but—"

"No," he said, putting his hand awkwardly to his cap, "people who are acting funny, people who aren't themselves?"

"No," I said, smiling. "I haven't noticed a thing."

I waited for Gary in Hunziger's office for nearly half an hour. "Sorry I took so long," he said when he finally got there. "My ex-wife called. What were you saying?"

"I was saying that even you have to admit it would be a good thing if Penny was taken over," I said. "What if the parasites aren't evil? What if they're those—what are those parasites that benefit the host called? You know, like the bacteria that help cows produce milk? Or those birds that pick insects off of rhinoceroses?"

"You mean symbiotes?" Gary said.

"Yes," I said eagerly. "What if this is some kind of symbiotic relationship? What if they're raising everyone's IQ or enhancing their emotional maturity, and it's having a good effect on us?"

"Things that sound too good to be true usually are. No," he said, shaking his head. "They're up to something, I know it. And we've got to find out what it is."

On the tenth when I came to work, Penny was putting up the Christmas decorations. They were, as she had promised, something special: wide swags of red velvet ribbons running all around the walls, with red velvet bows and large bunches of mistletoe every few feet. In between were gold calligraphic scrolls reading "And kiss me 'neath the mistletoe, For Christmas comes but once a year."

"What do you think?" Penny said, climbing down from her stepladder. "Evey floor has a different quotation." She reached into a large cardboard box. "Accounting's is 'Sweetest the kiss that's stolen under the mistletoe.' "

I came over and looked into the box. "Where did you get all the mistletoe?" I asked.

"This apple farmer I know," she said, moving the ladder.

I picked up a big branch of the green leaves and white berries. "It must have cost a fortune." I had bought a sprig of it last year that had cost six dollars.

Penny, climbing the ladder, shook her head. "It didn't cost anything. He was glad to get rid of it." She tied the bunch of mistletoe to the red velvet ribbon. "It's a parasite, you know. It kills the trees."

"Kills the trees?" I said blankly, staring at the white berries.

"Or deforms them," she said. "It steals nutrients from the tree's sap, and the tree gets these swellings and galls and things. The farmer told me all about it."

♣ ♣ ♣

As soon as I had the chance, I took the material Gary had downloaded on parasites into Hunziger's office and read through it.

Mistletoe caused grotesque swellings wherever its rootlets attached themselves to the tree. Anthracnose caused cracks and then spots of dead bark called cankers. Blight wilted trees' leaves. Witches' broom weakened limbs. Bacteria caused tumorlike growths on the trunk, called galls.

We had been focusing on the mental and psychological effects when we should have been looking at the physical ones. The heightened intelligence, the increase in civility and common sense, must simply be side effects of the parasites' stealing nutrients. And damaging the host.

I stuck the papers back into the file folder, went back to my desk, and called Sueann.

"Sueann, hi," I said. "I'm working on my Christmas newsletter, and I wanted to make sure I spelled David's name right. Is Carrington spelled C-A-R-R or C-E-R-R?"

"C-A-R-R. Oh, Nan, he's so wonderful! So different from the losers I usually date! He's considerate and sensitive and—"

"And how are you?" I said. "Everybody at work's been down with the flu."

"Really?" she said. "No, I'm fine."

What did I do now? I couldn't ask "Are you sure?" without making her suspicious. "C-A-R-R," I said, trying to think of another way to approach the subject.

Sueann saved me the trouble. "You won't believe what he did yesterday. Showed up at work to take me home. He knew my ankles had been hurting, and he brought me a tube of Ben-Gay and a dozen pink roses. He is so thoughtful."

"Your ankles have been hurting?" I said, trying not to sound anxious.

"Like crazy. It's this weather or something. I could hardly walk on them this morning."

I jammed the parasite papers back into the file folder, made sure

I hadn't left any on the desk like the hero in *Parasite People from Planet X,* and went up to see Gary.

He was on the phone.

"I've got to talk to you," I whispered.

"I'd like that," he said into the phone, an odd look on his face.

"What is it?" I said. "Have they found out we're on to them?"

"Shh," he said. "You know I do," he said into the phone.

"You don't understand," I said. "I've figured out what it's doing to people."

He held up a finger, motioning me to wait. "Can you hang on a minute?" he said into the phone, and put his hand over the receiver. "I'll meet you in Hunziger's office in five minutes," he said.

"No," I said. "It's not safe. Meet me at the post office."

He nodded, and went back to his conversation, still with that odd look on his face.

I ran back down to second for my purse and went to the post office. I had intended to wait on the corner, but it was crowded with people jockeying to drop money into the Salvation Army's Santa Claus kettle.

I looked down the sidewalk. Where was Gary? I went up the steps and scanned the street. There was no sign of him.

"Merry Christmas!" a man said, half-tipping a fedora and holding the door for me.

"Oh, no, I'm—" I began, and saw Tonya coming down the street. "Thank you," I said, and ducked inside.

It was freezing inside, and the line for the postal clerks wound out into the lobby. I got in it. It would take an hour at least to work my way to the front, which meant I could wait for Gary without looking suspicious.

Except that I was the only one not wearing a hat. Every single person in line had one on, and the clerks behind the counter were wearing mail carrier caps. And broad smiles.

"Packages going overseas should really have been mailed by November fifteenth," the middle clerk was saying, not at all disgruntledly, to a little Japanese woman in a red cap, "but don't worry; we'll figure out a way to get your presents there on time."

"The line's only about forty-five minutes long," the woman in front of me confided cheerfully. She was wearing a small black hat with a feather and carrying four enormous packages. I wondered if they were full of pods. "Which isn't bad at all, considering it's Christmas."

I nodded, looking toward the door. Where was he?

"Why are you here?" the woman said, smiling.

"What?" I said, whirling back around, my heart pounding.

"What are you here to mail?" she said. "I see you don't have any packages."

"S-stamps," I stammered.

"You can go ahead of me," she said. "If all you're buying is stamps. I've got all these packages to send. You don't want to wait for that."

I *do* want to wait, I thought. "No, that's all right. I'm buying a *lot* of stamps," I said. "I'm buying several sheets. For my Christmas newsletter."

She shook her head, balancing the packages. "Don't be silly. You don't want to wait while they weigh all these." She tapped the man in front of her. "This young lady's only buying stamps," she said. "Why don't we let her go ahead of us?"

"Certainly," the man, who was wearing a Russian karakul hat, said, and bowed slightly, stepping back.

"No, really," I began, but it was too late. The line had parted like the Red Sea.

"Thank you," I said, and walked up to the counter. "Merry Christmas."

The line closed behind me. They know, I thought. They know I was looking up plant parasites. I glanced desperately toward the door.

"Holly and Ivy?" the clerk said, beaming at me.

"What?" I said.

"Your stamps." He held up two sheets. "Holly and Ivy or Madonna and Child?"

"Holly and Ivy," I said weakly. "Three sheets, please."

I paid for the sheets, thanked the mob again, and went back out into the freezing cold lobby. And now what? Pretend I had a box and fiddle with the combination? Where was he?

I went over to the bulletin board, trying not to seem suspicious, and looked at the Wanted posters. They had probably all turned themselves in by now and were being model prisoners. And it really was a pity the parasites were going to have to be stopped, *if* they could be stopped.

It had been easy in the movies (in the movies, that is, in which they had managed to defeat them, which wasn't all that many. Over half the movies had ended with the whole world being turned into glowing green eyes). And in the ones where they did defeat them, there had been an awful lot of explosions and hanging precariously from helicopters. I hoped whatever we came up with didn't involve skydiving.

Or a virus or ultrasonic sound, because even if I knew a doctor or scientist to ask, I couldn't confide in them. "We can't trust anybody," Gary had said, and he was right. We couldn't risk it. There was too much at stake. And we couldn't call the police. "It's all in your imagination, Miss Johnson," they would say. "Stay right there. We're on our way."

We would have to do this on our own. And *where* was Gary?

I looked at the Wanted posters some more. I was sure the one in the middle looked like one of Sueann's old boyfriends. He—

"I'm sorry I'm late," Gary said breathlessly. His ears were red from the cold, and his hair was ruffled from running. "I had this phone call and—"

"Come on," I said, and hustled him out of the post office, down the steps, and past the Santa and his mob of donors.

"Keep walking," I said. "You were right about the parasites, but not because they turn people into zombies."

I hurriedly told him about the galls and Tonya's carpal tunnel syndrome. "My sister was infected at Thanksgiving, and now she can hardly walk," I said. "You were right. We've got to stop them."

"But you don't have any proof of this," he said. "It could be arthritis or something, couldn't it?"

I stopped walking. "What?"

"You don't have any proof that it's the aliens that are causing it. It's cold. People's arthritis always acts up when it's cold out. And even if the aliens are causing it, a few aches and pains is a small price to pay for all the benefits. You said yourself—"

I stared at his hair.

"Don't look at me like that," he said. "I haven't been taken over. I've just been thinking about what you said about your sister's engagement and—"

"Who was on the phone?"

He looked uncomfortable. "The thing is—"

"It was your ex-wife," I said. "She's been taken over, and now she's nice, and you want to get back together with her. That's it, isn't it?"

"You know how I've always felt about Marcie," he said guiltily. "She says she never stopped loving me."

When something sounds too good to be true, it probably is, I thought.

"She thinks I should move back in and see if we can't work things out. But that isn't the only reason," he said, grabbing my arm. "I've been looking at all those clippings— dropouts going back to school, escaped convicts turning themselves in—"

"People returning overdue library books," I said.

"Are we willing to be responsible for ruining all that? I think we should think about this before we do anything."

I pulled my arm away from him.

"I just think we should consider all the factors before we decide what to do. Waiting a few days can't hurt."

"You're right," I said, and started walking. "There's a lot we don't know about them."

"I just think we should do a little more research," he said, opening the door of our building.

"You're right," I said, and started up the stairs.

"I'll talk to you tomorrow, okay?" he said when we got to second.

I nodded and went back to my desk and put my head in my hands.

He was willing to let parasites take over the planet so he could get his ex-wife back, but were my motives any better than his? Why had I believed in an alien invasion in the first place, and spent all that time watching science fiction movies and having huddled conversations? So I could spend time with him.

He was right. A few aches and pains were worth it to have Sueann married to someone nice and postal workers nondisgruntled and passengers remaining seated till those people with connecting flights had deplaned.

"Are you okay?" Tonya said, leaning over my desk.

"I'm fine," I said. "How's your arm?"

"Fine," she said, rotating the elbow to show me. "It must have been a cramp or something."

I didn't *know* these parasites were like mistletoe. They might cause only temporary aches and pains. Gary was right. We needed to do more research. Waiting a few days couldn't hurt.

The phone rang. "I've been trying to get hold of you," Mom said. "Dakota's in the hospital. They don't know what it is. It's something wrong with her legs. You need to call Allison."

"I will," I said, and hung up the phone.

I logged on to my computer, called up the file I'd been working on, and scrolled halfway through it so it would look like I was away from my desk for just a minute, took off my high heels and changed into my sneakers, stuck the high heels into my desk drawer, grabbed my purse and coat, and took off.

The best place to look for information on how to get rid of the parasites was the library, but the card file was on-line, and you had to use your library card to get access. The next best was a bookstore. Not the independent on Sixteenth. Their clerks were far too helpful. And knowledgeable.

I went to the Barnes & Noble on Eighth, taking the back way (but no alleys). It was jammed, and there was some kind of book signing going on up front, but nobody paid any attention to me. Even so, I didn't go straight to the gardening section. I wandered casually through the aisles, looking at T-shirts and mugs and stopping to thumb through a copy of *How Irrational Fears Can Ruin Your Life,* gradually working my way back to the gardening section.

They had only two books on parasites: *Common Garden Parasites and Diseases* and *Organic Weed and Pest Control.* I grabbed them both, retreated to the literature section, and began to read.

"Fungicides such as Benomyl and Ferbam are effective against certain rusts," *Common Garden Parasites* said. "Streptomycin is effective against some viruses."

But which was this, if either? "Spraying with Diazinon or Malathion can be effective in most cases. Note: These are dangerous chemicals. Avoid all contact with skin. Do not breathe fumes."

That was out. I put down *Common Garden Parasites* and picked up *Organic Weed and Pest Control.* At least it didn't recommend spraying with deadly chemicals, but what it did recommend wasn't much more useful. Prune affected limbs. Remove and destroy berries. Cover branches with black plastic.

Too often it said simply: Destroy all infected plants.

"The main difficulty in the case of parasites is to destroy the parasite without also destroying the host." That sounded more like it. "It is therefore necessary to find a substance that the host can tolerate that is intolerable to the parasite. Some rusts, for instance, cannot tolerate a vinegar and ginger solution, which can be sprayed on the leaves of the host plant. Red mites, which infest honeybees, are allergic to peppermint. Frosting made with oil of peppermint can be fed to the bees. As it permeates the bees' systems, the red miles drop off harmlessly. Other parasites respond variously to spearmint, citrus oil, oil of garlic, and powdered aloe vera."

But which? And how could I find out? Wear a garlic necklace? Stick an orange under Tonya's nose? There was no way to find out without their figuring out what I was doing.

I kept reading. "Some parasites can be destroyed by rendering the environment unfavorable. For moisture-dependent rusts, draining the soil can be beneficial. For temperature-susceptible pests, freezing and/or use of smudge pots can kill the invader. For light-sensitive parasites, exposure to light can kill the parasite."

Temperature-sensitive. I thought about the hats. Were they to hide the parasites or to protect them from the cold?

No, that couldn't be it. The temperature in the building had been turned down to freezing for two weeks, and if they needed heat, why hadn't they landed in Florida?

I thought about Jackie Peterson's newsletter. She hadn't been affected. And neither had Uncle Marty, whose newsletter had come this morning. Or, rather, Uncle Marty's dog, who ostensibly dictated them. "Woof, woof!" the newsletter had said. "I'm lying here under a Christmas saguaro out on the desert, chewing on a bone and hoping Santa brings me a nice new flea collar."

So they hadn't landed in Arizona or Miami, and none of the newspaper articles Gary had circled had been from Mexico or California. They had all been datelined Minnesota and Michigan and Illinois. Places where it was cold. Cold and cloudy, I thought, thinking of Cousin Celia's Christmas newsletter. Cold and cloudy.

I flipped back through the pages, looking for the reference to light-sensitive parasites.

"It's right back here," a voice said.

I shut the book, jammed it in among Shakespeare's plays, and snatched up a copy of *Hamlet*.

"It's for my daughter," the customer, who was, thankfully, hatless, said appearing at the end of the aisle. "That's what she said she wanted for Christmas when I called her. I was so surprised. She hardly ever reads."

The clerk was right behind her, wearing a mobcap with red and green ribbons. "Everybody's reading Shakespeare right now," she said, smiling. "We can hardly keep it on the shelves."

I ducked my head and pretended to read *Hamlet*. "O villain, villain, smiling, damned villain!" Hamlet said. "I set it down, that one may smile, and smile, and be a villain."

The clerk started along the shelves, looking for the book. *"King Lear, King Lear* . . . let's see."

"Here it is," I said, handing it to her before she reached *Common Garden Parasites*.

"Thank you," she said, smiling. She handed it to the customer. "Have you been to our book signing yet? Darla Sheridan, the fashion designer, is in the store today, signing her new book, *In Your Easter Bonnet*. Hats are coming back, you know."

"Really?" the customer said.

"She's giving away a free hat with every copy of the book," the clerk said.

"*Really?*" the customer said. "Where, did you say?"

"I'll show you," the clerk said, still smiling, and led the customer away like a lamb to the slaughter.

As soon as they were gone, I pulled out *Organic Gardening* and looked up "light-sensitive" in the index. Page 264. "Pruning branches above the infection and cutting away surrounding leaves to expose the source to sunlight or artificial light will usually kill light-sensitive parasites."

I closed the book and hid it behind the Shakespeare plays, laying it on its side so it wouldn't show, and pulled out *Common Garden Pests.*

"Hi," Gary said, and I nearly dropped the book. "What are you doing here?"

"What are *you* doing here?" I said, cautiously closing the book.

He was looking at the title. I stuck it on the shelf between *Othello* and *The Riddle of Shakespeare's Identity.*

"I realized you were right." He looked cautiously around. "We've got to destroy them."

"I thought you said they were symbiotes, that they were beneficial," I said, watching him warily.

"You think I've been taken over by the aliens, don't you?" he said. He ran his hand through his hair. "See? No hat, no toupee."

But in *The Puppet Masters* the parasites had been able to attach themselves anywhere along the spine.

"I thought you said the benefits outweighed a few aches and pains," I said.

"I wanted to believe that," he said ruefully. "I guess what I really wanted to believe was that my ex-wife and I would get back together."

"What changed your mind?" I said, trying not to look at the bookshelf.

"You did," he said. "I realized somewhere along the way what a dope I'd been, mooning over her when you were right there in front of me. I was standing there, listening to her talk about how great it was going to be to get back together, and all of a sudden I realized that I didn't want to, that I'd found somebody nicer, prettier, someone I could trust. And that someone was you, Nan." He smiled at me. "So what have you found out? Something we can use to destroy them?"

I took a long, deep breath, and looked at him, deciding.

"Yes," I said, and pulled out the book. I handed it to him. "The section on bees. It says in here that introducing allergens into the bloodstream of the host can kill the parasite."

"Like in *Infiltrators from Space*."

"Yes." I told him about the red mites and the honeybees. "Oil of wintergreen, citrus oil, garlic, and powdered aloe vera are all used on various pests. So if we can introduce peppermint into the food of the affected people, it—"

"Peppermint?" he said blankly.

"Yes. Remember how Penny said nobody ate any of the candy canes she put out? I think it's because they're allergic to peppermint." I said, watching him.

"Peppermint," he said thoughtfully. "They didn't eat any of the ribbon candy Jan Gundell had on her desk either. I think you've hit it. So how are you going to get them to ingest it? Put it in the water cooler?"

"No," I said. "In cookies. Chocolate chip cookies. Everybody loves chocolate." I pushed the books into place on the shelf and started for the front. "It's my turn to bring Holiday Goodies tomorrow. I'll go to the grocery store and get the cookie ingredients—"

"I'll go with you," he said.

"No," I said. "I need you to buy the oil of peppermint. They should have it at a drugstore or a health food store. Buy the most concentrated form you can get, and make sure you buy it from somebody who hasn't been taken over. I'll meet you back at my apartment, and we'll make the cookies there."

"Great," he said.

"We'd better leave separately," I said. I handed him the *Othello*. "Here. Go buy this. It'll give you a bag to carry the oil of peppermint in."

He nodded and started for the checkout line. I walked out of

Barnes & Noble, went down Eighth to the grocery store, ducked out the side door, and went back to the office. I stopped at my desk for a metal ruler, and ran up to fifth. Jim Bridgeman, in his backward baseball cap, glanced up at me and then back down at his keyboard.

I went over to the thermostat.

And this was the moment when everyone surrounded you, pointing and squawking an unearthly screech at you. Or turned and stared at you with their glowing green eyes. I twisted the thermostat dial as far up as it would go, to ninety-five.

Nothing happened.

Nobody even looked up from their computers. Jim Bridgeman was typing intently.

I pried the dial and casing off with the metal ruler and stuck them into my coat pocket, bent the metal nub back so it couldn't be moved, and walked back out to the stairwell.

And now, please let it warm up fast enough to work before everybody goes home, I thought, clattering down the stairs to fourth. Let everybody start sweating and take of their hats. Let the aliens be light-sensitive. Let them not be telepathic

I jammed the thermostats on fourth and third, and clattered down to second. Our thermostat was on the far side next to Hunziger's office. I grabbed up a stack of memos from my desk, walked purposefully across the floor, dismantled the thermostat, and started back toward the stairs.

"Where do you think you're going?" Solveig said, planting herself firmly in front of me.

"To a meeting," I said, trying not to look as lame and frightened as the hero's girlfriend in the movies always did. She looked down at my sneakers. "Across town."

"You're not going anywhere," she said.

"Why not?" I said weakly.

"Because I've got to show you what I bought Jane for Christmas."

She reached for a shopping bag under her desk. "I know I'm not due till May, but I couldn't resist this," she said, rummaging in the bag. "It is so cute!"

She pulled out a tiny pink bonnet with white daisies on it. "Isn't it adorable?" she said. "It's newborn size. She can wear it home from the hospital. Oh, and I got her the cutest—"

"I lied," I said, and Solveig looked up alertly. "Don't tell anybody, but I completely forgot to buy a Secret Santa gift. Penny'll kill me if she finds out. If anybody asks where I've gone, tell them the ladies' room," I said, and took off down to first.

The thermostat was right by the door. I disabled it and the one in the basement, got my car (looking in the backseat first, unlike the people in the movies) and drove to the courthouse and the hospital and McDonald's, and then called my mother and invited myself to dinner. "I'll bring dessert," I said, drove out to the mall, and hit the bakery, the Gap, the video rental place, and the theater multiplex on the way.

Mom didn't have the TV on. She did have the hat on that Sueann had given her. "Don't you think it's adorable?" she said.

"I brought cheesecake," I said. "Have you heard from Allison and Mitch? How's Dakota?"

"Worse," she said. "She has these swellings on her knees and ankles. The doctors don't know what's causing them." She took the cheesecake into the kitchen, limping slightly. "I'm so worried."

I turned up the thermostats in the living room and the bedroom and was plugging the space heater in when she brought in the soup. "I got chilled on the way over," I said, turning the space heater up to high. "It's freezing out. I think it's going to snow."

We ate our soup, and Mom told me about Sueann's wedding. "She wants you to be her maid of honor," she said, fanning herself. "Aren't you warm yet?"

"No," I said, rubbing my arms.

"I'll get you a sweater," she said, and went into the bedroom, turning the space heater off as she went.

I turned it back on and went into the living room to build a fire in the fireplace.

"Have you met anyone at work lately?" she called in from the bedroom.

"What?" I said, sitting back on my knees.

She came back in without the sweater. Her hat was gone, and her hair was mussed up, as if something had thrashed around in it. "I hope you're not still refusing to write a Christmas newsletter," she said, going into the kitchen and coming out again with two plates of cheesecake. "Come sit down and eat your dessert," she said.

I did, still watching her warily.

"Making up things!" she said. "What an idea! Aunt Margaret wrote me just the other day to tell me how much she loves hearing from you girls and how interesting your newsletters always are." She cleared the table. "You can stay for a while, can't you? I hate waiting here alone for news about Dakota."

"No, I've got to go," I said, and stood up. "I've got to . . ."

I've got to . . . what? I thought, feeling suddenly overwhelmed. Fly to Spokane? And then, as soon as Dakota was okay, fly back and run wildly around town turning up thermostats until I fell over from exhaustion? And then what? It was when people fell asleep in the movies that the aliens took them over. And there was no way I could stay awake until every parasite was exposed to the light, even if they didn't catch me and turn me into one of them. Even if I didn't turn my ankle.

The phone rang.

"Tell them I'm not here," I said.

"Who?" Mom asked, picking it up. "Oh, dear, I hope it's not Mitch with bad news. Hello?" Pause. "It's Sueann," she said, putting her hand over the receiver, and listened for a long interval. "She broke up with her boyfriend."

"With David?" I said. "Give me the phone."

"I thought you said you weren't here," she said, handing the phone over.

"Sueann?" I said. "Why did you break up with David?"

"Because he's so deadly dull," she said. "He's always calling me and sending me flowers and being nice. He even wants to get married. And tonight at dinner, I just thought, 'Why am I dating him?' and we broke up."

Mom went over and turned on the TV. "In local news," the CNN guy said, "special interest groups banded together to donate fifteen thousand dollars to City Hall's Christmas display."

"Where were you having dinner?" I asked Sueann. "At McDonald's?"

"No, at this pizza place, which is another thing. All he ever wants is to go to dinner or the movies. We never do anything *interesting.*"

"Did you go to a movie tonight?" She might have been in the multiplex at the mall.

"*No.* I *told* you, I broke up with him."

This made no sense. I hadn't hit any pizza places.

"Weather is next," the guy on CNN said.

"Mom, can you turn that down?" I said. "Sueann, this is important. Tell me what you're wearing."

"Jeans and my blue top and my zodiac necklace. What does that have to do with my breaking up with David?"

"Are you wearing a hat?"

"In our forecast just ahead," the CNN guy said, "great weather for all you people trying to get your Christmas shopping d—"

Mom turned the TV down.

"Mom, turn it back up," I said, motioning wildly.

"No, I'm not wearing a hat," Sueann said. "What does that have to do with whether I broke up with David or not?"

The weather map behind the CNN guy was covered with 62, 65, 70, 68. "*Mom,*" I said.

She fumbled with the remote.

"You won't *believe* what he did the other day," Sueann said, outraged. "Gave me an engagement ring! Can you imag—"

"—unseasonably warm temperatures and *lots* of sunshine," the weather guy blared out. "Continuing right through Christmas."

"I mean, what was I thinking?" Sueann said.

"Shh," I said. "I'm trying to listen to the weather."

"It's supposed to be nice all next week," Mom said.

It was nice all the next week. Allison called to tell me Dakota was back home. "The doctors don't know what it was, some kind of bug or something, but whatever it was, it's completely gone. She's back taking ice skating and tap-dancing lessons, and next week I'm signing both girls up for Junior Band."

"You did the right thing," Gary said grudgingly. "Marcie told me her knee was really hurting. When she was still talking to me, that is."

"The reconciliation's off, huh?"

"Yeah," he said, "but I haven't given up. The way she acted proves to me that her love for me is still there, if I can only reach it."

All it proved to me was that it took an invasion from outer space to make her seem even marginally human, but I didn't say so.

"I've talked her into going into marriage counseling with me," he said. "You were right not to trust me either. That's the mistake they always make in those body snatcher movies, trusting people."

Well, yes and no. If I'd trusted Jim Bridgeman, I wouldn't have had to do all those thermostats alone.

"You were the one who turned the heat up at the pizza place where Sueann and her fiancé were having dinner," I said after Jim told me he'd figured out what the aliens' weakness was after seeing me turn up the thermostat on fifth. "You were the one who'd checked out *Attack of the Soul Killers.*"

"I tried to talk to you," he said. "I don't blame you for not trusting me. I should have taken my hat off, but I didn't want you to see my bald spot."

"You can't go by appearances," I said.

By December fifteenth, hat sales were down, the mall was jammed with ill-tempered shoppers, at City Hall an animal rights group was protesting Santa Claus's wearing fur, and Gary's wife had skipped their first marriage counseling session and then blamed it on him.

It's now four days till Christmas, and things are completely back to normal. Nobody at work's wearing a hat except Jim, Solveig's naming her baby Durango, Hunziger's suing management for firing him, antidepressant sales are up, and my mother called just now to tell me Sueann has a new boyfriend who's a terrorist, and to ask me if I'd sent out my Christmas newsletters yet. And had I met anyone lately at work.

"Yes," I said. "I'm bringing him to Christmas dinner."

Yesterday, Betty Holland filed a sexual harassment suit against Nathan Steinberg for kissing her under the mistletoe, and I was nearly run over on my way home from work. But the world has been made safe from cankers, leaf wilt, and galls.

And it makes an interesting Christmas Newsletter.

Whether it's true or not.

Wishing you and yours a very Merry Christmas and a Happy New Year,

*Nan Johnson*